THE

PARACLETE

A NOVEL

THE

PARACLETE

A NOVEL

JERRY
STUBBLEFIELD

LIFFEY
PRESS

an imprint of

OGHMA CREATIVE MEDIA

OGHMA

CREATIVE MEDIA

Liffey Press
An imprint of Oghma Creative Media, Inc.
2401 Beth Lane, Bentonville, Arkansas 72712

Library of Congress Cataloging-in-Publication Data

Names: Stubblefield, Jerry., author.
Title: The Paraclete/Jerry Stubblefield.
Description: First Edition. | Bentonville: Liffey, 2019.
Identifiers: LCCN: 2018952208 | ISBN: 978-1-63373-453-1 (hardcover) | ISBN: 978-1-63373-454-8 (trade paperback) | ISBN: 978-1-63373-455-5 (eBook)
Subjects: | BISAC: FICTION/Literary | FICTION/Psychological | FICTION/Southern
LC record available at: https://lccn.loc.gov/2018952208

Liffey Press trade paperback edition February, 2019

Cover & Interior Design by Casey W. Cowan
Editing by Michael Frizell and Cyndy Prasse Miller

to Adelia

ACKNOWLEDGMENTS

The author gratefully acknowledges the help of his wife Cindy and their daughter Phoebe, Dawn T. Jones, Peter Gregutt, Michael Hopping, Mary Prater, and Genève Bacon, all of whom offered encouragement, read drafts and provided critiques; also the Weymouth Center for the Arts and Humanities, which provided two weeks of quiet and comfort in a paradisiacal setting during a critical stage of writing; The Great Smokies Writing Program, in which several parts of the novel were workshopped; *The Great Smokies Review* and *The Chrysalis Reader,* both of which published excerpts from the novel; and for providing information on the American military presence on Wallis Island during World War II: the author's father Lester Stubblefield, Paul Sanford, Lieutenant Colonel James J. Ahern, and especially Andrew B. White, Sr. (Pai Pai), who provided insight about the native Wallisian language and customs.

"We are all damned together; the sons of men are lost in their webs of destiny. We are exiles, strange and alone. Our fathers forget, and set us free. Our mothers devour us if they can. Fatherless man is the son of his own child's flesh: our age is the lonely sonship of our cradles."

—from *O Lost* by Thomas Wolfe

"I, Antonin Artaud, am my son,
my father, my mother,
my self..."

"...I speak
from above
time
as if time
were not fried,
were not this dry fry
of all the crumbles
at the beginning
setting out once more in their coffins."

—from "Here Lies" by Antonin Artaud,
translated by F. Teri Wehn & Jack Hirschman

1

A COUPLE OF DIFFERENT TIMES when I was in first or second grade, Papa got in a sort of jolly mood that had a tinge of hysteria to it, and he laughed and told me I was an outdoorsy type. You'd have to know me to understand how funny that is. I'm smallish, nearsightedly bookish, indoorsy. So it was funny, a little bit, but more like strange. He tousled my hair and said, "Davy's an outdoors boy. A real outdoorsy type." And Mama just kind of smiled and told him to hush. It was a joke, not an attack on me at all, as Papa and I were the best of buddies. I just never understood why it was funny when he did that. I never will understand it, but you probably will.

I learned about time travel and omniscience from Papa. There are too many universes to number, and the one I inhabit is a little different from yours, even though in another sense it is the same one. You naturally think of a world as having "places" in it, and as having time that "passes by" so that you have a way to describe things. But I live in multiple dimensions of time, and that, as you can imagine, impacts how I exist in the dimensions of space. But I assure you I'm not just some emotionless reporter. I do fall in love. Maybe I should tell you about Joyce, and then Esbeidy. Diane Morgan too.

My universe *is* your universe, even though the differences I just outlined remain true. For you and me to talk with each other will require that you accept certain realities about me. I am a fourth grader in Miss Hamilton's class at Rhyne Elementary School in Oak Hollow, North Carolina. Yet I'm sixty years old, my school days long behind me. And I'm every age in between, and every age before and beyond, at all times. I can tell you, with good authority, any details about my grandparents—who died before I was born—and anybody else, whether or not I ever knew them or will know them, because

I can observe them without affecting them in any way. In this sense, I am older than my father, older than everybody. I can, and do, *know things I do not know*, things outside of my realm of experience. In short, I am omniscient. Consider me your narrator. And I am real. My name is Davy Nobles.

I should begin with important information about two people having sex in Cannon Shoals, North Carolina, in April of 1991. The two fornicators didn't rush, but they never paused, couldn't, trapped in time—the way it seems to move by. They were voracious, the desire giving way to selfish need. They were doing it on the sidewalk in front of her house.

Leo kept his weight on his elbows, considerate. They were on the hard ground, partly on concrete. Janet's eyes were closed, some of her butterscotch hair stuck in her parted lips' evaporated spittle glue. Last year's wild cherry leaf, fleshless lace, clung to her flushed cheek and Leo picked it off and kissed it, and dropped it into the grass and the trembling shadow of a dogwood blossom.

It was dogwood winter in Cannon Shoals, the white flowers like patches of snow visible through deciduous forests as yet sparsely foliated. The foothills were warm, Cannon Shoals sleepy, tired from the week, from the semester, from the decades of deterioration that seemed to be culminating along with the century. The sawmills were rusting away, the furniture factories closed, the work all gone to China and the war in an oil-slicked gulf on the other side of the world. Leo had sensed the air of denouement the moment he'd driven into Callan County. Nine more years might be enough for the millennium to sweep away the last rain-rotted eaves' timbers, the rusted square nails that held together these temporary shelters against the frontier cold, and the rubble of brick downtown stores that were built too solid and lasted too long.

Leo lifted his head and looked at Janet, and she was smiling, eyes closed tight against the sunlight, her mouth curled up at the corner near his face. He sucked into his nostrils the faint acrid decay from her exhalation, the smell of tea and honey and yogurt mingled in her all-night girlish breath, and he was delivered for the moment to life. That is how important she had become to him.

It was almost six o'clock, full daylight. They lay together side by side now on their backs. A patch of sunlight had crept across the gritty gray concrete and up to her breasts.

Distant, a car horn honked, *come on out, your ride is here*, first shift, no doubt. Apprehension began to erode his numb bliss. He rolled his head to the side, glanced at the dark windows of the house across the street, imagined that the pharmacist who lived alone there might have happened to look out his window and called the police. How many laws had he and Janet broken, lying there together naked, fornicating on the dawn sidewalk leading up to her house, the light of the butterscotch sun on her butterscotch hair and on her breasts. He was saved by sex on the sidewalk, saved by Janet, saved by her existence and by his lucky encounter with her. He was saved, and he breathed, but he knew nothing and could imagine nothing of what the future might bring now. It was the first time he'd ever been unfaithful to Leah.

———

That sexy daybreak was on a Friday. On the previous Monday, Leo was beginning his one-week residency. He nosed into room 204 and checked his watch. Either he had the time or the day wrong, or something had changed, because the room was vacant. He sat at the oaken teacher's desk, a heavy, ink-stained throwback to the fifties with stingy leg space facing the windowed wall. He could see the corner of the parking lot, but not his car down at the other end. A silver globe shone at the near horizon, an alien spaceship, marked CANN, that resolved itself into the water tower for Cannon Shoals. He rose from the desk and went to the window for a better look.

Fifth graders charged in around him, an emaciated blonde girl in a jumpsuit almost balling him with her elbow. He stepped out of the rushing traffic. He hadn't been off schedule, had just failed to allow for transit time between classes.

The waxy room flooded, daylight pouring through ceiling-high windows, green chalkboards on the other three walls, floors scarified by decades of metal desk feet, steam heat registers below the window sills, voices and desks clattering, notebooks dropping flat on the floor with maximized noise. Leo caught one or two little faces looking at him. He turned to face the windows again. In a moment the noise abated a few decibels. He would let the kids calm before walking to the back of the room, away from the teacher's desk, to confound them a little. They were fifth graders, the best age, he knew from the previous few weeks' experiences, as bright as they would ever be, and not yet ruined with body chemistry. Silence developed.

"There's a ship from Mars in Cannon Shoals," Leo said in his best deep voice. Tentative snickers erupted, quieted. "One Martian on board, injured, needing a safe place to hide while he repairs his craft and regains his strength."

The children were hanging on his words when the teacher came in chattering, breaking the spell.

"Hi, Mr. Nobles. I'm Miss Mabry. Well...." she raised her eyebrows and indicated with her soft blue eyes the quiet classroom.

He shook her hand. "We've already started." She smiled and took an empty student desk at the back, not uttering another word. He made his way along the windowed wall, aware that the glare of day was silhouetting his form.

"He has a name, but it's hard for Earthlings to pronounce. I'll need someone to supply that name." Several attentive students jerked toward pencil and paper. "He has a little machine with him, something he keeps close to him. He intends to use it to convince some Earthlings to help him. He's an ugly little critter, though, so it may not be so easy to get help. I need seven Martians."

Hands shot up everywhere. Mr. Nobles picked four girls and three boys. "I need Earthlings." Again, hands shot up. Two or three Earthlings teamed with each injured, stranded Martian, and Mr. Nobles had each team work out a skit to solve—or not solve— the Martian's problem. He made them understand, glanced at Miss Mabry and saw her appreciative—a little amazed?—eyebrows uplifted above those decidedly blue eyes.

Leaving his car at school, Leo walked home with her after school on Thursday, his penultimate day in her classroom. Ostensibly, she was going to show him a book about elementary theater improvisations she had at home. In Janet's classroom, there had been some unacknowledged but undeniable magnetism between them.

"I loved the Tennessee Williams improve you did today," Janet said. Leo smiled. "But that one where you had them secretly choose between love and money," she said. "I could tell which they'd chosen. And the way the boys chose love. I never would have thought, especially some of the ones who did. It was a safe way for them to express something they couldn't otherwise. What are you smiling at, Leo?"

"Oh, well, just at what you're saying, and I like the way you talk. We're being people now. You don't mind my saying so, do you?"

"It's more relaxed out of the school setting."

"Sure is."

"You brushed my arm with yours," she said, in mock warning as they walked along swinging their arms. "Fuzzy," she said. "Oh, look at that house. Oldest house in Cannon Shoals."

The wooden farmhouse stood out against bungalows from the fifties on either side. Too charmed by Janet to speak, Leo watched her beige profile in the blush afternoon light.

Her house was a frail octogenarian, drunk with honeysuckle and wisteria and morning glory vines, single-storied white wooden frame with steep roofs, deep eaves, and a front and side porch shaded by unkempt hedges.

"Just like Chicago, I guess," Janet said, smiling, having seen Chicago on his resume. They trudged through crabgrass around the side yard and toward the back door, the only one that could be unlocked from the outside. The backyard of a vintage 1970's rancher abutted Janet's yard, the squat construction showing its bricky windowless butt end. In a sense, that was just like Chicago.

Leo stood back as Janet opened the creaking screen door and unlocked the house. Giving her time, he took in the half dozen or so houses he could see from here, mostly their tops, and the trees obscuring them. Time in the neighborhood was cracked into shards a decade or so wide and strewn helter skelter over the space of several blocks. Leo liked that. He had always been a time traveler.

The door swung open, and he followed her inside. Something about the kitchen comforted him—the table and its spindled chairs as fragile as childhood, the linoleum tiles in a hideous pattern of white squares and maroon ones—Leo loved it instantly. Nothing in the room was modern. The countertop and cabinets were built in, not the manufactured kind. Handles on doors were chromed metal arcs designed to last forever. The gas stove, so old it had art deco design elements, was happily greasy of burner dial, confidently chipped of enamel, mature in its faint breath of natural gas odorant.

Janet indicated the slender table, and Leo sat. He felt the chair's joints give under his forearm, heard its complacent snap. Janet moved the other chair to one side of him rather than across. Leo picked up the little salt shaker and admired its kitschy details. It was a barn.

"The pepper was a silo, but I broke it," she said. "That was a walk! I'll make us something in a minute."

"I'm fine," he said, "I'm good. Just...."

"What?"

"I'd like you to tell me about yourself. You know."

Janet looked off to the side, as though she'd seen something. Leo wondered if he had put her off. She tilted her head, and he appreciated the new angle emphasizing the length of her neck.

"Most of the arts teachers in Callan County are afraid for their jobs," Janet said, taking up where part of their conversation had been interrupted earlier at school. "I guess you know the state cut our funding."

"Seems like that's all I ever hear. Funding cuts in the arts. I don't know how there can be any funding left at all."

"There's not much," she said and stood up. "Let's see what we have." She looked into the refrigerator.

"I don't want anything," Leo said, but he did.

"Having you in the county is a luxury," she told him. "We just barely get the use of a classroom. The art teachers go out and buy their own supplies. Music teachers buy their own sheet music. CDs? Forget it. So far I'm the only teacher I know of who has gotten an actual visiting artist."

"Do you think my salary could have been better spent?" Leo asked her.

"It's not out of the same fund," she said. "I checked." And she gave him a wicked smile, then sat down with a cold wooden bowl of grapes. "Sorry, these are a little used."

"I love grapes," he said.

"Once you're teaching in the arts, you're barely hanging onto a job," she said.

He liked the soft, slow cadence of her voice, pristinely Southern, none of the twang he knew from Texas.

"Good grapes," Leo said, mouth full.

"Some of them look too far gone, too soft, or too wrinkled. When does a grape become a raisin?"

"One of life's mysteries," Leo said, and then they were quiet together.

"Unmarried and childless," she said, cocking her elbow over the back of the chair and working her chin forward. It was, Leo felt, not so much a confession—not a sin, for heaven's sake, to be unmarried and childless—as an echo of some words she had thought, maybe even said out loud in a private moment, rehearsed for no future moment, or an unlikely moment. How often did she have a chance to say such a thing to someone?

"Same here." Leo nodded, agreeing to something. He met the loneliness of her dusty blue eyes, round and steady in their forbidden depth. Prettiest, though, was her comfortable mind. She was not afraid of their silences. "In a relationship, but...."

"But?"

"Only sort of. Really."

They picked through the bunch of decent grapes, bumping knuckles good-naturedly until only too soft or too wrinkled were left.

It was dark outside before they remembered the book of improvs. Janet retrieved it from somewhere in the house, and they looked it over for a few minutes. She made a pot of coffee, and they drank it.

"Let me show you the rest of the house," she said. Leo was so caffeinated he was afraid he might laugh out loud or bark like a dog.

"Sure," he said, managing a civil tone.

Just out of the kitchen they entered an amber-lit hallway. To the right was the bathroom, straight across was the bedroom. Leftward down the hall he followed her. Somehow she had lost her shoes. The cut of her blouse was tight around her thin waist, accentuating the flare of her wide hips.

"Bathroom back there, bedroom there. Here comes the—oh!" and she stopped at a framed print hanging on the wall. "This is my picture that was in my room when I was little."

It was not the sentimental pastoral scene that moved Leo, but Janet's sudden absorption in it. She seemed to forget him, tilting her head, eyes darting from detail to detail in the faded dime store print, a bemused smile curling her mouth. He felt abandoned and indignant and had a mad urge to kiss her, get her back here!

"See the bunny rabbit hiding under the bush?"

He was grateful when she turned and walked on.

The living room was cozy. He wanted to stay there for the rest of his life. Meals could be brought in. He would sleep on the huge old-fashioned lumpy brown couch. Janet turned the switch on a table lamp. More amber light washed out toward the walls where it soaked into the wallpaper.

"I love this room," he said. "Love this room. Can we sit?"

"Sure," she said and plopped into a stuffed chair. He sat on the couch.

"Your house smells all fresh and clean," he said.

"Thanks," she said, shrugging her shoulders.

"I'm buzzing. A whole pot of coffee, I never do that."

"Me too, I don't either," she said.

"Love this room," he said again, and they glanced around, Leo to take it in, Janet to help him. The front door had three small windows at the top end, arranged in stair step. Through them, he saw some vines on a trellis and the darkness beyond. Just inside the door squatted a three-shelved bookcase filled with thin paperbacks. Double full windows faced the front yard, framed by sheer curtains pulled back. They were covered with blinds of white brighter than anything else in the room.

"I want this to be my prison cell," he said.

She had no clever comeback. She gave him a half smile, but only because he looked to her for it, or for something. Then she said, "How did you come up with those improvisations for the kids?"

"Just made them up. I don't have a clue what I'm doing. I got the gig because the arts council in Springdale was hard up for a warm body with qualifications. I was there with my BFA. I mean, I turned in an application at the right place at the right time."

"They're good, the improvs. These kids don't respond to much of anything. Did you know that?"

"Fifth grade is not too bad. You should see eighth grade."

She smiled, "I know eighth grade, Leo. I've been there. I've done every grade except kindergarten and third."

"Including high school?"

"God yes."

"You like fifth?"

"It's a good age. But like I said, they don't respond to much. Not the whole class, the way you got them to do."

"Maybe it's because I'm a man, big ole man not supposed to be teaching school."

"No, that's true, but it's not the reason. You're good. They bought into the magic. It's been a wonderful experience for me."

It occurred to him that she was flattering him, but she didn't need to. He changed the subject.

They ate canned macaroni in the kitchen at about nine o'clock, then sat in the living room talking until three in the morning, releasing their easier secrets, Janet refusing to let him leave, insisting, illogically, that it was still early.

Finally, he said, "I really should go."

"Nope," she replied, lolling her head from side to side as though relaxing her neck muscles. "You should stay and keep talking all night." She stretched, smiling, looking pleased with Leo, her eyes sparkling at him. "I know," she said. "Let's walk around the block, stretch our legs."

Holding open the gate for Janet so she could take the lead, Leo said, "I feel like I'm in a dream."

She laughed. "When was the last time you did an all-nighter?"

"College, I'm sure."

It was a double block, one of the through streets having been closed decades earlier, Janet explained, and incorporated into the adjacent side yards. Mysterious were the ways of the small town. Untruths everywhere, unnoticed, the secret lies in Cannon Shoals. When they reached the end of the block, it was the end of Cannon Shoals itself. Beyond, a breeze whispered across the scrubby dogwoods under the jack pines.

Janet had been right. It felt good to stretch. Leo was intoxicated by the night air, the smells carried on it, unidentifiable scents from the nests of arboreals, wafts of the disintegrated corpses of multitudes of insects, almost soil, the bacterial off-gassing from last year's grasses, retreating asphalt chemistry, floral eflations, dust from the stars. He took her hand in his. It was meet—it was right.

———

Back in the living room, Leo didn't sit, again offered to go, but Janet plopped onto the couch with a sigh and a smile, and Leo was assuaged.

"Why don't you sit here with me?"

Leo sat on the couch next to her, their silence not as comfortable as before, the sense of expectation undeniable but still unspoken. He mentioned leaving once again, and she grasped his forearm with both of her hands and told him she would not allow it. "I want to discuss bioluminescence," she said. She spoke of foxfire, which she had seen and Leo had not. She said, "I'll show you some sometime," and it sounded, Leo thought, like a commitment.

Janet went to the kitchen and brought hot cups of tea back.

"Oh, my god, more caffeine!" Leo laughed.

Whistling steam off the liquid surface, Leo noticed Janet staring at the blinded window. "See anything out there?" he offered.

"Sometimes I do," she said. "I look out sometimes and think I see designs in my yard and beyond. Have to wonder if they're really there."

They were slow, lying on the couch, holding each other, kissing more like school kids making out. Leo was aware that the night would be ending soon, and finally they began to undress each other.

Suddenly Janet stood up, wearing by then only her panties and bra. Leo was down to his shorts.

"I want to go outside," she said.

Leo could see the faint first light of day through the window. He laughed.

"I'm serious," she said.

"I like the concept," he said, "but there are quite a few houses on the block."

She moved a little toward the window and looked outside, tilting her head like a kitten, saying, "It's still dark. Everybody's asleep this early." And then she turned to Leo and smiled at him before lowering her eyes like a shy, sly little girl.

Through the long night, Leo had tried to charm her. This he must acknowledge. He had amazed himself with wit and bashful sincerity. He had used his every wile to win this woman over to him, not anticipating any consequences necessarily, sexual or otherwise. It was as if he had fallen in love.

It's as if I've fallen in love.

She stood between Leo and the window, her face glowing with a wild confidence that something was right about her suggestion. And he knew she was right. She reached behind her and unhooked her bra, letting it fall to the floor like a burst balloon. After a moment, she took off her panties, and then moved to the front door and opened it, where she turned and looked at Leo, waiting.

2

U P ALL NIGHT. CULMINATE WITH love on the sidewalk. Leo's elation was uncontainable. That this was possible in his life! His mind amped and spinning from the all-nighter-cum-caffeine, he drove the fifteen miles from Cannon Shoals back to Cadbury, the Callan County seat where he was staying during his residency. He could barely restrain himself from smiling and waving at the farmers passing in their pickups, making their morning rounds. He arrived back at his room dazed, relieved to be out of his car. After a shower, shave, change of clothes, it was time to head back to Cannon Shoals for breakfast before starting his last day at the elementary school.

By nine o'clock, he was pulling a copy of *The Cadbury News-Topic* out of the vending trap in front of the Cannon Shoals Café. Here was an earnest, old fashioned, generously spaced and paced little establishment dead-center of downtown, its raked and recessed entrance vestibule paved with the original octagonal white tiles, well worn.

Inside, giant chrome coffee urns dominated the mirrored wall behind a short lunch counter, and suffused the air with their wood-pithy aromas. Café-curtained windows stretched across the front. One black fan hung from the beaded ceiling twelve feet up, motionless and cobwebby in the motor vents.

Of the six square tables spaced around the room, each clothed with gingham and set with cups upside down in saucers, Leo chose the one nearest the windows. The curtain near him was pushed back, revealing the street view. Downtown consisted of three blocks of businesses along Center Avenue. *Howard's Pipe Fittings. Wellworth Real Estate. Emmendee's Janitorial Supplies. USDA SCS. Bill's Barber Shop,* apparently out of business. A modernized storefront with some corporate symbol. *Lou's Bath and Beauty.*

And, directly across the street, Leo could see the pharmacy. He opened the newspaper to the sports on page four.

Driver Burned as '76 Diplomat Explodes on Ramming '70 Riviera. How odd, to name the car models in the headline. The Demolition Derby, a week-long elimination event at the Callan County fairgrounds, had racked up its first serious injury.

More coffee? Please, and soon. He ordered chicken and dumplings. It was an unusual breakfast, but he had been up all night, and it was on the menu, and it appealed.

He felt cocky, and also guilty in spite of all humanity's proclaiming his innocence, in spite of all reason, history, literature and drama, kings and scholars and the avidly held opinions of the meat in the seats at the Demolition Derby. In spite of all their chuckling forgiveness of sexual transgressions, he knew he was guilty—because of Leah. Cocky he felt, and sweetly too, though knowing that Janet had been no conquest. It had been easy for both of them, meet and right, and with time and a clear head, he might figure out why.

The waitress, her plump prettiness harking back to scrapple and bacon, placed the bowl of chicken and dumplings beside the coffee cup. Then she placed a soup spoon into the food, wedging it beneath a morsel of white meat like Leah would have done, but self-consciously for Leo, the customer, the stranger—stranger still, wanting chicken and dumplings for breakfast.

"Pretty nice morning," she checked the creamer on his table and gave him a smile that reddened her cheeks.

"Real nice," Leo said, grateful as she put the full cup before him.

"I mean, real, real nice, for you," she seemed to say. Leo just caught her thinning smile. Had she said that? She was walking away when she said it, whatever she said. What he heard niggled in his head. He was hungry. He ate. The food was tasty.

The new caffeine kicked in atop the buzz from the first cup and the comfort of a full stomach and the jagged stupefaction of sleep deprivation and reading about Demolition Derbies. A swirling scenario began to form in his jolly mind, and he recognized the force of paranoia but enjoyed giving it some rein. *Now, the drug store was straight across the street from this cafe. The pharmacist had said good morning to the waitress half an hour—maybe an hour ago, then proceeded to tell her of the spectacle he had witnessed in the early morning light. Janet told me twice, and started to tell me a third time, that the pharmacist lived in the house across the street from her. How, then, did the waitress know that it was him, since she'd never seen him before? Well, of course, the pharmacist had signaled her, flashed a mirror through the street-facing windows of*

the two establishments to get her attention, then pointed and nodded as Leo was taking
his seat. "That's him," the pharmacist mouthed at the waitress. "That's the one I was
telling you about, the one with Janet Mabry, on the sidewalk in front of her house this
morning. That's him!"

Leo allowed himself a little smile on reflection of his unreasonable scenario. Life
in Cannon Shoals, he thought, backdrop for a drama of peculiarly American love.
Here was a town as fragile as the dogwood blossoms covering the foothills where it
nestled, the hinterlands, the aging Camaro back roads convenience store land of six-
packs and churches.

Leo had passed Meredith in the hall every day that week. He found her in the
teachers' lounge this morning on his 10:55 break. She was on her feet, leaning back
against the refrigerator, reading a document. She wore half glasses in silver wire rims.
She did not look up, but her readers slipped off the bridge of her pug nose, the upturned
tip of which caught the glasses. "Morning," Leo said. She ignored him. He sat down.

Ugly as pooting in church, Leo thought. He was assessing the considerable similarity
between her body and the appliance against which she was leaning. She looked at him,
caught his eye.

"Now, who are you?" she said.

Now, who am I? "I'm the artist in residence," Leo said with a cool, brief smile. He
was sure she knew who he was. "Leo Nobles," he added with an even briefer smile.

"Actually, you're not supposed to use this room. It's for teachers," Meredith said.

"Oh," Leo said. Could she be for real? He started to rise.

"No, no, no, no, no, no, no. Who cares? Besides, you're sort of a teacher, anyway
aren't you?"

"Well, not exactly. I wouldn't want to break any rules."

"Forget it. Artist in residence. Close enough." She bounded across the room to the
couch and sat next to him. "Listen, Leo, you use the teachers' lounge all you want to.
Nobody's going to say a word. How long you here for? A week?"

"Well, a week, but...."

"Use the lounge all week long. Believe me, nobody's going to care. If you can
stand the smoke smell. Can you believe this air? God! Lack thereof. Gryder is the only

principal in the state of North Carolina who allows smoking in the teacher's lounge. I know that for a fact." She sighed and collapsed back on the couch.

"I'm only here one more day," Leo said. "I'm covering the whole county one town at a time."

"No problem," Meredith said, toasting him with her soda can.

She tells me I'm not supposed to be here and then, so generous, makes an exception for me and now we're old buddies, the best of friends.

Leo caught a languid smile on Meredith's face.

"How do you like working with Janet?"

The hard vinyl upholstery of the couch now seemed to chill Leo and crease under his buttocks.

"Well, it's not so much working *with* her as it is working *in front* of her. The teacher hangs out at the back of the room and keeps an eye on things."

"Clobbers the ones that act the worst, right?"

"The kids seem to respect Janet a lot. I haven't had any problems with them."

"Yeah, everybody loves Janet." Meredith nodded, managing a hint of derisiveness.

Then she leaned over toward Leo, stuck her face right up to his and showed him a gross, fake, squinty-eyed grin.

"What the hell are you doing?" he said, smiling to mitigate his little profanity.

She fell back on the couch again and reached for her can of Diet Pepsi.

Time to go, he put his hands on his knees and leaned forward.

"You can't do anything around here without everybody knowing it." Meredith sniffed, looked sideways at Leo. "I guess you've found that out by now."

Leo assumed his reaction didn't show. "That's why I don't do anything," he said, feeling suckered into a conversation he did not want to have.

"Neither does Janet. She just... oh, well...." Meredith was shameless, Leo thought. Speaking in ellipses, no less.

But he was trapped and knew it. "What do you mean?"

Meredith averted her eyes, and Leo had the impression she was formulating some different approach now, some diversion. He looked toward the exit door.

"Why do you think we call her Evangeline?"

"I didn't know you did."

"She's pining away for her true love," Meredith wheezed. She laughed into her Diet Pepsi can, then glanced around furtively. "She was seventeen."

Meredith hunched over her soda can and waited for Leo's glance, which he gave her. But apparently, she wanted him to beg. She leaned back again and curled her upper lip over the sharp aluminum edge separating her from her cola, and she waited.

Disgusted, Leo guessed he would find out what she wanted to tell him precisely because she wanted so badly to tell him.

"Did *you* have a true love at seventeen?" he asked her. He hoped to be cruel with impunity. She slurped, didn't look at him, didn't answer.

Leo tried to imagine Janet having said something about them to her colleagues. He couldn't see it. Meredith might have picked up on the chemistry Janet and Leo had felt, but he doubted even that. He thought Meredith was fishing. If she had anything more to say, she would say it.

"When I was seventeen," Leo mused, "I acted in my first play. I was Richard in *Ah! Wilderness.*"

Meredith slurped up the drop of soda trapped at the rim of her can, struggled to her feet, and sauntered out of the room.

Leo walked through the pleasant spring midday back toward the café for coffee and a light lunch, thinking how incredibly light his schedules had been in the several Callan County schools he'd covered so far. The morning had gone well, the improvs effective, his caffeine energy up to it, but now depleted. Crossing the street, he glanced back at the school, a 1920s era three-story brick structure flanked by a playground. A dozen swings, their chains raw and still, stood in A-frames, stark against a row of houses across the street beyond the parking lot.

When he reached Center Avenue, the main downtown street, he saw a small crowd—ten, twelve people—gathered in front of the café staring at some police action across the street at the pharmacy. An ambulance and three police cars, one with its blue lights flashing, were pulled onto the sidewalk at dramatic angles. Two policemen stood chatting on the walk in front of the pharmacy. A few pedestrians on that side of the street veered away, crossed the street and, like Leo, joined the crowd in front of the cafe.

Sidling to a young woman hypnotized by the event, Leo asked, "What happened?"

"The guy in the drug store is dead," she said without taking her eyes off the pharmacy.

"The pharmacist," said a well-groomed, flannel-shirted man of about seventy. He also did not look at Leo.

"Johnny Bishop," said a middle-aged woman, not looking at Leo.

"Suicide," said the well-groomed man.

"Definitely *not* suicide," the woman said.

Leo said to her, "How do you know?" but she didn't answer.

The man looked at Leo and said, "My wife *found* him. That's her, see right through the front window there? Inside talking with the detective."

All Leo could see in the window was a reflection of one of the police cars and a display of Dr. Scholl's footpads.

"See her?" the man asked.

"Oh, yeah. Now I see her," Leo lied, hoping the man would tell him more.

"She's the one that called the police. I'm waiting for her to come on out so I can take her home. They didn't want me in there."

"Chances are he was on some medication, and it gave him a stroke or a heart attack," the woman said.

"Medication," said another woman, younger, standing beside the first woman. Leo thought he detected a note of irony in her voice, looked at her. She averted her eyes.

Out of habit, Leo dramatized the situation in his mind. Johnny Bishop—but change his name to something more real sounding—epitomized the paralyzing timidity—disguised, in his case, as morality—of small-town folk. He would be a minor character, the hero's brother, his overuse of the drugs he had so readily at hand, a foreboding, a foreshadowing, a warning of the consequences of succumbing to the monstrous burden of living without prospects.

"Suicide, huh?" Leo said, almost whispering it to the man.

The man turned to look at Leo. "Johnny's a bachelor. Always was, except for one time. No family, not around here anyway. Unless you count that one. Seemed to keep to himself pretty much. Had to do it in the store I guess, or nobody might have found him for a while."

"You're speculating about that, right?" Leo said.

The man continued, "Wife said she found him sitting on the floor, propped up against the wall. Like he planned it."

"Like he had to sit down fast, you mean," said the woman.

"Come on, we need to get to Lucy's," said the younger woman, and they left.

Leo gazed at the front of the pharmacy, at the two policemen. He felt removed from the whole situation, and yet at the same time had an insane notion of walking over to the pharmacy, pretending to be a relative—something like that—and walking in. *The urge to jump, tied with the fear of jumping.* Leo headed for the café. But as soon as he approached it, he saw the waitress from that morning standing at the window, arms folded across her chest, but not watching the pharmacy.

She was looking at him.

He reached the school parking lot. He had plenty of time to drive somewhere and have lunch. Inside his car, the air and surfaces were still cool from the early morning, though the day had warmed up. He remembered a rattling old car he had owned at the university for a while during his senior year. It had been a boon for him, a spaceship into which he could retreat and travel. His current car, chosen by Leah, was never any good at space travel. It rolled along the roads and streets and delivered him to preset destinations. Its time travel mechanism was busted. It was hardly worth the trouble, good only for the needs of linear existence.

At Dixie Burger, he drove-thru and then parked. Chewing the rubbery sandwich, he conjured the sound of Janet's soft voice, the dry warmth of her hand in his on their nocturnal walk around the block again. He and Janet were coming to terms in small but steady increments. Last night. Just a few hours ago.

At 2:30 Leo pulled back into the school parking lot. Two of the three buses there were idling, their lights burning, doors open, and Leo watched as an older man emerged from the cafeteria door, crossed the lot to the third bus and unlocked it. What an unconquerable task, driving a school bus, Leo thought. The first wave of children exploded out the side door of the school building and gathered around the doors of the front two buses. Arms flailing, feet tramping, every kid vibrated with energy, and then they were on the buses.

A moment later, older children exited the school, and Janet came out after them, monitoring their kicking and jostling toward their assigned rides home. Full of appreciation for her slim good looks, Leo watched her feminine manner applied to excellent effect in herding the fifth graders.

The second bus loaded and disappearing down the street, Janet held up a hand to still the remaining children until the third bus pulled into position. Leo saw Janet catch sight of him. He smiled, but she had already looked away, bent down to the level of a wronged younger child on whose quivering shoulders she placed her reassuring hands. Janet matched each car-rider with their ride, received and returned thumbs-up for each bus before it left the lot, and resolved each dirty-handed little dilemma as it arrived in front of her. Then, as the last bus pulled away in a dense blue cloud of its exhaust, she hurried across the parking lot to her car.

It was as though she had forgotten Leo was sitting there waiting for her. He hurried out of his car and across the lot, catching her before she had her car door open.

"Hey," he panted.

"Hi, Leo."

"Would you like to meet somewhere for a Coke or something?"

"Oh, I can't right now," she said.

He searched her face for meaning. She smiled. Was it a polite smile? And there was an urgency in her struggle to unlock the car door.

The sexual afterglow Leo had been enjoying all day began to evaporate. The anticipation he'd felt, knowing he could be with Janet again for a while after school, suddenly turned murky.

"Tired?" he offered with a quick smile, and now she was in her car. He held the door open, not letting her close it when she tried. "Look, Janet, you don't feel embarrassed or anything, do you?"

"Embarrassed? About what?"

"About last night, this morning."

"What about this morning?" she said, gazing, it seemed to Leo, straight through his face. Confused, Leo loosened his grip on the door, which she then closed. He knocked on the window, and she rolled it down, but then started the engine.

"Can I drop by to see you about five o'clock?" he asked.

"That's fine," she said, glancing at him. She put the car in gear and Leo had to back away or have his feet run over.

Normally Leo would have driven the hundred miles straight back to Springdale and Leah for the weekend. Instead, he drove to Cadbury. His room was in a squarish house located in an old residential area ruined when the interstate was put through.

He avoided the bed, knowing that in his exhaustion, he would pass out if he lay down. He intended to return to Cannon Shoals by five o'clock to re-connect with Janet.

Sitting in the wooden chair at the writing table, Leo stared out the window. *Done with Cannon Shoals. Janet will write a nice report for the Arts Council, Gryder will rubber stamp it. My work accomplished little, will make a decent addition to my resume.*

What resume? My resume makes one thing clear—do you have to read between the lines? Not really. I was a teacher and was fired and couldn't go back to it. After that, it's piddling little residencies, few and infrequent.

His eyelids grew heavy. He could go out for a cup of coffee, but he was so tired he could scarcely entertain that idea. Instead, he let his mind relax along with the rest of his head. *Unfaithful to Leah. First time ever. What does it mean? What does unfaithful have to do with anything? Well, Leo, everything, of course. None of this will mean anything later on. It can't, can it? Can you give up the pretense? Do you want to? Of course, I do. But can you? I could. I think I could. But is this love? How can one know? How can one ever know, given my history, given my enslavement? What is that adrenaline all about? Well, it's love, or guilt… hope… head about to fall onto the table….*

He pulled himself up, body unwilling, and trudged down the hall to the bathroom. He showered, put on fresh clothes. He would just have time for that cup of coffee before driving back to Cannon Shoals. Assuming that after seeing Janet he would drive the hundred miles back to Springdale, he gathered the items he needed for the weekend and threw them into the car.

His punctuality was wasted. At five o'clock, Janet was not home. Her car was gone. The house was locked, front and back. The kitchen looked dark and cold through the window. He poked around the other side of the house, glancing in windows. At the front again, he took a seat on the rickety porch swing. He would wait for her.

The air was hot, and some insects—gnats of some sort—bothered around his head. The edge of the swing's seat began to cut into the backs of his legs. In five minutes he was up again, roaming once more around the house, then venturing to the significant locus on the front sidewalk. He didn't linger there, though, out of some odd sense of propriety, but circled again to the backyard.

He heard a car pull up and stop. Relieved, he headed around the house, intending to put his arms around Janet without delay, and kiss her and give up his fear and find happiness with her now, right now, and forevermore. However, the car was not hers, nor was it parked at her house, but across the street. It was a police car.

Leo stopped, edged back close to the house. He castigated himself for the ridiculous, unfounded feeling of guilt, but he was not able to come out in plain sight. Instead, he watched as two men, one in uniform, the other dressed casually, walked up to the house across the street and went inside without even having to unlock the door.

My car is parked right in front, in plain sight. But then, so what?

For a quarter of an hour, Leo sat on the single stone step at the back door. His tailbone hurting, he rose and crept to the side of the house. The police car was still there. He scouted the back of Janet's yard, annoyed that there was no egress there because of the way the house opposite abutted her property.

And why should I even be thinking about sneaking away?

Leah would be wondering why he was late. He would have to make up some excuse. No matter what, he intended to see Janet before he left Cannon Shoals. He would find himself some dinner somewhere and come back later. Surely she was delayed somewhere and would apologize, and they would laugh about it.

Leo heard men's voices coming from across the street, and then the sound of two car doors opening, closing, the cessation of voices, the car engine starting, idling, idling, idling. *What the hell are they doing sitting there?* At last, the car pulled away, its growl fading to nothing in the space of one, two, three blocks, four? Gone.

3

ALL OF WHICH HAPPENED BEFORE I was even born, so you see why I had to explain the thing about omniscience and the dimensions of time. Once, I asked Papa about God. I was curious as to whether our God also existed in other universes, or just in ours. And I wondered if, in the event that our God only exists in our universe, would there be another God in another universe, and if so, how that God would compare to ours.

God does exist, clearly, for those who can know it. God is the goodness and the grace. I thought, for a while, that this meant that God *is* because God is *believed*, but actually God is anyway, believe it or not.

This sounds odd, but God is also nonexistent, and every atheist is right about that. No disputing it. They are correct. And yet God is no less present in the life of an atheist than in the life of a believer. This is a paradox.

I have to go back several decades now, but you should know the story I'm telling contains some brushes with religion—in a way. To answer my question about God and other universes, Papa narrowed it down to the universe where he lives. God exists in Nothingness, and because that is a paradox, and because Papa is a theater person, he calls God "a parody of nothingness." Meanwhile, Miss Hamilton has pointed out that in the Second Letter of Peter, the Bible says "…with the Lord one day is like a thousand years, and a thousand years are like one day." So the six days of creation can be construed as a metaphor for a much longer period of time, although apparently that argument doesn't cut it for a whole contingent of individuals. To me, the Bible is saying that time is variable in many ways including the direction of its travel, that existence is eternal, and man is, at least for now, trapped in an illusion of existence that is just the plane surface of a multi-dimensional continuum in God's mind. We are silly to sit around and argue about the Big Bang—or the Big Bounce—versus the creation story in the Bible. But we do anyway.

We would do better to try and see our history and our future as the whole of our existence, instead of believing that yesterday, or even a billionth of a second ago, no longer exists. And likewise, believing a billionth of a second from now does not yet exist, nor does a minute or a year from now. If that were true, then what would exist? The answer is "now" would exist. But "now" is infinitely small, and one could argue that if something is infinitely small, it is equal to zero. And by that logic, we don't exist at all. But of course, we do exist. Meanwhile the rocks, the fish, the trees, the stars, the cows, the sand—everything except us—exist without introducing the argument of time. The rock and the fish "know" that they exist always. It's not that they know it, of course— they just don't unknow it like we do.

I'll continue to contemplate paradoxes throughout my life. As early as next year, in the fifth grade, I'll start looking at self-referential sentences like, "This is the first lie I have ever told." I'll be hooked for life. In 2019 I did—excuse me, *will* do a paper on the idea that consciousness is an illusion—a paradox of the first order, no?

For you to understand Leo, you must know certain things about his family. The Great Depression was eating Milton alive, and that's why he was a drunk. "Brownwood." His wife heard him complaining as he gave the screen door into the front room a good pop, sending it shuddering open. "Brownwood." He cleared his throat and chuckled. Milton and Ina would be Leo's grandparents later, once their daughter Lulu brought him into their world.

Ina was standing at the stove, leaned toward the kitchen door to see into the front room. "You home?" she asked.

He stumbled through the dining room, held himself steady against the kitchen door frame, leaned there, his grin challenging her to say anything about his condition. She escaped his breath, crumpled down to her hands and knees to light the oven. She remembered a time when he had been standing there at the door before he was drinking much, and Drew was not yet a year old, she had done this very thing, lighting the malfunctioning pilot in the oven, and he had suddenly been on top of her.

He mumbled something and cleared his throat.

"What?" she said, striking a match.

"You have a big butt," he said.

"Thank you," she said, though she knew it was neither an insult nor a compliment. He had, in the early years, told her he liked her big butt.

The oven lit and Ina stood up. She looked toward the quiet coming from her husband and saw sadness in his eyes that stopped her short.

"How is your back?" she asked him.

"It's throbbing."

"The booze helps a little?"

When he didn't answer, she looked at him again from where she was reaching up for a bowl to mix the cornbread.

"Drinking... so much easier than fucking," she heard him say, but he was turning away, back into the dining room. "Brownwood," he announced.

"What about it?"

"You know why it's called Brownwood? Because everything is brown. I was looking around on the way home, and you know what? This whole town is brown. Brown ever god damn where you look."

She adjusted the gas, turned to the sink where greens were piled in a colander.

"Shit brown." Now he was back in the doorway, grinning at her, sounding amused at his own acumen. "Ever single shade of shit brown."

"I never noticed," Ina said, pulling the first big collard leaf free from the bunch.

"Well, look around next time you're outside," Milton was expansive now. "They oughta call it Shitwood. That's more like it." He pushed himself away from the door frame and staggered toward the bathroom, muttering *Shitwood* over and over. *Shit-tit-titwood, boy, where we live.*

Drew appeared now at the kitchen door.

"*Shitwood,*" Russell exclaimed from somewhere in the house.

Ina gave up a sigh, and Milton laughed and said something Ina could not make out. "Don't you dare, young man," she yelled toward Russell.

Drew eased into the exact position his father had just vacated at the kitchen door. Nine years old, Drew sometimes frightened Ina with the way he mirrored his father's action. "He's drunk," Drew whispered. It was almost an apology.

"He sure is," she said, scrubbing the leaf with her thumb. "Why don't you find Russell and y'all get your hands clean, and then you come back here and help."

"Help do what?"

"You can set the table after while. These don't take too long. Where's Russell?"

"In the living room."

"He tearing anything up in there?"

"Hiding behind the couch."

"Go get him and y'all clean up. Tell him I said so and I better not hear any fussing."

Ina saw a brown spot on the greens and punched it out with her thumbnail, thinking *That's right, Brownwood. Wouldn't mind leaving the place, but not to go back to some mud hole like Cross Timbers.* Coming to Brownwood—it was not so much a memory at first as a pleasuring along her nerves, giving her a shiver before she formed mental pictures of the deep green of oaks that were common along through-streets here. She had desired, the first time she and Milton walked along Austin Avenue, to sit down under a big tree and breathe in the different air of the big town.

Milton had been excited about transforming alternating current to power radio sets. Ina could see that he was a discerning man, able to read people—when he was interested enough—as well as the laws of physics. He could see not just the surface of a piece of cast metal or a person, but the subtle clues to what flaws might be hidden within, what invisible fissures threatened to crack and rupture the marriage of zinc to iron, or man to woman. He had taken the remnants of an old grinding stone and used small chunks of the embedded silicon carbide to construct the receiving elements of an assortment of simple crystal radios. He had already constructed a successful transformer, using materials he'd scavenged, tooling them at his boss's shop on Depot Street after hours. But late in 1929, the Depression had hit, and after a struggle, the electrician's shop had closed down.

"Mama, he's got the pillows behind the couch and probably getting em dirty."

"Tell him I'm gonna tan his hide," she mumbled. She remembered Dr. Wilks, the preacher who'd performed the wedding, and the long, long talk in his office a few days before the ceremony. He'd spoken straight to Milton, about how he must be a gentleman, and remember the responsibility that God gave men along with their superior strength. Ina still recalled every word the preacher spoke, and she now pictured him, his gentle countenance set off by large eyes magnified further by rimless spectacles, the bulbous nose and straight, lipless mouth that curled into a smile on one side. And she had watched Milton trying to pay attention, but his hands were finding his face and his knees and his arms, his smiles forced into the room at inappropriate times, his fine hooked nose set between intelligent brown eyes, and she saw the working inside the square set of his noble jaws. Ina had noted Dr. Wilks' obsequious behavior and, because part of it was accepting, forgiving that Milton was not paying attention, she felt comforted by it.

Brownshitwood. Hee, hee, hee. He clattered out the back door. *Good. Go down by the creek and stay there 'til supper time.*

"Mama, he won't give me them pillows."

Ina had loved the big, new First Baptist Church with its huge stained glass windows, where Dr. Wilks joined Milton and Ina in holy wedlock on Saturday, June 19, 1926. All during the day of the wedding, Ina had felt ghosts hurrying past her at the Bledsoe house, disappearing behind her. Other brides might have called the feeling butterflies in the stomach, but to Ina, the ghosts had felt like warm breezes, and more than once she'd checked her hair to see if the ghosts had mussed it. Cross Timbers was receding, sucking the hayfield air with it like a sinking ship sucks water.

Milton, meanwhile, spent the first part of his wedding day at his cousin Klaus's house east of town. To Klaus's annoyance, Milton would not partake in the drinking. Secretly he had longed to, he admitted to Ina. He believed, though, that he would enjoy his wedding night more if he was sober.

And did you? Where was he? That better not be him out in the front. *Shitwood for sale.* Was that what he was yelling? *tit tit tit tit kablooo...* She jammed the greens into the big pot and ran water into them.

———

Years of the depression reaching the biblical number seven, Drew and Russell played barefoot in the dusty yard, indifferent to the baby in the house, their minds tuned to poverty, Lindy their hero for a day or two but then forgotten along with the *Spirit of St. Louis* they'd made from two rotten planks. Mashed potatoes eaten up or else seen again browned in skillet grease, the boys never missed what they'd never had, and were content. Willis Creek carved its dusty lazy gully behind their house at the eastern edge of town, a flaw on the landscape to Brownwoodian eyes, an annoying depression, the banks of which, in the coming years, would be bulldozed, bridged and otherwise tamed by spitting, impatient men until its modest native beauty was forever lost. It sometimes ran clear in the spring but was usually dry unless it was raging after a downpour, scouring up the brown wood and mud and dumping it into Pecan Bayou.

There was always milkweed in the forty or fifty feet between the back door and the creek, and in the spring, Ina let the noxious, bristly plants stand until the Monarch caterpillars had eaten their fill, turned to shimmering green chrysalises, and metamorphosed into butterflies.

For some years Ina had been letting Drew go down the footpath to the creek by himself. Milton had shown him how to catch crawdads with a string and tiny bit of bacon fat. She had warned him about scaring Lulu with the creatures. He sometimes brought dozens of the crustaceans to the back door. Ina did not consider them edible, though she knew people in Louisiana did. Once, when food was scarce, she'd looked down on Drew's beaming face and the lard can teeming with crawdads and considered looking for one of those Cajun recipes. But Drew considered the animals his pets.

Drew, satisfied to have shown his catch to his mother, would then engage Russell in crustacean play in the patch of dirt outside the back door. The animals would struggle through the dry dirt searching for escape and moisture, and, one by one, get themselves lost in the milkweed where they would dehydrate and die, the boys having moved on to another sport.

Sometimes, not often, Milton would order a block of ice for the icebox. He rarely told Ina in advance, so when the ice man knocked at the back door, it was unexpected.

"What you boys got there?" Boyd Gene, the ice man, asked Drew and Russell one hot afternoon. He wore a felt hat and a funny shirt with a patch on it like a badge, the dripping block of ice dangling from tongs, wetting the trousers at his knee.

"Crawdads," Drew said, already hoping for a chip of ice off the wagon.

Boyd Gene looked into the lard bucket. There were dozens, some good-sized. "You selling those?" he asked.

The boys giggled.

"Git them loose ones back in the can, and I might buy the whole bunch from you." He gave them a look to assure them he was serious, then knocked on the door. Ina soon appeared and smiled, pleased to see Boyd Gene and his cold delivery.

"Oh, good," she said. "He never tells me this is coming."

"Paid in advance at the dock, as usual," Boyd Gene announced. When she pushed open the screen door, he quickly carried the block to the icebox, trying to minimize the drip on the floor, always considerate. But as he turned to go back outside, he paused and said, "You want to sell them crawdads?"

"Sell?"

"I like em. That's a good mess of em. If your boys are just playing with em, I might want to give a little something for em." Ina had never noticed the ice man's strange lilting accent before.

"Well, I don't know. How much are they worth?"

"I'd give em a nickel for the mess of em."

Ina nodded, considering, then stepped to the screen and said to the boys, "Y'all want a nickel for them crawdads?"

The boys, wide-eyed, jumped up and yelled, "*Yeah, yeah, yeah.*"

The ice man stepped outside and made sure the animals that had been retrieved from the ground were still alive. He ceremoniously pulled a nickel from his trouser pocket and held it out. "Who's the banker?"

"Me," said Drew, and then he received the money.

Ina was standing at the door, watching through the screen.

"I'll bring your bucket back next time I'm out this way. Might be a day or two," Boyd Gene said. Then he turned to look at Ina and said with a pleasant smile, "If that'd be all right."

The boys harvested more crawdads the next day. The rusty motor oil can was murder on the crawdads. Boyd Gene didn't show up, anyway. When he did come a week later to return the lard bucket, the creek was dry. He gave the boys chips of ice and, seeing Ina standing at the back door, he offered her free a substantial sliver for the ice box. She declined the offer. There was nothing in the icebox to keep cool, anyway, and it might have been difficult to explain to Milton why the ice man was so generous.

———

The house was quiet. Milton had left for the dairy at four that morning. Lulu was entering first grade, and as always, she seemed game, ready for anything. The children had walked away half an hour ago, each big brother holding one of Lulu's hands. Alone in the house for the first time in six years, Ina had felt a shiver of relief. She'd sat on the couch, then laid down on it for fifteen minutes before stepping outside. Now she stretched and felt the pleasant tingling of awakening muscles, felt like getting cleaned up, thought about being always dirty, had been dirty all summer, sweaty, covered with dirty hand prints from her boys, dirty somehow ever since Lulu had come along.

Ina stood on the earth in her bathrobe, leaning on the shiplap outside the kitchen, letting the morning sunlight collect on the side of her face and in her hair. Sleepy, she stared toward the remains of a long-abandoned spider web on the screen door's gray, paint-flaked frame. Hanging in the web, the single hindwing of a Monarch fluttered in the otherwise imperceptible breeze. The butterflies had gone. The late summer's sparse showing of green along the creek was turning yellow and brown, spotty leaves falling into the slow trickle of the stream.

The tub could run only cold water. Milton had promised her a water heater, but for now hot had to be added from pots heated on the stove, a tedious chore because Ina liked her bath hot. It was almost ten before she disrobed and stepped into the water, but it had been worth the effort. Immersed in ecstatic warmth, she began exploring her body. Was the skin still smooth on her forearms? It was, in the water anyway. Had the three babies left her lower abdomen awful and flabby? Whimsically, she pinched up the belly skin and imagined it sliced off. It was all unimportant. Milton was a drunk, and they rarely touched, let alone made love.

Though the dress she pulled from the closet was old and a little out of fashion, it was at least clean. She was checking the cupboard, also feeling the exquisite warmth of her bath escaping her skin. Milton always ate when he arrived home. Then he would make himself scarce, often sequestering himself in the cramped workshop he'd made from a room that used to be a side porch.

Potatoes, onions. She would make soup for a change. He'd probably like it.

There was a knock on the front door. Through the living room window, Ina saw the ice truck. Good. She would make an iced drink to go with the soup. Milton might admonish her for wasting the ice, but he would enjoy the drink.

She opened the door. Boyd Gene was holding a half block with the tongs. "I'll bring it around back," he said, tipping his hat, a wide-brimmed felt one, becoming on him. He was off toward the back of the house. Ina met him at the back door.

As he swung the block toward the ice box, the ice compartment of which Ina had already opened, he met her eyes. Once the block was secured inside the box, Boyd Gene looked at Ina again and smiled with a hint of expectancy. She looked away.

"Paid for at the dock?"

"Yes," he said, still smiling. "Sorry. You look so... I like your perfume. Very... it's...."

"I'm not wearing perfume."

He nodded at her.

On that day, he went on his way. But on another day, another ice delivery some months later, when Ina reached for the cool brass lever that was the latch on the oaken icebox door, and her thumb found its place at the fulcrum, and her fingers slid around the flesh-smoothed golden metal, another hand, helpful, warm, layered quickly upon the back of hers, adding its strength for opening the cranky door, those stronger fingers finding the spaces between hers in the tight spot between metal and wood.

———

At fourteen, Drew suddenly grew rangy, his Adam's apple protruding alarmingly. His face began to break out, and the acne, unchecked, had its way with his skin. He saw a picture of a GI with a crew cut in *Look Magazine* and nagged Ina to cut his hair in that style. When she finally did, the results caused her to laugh—the boy's head looked like a peanut. But he liked the look. His teacher called attention to it in class, complimenting him for his stylish, forward-looking attitude. He felt less poor.

Drew no longer expected approval, or even notice, from his father. Milton had drunk his way through the Depression. He'd been lucky to get the job with the dairy but had felt cheated of his career as an electrician. He often complained that science was moving forward and leaving him behind in this shithole of a town where nobody even owned a refrigerator. When he tried to enlist after Pearl Harbor, he was rejected, even though he had not yet turned forty. He could not pass the physical exam, could not bend his right knee to a squatting position. He borrowed a fifth of whiskey from his bootlegger friend, to be paid off over time in the milk he would pilfer from the delivery truck. He hardly noticed Drew's crew cut hair.

Drew was the one who knew about his mother and the ice man. He remembered what Boyd Gene looked like, even though he'd stopped delivering ice after the summer of 1938 when the ice factory closed down and only people on the south side of town, the rich side, who had refrigerators, could keep anything cold.

It was a day in 1943 when school routines were set, and Christmas was still too distant to contemplate. Drew skulked along the sidewalk toward school, irritated at the way Russell hopped around, kicking every rock and stick and kept dropping his lunch sack.

"Russell, get over here and listen to me." Drew stopped and waited. Russell had picked up a tin can smashed flat. "What are you going to do with that piece of junk? Put that down and come here."

"Sell it for scrap metal," Russell said, but then dropped it on the sidewalk. "What?"

Drew pointed down the street. "There's school. You know how to get there by yourself, so go on. I'm not going."

"You're not going!"

"I'm sixteen, by god. If I don't feel like going, I don't have to."

"You're going to play hooky? Me, too!"

"Shut up and get going. And if anybody asks, you can tell them I didn't feel like going to school so they can kiss my ass."

"I will. I said I *will.*"

"I'll kill you. I stayed home sick today. Now git."

Not knowing what to do with his sudden free time, Drew walked around a block and then back home. He would tell his mother he needed a day off to plan his future and consider what to do if the Nazis took over the world. He held the front door from slamming so he made no noise. Feeling less sure now how to explain himself to Ina, he stood in the front room listening until he thought he could hear her in the bedroom. She might have been folding clothes or making the bed. He moved like a shadow into the dining room.

The ice man came clattering in through the back door, and Drew, unnoticed beyond the kitchen door, saw him and noted the ease, the unmistakable familiarity with the room that had nothing to do with ice deliveries years ago. He was wearing a crisp U.S. Army uniform, the hat worn at a jaunty angle. Ina, hurrying to the kitchen from the bedroom, stopped abruptly when she saw her son, and her eyes widened. She was flushed, made up prettily, wearing a nice skirt and blouse that flattered her angular body. "Did I hear someone at the back door? The back, the door." She was stammering, Drew noticed. She never stammered. "I didn't know you were home, hon."

Drew walked out the front door. He began running as he rounded the corner at the end of the block, but then walked quickly around the block and approached the house. The cedar at the back of the house partially covered the window, but Drew could see in through the dining room to the bathroom door and, next to it, his parents' bedroom.

They were talking sadly in the dining room. He could hear most of it. After a while, Boyd Gene came up behind her and spoke words of reassurance. *He's a big kid, he'll understand how it is soon enough. He knows his dad's a drunk. Well, it's the truth, and it's probably just as well this way.* He was embracing her from the back and tried scrunching her skirt up into his hands. She said no, but she didn't seem to mind. He said this might be their last chance before he shipped out Friday. She let him pull her skirt up, and let him walk her, still holding her from the back, two crawdads stumbling back to the bedroom where they had been about to do this, anyway.

4

FROM THE IRONING BOARD, INA watched Lulu at the crib gazing at the beautiful new baby. Ina had already warned Lulu not to touch Leah too much, but her hand, seeming to have its own will, cupped itself and began inching toward the luxurious black hair.

"Remember what I told you about germs on your hands," Ina warned from the ironing board, keeping an eye on her older daughter, whom she had maimed and therefore feared.

Lulu retracted her hand. "I washed them, Mama," she said, then went ahead with adjusting covers in the crib, making sure the blanket was not too tight or too loose. "She's opening her eyes."

"Well be quiet and don't wake her up. Let her sleep."

Lulu backed away from the crib but watched Leah, who closed her eyes again.

At twelve, Lulu was well able to change diapers, walk the baby when she cried, bathe the baby, and keep her amused. Ina wanted to tell Lulu to run and play, to leave the baby alone, but she knew it would sadden Lulu, and Lulu would have a bad day, disappear somewhere. The boys would have to go and find her in some tree or way off down Willis creek on a sandbar. The boys would be angry because Lulu would hide from them. So, rather than upset the day, Ina let Lulu inch back toward the crib until she was again leaning over it, listening to the baby's breathing, making sure it didn't stop, noting the subtle undulations in Leah's eyelids as she followed images in her baby dreams.

"She's a beautiful baby, isn't she Mama?" Lulu said. Ina still had a pile of clothes sprinkled, to be ironed.

"Yes. We've already said that over and over."

"Don't you love her?"

Ina laughed, embarrassed. "You don't have to watch her all day long, Lulu. I'm her mother, you know."

"But you're thirty-nine."

"And you're twelve. Go outside and play." Ina felt the pang in her back, the same rock was thrown at her every time she stood too long and ironed. She checked her anger. It was the anger that had caused her to injure Lulu. She would not let that happen again. And Lulu was such a sweet child. "Thirty-nine is not too old to be a mother," Ina said, trying to sound instructional, raising herself above her child, playing the teacher, the way she did with the boys, but it was never as comfortable or natural with Lulu.

That the baby was beautiful was obvious to everyone. Ina allowed Lulu to take care of Leah as much as seemed prudent, or defensible. It was a genuine help, for one thing.

Drew, almost grown now, was seldom home. Russell, having established himself among some of the neighbors as a reliable yard man, was intensely interested in his personal finances. He tried to remember to compliment the good baby often, usually in passing, mainly to please Lulu.

The ironing finally done, Ina walked out back and down to the creek, pushing her back with both fists, hoping for a spinal snap to bring relief. She stood at the edge of the gully, watching the slow clear trickle that had just yesterday been a muddy rush. She never let herself think of Boyd Gene, but Boyd Gene, somewhere overseas, incommunicado of course, did have a way of flashing across her mind.

Lulu lavished the infant with attention throughout the summer. When school started in the fall, she would run home in the afternoon and go straight to the baby, quizzing Ina about anything Leah might have done that day.

Ina watched for signs that Lulu was not damaged beyond the one eye, the left eye, but she could never convince herself. The little girl who'd been so personable, so attuned to the feelings of those around her at all times, had not always been so since the unwarranted whack across her face. In school, her teachers reported the child's bright personality, her intelligence, her natural ability to bring the other children together in happy games and activities. But they also reported certain lapses in which Lulu would drift away mentally, favoring a facial twitch that was usually not noticeable. These reports worried Ina and fed her guilt.

———

On Halloween, when Leah was six months old, her hair raven black and her lips dark and defined, her eyes sapphire and wide with wonder, Ina waited in the twilit room to see if trick-or-treaters would come by the house on Willis Creek. There were few children in the neighborhood, Drew had taken Russell with him to some function at the high school, and the dusk was quiet.

Ina sat in the living room, thinking Leah was an easy baby, playing by herself with a box of yarns on the floor like that. The gloom accumulated around Ina and the small bowl of peppermint sticks she had purchased to fend off tricksters. Lulu was several blocks away at the home of Pete Charles, a friend from school who had two brothers and two sisters. They would be making popcorn and playing games. And Ina felt afraid.

It was not that Milton was drunk and sullen again, somewhere in the house tinkering with an electric motor he'd found abandoned on the loading dock at the dairy. She was used to his drinking, his depression, his solitude. Rather, she tried to attribute the unwonted emotion to the holiday spirit, though she knew that was not all of it. The monsters, or whatever was frightening her, came out of the kitchen and the dining room in the house, not from the dark sky and not from witches or goblins. For a second, when the shadow of a memory crossed her mind—a smell of surrender and something as evil as satisfaction—she thought that she existed somewhere else, somewhere in addition to the here and now, and it was that place from whence the fear came. But Ina knew it was a useless thought and put it out of her head.

Milton clomped through the house, appeared in the doorway and glared at Ina. "You want to go on over and visit with the Charleses? I can watch Leah."

5

THERE'S ANOTHER WAY OF LOOKING at this. It's called "dream time." Time acts differently in dreams. For example, say your Papa picks you up because you've fallen asleep on the couch and he wants to put you in your bed without waking you. You might dream that you're in a forest and you see a bear, and the bear grabs you and carries you off. The dream is prompted by the physical sensations you experience when your Papa picks you up. But the dream retroactively shows the bear walking through the forest and coming after you. You have experienced the passage of time out of order.

Fortunately, the book of the universe contains much more than just facts, but also Truth as well as Deception, so we are free to tell our stories in whatever way we wish. "And all the fictions bards pursue, do but insinuate what's true," wrote Jonathan Swift.

The question for a kid such as me is, am I good? And if I'm good, can I turn bad? Papa says that it's a good question, and it doesn't have an easy answer, such as "Yes, you are a good kid, and yes, you could turn bad like Drew." Drew is a family legend. Or, "Yes, you're a good kid, and although bad things might happen and you might do bad things, you will always remain a good person." It's not so simple. It's one of those fictions bards pursue.

When Milton had a stroke, mid-summer of 1957, he bedded in Brownwood Memorial Hospital for a week, semi-conscious. Ina sat with him most of the time, listening to him babbling about electricity, something about Shitwood, about the gearshift in the milk truck getting stuck in second. He would be quiet for an hour or so, then start again. The gear shift would not go from second to third. It needs to be fixed.

It wastes gas to go all the way from Avenue K to Coggin Avenue in second gear, no no no in third, the motor lugs, it's going to grind the whole transmission down to nothing. It had been years since he drove the truck for the dairy.

They brought him home from the hospital in an ambulance. He was stable but was not going to improve. The next day Lulu brought her little boy Leo to see his grandfather, most likely for the last time. Lulu had married Cord Nobles in 1949, and Leo was born in 1952. Ina had warmed to the baby instantly.

Milton lived another four days, Ina lying beside him in bed all night. He began choking around dawn on the fourth morning and suffocated.

At the funeral, Ina sought comfort from nearness to Lulu, but Russell was the one who held her arm. Drew was absent, not yet in jail, but awaiting trial in Abilene and unable to leave. He cried for his father over the phone with Ina. Lulu brought Leo to the funeral, held him close. She did not let go of her precious son even when they were back at Ina's house. He began to cry late in the afternoon, his tears darkening little spots on Lulu's navy dress, and then he fell asleep. Lulu continued to hold her sleeping boy until suppertime, then put him on Ina's bed, still in his dress clothes, and lay down beside him. Leah came into the room and undressed the sleeping Leo and then the drowsing Lulu. Cord had gone out back, pulled out his pocket knife and found a good piece of dead mesquite. He stood at the edge of the creek whittling a small rough figure of a big breasted woman in a grass skirt.

Ina wandered through the house, answered the door when a neighbor brought a plate of sandwiches, the only visitor that day, and ventured once to the backyard, where she spotted Cord down past the milkweeds whittling a stick, the shavings falling into Willis Creek's dry bed.

"Doing some carving?" she said, approaching Cord.

"Don't know what else to do," he answered. Ina knew that he was uncomfortable, wanted to take Lulu and Leo home and let this day be over.

"Cord, we'll have some supper and then y'all can go home. Leah's helping me in the kitchen. She's been talking about going to be thirteen soon."

"She sure ain't letting anybody forget that," Cord said.

"I know it's been a long day for all of us." Ina waited for Cord to offer some word of condolence to her. He finally looked up from his whittling and nodded to her. She went back inside the house.

A few days after the funeral, Lulu asked Ina to take her downtown and help her buy some slacks. Ina thought it strange since Lulu had just lost her job at Kimball's and didn't need to be spending money on clothes when she wasn't going anywhere anyway. When Ina came to pick her up the next day as planned, Lulu had forgotten that she wanted or needed slacks, and was still in bed and would not get up. Ina spent the day watching over Leo.

———

A season passed. It was late October and the leaves were turning brown, the trees looking scrubby, an unpleasant wind blowing. Ina's visits to Lulu and Cord, begun after Milton's passing, had become less frequent—only on Saturday mornings now instead of every day or two. Recently she'd even let a Saturday go by now and then without visiting. Driving back home from a trip to the grocery store, feeling miffed by an experience with a rude clerk, Ina let her nervous mind wander into familiar territory, her family. *You'd think they would come see me and look after me, not the other way around. I'm the widow. Y'all are still young. But then, I'm only fifty-two. I'm young too, for a widow.* But in truth, she knew that she preferred her own company to theirs.

Leah had moved out of the house and moved in with Lulu and Cord after Milton died. Ina had not protested. Leah had never been a help, not a comfort, just a thirteen-year-old interested in her magazines and dolls, and generally unpleasant to her mother. She was nicer now that she was out of the house. She was helping Lulu take care of baby Leo, not such a baby any more, five years old in a few weeks—a fair situation, it seemed to Ina, since Lulu had taken such great care of baby Leah. Lulu had been sick ever since taking the awful job at Kimball's. Cord and his fussing and fuming and yelling... they would be better off without him. *We all would be.*

When Ina pulled up to her house, she saw Leah waiting on the front porch.

"Hi Leah," Ina said, getting out of the car. "Came to see me?"

"Hi Mama." Leah walked toward the car, pulling the cuffs of her shorts down. "I was going to wait one more minute."

"Oh, glad I didn't stop at the bakery. Decided I didn't need a pie."

Seeing two bags of groceries, Leah opened the door and took one of them. "You still shop at Emerson's?"

"Usually. Is everything all right?"

"Oh yeah. I went for a walk and decided to come say hello."

"Glad you did," Ina said. "I was just thinking of y'all. I sit down and flat don't want to get up," Ina said, throwing her daughter a smile that was not returned. "How's Lulu?"

"Doesn't ever do anything." She waited as Ina opened the front door. Ina knew that Lulu was ever more withdrawn from the world. She still harbored her guilt, did not like to talk about it.

"I was thinking about Leo. Why don't I take him for an afternoon?"

"You?"

"Well, why not? I'm his granny."

Leah hunched her shoulders. "What do you want to do with him?"

"I was thinking I might take him for a little drive tomorrow, maybe all the way out to Cross Timbers, show him where I grew up. We could get a hamburger somewhere. I bet he'd love it. I could buy him a toy."

Leah set the grocery bag on the kitchen counter. "Cord spanks him too much."

"He does?"

"Whips him with a belt. Five years old, Ma. You ought to keep him all the time. What time you want him tomorrow?"

"I don't know. After lunch I guess." Ina had no context for the propriety of whipping a child. She had rarely struck her own children, and lived every day with regret for having injured Lulu out of anger. That Cord used a belt on little Leo, regardless of any context there might be, inflicted Ina with a vast chasm in which only sadness and evil could dwell.

"I'll make sure he's clean."

"That'll be good. You let Lulu know."

"I'll tell her. She won't even say anything, though."

Ina peered into the grocery bag. "Is everything going all right for you over there?"

"It is, I guess. Cord gets mad and yells all the time."

"Does it scare you? You can come back home, you know."

"No. It scares Leo though."

"Well, that's the way men are, I guess. Leo's bound to grow up and yell at his kids then."

"I think it makes Lulu go to bed and close her eyes."

This stopped Ina mid-thought, but she continued unloading the groceries. Could some of the blame be placed on Cord? All of it?

"I can't eat ten pounds of potatoes before they go bad," Ina said, opening the mesh bag and taking out potatoes, putting them in one of the empty grocery bags. "You're going to take half of these home with you."

"Oh, thanks."

"You want me to drive you?"

"No, I like to walk."

"You're so pretty, Leah. You always have been."

"Thank you."

"You be careful. There's a lot of sad and lonely men in Brownwood."

"I will."

"When I was your age, I used to see a man walking along the road in front of our place, way out on what we called the highway, but it was not even paved. I saw him several times, over… I don't know, must have been several years. He seemed to be walking slow, and at least one time, no, I think three or four times, he stopped and looked at our house. I remember thinking he could see me and I thought about waving to him but for some reason I didn't."

"I wouldn't have."

"Well, nowadays you wouldn't, but this was different. You can't imagine how isolated it was out there. The only way people even saw each other was if they went to church, and we didn't. We didn't know many people." Ina paused, drifted for a moment. "That whole place is gone now."

"Well, you can show him where it used to be anyway."

"What?"

"Leo."

"Oh, yes, I'm going to drive by the place. There's not much out there. Cross Timbers never did grow like other towns. Everybody moved to Brownwood, I guess." Ina looked at Leah to see if she was listening. Leah was picking at something on her knee. "My folks didn't see any connection between religion and real life. Some people were like that, but others seemed to get the connection. I never have been able to figure it out. I think there's religion and then there's the thing that religion is supposed to be about. Spiritual things. I never have figured it out."

"Me neither. I better get on my way back, Ma."

They both moved toward the front door. "You want me to drive you? Those potatoes are kind of heavy."

"No it's only eight blocks."

"Really? I never counted them."

"I did."

"Well. I'll come pick him up right after lunch."

"I'll have him ready."

Ina watched Leah disappear down the block. She felt as wooden as the porch on which she stood, and as dry as its flaked and detaching green paint. When Boyd Gene came into her memory, she put him away, the man who was Leah's real father but never came back. There was no reason to think of him. From the back door you could no longer glimpse Willis Creek because the privet hedges had grown so thick over the years.

Ina's house had plenty of room for Leah, more than enough. At Lulu's house, there were only two bedrooms, one for Cord and Lulu, and one for Leo. Yet when Leah had announced she wanted to move there, nobody had objected. Ina had assumed Cord would disallow it, but even he had just snorted and said, "She'll have to sleep on the damn couch." Ina had helped load her daughter's belongings into the car, with scarcely more resistance than, "Are you sure you want to stay over there?"

The wind was coarse, like sand, even though it was just air. Brown leaves. Brownwood. A crape myrtle bough was switching against the house, and now, as then, to Ina it seemed meet and right that her two daughters and her grandson would live together.

———

After the day Ina showed Leo the ghost town of Cross Timbers, she began keeping the boy more often. She taught him to call her Granny. A routine began to take shape, and after a few months, Cord was often dropping Leo off at Ina's house on a workday morning and leaving him there all day. Sometimes Ina would drive over early and pick up Leo while he was still sleeping, take him home, make him breakfast. "You're going to be in school after summer's over," she told him. "You want Granny to help you work on your name?"

Ina was surprised at how quickly Leo learned to hold the pencil, control it, draw lines and circles and, within days, write *LEO* in such a large script that it made her laugh.

"That's very good," she told him. "See if you can make space for your name two times on one sheet of paper now."

"I want to do Nobles," he said. And she taught him *NOBLES* on another piece of paper, and soon he had his whole name down.

One afternoon Ina took Leo to the Carnegie Library, a massive neoclassical structure downtown, and checked out a half-dozen books for him. Each day for the next two weeks, Leo spent hours in Ina's lap, watching the pictures in *Charlotte's Web, Scuffy the Tugboat, Tawny Scrawny Lion, The Little Engine that Could,* listening to the stories unfold as Ina read to him in a clear, lilting voice. When Leo finally began squirming, needing to expend some physical energy, she found that she hated to give him up, missed the weight of his little body on her lap. He would bounce away from her, sometimes quoting passages from the book she'd been reading to him, and she would catch herself envisioning him in the deep future, when he would be a man.

When they weren't reading, Ina and Leo explored the house and yard, sometimes venturing down to the creek. They would settle into a spot of lawn and see what they could find in the grass and the dirt. Ina would tell Leo all she knew about each item they found, and when she knew nothing, or little, she would entertain him with stories she made up on the spot. "That's a sandwich bug. We can gather a bunch of them and make sandwiches." "Nooooo, Granny!" Leo would laugh. "Sure! And we'll mix them into the peanut butter." More than once, they languished in a shady spot, Ina making up stories until Leo exhausted himself laughing and fell asleep with his head in her lap.

Once Leo could write his name, Ina helped him perfect it for several weeks before finally mentioning it to Lulu one afternoon. Lulu had been out of bed for a few hours that day, had put on some clothes, and was sitting at the dining table.

"Leo, you want to show your mama what you can do?"

Leo reached for the pencil Ina proffered, then took the sheet of paper from her other hand.

"What can you do?" Lulu was looking through the door into the kitchen.

"Here, Leo," Ina said, clearing a pile of teen magazines from a spot on the table. "Show us what you can do."

Leah came into the room, placed her knee on the chair Leo was kneeling on to reach the table.

"Let Leo show us," Ina said. "Let him have the chair, Leah."

"Where are my magazines?" Leah demanded. "I had them right here."

"Here," Ina said, patting the stack of *Teen Idol*. "Don't you want to see what Leo can do?"

Leah took her knee off the chair and watched Leo take the pencil carefully between his thumb and fingers. "See how he holds it," Ina's pride sounded odd, oily, even to her, and she tried to tone down the smile on her face.

Leo positioned the tip of his tongue at the outside corner of his mouth and went to work. Leah and Ina watched in silence as he formed the letters carefully, never making a mistake, his writing impressively small.

"Perfect!" Ina exclaimed.

"That's good, Leo," Leah said, hugging the boy, claiming him. "I'm impressed."

Ina looked at Lulu, who stared at the paper with a bemused smile, but said nothing.

"Leah, why don't you take Leo and y'all go play," Ina said, watching Lulu.

Leah picked Leo up like a baby, grunting, saying "You are getting to be such a big boy...." as she carried him from the room. "Are you excited about school?"

"Uh-huh," Leo was saying. "I can read."

"No, you can't!"

"Uh-huh, if I can see the pictures...."

Ina heard the backdoor squeak and slam and then Leo's distant laughter. She was still watching Lulu, the blank stare, the bemused smile.

"Aren't you proud?" Ina said, laying her hand on Lulu's shoulder, offering a gentle stroke across her back.

"I was going to teach him that," Lulu said.

Ina removed her hand. She moved to the kitchen door, thought about helping with dinner, realized she would just be in the way when Cord blustered in from work. She looked at the stove, the crusted old grease around the bottom of the little pan, the broken handle on the big pan.

"I'm sorry," she whispered. She was sorry, but not about Leo. She would have him reading before school started. He would also know some arithmetic. He would get everything he needed, if not at home, then at her house.

6

ISS HAMILTON, A GENIUS, A fourth-grade teacher whose mind operates in depths and dimensions that would baffle most of us, understands time travel. Miss Hamilton will comfort a student in her class who is upset. Mrs. Wall never did that, and even Mrs. Bringfirth, who is nice, never made sure she was completely fixing a problem. If you are crying, Miss Hamilton can assess the situation, formulate a plan of action, and execute it. The result is a student who is not only calmed down, but now has a deeper understanding and a better perspective on whatever upset them. You get the feeling that it's second nature for Miss Hamilton, that she could take on much bigger problems than the little classroom fires she puts out all the time.

She sees life in symbols a lot. We have an inclusive in class, Greg Hume, who picks apart pieces of paper and makes little messes, but he'll ask questions once in a while, and everybody laughs when he does. That bothers me, because the questions could be used to deepen our discussion, and instead everybody reacts like he's on the wrong track. We were learning about habits one day, and after we learned what a habit is, everybody had to get out pencil and paper and write down as many of their own habits as they could. Habit was just a spelling word, but Miss Hamilton was making a whole lesson out of it. It turned out that it was harder to think of your own habits than we expected. All you could hear was somebody sighing, some pencils scratching a little bit, and the air conditioner. Then Greg Hume says right out loud, "Who are my habits?"

So of course, everybody laughed. Miss Hamilton doesn't fuss about it when the class laughs like that, at Greg, but if you look at her face you can see she doesn't like it.

She's thinking, *'Oh, well, these are stupid kids and one day they'll grow up and know better.'* But then she said, "When you have listed all your habits, go back and give each one a name, like you would name your children or your pets. I know I always sit in the same chair in my kitchen when I eat breakfast. I call that habit Jimmy." You should have heard the quiet then. "When I take a shower, I always soap myself from the top down, and never from the bottom up. That habit is named Gail. Capital G-a-i-l."

Then when everybody had finally named all their habits—and you wouldn't believe how some of my classmates could be confused by a simple assignment like this—she made everybody choose one of their habits and write how tall it is, what it's wearing, what color hair it has, what kind of haircut, and some other qualities.

Papa liked this exercise when I told him about it, but he said it's probably not part of the curriculum. He said the *real* lesson was about Greg and other people who have different perspectives from us, and I said I knew that already. He said Miss Hamilton is a treasure, and I agree.

I think habits are more important than symbols—another spelling word. Young Leo's mind operated without symbols. On the contrary, he pushed thinking outward toward intangibles.

Dark, safe in bed, the summer ripe and no school to worry about, Leo sometimes lay awake. Mixture of aromas, rust and dust and must on the window screen, honeysuckle from next door, wisteria thick and heavy on the vine in the backyard, the precipitate night air itself, together soothed him and assuaged the lonesome, incognizant yearning for father that lay at the base of his perversion. This is ecstasy, he thought, his cheek on the windowsill, his tender hairless nostrils rimmed with chill from the rush of inhaled air.

On a warm summer afternoon when Cord was at work, Lulu sat at the picnic table in the backyard enjoying the sunshine and the company of her boy. Cord had whipped him earlier that morning, and his eyes were still rimmed with redness, but his spirit was lifted up by Lulu's receptive demeanor. He was trying to explain to her about his ecstasies.

"Can you say somewhen, Mama?"

"You sure can."

"Somewhen, not in this life, but in one before or not yet, I can feel things that happened, but I only feel them and don't remember them. Sometimes I see little bits, but it's mostly just feelings that come in through my nose, I guess."

"Carried on the aromas of the wisteria, you mean?"

"Uh-huh, and honeysuckle and the screen wire. But Mama, can I have somebody else's memories"

"I don't know. Maybe."

"He may have been another person and I was thinking about it, he may not have died before I was born. He may have lived until I was about four years old. I think I got some of his memories when I was a baby, but I didn't know anything so I only have the feelings."

"And the feelings are ecstasy?"

"They are to me."

"You have a very special gift, Sugar. You might never find anybody who understands what you understand."

"It's hard to explain. Do you understand it?"

"That's not important. What's important is that I believe it. And I do."

All of this he would eventually tell me, and it has helped me to understand. Leo was of course himself again in the mornings, not the father of himself, not some stranger's leftover beingness. Leo had figured out time travel. He learned not to talk about it, even to Lulu, but to practice it for fun. Back here at age ten, it was marvelous how little he knew, how little he'd experienced so far. It was a fine place to visit, full of mystery and ignorance. Something told him he'd know more, later on, about ecstasy.

He wondered about the man whose soul he'd inherited. Was it the Rain Man—an especially clear character among Leo's nocturnal receivings—who walked down the muddy, silty-puddled alleyway behind the backyard when the petrichor lingered in the air? Who walked out of town afterward, into the mesquites, where he threw off his clothes, vomited and emptied his bowels and vomited again until, trembling, he was nothing except himself, and contained nothing that was not him, and only then stepped into gullies swollen with muddy torrent and submerged himself and felt the grit and twigs scouring him.

Leo had visions of places sometimes. Common scenes, but specific to some "other," leaks through the cosmic ether from mind to new mind. Lonely landscapes, too, like dreams, beckoning, mysterious. He wondered if he'd see some of the scenes later in his life and remember them, startled, or re-set to this childhood time—travel back to 1962, a night of cool late summer when the aromas floated, and days that were almost intolerable.

———

Leah, his mother's sister, had lived with them since she was thirteen and Milton
had died. Now she was eighteen, Leo ten. They were playing on the picnic table in
the backyard, shaping fantasy figures with oil-based clays that never dry. They sat cross-
legged at opposite ends of the slab, leaning toward each other, working the clay, her
flannel skirt so long it covered her knees.

"This is a flying shoe," she showed him. Inside the elf shoe she had encapsulated
a little elf man, no more than a tiny ball for his head, another ball for body, and
serpentine arms and legs. She moved it in a graceful arc through the air above their
heads. She was pretty, slender, tall, buoyant dark hair down past her shoulders. She
never wore makeup, or just a little. She looked a little like Elizabeth Taylor in *Look*.
The little elf man's head fell off when she made him loop the loop. As she bowed
toward reattaching the head, Leo went back to work on the figure he was making, not
sure what it would become.

"This is a *Shingaru*," he said.

She glanced at it. "Creepy-weepy."

"It eats elves."

"Not my elves, it doesn't," she said, giving a half smile.

The perlaceous Brownwood afternoon was fading into white twilight, and they
were as lost in play as two children, though only one of them was a child. Leah molded
a squadron of flying shoes, each piloted by an elf sealed within. Leo smoothed the
Shingaru all over. Paint hung in oak leaf shapes from the siding on the back of the house,
and nut grass choked the flower beds at the picket fence along the alley and the unliked
neighbors'. Two mourning doves carried on their simple exchanges, one near, one a
house or two away. Leah knew her brother-in-law Cord would be home from the store
before dark. Her sister Lulu, working second shift at Kimball's, would be home shortly
after eleven p.m.

The distant carillon at Glynn Daniels Baptist College insinuated the air with off
tones, unfamiliar old hymns.

Leah put down the toy putty, watched Leo—who was named after her—until he
looked up at her. "Where did that Shingaling come from?" she said.

"Shingaru."

"You made it up."

Still working with the Shingaru's facial features, Leo said, "They come from memories you don't remember."

"Not my memories."

"Mine."

Leah watched the Shingaru develop a long, conical nose. "The devil is real," she said. "This is the thing you learn when you become a grownup at eighteen. And the devil will hurt you, and punish you for your awful sins, like he did Lulu, even if she didn't even have any sins."

Hearing his mother's name, Leo looked away, listening more intently.

Leah poked at the Shingaru with her finger, and Leo protected it. "When Lulu was a little girl," Leah confided, "before I was born, the devil came into our mama and took her mind from her temporarily and made her hurt Lulu. He wanted Lulu crippled because she was so nice. He hates nice people." She poked Leo in his ribs so he would look at her. "So, you better watch out."

"Shut up," Leo said. "Mother's not a cripple."

"What about her *eyes!*" Leah took a handful of Leo's hair in her hand and bent his head back.

"Stop it."

"That's what the devil did!"

"Let go or I'm gonna tell."

Leah let him go, then whispered, "Just remember, it's not her fault. She would have looked normal if the devil hadn't put his mark on her."

"Shut up," Leo repeated, frowning.

Suddenly Leah laughed, grabbed Leo and began tickling his ribs, but he broke loose angrily and ran toward the front yard, leaving Leah laughing across the distance.

7

FROM HIS PERCH ON THE arm of the couch where Leah was sound asleep, Leo could see through the open door into his parents' bedroom, both of them in there day-sleeping, both on late shifts, Lulu at Kimball's, Cord at Monkey Wards. Against the bedroom wall stood the "cabinet," as they called it, a display case for some of Cord's whittlings and constructions. Dozens of small carvings posed on the shelves—animals, a miniature naked woman of some dark hardwood, mechanical toys made from various woods, and other mysteries. Leo's favorite was the chain and cage. From a single piece of white pine, Cord had carved a chain with twenty links, and at one end, the chain was connected to a square cage inside of which were forever captured a perfect sphere and a representation of a stoppered jug. Leo gazed at the chain and cage for long minutes, imagining the skill required to create it, and also desiring to own it, to have it in his hands, put it in his room, display it on his shelf. He knew he must not climb up on the cabinet and take down any of the items. He remembered the belting he received for doing so when he was little more than a toddler. Now, at eleven, he was wary of unfair whippings for unintentional offenses.

Leah stabbed at him with a big toe. "Quit it," he mumbled, and turned to look at her. She was awake, stretching.

Wandering through the house with empty hours ahead of him, he caught sight of Leah disappearing into the bathroom, her morning, like his, lacking an agenda. His summer was filled with such nothingness, Cord getting up late and smoking cigarettes, Leah sprawled on the couch in the living room, and his mother, Lulu, lying in bed all day except on her work days.

He stopped again at the doorway and gazed at the chain and cage. He leaned his head into the room. Cord was awake, shaking a cigarette from the pack, and Lulu was in the bed. Cord said, "What you want?"

"Nothing," Leo said, and backed away. He hurried to the back door and went outside, grabbing a paring knife as he passed through the kitchen.

Beside the house on the unliked neighbors' side, scraps of lumber lay rotting in a heap. On his knees at this woody altar, Leo rifled until he found a scrap about an inch thick, almost two inches wide, well over a foot long. It was soft white pine, and yielded to the paring knife, but split with the grain if the knife bit too deeply. Leo intended to carve a chain, and it seemed to him that a good first step would be to smooth off all the edges.

Leo believed Cord worked at a place called Monkey Wards. That was all he had ever heard his father call the place, mostly in short snatches of conversation with Leah or Lulu. At Monkey Wards, Cord unloaded trucks, broke down cartons, maintained things. At the moment he was working from 1:00 p.m. until 6:00 p.m. He had his eye on a television set in the store. He had already announced, in front of Leo, Leah, and Lulu, that he intended to buy it, and maybe sooner than anyone thought.

Leo worked on his carving in the backyard until he heard Cord go out the front door. Running around to the front of the house, Leo brought the stick to his father.

"Daddy, look," he said, holding the stick out, its edges all gnawed off and splintered.

"What's that?"

"Is this the way you start making a chain?" Leo delivered a copious dollop of doubt in his voice.

"No," Cord said, and he opened the car door, spat onto the curb, folded himself into the car and drove away to Monkey Wards.

Leo found a brick, once part of a flowerbed border, and pounded his incipient chain straight down into the soft clay soil near the hydrant until it disappeared.

In the catch-all drawer, Leo found lighter fluid in a can with a squirt nozzle, and some matches. Lulu was having an all day in bed day. Leah was in the living room, sprawled on the divan, staring at the ceiling, wearing the shorts and blouse from yesterday. She would stay there a long time because she had nothing to do except be there at home with Leo, and lately she never read, never even listened to the radio because it bothered Lulu.

The narrow passage of packed clay and cat smell and sow bugs and shade and yard detritus ran between the house and the unliked neighbors'. The scrap lumber was also piled there. The privacy of the space sometimes gave Leo the urge to defecate, and he'd learned to enjoy crouching there, one heel wedged against the urge until it faded. Crouched just so, he wrote his name in cursive on the damp clay with the pungent lighter fluid. Setting the can aside, he struck a kitchen match and set it to the capital L. The effect was better than he expected, a slow rewriting of his name in the devil's own candescent hand.

He wrote some dirty words and burned those. With a broken length of maple dowel, found half rotted and slimy amongst old tongue and groove flooring laid to the bare ground, he dug a hole half the size of a cup and squirted copious lighter fluid into it. When the dirt was saturated, the fluid began to pool, and before the standing liquid could sink away, Leo struck a match and tossed it into the hole. The orange fire was tall and its upper tips gave off smudge that curled into writhing black filaments before Leo's face. He had to move back. By now Leah was watching him from behind the blinds in the front bedroom window.

———

"You coulda burned down the god damn house," Cord said the next day. "Get in that bathroom."

Leo hung his head and marched with dread into the bathroom. Sometimes there was a wait before the whipping.

"Shut them god damn doors."

Two doors led into the bathroom, one from each bedroom, the house having no hallway. There were no locks on these or any other doors in the house. Leo closed the doors and sat on the floor. It was quiet. He listened more carefully and thought he heard Cord and Leah speaking, but then that stopped. He imagined his father would never come with the belt, that he would somehow forget for a while and then his temper would cool and he would decide that starting fires in the dirt was not a whipping offense. He also knew that it was hopeless. Cord was about to hurt him again.

There was no shower, but a tub on ball and claw feet. He could see the green linoleum was blackened underneath the tub where a mop couldn't reach. After a while, when he was convinced the wait would be a long one, he lay on his side, letting his cheek warm the cool green linoleum. From there he could see some of Leah's hair, long and dark, around the base of the commode, several strands pasted to the porcelain in twisted shapes like letters from an alien alphabet. His mother's hair was short and gray even though she was just thirty.

The door of the linen closet was ajar several inches, and when he rolled over to his other side, he could see a basket tipped under the weight of a box of feminine napkins. He also saw other mysterious items, some of them consisting of translucent brown rubber tubes and nodes and bulbs, some made of metal and glass. The light from the frosted glass of the room's one high square window was fading in the late afternoon.

Leo was in the middle of a deep breath, a sigh of relaxation and boredom, when he heard the heavy footsteps through the front bedroom, the top drawer of the dresser scraping open, the clatter of the belt buckle against the thin wood and veneer of the drawer, and then the brassy jingling of the chape against the buckle's rim, which jingling continued as the drawer scraped closed with a dull and hollow thump, and the heavy footsteps approached and the bathroom door imploded. In those few warning seconds, Leo sat up so the door would not bang his head.

"All right, get them hands in the tub." There was no sorrow, no compromise or warmth of any kind in Cord's voice—only anger. Leo let out a soft moan between lips stretched taut, tears flooded his eyes and ran down his cheeks, even before he began to get to his feet. And when he was on his feet, he trod in place, left and right, up and down, like a child needing to pee.

"Get em in there, hurry it up," Cord said, the mean spirit in the words powerful and menacing. Leo could not move toward the tub, and Cord grabbed a thin arm at the bicep and jerked it toward the tub, slamming the tops of his son's thighs against the turned back lip of the basin. Old rage pooled at the upheld fist clasping both ends of the doubled leather strap, and it came down through the astringent bathroom air just as it came down through the decades and tried to find release at the tender flesh of Leo's bony rump, and then on his thin legs, and once on his face when he writhed and turned his agonized countenance toward the hurting big man, and again on his legs, and on his back and on the top of his head, Daddy whispering and spitting words… "Thinks he's so special… lays there in that god damn bed…." Leo danced around the bathroom, abandoning the pretense of obeying repeated commands, "Git your hands down in that tub…." trying to protect himself at every point of assault, twisting into strange postures, knee seeking knee, "…Had me some real pussy on Uvea, could've… " elbows over ears "…bus stop girls, could've had any one of em…." fingers splayed on hand jutted to deflect blows away from the immature gonads… "Should've got off the god damn bus… Git them hands down in that tub or I'll show you what a real belting feels like...." But Leo was beyond obedience, none of his movement was from knowing—all of it out of instinct, and useless. His daddy flayed now like a harried man after a fly in the air, "...Worthless whelp... stick you in the god damn closet...." raising red welts all over the little boy, letting the shrill cries fan the flames of his ire. "I'll set your little hide on fire!" he declared, giving extra force to a lash that found a breast and ignited the tiny nipple there in sparkling pain. "Scream, worthless whelp...." muttered through clenched teeth. It might never end. It seemed that it would never end. "I'm the man around here... I didn't hit her... was her god damn mama... do him good... do him real good... teach him a thing or two... burn down the god damn house...." And when Leo felt his consciousness receding to a safer place, and hadn't the reasoning left to wish for the place or even hope for it, the whipping went on. He felt the tip of the belt snap at the bottom of his foot and he was on the floor with his legs up, trying to protect. He pulled his knees to his chest and the belt came to his face and then to the hands he'd put in front of his face and then along his ribs when he curled up and rolled onto one side and then it stopped and his daddy was gone to put the belt away and leave the house.

Leo wailed and sobbed, and after a while he was able to stop the flow of snot from his nose with some toilet paper. In half an hour, he was sitting with his back against the linen cabinet door, holding his knees to his chest, his lips held still for a few moments and then quivering in reprise.

———

Leah had not told Cord about the little fires. She had told Lulu. Later, in a drugged haze, Lulu had alluded to the fires when Cord had come home from work, and he had ferreted the story out of her. Leah had tried to stop Cord from whipping Leo, but it was futile.

Days later Leo sat at the picnic table in the sunny backyard morning. Spread before him, a can of 3-in-1 oil, a rag, a screwdriver, and his BB gun. He had the stock off and was oiling and cleaning the metal parts he could reach. He heard the screen door open and shut, did not have to look. It would be Leah, bored, wanting to talk or fuss.

"Did you break it?" she asked, strolling up behind him.

"Nope. Just cleaning it."

She sat down next to him on the bench, put her arms on the table and laid her head down on them.

He sighed, "You're in my way, Leah."

"Sorry," she muttered, not moving.

He continued to work, wiping and oiling. After a few minutes, he became aware of Leah's leg crowding him. He glanced at her thick, fluffy hair, iridescent blue and orange highlights where light from the sky was hitting it.

The screen door creaked. Leo turned around to see Cord leaning against the door frame, holding the screen door open.

"I thought you was looking after Lulu," Cord said.

Leah raised her head and sat up straight. "She's asleep, Cord."

"She mighta been when you come out here but right now she's awake and she has a headache."

"Well, she knows where the aspirin is, and everything else she has in there."

"What're you doing?" Cord said to Leo.

"Cleaning it," Leo said, a touch of pride in his voice.

"If you're not going to help her, Leah, then what're you doing here all day?"

Leah sighed, "I don't know, Cord."

"Well it wouldn't hurt you to get out and look around a little. Wouldn't hurt you to work and put something into some groceries or something."

"Okay."

"Well, it wouldn't."

Cord let the screen door close, disappeared back into the house. Leah mumbled some mild complaint that Leo couldn't make out. She laid her head back down on the table.

"You're in my way again," Leo said.

"Oh, yeah, I'm in everybody's way," Leah said. "Am I in your way, Leo?"

"Yeah."

"I don't mean now. I mean every day. Am I in your way sleeping on the couch and living here and everything?"

"No. Mama wants you to be here taking care of her."

"I know."

"I wish you'd give me some room."

Leah sat up and Leo moved the gun barrel to the available spot.

"It's kind of odd, I guess," Leah said, brushing her hair away from her face.

"What is?"

"You know, me being finished with high school, laying around the house all day."

She swung her legs around and sprang up, moved out toward the alley, thumped a clothespin to make it spin on the line.

Cord reappeared at the back door, this time pushing it open and going to the table where he stared down at the gun parts. Leo picked up a screw. Cord hacked, cleared his throat, turned to a shady spot against the house underpinning and spat there.

"Daddy, is 3-in-1 oil right for guns?"

"No, it's not. You're gonna ruin the god damn thing."

"I'll leave if you want me to, Cord," Leah said from the yard.

"I don't care what you do," Cord said. "I don't see how you can sit around on your butt all day, that's all." He started back for the house.

"You're right," Leah said, turning around to face the alley. Then louder, "I'll ask Roland if he knows of any jobs that'd be good for me."

Cord stopped. "Ask who?"

Now she turned around and looked at him, his face hanging there halfway to the house, slack, curious.

"You know. Roland. Did I not tell you about him? Real nice, goes to Glynn Daniels."

Cord stood speechless for a few seconds. Leo turned around to look at his silent father, saw an involuntary twitch in the man's upper lip before he spoke again. "Ask him, then. Good idea." He turned and went inside.

Leah returned to the table and crowded Leo again, laid her head on the table, one arm her pillow. With her other hand, she caressed Leo's thigh once, then stopped. "I'm sorry," she said, and the shaking in her voice made Leo look at her, see the redness forming around her eyes.

"At least he doesn't whip you," Leo said.

"He knows better." She glanced at the back door. "He thinks about me all the time. He hardly even tries to hide it."

"Thinks what?"

"Maybe Roland can get me a nice job at Glynn Daniels. You think?"

"I don't know." Leo lined up the screw holes in the stock and the pump assembly.

"Look at me," Leah said, and Leo turned to look at her.

"What?"

Leah stared at the blue and yellow bruise on his face for a moment, then turned away from him.

8

WHEN SCHOOL STARTED THE BRUISE on his face had faded to ocher, and where there had been bright red stripes on his legs and arms and trunk, there were, in the cool September air of regenesis, fading brown lines and speckles that were covered with long shirtsleeves and bluejeans.

The Saturday after the first week of school, Leah found Leo rummaging through the dirty clothes basket inside the back door. "You want a 400?" Leah asked. She had just finished having cereal with Lulu in the bedroom. Leo, sleep in his eyes, had been padding around the house in his cutoff blue jeans, no shirt, no shoes.

"What is it?" he asked, looking for the T-shirt he'd discarded the night before somewhere in the house.

"Put on some shoes. We have to walk."

"Is it good?"

"It's good."

"Walk where?"

"Coggin Drug."

Leo located the T-shirt in the hamper, slipped it on as he returned to his room for the blue deck shoes without socks. He found Leah waiting for him on the front porch.

"What's a 400?" he asked her. She was already walking and he fell in step with her.

"You'll see. It's good."

"Ice cream?"

"No. It's a drink."

"Coke float?

"It's chocolate milk."

"Okay."

"With ice in it, too."

They stepped into the morning sun, already hot on the pavement. Leo realized Leah was walking fast, too fast for his comfort.

"Slow down," he said, and he stopped trying to keep up with her.

"And then I'm going to call Roland," she said, slowing to his pace.

"Who is that, anyway?"

"I met him at Safeway. He was tall so I told him to reach me down a can of peaches."

"Did he?"

"Course. Then he started trying to talk with me."

"Because you're pretty."

"He had to tell me he plays basketball and majors in economics. He wanted to know if I ever went to any Glynn Daniels games."

"You never have."

"No, and I just wanted to get the rest of the groceries and get out of there. But he kept talking and talking."

"Did you like him?"

Leah made a puff of air with her lips.

"Well, did you?"

"He got my name and told me his and then the next day he called me. My name's not even in the phone book so I don't know how he found the number. Had to do some looking, I imagine."

"He ask you for a date?"

"Of course."

"Did you?"

"No," she said, and tried to hit him on the arm, but he ducked.

They turned the corner onto Coggin Avenue, heading for the drugstore, the soda fountain, the cool privacy of the wooden booths, the table tops carved with names of boyfriends and girlfriends from years and decades back.

"But now I'm going to," Leah said as the store came into view.

"Why?"

"Because Cord is such a stupid stupe." Leo kept his agreement private. "Well, he is."

This, Leo surmised, was the subject of the conversation, the reason he was getting a 400, because she wanted to tell him this, wanted him to agree. "He looks at me all the time, you know. Wants me to get a job. He better stop looking at me and thinking things."

They pushed through the heavy wooden and glass doors. The air conditioning hit them hard, induced violent pleasure, evaporating the sweat they'd worked up on their walk. They headed straight back to the soda fountain and found the booth most distant from the counter.

"He was already jealous when I just said Roland's name," Leah continued. "'Who?' Why are you so interested, Co-ord?"

Leo didn't remember Cord being all that interested, but he might have been.

"I'm going to show him a thing or two," Leah confided.

"What?"

"Oh, like maybe I can go out on dates, and he might not get to look at me so much from now on."

"I don't think he cares."

"I think he does. He *will*."

"Are you really going to get a job?"

"Maybe Roland can help me find one," Leah said, less interested. "I'll go get us our 400s." She slid out of the booth and bounded over to the counter and ordered. Waiting for the drinks, Leah smiled back at Leo and posed like a movie star for him, making him blush. She paid for the drinks, carried them back to the booth.

"What if he already has a girlfriend?" Leo said as he took his 400.

Leah smiled at him.

—

Late Monday afternoon Leo, tired from school, sprawled on the dining room floor and watched Leah perusing the want ads in the *Brownwood Bulletin*.

"I could get a job in this town if I wanted one, I bet," she told Leo. "And I don't need Roland Brunck to help me." Leo closed his eyes, wondered what it would mean, Leah having a job.

"The Lyric Theater's looking for someone for a ticket booth girl. I could do that. How hard could that be?" She took the paper to the phone and dialed the number.

"I'm calling about the ad in the *Bulletin* for a ticket booth operator." She sounded so breathy and polite that Leo looked to see if it was still Leah he was hearing. The person on the other end was doing all the talking, it seemed, and Leah was only saying "Yes, sir," and finally a few words about Wednesday at eleven a.m.

When she hung up, she fell to her knees beside Leo and started tickling his ribs violently. "See? Nothing to it!" she laughed.

"Quit it!" Leo pushed her away. "You mean you found a job already?"

"I got an interview," she said. "Same thing."

—

Cat Ballou was showing on the night Leah began work. There was little to learn, and she learned it quickly. By November she was beside herself with boredom. At home, she confounded Leo with sudden conversations. *South Pacific* had been showing for two weeks, a huge hit and already scheduled to be held over for another week. Her boss Tom Miller, Leah had reported to Leo right away, liked to squeeze into the booth with her and explain things that didn't necessarily need explanation and start discussions about how good she smelled. When his wife came downtown to check out the new ticket girl and sniffed around the lobby all one evening, Tom stayed away from Leah, but Leah was bored. "I just acted the way Tom always liked me to act around him," she told Leo.

The day after she was fired, late that night, Leo rested his cheek on the sill at his window, the sash raised about a foot, the night breezy but warm for December. He liked to lie in the dark and watch a giant elm two backyards away. He'd long ago memorized the lines of it, the play of the night skyshine through its branches. He made pictures from its parts, some of them characters who became strong in his mind. The left lobe of the crown was a grinning horse-faced man who nodded his assent to Leo's questions when the wind blew. Crouched beneath him was a little girl, her face turned away but her dress all billowy. She held her legs together always, as they were the trunk of the tree, tonight around her head a halo that was the Milky Way.

The floor creaked and he rolled over to see Leah standing inside the doorway. It was dark, but she was wearing a white nightie that glowed against everything else in the room.

"You 'sleep?"

"Not yet."

She glided across the room and sat on the edge of his bed.

"What do you want?" he asked, annoyed.

She breathed once, twice, before answering. "You're going to get a cold laying like that."

"Who cares." His thoughts spun off to the homework he hadn't done, and wouldn't. He felt a pang of dread for tomorrow when he'd have to announce his grade in class out loud. Zero. Again? Yes, ma'am.

Leah told him all about a movie, a western with Audie Murphy, and she chuckled at parts that were not funny, and she made the story go long, long and boring, and he was sleepy. When he was almost drowsing into sleep, she placed her hand gently just below his belly.

Then she continued telling the story of a movie, but it seemed that it was a different movie now, about Vikings, with lots of scenery and not much happening. And as she talked, little more than a whisper, she began touching him. At first he questioned her, told her to stop, but her hand kept on caressing him until he no longer wanted her to stop, and her hand kept on until he understood the end of it and there was no more need for it. It was later, the next day and days following, that he considered whether he, or she, or both of them had been bad.

9

ALMOST EVERYTHING PHYSICAL, NOT COUNTING space, is opaque except for things like air, water, glass, etc. Opaque things are invisible except for the surface. The surface is almost nothing, just some light waves bouncing. We can't see the real thing, which is all inside. I thought this up and told my teacher, and she liked it. I told Papa and he liked it even more than my teacher. He said it was profound, even though it was not informed by all that much wisdom because I'm not old enough to be wise. I probably will be wise, though, when I get old. I've been verbal right from the start. Too verbal, I imagine you are thinking right now.

As I have said before to anyone who will listen, I like Joyce Heffernan. She came from somewhere else, I think Atlanta, Georgia, in the middle of the year because of her father's job. He's a hospital lawyer. Joyce is a nice girl, and the reason I like her— one of the main reasons—is the way she talks about subtraction. She doesn't say minus and she doesn't say equals. Where she came from, they say "take-away" and "makes" instead. But what I like about her is that she doesn't say "take-away" either. She says "cake-away." "Eleven cake-away eight makes three." I'm sure she just heard it wrong and thinks that's the way it's supposed to go. If my hormones were raging yet, I would be in love with Joyce, but of course that's years away, so for now I like her a lot and think I'm in love with her.

Roland wore his letter sweater, sitting with Leah in the car at the Dairy Maid, sipping Dr. Pepper. He'd won the game against Stephenville the previous night. Maybe thinking you're in love with someone is the same as being in love with them.

"Have you ever thought about going to college?" he asked her.

"Mmm," she said, swallowing, disengaging from the straw. "I was good in biology. Thought about pre-med."

"Pre-med, well well."

"Still thinking about it. Haven't had a chance to do much serious looking yet."

"Why not?"

"Well, because of my sister Lulu." She had already told him she was a full-time caregiver for her invalid sister.

Roland reached over and took Leah's hand in both of his, a move that reminded Leah of a Rock Hudson movie.

"I think you're a very special girl, Leah, and I hope you don't mind my saying so."

"No, I don't. Thank you. I'm nothing special though."

"Oh yes, you are."

Roland let go of her hand. "So anyway," he said.

"What?"

"Want to go out with me tomorrow night?"

"To do what?"

"I don't know. Drive around. Whatever you feel like."

Bangs Hill was a bluff northwest of Brownwood. At the summit, a small parking lot was flanked by four picnic areas outfitted with tables. Brownwood, nestled in the little geographic niche known as Pecan Valley, sparkled on a clear Texas night far up toward the eastern horizon. Even Leah, who had no friends her own age, but who had socialized during high school, was aware of Bangs Hill's function in the scheme of Brownwood's romantic life. Roland was content to kiss her, then tell her about his master plan—get his undergraduate degree at Glynn Daniel, take an MBA elsewhere, start a business, buy a car and a house, then get married to someone wonderful—and when she reached her arms around his neck and pulled him to her, his joy was transcendent. A half-hour of heavy petting, and Roland seemed satisfied for the time being.

"I better get you home," he announced, manly, as though to say he could not go any further without wanting to go *further*. "Homework, you know."

This is perfect, thought Leah. Under control.

—

On Tuesday flowers arrived at the front door. Leah answered the knock. She saw the white Davis Floral van parked at the curb. A woman in her fifties, stocky and ruddy, with short curly orange hair, handed the flowers to Leah with a smile. "I bet these are for you. Leah?"

"Yes, I'm Leah."

A bigger smile, a sort of wink, and the woman was gone.

Leah stood at the door for a minute and watched the van disappear down the street. Something stirred in her, but she was not sure what, or what it meant. She had no feelings for Roland, and the flowers would not change that, nor would all the flowers in the world.

She heard her name called out weakly. Taking the card and crumpling it into her pocket, she carried the bouquet into the bedroom where Lulu lay in bed under blankets.

"What?"

"Oh, you got flowers? Are they from Roland?"

"No. A lady from Davis Floral brought them and said they're for you, from a secret admirer."

"Oh Leah, you're a liar."

Leah crawled onto the bed and held the flowers for Lulu to smell.

"Oh, they're beautiful," Lulu sighed.

"And they come with a kiss," Leah said, smoothing Lulu's hair away with her hand. She leaned over to Lulu and kissed her cheek, lingered there, kissed her on the mouth.

"Oh Leah, quit it," Lulu said, but she didn't seem to mind it. Leah kissed her on the mouth again, this time wetly. "Now stop that, Leah."

Leah stopped it, but snuggled close to her sister where she was able to put all thoughts out of her mind and relax. Lulu began snoring, and Leah pulled off her jeans and T-shirt and crawled under the covers to be close. The flowers fell to the floor in the rustle of covers, and when Leah found her comfortable position with one knee wedged between Lulu's bony thighs, she fell into a midday sleep full of colorful dreams.

—

Roland seemed comfortable with not meeting Leah's family, nor setting foot into her house. He himself came from a working class family, good Baptists, little money, decent enough status in their small east Texas town. He would make his own way in life with whomever he chose. Too soon even to think about it, he assured Leah. Drive-

In movies and Bangs Hill became their routine–perfect opportunities for leisurely kissing until passion began to get out of hand, at which time Roland exercised self-control and called time.

The wet winter winds gradually gave way to some spring-like days. At the first opportunity, they lay on their backs in a grove of pecan trees in Coggin Park opposite the playground. The late February sky was alive with clouds, swift little fluff in a field of blue. Roland's transistor radio issued tinny harmonies, ecstatic sound track to the romance. *I cry each time... I hear this sound... Here he comes... that's Cathy's clown.*

Roland went up on his elbow, unable to bear not gazing upon his girlfriend, so petite there on his blanket, beside his front guard body. "You're so beautiful," he said to her. She knew already, but it was nice to hear it, also a little disturbing that he had found the courage to say it. She had already ascertained that he'd been dating a girl at Glynn Daniel, a Bible major, and had quickly dumped her after Leah had first called him. Leah invented a boyfriend who'd moved away a year ago to take a job in Enid, Oklahoma. More than that, she would not say.

He leaned over and kissed her. Safe from the possibility of sex, clothed in the bright daytime, they worked torso to torso, spinal twisting hip to hip, passion building over the better part of an hour.

She'd been letting him put his tongue in her mouth on the last several dates they'd had, and here in the park, under the sheepie ghost clouds and the pecan trees not yet budding out, they kissed again and her arms wrapped around him again and her hands caressed his back and now *her* tongue went into *his* mouth, and when it did he humped toward her in a surge of passion.

He suddenly made a guttural, involuntary sound. Leah felt his body tense violently. Lying back, he struggled to conceal his embarrassment. Leah could hear him panting, and was in fact aroused herself, but had no idea what had just occurred. She uttered a small giggle. "We better cool it a little, huh?" she offered.

But Roland sat up. "I need to get you home and get back to the dorm," he said.

"Oh," she said.

"No, it's just... I have something I need to get done. I'll call you tonight." He hurried her to the car, and tried for small talk until he dropped her off in front of her house. He drove off toward Glynn Daniel, Baptist College of the Southwest.

—

Cougar windshield wipers cleared away the thick late winter mist as Roland drove the two lane toward Indian Gap, a defunct community—some called it a ghost town— some twenty miles from Brownwood.

When they reached the stretch of abandoned, rotting buildings, Leah frowned at the decay. They got out of the car and strolled along the weedy gravel road. Leah turned to Roland, looked up with her eyes big. Hypnotized, he embraced her and they kissed, long and French, bodies pressed together.

"I have to...." Roland croaked, but couldn't finish.

"Have to...?"

"...tell you something. Leah, I feel... I need to... I think I...."

"Hush," she whispered, and kissed him again. "I know how you feel. Let's get back in the car before the redbugs get us."

Back in the car, they pulled away down the road, out of Indian Gap. Aware of Roland's darkened mood, Leah placed her hand on his thigh and rubbed it soothingly.

"Maybe you shouldn't do that," he said, none too brightly.

"I'm sorry."

"No, *I'm* sorry. It's just... when we're making out, I get so...." He saw a small dirt road to the right and pulled into it, drove down it a few feet and stopped.

"What's the matter, Roland?"

He jammed his hand into his pocket and pulled out a pack of Trojans, tossed them on the dashboard. Leah stared at the item, her lips parted, her eyes open wide at first, but slowly narrowing. Watching her, Roland finally said, "I'm sorry."

"I'm not that kind of girl, Roland."

"Oh god! I *know* that, Leah." He took her hand in both of his. "I *know* that, and that's why I feel so... I'm just...."

"Don't worry, Roland. I know it's frustrating. We have to cool it, that's all. Don't you agree?"

He hung his head. "Yes. You're right."

They sat looking down the dirt road to where it bent out of sight behind a growth of Johnson grass. A light mist began falling again, the world pointillist through the windshield, and a rain crow nagged the gray sky with its harsh cry.

"Does this mean we can't... kiss anymore?" Roland said.

"Oh, Roland, I hope not. Do you think we shouldn't?"

"I think we *should*."

"I do, too. We have to not be so passionate about it. That's why it gets frustrating. Don't you agree?"

"Yes. I just don't know if that's possible."

"Here," Leah said, leaning across the gearshift console to him. "We can still kiss without getting carried away." She offered him a kiss, which he took, and they shifted to gain more intimacy and kiss some more. Leah guided his hand to her breast and kissed him harder, and worked his lips apart with her tongue. She took his tongue into her mouth and sucked it in and out until it was clear he was losing control. Within a minute, she was practically astraddle him, and he was undulating under her. She reached down to his crotch and cupped the bulge there in her hand. As soon as she moved her hand along the bulge, he tensed and moaned, and in a moment he pushed her away.

"Oops," she joked. "There we go again. Hard to not get carried away."

"I know," he said darkly, settling back in his seat.

On the hurried drive back to Brownwood, Leah realized in a slow epiphany that Roland had had an orgasm. By the time they reached town, she had also figured out that the same thing had happened before, in the park. What to her had been amusing—these heavy petting sessions—to him had been overwhelming. She was pleased to realize this. She was strangely empowered, but also troubled by the situation, and she searched hard, in the silent ride back toward Brownwood, for the truth.

"I want to try and tell you how I feel about you," he said.

"Okay."

But he said nothing until he had found a place to pull off the road and stop. He swallowed hard. "I love you." He was staring straight ahead.

She was silent for a few seconds. Just long enough to let him worry.

"Well, I love you too," she said.

"I mean I'm in love with you," he said. "I never want to leave you. Someday, when I'm at the right place in my career, I think we ought to get married." This time she gave him indefinite silence. "What do you think?"

"I don't know. You have another year at Glynn Daniels and then you'll have to move on. Don't you have to get a Masters degree?"

"Sure. So what?"

"Oh, Roland. I never thought you would ask me to marry you. Don't you see? A low class girl like me. I thought you were playing with me. I thought... I don't know what I thought." She buried her face in her hands and sobbed.

THE PARACLETE
69

"Leah, how could you ever think that?" He sat speechless and waited for her crying to subside, which it soon did. "I should have told you I loved you when I first knew."

"When was that?" she asked, face still hidden in her hands.

"Almost the first time we went out."

"Oh, Roland. I wish you had told me." She offered herself up for a kiss, and he obliged. They continued to kiss, and the passion mounted.

"So you'll marry me... someday?" he managed in a moment when he had possession of his tongue.

"Let's give ourselves some time to think about it," she said, and quickly took his tongue back.

But he broke away again.

"What's the matter?"

"Nothing, Leah. But I think it's time to stop this until we come to some kind of decision. I mean, really. I can't stand it anymore."

Leah registered his attempt at coercion.

"I know you're right, Roland. I'm sorry. I shouldn't let my feelings make me do that to you. I'm being selfish."

"No, I want it as bad as you do. But, you know, I want it all."

"I'm going to be better. I'll be a good girl. I promise." She knew this was not exactly what he wanted.

"Yeah, I will too."

"Oh don't be so glum. You know what?" she said, resolve rising in her voice. "Let's get me home now so I can go to the bathroom like I need to do real bad, and tomorrow is a new day. When I said I love you, I meant it, and a person doesn't try to frustrate someone they love. You agree?"

"Yeah. You're right," he guessed. But she had to prompt him again to start the car, and when they arrived at her house, she denied him a good night kiss.

—

The next day Leo was sitting on the front steps petting a friendly cat belonging to the unliked neighbor. He saw Roland drive by the house, recognizing by now the car and the driver. Strange that he drove by and didn't stop. The cat plopped down and turned belly up, an invitation for more intimate petting, then attacked Leo's hand when he tried to pet it.

"You're a stupid kitty, aren't you? Yesh you am."

"Don't be mean to the little kitty," Leah said from behind the screen door.

"Him's a bad kitty, trying to scratch my hand," Leo said. "Your boyfriend just drove by."

"I saw him." She stepped out to the porch, her first foray into daylight today. She sat on the step next to Leo. She was wearing bright white short shorts and a white sleeveless blouse.

"I see you noticing my shorts," Leah said.

"So?"

As Leo petted the cat, Leah straightened her legs and rested them across the bottom two steps. "Don't call him my boyfriend."

"Why not?"

"When he's my boyfriend, I'll tell you. Don't be so quick to judge everything. You don't know anything."

—

Roland phoned her that evening. "I need to see you. Can I come pick you up?"

"I'm making dinner for everybody. Can you wait 'til we finish eating?"

"How long?"

"I guess about thirty minutes."

Leah had not finished her pimento cheese sandwich when she heard the honk out front.

"Don't go running out there," Cord grumbled when she started to get up. "Finish your sandwich. How come he don't ever come in the house?"

"I can't eat any more," Leah said, getting up and hurrying to the front door.

They drove up Bangs Hill and parked. The day was warm and hazy, the sky almost blue through the moist air. The scrub oaks were beginning to send out leaves, from the hill Brownwood looked gray-green, and even the old hotel, a twelve-story red brick structure, appeared grayish.

Staring through the windshield at the pale sky, Roland measured his words. "I want us to be together. I love you, Leah."

"Well, I love you, too."

"Getting married would—I mean, not be according to my plans, but...." He looked at her and found that she was watching him. "I had this all planned how to say this, but now...."

"Are you officially proposing to me? Because...."

"No," he interrupted. "Well, in a way. I mean, it's up to you." Flustered, he took a deep breath, put his hands on the steering wheel and gripped it. "Let me tell you what I came up with, and don't take this wrong. I know you won't. It's about the frustration."

"Oh, yeah, that."

"Yeah. Well... I'd be willing, if you agree, to keep to my plan and not get married right now, but I wouldn't want to keep on, you know, the way we're going.... It's not *healthy*, for one thing. You know what I mean?"

Leah now leaned her head back against the seat. "You mean about sex and everything, right?

"Right. Not... having it. You know?"

Leah looked for a long time at the sky, wondering if she was looking at cloud cover or just haze.

"You know what I mean about it not being healthy, don't you?" Roland said.

Leah leaned forward so that she could look down on Brownwood. "You're saying we should go ahead and have sex now so that you don't have to mess up your plan about getting your job first and everything."

"Not saying we *should*. Just saying it would be healthier, at least for me."

"I'm not that kind of girl."

"I know that." Plan B, he might as well have said. Leah almost smiled. "I know that. And I'm willing to get married now, even though it trashes major portions of my plans. To me, you're more important than all the plans in the world."

He had now made the ultimate offer, Leah realized. This was as far as he would go. He wanted sex, and was even willing to marry her for it, even though he'd prefer not to.

Leah felt herself floating in a kind of void—not a void of gravity, nor of atmosphere, but a void of power. She knew Roland had none over her, but she felt little power herself, either.

"What are you thinking?" he asked.

"This is the first you've talked about marriage in the present tense, Roland. I wasn't thinking about that. To me, it was just dating. I mean, I have plans too."

"I know that."

"I mean, I love you as a boyfriend, I do. And I was flattered when you said you were thinking about marriage. But to talk about marriage, I mean... I know we're old enough, sort of, but I haven't thought about that, and...."

"And what?"

"Well, when I think about that, it brings in some other... some other... people."

"You think they wouldn't approve of me?"

"I'm not talking about them. I'm talking about somebody I knew before you."

"What... who are you talking about?"

"Well, he's been out of town. He actually *lives* out of town. But, I mean...."

"Are you saying you've been dating somebody else?"

She stared hard at the dashboard.

"Leah?"

"Not since I've been dating you, but he and I didn't break up either or anything."

Leah turned her face away from him and let the silence push in on them.

"You mean.... Not the guy you said moved to Oklahoma. You said y'all were broken up."

"No, I didn't say that. I was supposed to be waiting for him."

"But it's been all this time and...." He opened his car door violently, sprang out and slammed it shut. Leah watched him stalking toward the bluff. He stopped where the guardrail edged the drop-off.

He stewed for a minute or two, then turned back to the car and approached it, a frightening deadpan expression on his flushed face. He jerked open the passenger side door.

"Do you mind getting out?" he said, choking on his own words.

Leah climbed out, waited for him to close the door. He slammed it. Leah spoke firmly, "I didn't mean to upset you. This is no time for me to be holding anything back, is it? You sprang this on me."

"*Sprang* it on you!" He stalked off again and stopped at the guardrail. Clearly, he was too overwrought even to talk. She went to his side and stood looking down the drop-off. It was a sheer thirty-foot drop onto rocks and many broken beer bottles.

"I never meant to upset you, Roland. I thought we were dating, having a good time."

"We weren't talking about having a good time," he sputtered. "We were talking about love. We said... I told you I love you, and you said you did too. Now, you.... Oh god." He turned and walked away. She could see that he was breaking into tears. She started to follow but he quickened his pace. She let him go, watched him until he disappeared down a trashy little trail into a thicket of mesquites and tickle tongue bushes. She sat on top of a picnic table. A catchy little tune was running through her mind, and she tried to identify it. It was from that movie she'd seen with Roland a few weeks ago, *Tom Jones*. It always played at the funny parts when they used fast motion.

He was gone ten minutes, then returned, red-faced but not tearful. He started speaking before he even reached the picnic table. "Say you'll marry me," he demanded. "Just say it."

"Let's go to the park. We need some time to...."

"Tell me you will marry me."

"We have plans, Roland. Maybe we will get married sometime...."

"Today. We'll get married today or I will kill myself."

"What?"

"Today. Or I will kill myself."

She didn't judge him to be suicidal. She folded her arms across her chest, set her mouth, and looked down at the ground, frowning.

"Fine, then," he said, and walked toward the guard rail.

"What are you doing?"

He whirled around to face her, stretched his arm toward the bluff. "I'm jumping off the cliff. *Right now,*" he shouted, and she saw the tears flowing from his eyes and heard the fervor in his voice. He turned and hurried toward the bluff.

"*All right,*" she screamed. "All right." He stopped. She slid off the table and walked to him, placed her hand on his shoulder. "Roland. Roland."

Before turning to her, he said "We'll be fine. We'll find a little apartment in Brownwood and everything. Roaches, the works."

He had no intention of marrying her and she knew it well. Neither did she believe he would have jumped. Those opinions solidified in the low humming of the Cougar as he drove her home.

He turned off the motor in front of her house. "I'm sorry I acted that way," he said.

"I understand," she said. "But we're not going to see each other for a while."

She was out of the car in a flurry, straight to the house, noticing that he was not starting the car, not driving away.

Five minutes passed. Then, sitting on the couch where she slept at night, Leah heard Roland's car start up, then the engine revving over and over, louder and louder. She heard the gears grind and then the tires squealing against the pavement as the car careened away. Then more loud squealing of tires as the car swerved around a corner, she judged two blocks down the street. Moments passed, Leah could still hear the car's engine revving, tires squealing some blocks away, but the sound getting fainter. When she realized that the sound was beginning to get louder again, she went to the front window, stood beside it and peeked from behind the shade. She could tell when he turned back onto McKavett street, several blocks down the other direction now. He was driving like a maniac. She saw the car for a brief moment as it roared past her house and on down the street. The sound was fading, but still audible when she heard a loud shriek of distressed tires on pavement and then a louder crunching thud followed by some crashing of glass and metal. He had wrecked his car. Leah sat back down on the couch, felt tired, wondered if there was any milk.

10

THE NEXT EVENING, CORD WAS watching TV when Leah walked by him carrying a bag of potato chips and half a bottle of root beer.

"Where's Leo?" Leah asked him.

"I don't know. Out in the back."

She found him in his room, lying on his bed staring at the ceiling.

"Whatcha thinking about?" she asked him from the doorway.

"Homework."

"You done it?"

"No."

"You're going to fail seventh grade."

"Don't care. I can't do it with the TV blaring all day and night."

"You hate me?"

"I didn't say I hated you."

"You have said it."

"I don't hate you."

Still standing in the doorway, Leah shifted and turned to leave.

"I like you," Leo said.

She stopped, turned to look at him. He lay still, staring wide-eyed at the ceiling. She meandered across the room to him and looked down into his face. He refused to look at her. "You do?" she whispered.

"Yes, I do," he said, frowning as severely as he could.

"Well, well," she whispered. "I'm glad." Then, as she turned to leave, she whispered even more softly, but above the gentle crinkling sound of the potato chip bag as it pressed against her soda bottle, "Took you long enough."

———

For an hour after lunch on Thursdays, Leo could relax and enjoy math club with Sterling "Turtle" Terrence, Kenneth Triplett, and Dean Warburton, the only three kids who enjoyed numbers. Leo was bad at math, but it was just a club, no grade. Mrs. Oberman put Mary Jane Bowen and Debbie Bradford in the math club because they had no interest at all in any of the clubs.

Even on Thursdays, though, Leo's unease lingered throughout the afternoon and evening. Each school day ended with a recap of grades, read out loud by Miss Ater. His marks publicized that he never did his homework. Miss Ater glared at him as the class filed out of the room, but she didn't call his name, made no attempt to stop him. First Lulu and then Cord had already frustrated her attempts to communicate about Leo's homework. She had given up on him.

He ambled home. No hurry. Nothing there was going to be any different from before. He stopped in front of a gray frame house when he saw a cat approaching him from the brick walk. He let the cat smear its scent on his pants legs. He started walking again, checking to see if the cat would follow him, which it did for a short distance, but didn't make the turn onto McKavett Street. The wet, tepid air carried faint, tarry scents of decay, and Leo remembered something, but it was nothing, just one of the memories from before he was born, and he was too tired to try and let it ripen.

Pausing again on the front steps at home, he looked up and down the quiet street. Nothing. No activity, no possibility.

He opened the door with his foot, stepped into the fumy house, closed the door with his heel. Staggering toward his room, he dropped his schoolbooks on the couch where Leah slept at night. He refused to accept that he would not touch the books again until he left for school in the morning, vowing to do his homework this time, no more humiliation in class. How difficult could it be? The lessons were easy. There must be a way to set up a little table in his room, close the door against the TV noise.

From his window he saw Leah in the backyard. It was a warm, overcast day, and she was wearing Bermuda shorts and a pink short-sleeve blouse tucked in to accentuate her narrow waist. She had tortured Roland for almost a year. Leo had watched it with only passing interest, but wondered now if his impressions had been correct. He knew little about sex. His one experience was associated with her billowing white nightie, her long painted fingernails, her soft voice. He knew his scruffy friends at school bandied half-understood misinformation from which he might glean some truth, but he hadn't done so. Certainly, neither Lulu nor Cord had been moved to educate him in any way. He didn't care.

She was taking down some items from the clothesline, placing them in the same worn out blue basket they'd used forever. Leo collapsed on his bed, stared at the ceiling for a moment, then closed his eyes against life.

Leah clattered in the back door, and he waited for her sounds in the house. Lulu, he knew, was asleep in the front bedroom. Cord was at work. The unexplained silence opened his eyes. He caught a glimpse of pink at his doorway where Leah was standing, leaning on the frame, looking at him. She was not smiling, was not frowning, but merely looking at him with... what? Curiosity? Interest?

"What'sa matter?" he asked her.

"Nothing. What'sa matter with you?"

"Nothing. Go away."

"Thought you liked me."

He didn't answer, closed his eyes, then opened them to keep watch on Leah. She wandered into his room, gently pushing the door closed behind her, went to the bed by way of checking the items on his dresser—a broken clock, some socks—no pairs—a small piece of wood, a magnifying glass, the remains of a pad of lined paper, butch wax from crew cut days last year. She sat on the foot of the bed, turning profile to Leo, who pressed his chin into his chest to keep an eye on her.

"Gonna take a nap?" she asked.

"No."

"You can't lay on the bed with your shoes on. It'll get the bedclothes dirty."

This was news to Leo, and he ignored it. Leah turned, shifted with a bounce, and in a swift motion lifted Leo's sneaker-shod feet into her lap, where she went to work untying shoelaces. Leo reacted by pulling his feet away from her, but she held onto them, gave him a stern look.

"Shhhh."

Not sure why, he stilled himself, and she removed his shoes.

"Stinky...," she whispered. Leo knew it, said nothing. She put her hand up into his pants leg, held the small calf in her warm hand. And then Leo looked at her again, and she looked at him.

This was something they could do together, and, on balance, he did like Leah, and he knew she was more than pretty. So he lay still, tried closing his eyes.

"You have to help a little," she said. But he did not.

"How come you like to do this?" he asked, eyes open now.

"Don't you like it?"

"No. It's stupid."

"You liked it before," she said.

"It felt funny."

"Didn't you like it, though?"

He couldn't remember—it had been a year ago.

"I think you did like it," she said, and Leo felt her hand.

It does feel nice. Very nice. Yes. Now I remember. This is what it felt like.

"Am I pretty?"

He sighed, and it was enough of an answer. With his eyes closed, he began picturing Leah's red, long fingernails, how many times he'd noticed them, their perfection. He vowed he would think about them often.

"It's bad, isn't it," Leo said, and opened his eyes to look to his aunt for an answer.

"Yeah," she said, and she smiled and winked.

—

She came to Leo every once in a while at first, but two years later he was wanting it all the time. They planned it together, figured out when they were going to be alone in the house. She'd done some of his homework for him in seventh grade, when he'd been about to fail, and he squeaked through. Now Leah said most of the work was too hard for her, why didn't he get help from other kids who were good at it? But it was not that the work was hard for him. The work was easy. He just didn't do it sometimes. He didn't have an excuse. Sometimes, when Cord was at work, he walked by his parents' bedroom and saw his mother asleep, and even though it would be a good, quiet time to do homework, he plopped down on his bed and stared at the ceiling.

Evenings, Cord was home and turned on the TV. On the news there were stories, complete with movies, of war in Vietnam. Leo sometimes sat and watched, other times went outside to get away from the noise. He was fourteen now, technically a high school freshman although ninth grade was housed at the junior high school. But he was still small in physical stature. Some of the boys in his class were growing bigger, more muscular, shaving, a few of them starting to look swarthy. Leah made him feel fine about himself when she snuck into his room, telling him things he liked to hear while she touched him.

11

O N ONE OF THE AFTERNOONS of neglected homework, Dean Warburton, from math club back in seventh grade, rode up the street on an old blue bicycle. He was the kind of guy who picked his nose without a tissue. One thing about Dean, though, he was always nice. Like Leo, Dean had not yet grown larger, though his hair was coarser and he had a feral look.

The seat of Dean's bike was too low so he rode with knees bent, struggling to pedal along the level street. The tires needed air. He said, "Hey Nobles." Leo returned a small wave. Dean pulled up to the curb and put down a toe.

"This where you live?"

"Yeah."

Dean nodded and showed Leo his broad smile. Leo had been stepping on ants, and now looked for activity befitting his age. He began easing off toward the side of the house.

"I know a place," said Dean.

"Huh?"

"I know a place you wouldn't believe. I found money there."

"How much?"

"A quarter. But there's probably more. Come on, get on the back."

"No, I don't want to."

"It's not far. I'll pump you over there. You'll like it."

Leo lowered himself onto the back fender, saw the tire go flatter than ever.

"You sure this crate'll make it?"

"Yeah. It never breaks. Never has yet."

Leo held his feet away from the spokes as Dean, smaller even than Leo, stood on the pedals to get going. They wobbled top-heavy down the street. The humid air carried Dean's scent to Leo, a strange mixture of camphor and stale bacon grease. Leo regretted getting on the bike.

They crossed Coggin Avenue, entered a neighborhood Leo seldom attended. Two blocks in, Dean stopped the bike at a derelict wooden frame house, its graying asbestos siding corrupted by honeysuckle, underpinning loose and rotted and crowded with Johnson grass. The front windows were paned with cardboard or glass or nothing, shards of glass like the blades of pirate sabers splayed on the ground. The yard was waist high in milkweed. Beggar-lice clumped along the walk to the front door, which stood open behind a screen hanging twisted on one hinge. Russet dead morning glory vines rose from the tangle in front of the concrete slab of porch, and crossing it, clung to the screen and spread around the front door frame. Dean sidled toward the house, avoiding the beggar-lice, up a crumbling concrete walk whose upper surface was eroded away.

"Come on. It's great."

"Who owns this place?"

"I don't know. Come on in." He was standing at the door.

Leo moved up the walk, through the forlorn white glare of day, and followed Dean inside.

Inexplicably, dozens of empty, smashed Milk Duds boxes littered the floor. Window light fell on trash, a tumult of ill-used personal items, a *People* with a single, alienated Beach Boy on the cover, a nylon stocking, sere and partially submerged in a pile of hair conditioner bottles. At the doorway to the next room, a stack of acoustical ceiling tiles, high enough to make a seat, and compacted by such use, lay damaged around the edges. In the dining room, a gallon paint can, its lid off and pale blue tint spilled, long dried, to a newspaper, and other newspapers scattered, as though spread and then kicked and disregarded. The house smelled of stale humanity and its rotting accoutrements. Damp odors from the trash and sediment on the floor rose and mingled with the cooler air in the still rooms.

Leo picked his way through the dining room, stopping to flip over a magazine with his toe, curious to see if it might be nasty. It was only a *Look*, its cover proclaiming Lyndon Johnson and NASA at odds over the race to the moon.

"In here, hurry."

The voice was more than a room away. Leo didn't hurry. He glanced once more around the dining room, looking for anything that might be worth examining. A Milk Duds box on the windowsill appeared unopened, but Leo wouldn't touch it. He stepped into a narrow hallway. Darker, less defined masses were piled along the baseboard. He looked for an object he could use to prod—a stick, coat hanger—but there was nothing useful. He tapped a shadow with his shoe. It was cloth. He leaned closer. It was a garment of some kind, dark blue or black, corduroy. A few feet to the right there was a closed door. In front of him, a bathroom with no door at all. To his left, an open door, Dean poking around in a room that would be a bedroom. Leo went in there.

"Where's all this money?"

"This is where I found it. In here."

"Where?"

"Under this stuff." Dean was tentative, though. Leo felt unsure as he watched the boy turn to a mound of magazines and newspapers in front of a portable record player missing its chassis. Dean stooped, tossed some magazines aside. "Under here." He stood up, unpocketed the quarter he'd referred to, and held it toward Leo.

"There's not any money in here," Leo said. "Why'd you want to show me this place?"

Suddenly Dean was squirming, putting the quarter back in his pocket, looking embarrassed but desperate and driven. "I think it's cool. It's a hideout. I thought you might like it."

Leo had never felt such pity. "Yeah, it's cool, man, but it's nasty in here." Now Dean was hanging his head, embarrassed. "What do you want? To be friends?"

"Yeah," Dean said, and looked up hopefully.

"Well I don't have friends," Leo said, as firmly as he could. "No offense." He met Dean's eyes and then quickly turned away. Passing back through the dining room, Leo could hear Dean in the bedroom saying "Please." And then louder, his voice strained with imminent crying, "Please."

Outside, Leo gave the bike an assessing glance as he strode past it. It was the old style, and now he noticed it was a girl's bike. That poor kid was exactly the type to get bullied, and Leo felt more than pity, something else, unfamiliar and disturbing. He felt superior to Dean.

Taking a right down the sidewalk, he marched in the direction of home. He heard but did not look back to see Dean at the front door of the house. "I can't help it," Dean was whining toward Leo. Then, it sounded like he said, "Help it." Or just "Help." Then, as Leo increased the distance between him and Dean, the vocal sounds were more like angry grumbling, and then Dean must have slammed something against the door or the doorway. Then the door might have fallen off its hinge, or Dean might have kicked something, because there was more thumping and thudding before Leo turned the corner.

On his walk home, Leo remembered hearing Cord disparage individuals as wimps, for no apparent reason, and Leah giggling, on at least one occasion, when Cord did that. Dean, it seemed to Leo, was not a coward, though. It must have taken courage to try and make a friend. Why was there any reason to hold that against him? By the time Leo reached home, he was sorry he had abandoned Dean.

Still, he saw no reason to pursue a friendship with him. Just in case Dean came riding back by, Leo walked around the house to the backyard, out of sight. Looking for something to do, he found nothing but a small pile of nut grass someone had pulled from around the back steps and left there, roots dying now of thirst and scorch.

—

What was in the boxes? Stare at the crack in the wallpaper.

His feet hung off the end of his bed. It was the same bed he'd always had. It had always been pushed up against the window and he used to nuzzle up to the screen, place his cheek on the cool sill and breathe the backyard air and remember feelings from another timeplace. Back when he was little.

Nobody ever changed his sheets. Lulu almost always stayed in her bed, but she was somewhere now, gone to the drug store with Leah to get something. He lay on the bed, looked at the cardboard boxes, five of them, stacked against the opposite wall in his bedroom. They'd been there so long he'd forgotten what was in them, if he ever knew. Relics from past school years?

He felt the first buzzing numbness of dozing. Rather than succumb, he pulled himself off the fatigued mattress and slouched across the littered floor to the boxes.

The one he opened contained a set of stainless mixing bowls that nested into each other, some spiral notebooks from fifth and sixth grades, a plastic ruler, a compass with no pencil lead, a cardboard stencil with the whole alphabet and all ten numerals and punctuation marks.

He took the 12-inch ruler and fell back onto the bed, pulling down his jeans and skivvies in one motion. *No girl could get that in. You'd rupture her,* she'd told him. And the ugly word "rupture" echoed, and brought vague reds and whites and grays into his mind.

Worried, he wondered how much too big he was. He thought about Leah. He took a deep breath, imagined her, went over her in his mind until he was hard.

His idea was to measure himself. When he placed the ruler along the shaft of his penis, he began to lose his erection—the task was clinical, not sexy. He hurried, tried to decide where the base of it was. Should he measure from the scrotum or from the topside of the base? He lost firmness as he tried to position the cold, sharp-edged instrument. The measurement would not be accurate now. His frustration further deflated him. He gave up in disgust. Should he think about her some more, get it hard again, try again?

He let his hand drop off the edge of the bed and flipped the ruler underneath the bed with whatever else was lost there. *It's so big.* She said that almost every time. Was he so big he would have to miss out on the real thing, the vagina, his entire life?

—

In 1967 Leo turned 15. He'd considered the best way to convince Cord to let him put a latch on his bedroom door. He knew that if he did it without asking, Cord would rip it back off in a fury, and that if he asked for permission, Cord would not give it. He waited until his father had a day off, had had plenty of rest, and had consumed three cans of beer.

It was afternoon, and Cord was wandering around the backyard picking an odd weed and tossing it over the fence into the unliked neighbor's yard, placing his third empty on the ground like a football, backing off two steps, then kicking a field goal far off to the right.

"Let me," Leo said cheerfully, approaching from the back door, careful not to let the screen slam.

Cord glanced at his boy. "You? Shit."

Leo picked up the dented can and set it upright. Imitating Cord, he backed off two steps, then approached and kicked. The can went awry. Cord laughed.

"Hey Daddy, can I ask you something?"

"Like what?" He found a loose picket in the fence and jiggled it.

"I have something I want to do, and I don't want to ask Mama."

"Well, if she don't want you doing it, then you can't do it."

"It's something I ought to ask you."

Cord looked at him. "What you talking about? Ask me, then."

"I don't want to keep anybody out of my room or anything, but I want to put me a latch on the door for when I'm in there and nobody needs to get in or anything."

"A latch? What the hell for? Them things messes up the door frame."

Leo now started his act. With no more words, he shoved his hands into his pockets, hung his head low, nodded his ascent, and slowly turned and walked, not toward the house—this wasn't over yet—but to the back of the yard, his father watching him.

It took only a few moments. Cord would figure out that Leo was a teenager now. He needed to have a private place to do what boys had to do. He would probably say something stupid now, something about growing hair on the palms of your hands, or going crazy, or turning into a pervert. But then he would give his permission. Unless Leo had miscalculated.

"You go ahead," Cord said from half the backyard distant. "Don't make a mess on that door and door frame."

"I won't." Leo did not smile, but ambled toward the back door, past his father, avoiding eye contact though Cord wasn't looking at him anyway. He already had the latch, just needed now to find a drill and a screwdriver.

12

DEAN AND LEO BECAME FRIENDS their sophomore year in high school, having begun a polite relationship as they routinely ran into each other going to Geometry class, after which they both had their lunch break. They defaulted to a table in the cafeteria occupied by a few boys who belonged to no social group. Leo was entertained by the cartoons of cruelty that Dean was always sketching on notebook paper when he was supposed to be eating. The sketches lampooned the teachers, the football players, the in-crowd girls, the blacks, the eggheads—all the groups the boys at this table felt were not open to them, and some groups with whom they considered themselves too clean to associate—the smokers, and the greasers who wore metal taps on their pointed shoes and snuck off campus during the lunch hour. Occasionally a misfit girl would try joining them, and they would all ignore her.

Through these lunches, as Dean doodled in his notebook, claiming not to be hungry, Leo looked on, giving an approving snort to the best of Dean's inventions. "This is Mrs. Goynes," Dean mumbled, his pencil swirling, magically creating a good image of their geometry teacher. "Here comes…," increased magical swirling "…*Mister* Goynes…," foisting unspeakable acts on Mrs. Goynes's left ear. Leo grunted his approval while the other boys suddenly grew excited. They had spotted a beaver, blue panties, Carmen Sayers, the redhead varsity cheerleader. *Oh god, man, she knows what she's doing.*

"Nobles, you're missing it," an urgent, pimpled boy said.

"I've seen it before," Leo said. "In my car." He had no car.

"Dean couldn't care less," someone said. Which Dean ignored as he penciled in Mr. Goynes's appendage protruding now from Mrs. Goynes's right ear, and Leo laughed out loud. Comrades in unrequited lust, the importance of their kinship unrecognized in the glare of their raging, unfilled sexual needs, the other boys at the table jostled. Dean doodled his sad cry. Leo retreated inwardly, leaned into the trace of Leah, whose hand he had known for years now.

Leo and Dean began finding opportunities to talk alone. At first Leo told himself he was being nice, yet he also enjoyed the sensation of having a friend.

They planned an excavation. In the vacant lot beside Dean's house they began digging each day after school. They drew a square three feet on a side, and with a discarded license plate scraped off the nut grass first, then the mauve topsoil with its decaying snail shells, millipede exoskeletons and other death, to reveal the flat red surface of the moist, pristine, and primordial clay. Never once discussing their reason to dig—never even considering that there might be a reason—they conversed in tones of engineering, dread, inevitability, apocalypse, atheism. They were digging to the center of the earth, where gravity would reverse, and everything would be upside down. To this end, they acquired from Dean's mother's garage two shovels.

Dean had developed a gamy, compact body that hunched over the project, very different from the pasty boy on the girl's bike that Leo had by now almost forgotten. Dean was already shaving, the black stubble apparent as a shading beyond the sideburns he maintained to the legal limit. A shock of black, greasy hair bobbed before his eyelashes as he used both hands to drive the blade into the dirt. Bad pimples thrived in the oil running from his facial pores, and yet it was a handsome face with a slender nose, well defined lips, the blue eyes perpetually reddened with poor routine.

Some afternoons, they met at the hole but didn't dig, just talked. Dean liked to read, and seemed to enjoy ribbing Leo for not having read certain books or authors.

"You haven't read any Morris West? Seriously? You haven't read *The Devil's Advocate?* What kind of Catholic are you?"

"A Methodist one."

"Methodist, huh? You think God is omnipotent?"

"Sure. Don't you?"

"It appears that God is not omnipotent. If God was omnipotent, you could ask for a sign and you'd get one."

Leo considered himself an atheist, but was game for the polemic. He countered, "Only if he wanted to. And anyway, you might have to wait for the sign your whole life before it came."

"True," Dean said. "And you might not even know what kind of sign you're looking for. Or what you want from God in the first place."

"I thought you were an atheist," Leo said.

"We both are, but I'm playing the devil's advocate."

"You got a copy of the book?"

———

Other days they dug, punishing the earth for the day's humiliations.

"Do you get along with your brother?" Leo asked.

"He's an asshole," Dean said, stomping a spade to break new depth. "He's mean, and he's a son of a bitch. He took me on the back of his motor once, just so I'd know what I was missing. Wouldn't let me ride it myself. You know what he says to me every night when I go to bed?"

"What?"

"Suck my dick, queer."

"Nice."

"Instead of 'good night.' Like he was saying good night, except 'Suck my dick, queer,' instead."

"Probably thinks it's funny."

"I think he'd like it if I would, too."

"You mean he's a...?"

"No, he's not a fag. He screws these tramps all the time. I think he has one knocked up right now."

"Nice."

"Treats Mom terrible. Calls her a bitch sometimes. Makes her do everything for him. Cook. Wash his clothes."

"Man...."

"It doesn't matter. He's going to 'Nam anyway. They already snagged his sorry ass. He's trying to sell his motor, leaving for boot camp next month."

The specter of the war seeped out of the cold clay where they were fox holed, five or six feet down now, the original dimensions of the opening having increased to six feet by three to accommodate both their bodies. The hole, and the pile of dirt next to it, were hidden from the street by a large mesquite and a tangle of honeysuckle engulfing a cedar post, vestige of a fence. They sat in the bottom of the pit, resting chins to their knees, staring at the earth in front of their faces or upward to the sky.

"Mom said we have to fill this up pretty soon," Dean said.

"No problem. Have fun."

"Bull*shit*," Dean grinned. They had dug together for weeks, almost every day after school. It had been a stab at boyhood fun, like playing trucks in the sandbox or climbing trees, but it had begun to smack of denouement in the storybook of childhood. The issues of sex and war and human hostility had often encroached, and the earth, six feet in, or at the center of the planet, had failed to comfort.

"I saw your sister pick you up yesterday," Dean said. "She's pretty, man."

"That was my aunt."

"Yeah? She lives with you, right?"

"Yeah." Leo knew he had never told Dean this bit of information. It must have come from another source. Gossip. Was there much gossip, he wondered? Did it seem unusual to have an aunt living in your house?

"Do y'all get along with each other?" Dean asked.

"Oh yeah," Leo said. "She's great in the sack."

Dean seemed almost ready to believe it.

"Leah usually has a job," Leo said. "She has to sleep on the couch."

"Part of the family."

"Yeah," Leo muttered. "How'd you know she lives with us?"

"You just told me."

"You already knew."

Dean coughed once, twice, turning red in the face. "My asshole brother told me. He was telling all about what he wouldn't mind doing."

Leo managed an offhanded tone, "Wouldn't mind doing to Leah?"

"Yeah. He thought she was your sister."

Leo forced a grin, held it there, still. Turning away, feigning interest in a clod of dirt, he breathed, breathed.

"My mother's kind of out of it," Leo said. "She stays in bed all the time."

"*All* the time?"

"No. Half the time, though. Sixty percent of the time. And when she's not in bed, she's kind of, I don't know, staring."

"What's wrong with her?"

"Something. I don't know."

"Female?"

"No. Brain dead, I think. She has all kinds of drugs to take, but nothing gets her out of bed."

Dean nodded. "Can't walk or anything?"

"She can walk, but she never does. Just to the bathroom. She'll get up and act normal some days, sort of, but mostly not." It was better, off the subject of Leah now.

"Too bad, man. Is she supposed to get better?"

"I don't know. I don't think so. Maybe." Leo tried for a smile, or an ironic snort, but it was wrong. He felt a dizzying confusion of emotion, and gave himself a moment to let it clear from his chest. "She used to be nice. Sometimes, I mean. Not always."

"How often?"

"About once every century. One time she took me to Coggin Drug, and got me a doughnut, and she talked to people and was really nice, smart. Now that I think of it, she acted like a completely different person. Everybody was her friend all of a sudden. Everything was interesting and worth talking about. I was just little, but I remember that day. We walked over to the park, she let me play near the pond, she talked to people and laughed. But then, I don't know when it stopped, but she was back in bed and like she is now."

Dean nodded, "Uh-huh. Just that one day?"

"That's the day I remember best. I mean, there were other times she perked up a little. Not many. Not for a long time now."

"Sounds fucked, man."

"Pretty much." For a moment, Leo thought he was finished talking about his mother. Then his need fell upon the cushion of his friendship, and he went on. "We used to talk some. Long time ago. I'm a time traveler, which you are too dumb to understand, but I am. Mama's the only one I ever told. I used to be another person, before I was born, but things got slightly screwed up, and this man who I was before I was born, forgot to die, and we both were the same person until he died when I was about four." Leo looked at Dean and found that his friend was nodding, staring at the dirt but taking in what Leo was saying.

"You mean you had the same soul, right?"

"That's one way to put it. I ended up with feelings from his memories, but I couldn't remember it myself—just little glimpses."

"You know what?"

"What?"

"This hole is shaped like a grave."

Leo looked up, scanned the shape of the opening, the uneven surfaces they'd created. He and Dean looked at each other, both feigning horror. They lunged for the top, laughing, pushing each other back, vying for first escape. Leo put his foot into Dean's chest and hoisted himself up and out, pushing Dean back to the bottom of the hole. Then he gave Dean a hand out, and they sat, panting, examining their handiwork from the perspective of the weeds and the fetid air in the vacant lot, no longer masked by the deep earth's scent.

"What about your dad?" Dean asked.

"He works. I hardly ever see him. When he is home, he's drunk half the time."

"Nice."

"No, he's not bad. He's not like a drunk drunk. He's on the night shift, so...."

"Not around too much," Dean said, nodding.

Leo let it end. He stared into the clay, remembered the exact moment, days ago, that the shovel bit at an angle and left the indentation he was staring at now. He liked Dean. He would like to have told him how he feared his father, how the whippings he'd suffered all through his childhood had left him unable to look men in the eye. And there were other complaints and mysteries he'd like to have shared.

—

Leah routinely picked Leo up after school, and often saw Dean hanging around with Leo as he waited for his ride.

"I wouldn't get too close to Dean," Leah said as she drove away, before Leo had even said hello. "I don't like the way he looks at me."

"Everybody looks at you. What do you expect?"

"Well they don't all look at me the way he does."

"He's not interested, believe me."

"Really? What makes you so sure?"

Leo sighed.

"What, he doesn't like girls?"

"He sucks his brother's dick every night." *Why the hell did I say that?*

"He told you that?"

"No, I'm sorry. He does not suck his brother's dick every night." He could not look at Leah. "He never sucks... he never does that. He told me."

"Leo?"

"*What!*"

"You never talked like this before. I don't like it. And it's not you. And I think your friend Dean is a bad influence."

"Yeah, okay."

"Well, I do. That's all I'm saying. It's for your own good." He still could not look at her, but heard her continue, *"Our* own good."

—

Leo was mindful of Leah's caution, but he valued Dean's friendship. Dean was a bad student and untidy, yet his continual references to his reading intrigued Leo. He was increasingly interested in certain books and other writings Dean talked about. Because of Dean, Leo read Djuna Barnes' *Nightwood,* and then Joyce's *A Portrait of the Artist as a Young Man.* Then Dean handed him *Steppenwolf,* and after reading it, Leo asked for more from Hesse. Dean laughed and directed Leo to the library downtown, where he found *Siddhartha.* As soon as he finished that, Dean presented him with a deteriorating copy of Carlos Casteneda's *Tales of Power.*

Leo was more than delighted. It was as though these yellowed paperbacks, brought forth from filthy corners of the floor in Dean's house, were doors to time-places much like the partially perceived ones he had wondered about in his moments of ecstasy, the ones carried to him on the fragrance of backyard wisteria. But Leah was unsettled. She saw that Leo was ignoring her warnings about Dean. On a cold day shortly after Thanksgiving had come and gone with little celebration, Leo became aware that Leah was not approaching him in his room. He had never had to encourage her before, and didn't know how. But she knew what he wanted without his asking, and she let him know that it would not be so easy unless he distanced himself from Dean. So Leo did make an effort to end it, but the friendship was strong, and while Leo thought things cooled somewhat, Dean hardly noticed.

—

In the lunchroom on a hot March day Dean approached Leo at a table, too stupefied with hormones to notice Leo's cool demeanor. "Try this one," he said, tossing not a book but some chalky gray photocopied pages onto the table.

"What the hell is it?" grumbled Leo, who was often finding his own reading now. Pressing an index finger down hard onto a corner of the stapled sheets, he dragged the bundle toward him across the foody surface of the table.

"Kafka. 'A Letter to His Father.' Franz Kafka."

"I've heard of him."

"You think you've got an asshole for a father. Read this." Dean waited a moment, long enough to see Leo start reading, then he sat down and opened a candy bar.

The bell for fifth period rang while Leo was still reading. He ignored it, finishing the piece. He looked around the noisy room, saw an unfamiliar lunch crowd, realized he was absent from Algebra class, had not seen Dean leave. Yet he sat still, stared across the white and gray space. *Did he really write that to his father? Did his father read it?* Stunned by Kafka's tirade and his own scarified rage at Cord, Leo delayed heading for class. Carrying the pages rolled into a tube, he stopped for a long drink at the water cooler in the locker bay. He went into the boys' room and took a leak he did not need. He dropped the pages into the lavatory, watching them start to uncurl, the back page getting damp in the water drops on the stainless steel, and he left it there, like a curse, for another traveler to find.

Another day, Dean handed Leo a library-copy of *The Catcher in the Rye*, which Leo would read, return to the library, and then purloin—the very same copy—and keep for his own to read again and again.

Nevertheless, mindful of Leah, Leo was set to end the friendship. His plan was to cool gradually, with no fights, no arguments, not even any uncomfortable silences if he could manage it—nothing that would make Dean suspicious. There was no hurry, but Leo knew that if the friendship grew, he would be tempted to confide in Dean. That, he and Leah had agreed, would be the worst thing that could happen.

—

The latch, in practice, was unnecessary, since Leah left the house any time Dean was there, Leo wondering whether she was giving him space, or expressing irritation with him. And though Dean asked Leo several times if Lulu could hear through the walls, Leo just laughed at him.

After a few weeks during which Leo felt Leah's growing irritation with him, he found himself routinely hanging out at Dean's house again. His station became the filthy sofabed Dean slept on. Leo tried to hide his disdain for the mounds of clutter banked up the walls.

"I'm going to change my name," Dean said. He was leaning in the doorway, looking uncomfortable, Leo thought.

"To what?"

"The Wanderer."

Leo let himself fall back on the yellowed sheets. He stared at the ceiling, hooked his fingers behind his head. "So, can people call you 'Thuh' for short?"

"Close friends can." Dean disappeared, and a moment later Leo heard the back door open. Uncomfortable in the house by himself, he followed Dean out to the backyard, spotted him at the ancient site of their dig, now grown over in nut grass and beggar lice. The sense of their friendship's longevity weighed on Leo. It was clear that dropping a friend was not easy.

13

I HAVE A FRIEND IN MISS Hamilton's class. His name is Perry and we both like planets and stars. He comes over to my house to play, and I go to his. Last year I was friends with Rita Caldclieu and Zeb Hunt. It's always easier to be friends with people in your classroom. Yes, when I get older, some of my friendships will be more complicated. When I get to Charles Konstandinos my junior year of college, that will be a doozy due to his OCD and his relationship with Anne Krasner, whom I will also know. In general, friendships come and go. Leo's world of friendship was sparsely populated, though. You can begin to understand how Leah was causing that, though it would already have been limited by the small town and the poverty of culture and intellect Leo sometimes found himself up against.

When Dean went outside and stood over the hole he and Leo had been digging, there was a moment when Leo felt the most profound sense of loss he had ever experienced. It was because of what he was planning, and he almost decided to abandon the plan, the loss not worth protecting his shameful secret. He was not sure, in that moment, that he would ever find another friend—how could he be sure? He had not found one, after all, in his entire life before, had he? But he stood up and renewed his resolve to preserve the fidelity to Leah that had defined him for years now. What he had with Leah was dangerous, he knew, but it felt safer to preserve it. He followed Dean out the door.

"I forgot to tell you," Dean said, "I have established a private society, extremely exclusive. Some of the members mentioned you might be interested, and authorized me to approach you about it."

"Does membership come with a salary, Thuh?"

"Mister Wanderer to you." Dean kicked at a clod of clay leftover from the dig. It burst into a dusty cloud. Turning toward the street, he said, "Let's go. I got to get out of here. I need to wander. I need, in fact," and he looked to make sure Leo was following him to the street, "to wander away and get as far from this cocksucking, motherfucking...."

"Shit-eating."

"Asshole-licking place as I can."

"How's your brother liking Nam?"

"Who the fuck knows, my friend. You actually think he writes or anything?"

"That would be out of character, I guess."

"Mom seems to have found a friend."

"So, she's never home, or she is and he's there too?"

"No 'he' about it. She has this girlfriend. They work together. And now, apparently, they sleep together too."

Leo said nothing, trying to let the image form in his mind.

"But not at my house," Dean went on.

"Aha. I see. So, you're basically living alone, then."

"I am, and I don't care for it."

Leo heard something in Dean's voice. A slight crack, a little loss of control. Dean walked a bit faster, showing Leo only the back of his head now.

"Fuck it," Dean said, and took off running.

Leo hurried after him, but decided not to run. By the time he lost sight of Dean, several blocks on, he knew that they were going to the park. He took his time, his purpose to let Dean regain his composure.

There was an open drainage canal through the park, dry except during rain storms. Leo spotted Dean taking a run at the canal and jumping it, then doing the same again in the opposite direction.

"Remember when this was way too wide to jump when we were little kids?" Dean was grinning broadly and breathing heavily as Leo approached.

"I never saw you here," Leo said. "Did you play here?"

"Once in a while. You're not the only one who used to have a mother."

Dean lined up to the canal again, posturing like a field goal kicker, then suddenly relaxed and turned to Leo. "It's called the Fidelity and Realness Team. A majority of the members would like you to give us a try. Trial membership. Would of course have to be a probationary period."

—

FaRT had its first meeting right there at the park, after Dean had jumped the canal once again, and Leo had walked off toward the pond. Dean joined Leo, who was watching a giant goldfish foraging in the mossy depths.

"We should write down some bylaws, though," Dean said as he sat, panting, next to Leo on the bench.

Leo was still unsure of the group's actual function. "So we need to acquire pencil and paper."

"Correct. Can you do that?"

"As part of my probation?"

"That's over. You passed, *compadre*."

"So, I'm in?"

"Whether you like it or not. I'll be needing your dues."

"For a long time, no doubt."

For a while they spoke of what they would do with unlimited funds. By lunch time, they had arrived at Leo's house. Leah was sitting in the kitchen, finished with a bowl of cereal. She eyed the two boys as Leo looked into the refrigerator.

"Leave that hamburger alone." She pushed away from the table. "That's for supper."

"No problem," Leo said. He noticed Dean eyeing Leah as she put her dishes into the sink, wiped a bit of milk off the table with a washcloth, and walked without purpose out the back door, pausing before choosing to walk toward the street.

"She is one beautiful lady," Dean said.

"My aunt? Yeah, I guess she's good looking."

"Good looking? Shit, man. That's like saying water is slightly damp."

Leo tossed the plastic bag of bread onto the table, noticed that Dean was straining to watch Leah as she disappeared around the side yard.

After lunch, Leo looked in on Lulu. She was lying in bed, staring at the closed blinds on the window. "Mama," he said softly, and she did not respond. "Mother?"

Dean had crept up behind him, and Leo shut the bedroom door and led Dean to the front door and out to the street. He headed toward Coggin Drug.

"Where we going?" Dean said.

"Let's go find my aunt and bang her," Leo said.

"Hey, man, I'm sorry, but she is *beautiful.*"

"No problem. I know it. How about a Coke at Coggin Drug?" Leo said.

"You buying?"

"You are."

Instead, they walked along some quiet streets in the neighborhood on the other side of Coggin Avenue. The day was pleasant. They meandered, spoke little, and without intending to, Leo led them toward Ina's house out at Willis Creek.

"Oh shit, man," Leo said.

"What?"

"There's my grandmother's house."

"Can she give us a Coke?"

"I don't know. Maybe." They approached the house. "Shit, her car's not here."

"Knock anyway."

"She won't be here," Leo said, and she wasn't. They sat on the front steps, resting.

"What's your granny like?"

"She's cool. She used to take care of me."

"Yeah?"

"Yeah, she taught me to read. Taught me arithmetic, too."

"*Tried* to teach you arithmetic."

"Main thing is...." Leo trailed off.

"Main thing is what?"

"She's fucking sane." Leo looked at Dean, saw him kill a small beetle that had ventured near his shoe.

"Sane, no shit. What about your aunt? She's sane, isn't she?"

"Leah's pretty cool," Leo said, nonchalant. It didn't seem like enough, so he added, "She's kind of lazy, but you know, not fucking crazy like the rest of my family."

"She could be in my family if she wants," Dean said.

Leo felt somewhat tested. Or was it just a backhanded compliment? Leo saw another beetle of the same type Dean had killed. "You missed one," he pointed to it.

"Die, scumbag," Dean said, and slowly brought down his shoe on the bug, then twisted his foot back and forth to liquefy the creature.

"Leah's a little crazy too," Leo said, surprising himself. *What am I doing?*

"Yeah? I could deal with some of that."

"Some of what? Some of her craziness?"

"Some of her," Dean said. Leo looked at him. He was grinning, risked a glance back at Leo, looked away quickly. "Well, shit, man, what's wrong with that? She's a fucking bomb, man. I mean, I know she's your aunt, but...."

"I know she's a bomb. So what, Dean? So you think I should get all hot and bothered over my *aunt?*" Leo felt himself losing control. He sat very still, took in air as slowly as he could.

Dean laughed. "Hey, I don't care what you do, but she ain't my fucking aunt, and I likes what I sees, hope you don't mind."

"Yeah, well, you're a pervert, so I guess it's okay."

"Yeah, well, you're a pervert, so I guess it's okay if you don't like women."

"Yeah, fuck you, Dean."

"See? No, thanks, I don't want you to fuck me, thank you for the offer, though."

—

In Leo's bedroom a few days later, Dean dictated, and Leo wrote on the Big Chief tablet he'd found under his bed. He used a fountain pen, the ink from which spread into the pulpy paper and settled into fat, hairy letters.

SICKENINGLY LARGE NUMBER #1—Nine to the power of nine, the result of that to the power of nine, etc. for nine iterations. Final result: higher number by far than the total number of all atoms. So large it will make you throw up blood. Hamlet would be typed by a monkey at least once.

Each SLN, they decided, would be characterized by a "final result" and a "monkey typing Hamlet" rating. Leo wrote,

SICKENINGLY LARGE NUMBER #2—A series of nines, each figure written the size of the nucleus of a hydrogen atom and touching the next figure, the series extending the length of the universe, or twenty billion light years, whichever is longer.

He read that much to Dean, who amended it verbally, and Leo wrote,

Each integer in the above series of nines to be considered the exponent of the preceding result rather than the next place in the base ten number system. Final result: Contemplation of size of number brings on two to three hours of vomiting and simultaneous diarrhea followed by dry heaves and hemorrhoid-producing spasms of sphincter muscle. Hamlet would be written by monkey so many times this number alone would exceed number of atoms that exist.

As the afternoon wore on, page after page of the Big Chief filled with descriptions of SLNs. SLN #8 read,

...a series of nines, each the exponent of the preceding result, each written only the size of a hydrogen atom's nucleus and shoulder to shoulder with the next integer, packed three dimensionally into the known universe. Final result: Upon sixty seconds of contemplation of the number, you will begin throwing up, and after ten minutes, you will dry heave for twenty more minutes, after which you will begin regurgitating internal organs, first the stomach and intestines, then the liver, the pancreas and kidney, followed by the testicles, after which the dick itself will turn inside out and stretch upward trying to break off and come out the mouth. However, death will occur during this time frame and probability of actual dick vomit is quite small, though possible. Monkey will type Hamlet so many times that the number is an SLN itself, comparable in size to SLN #2. Monkey would also type entire contents of Library of Congress, in alphabetical order by book title, quite a few times.

"SLN number... what are we on?" began Leo.

"That was eight. This'll be nine."

"All right. SLN number nine is SLN # 8 cubed."

This was good for only a chuckle. Dean, however, was ready with the result, but Leo was laughing too hard to write it down.

"SLN # 9, then," Dean began. "Any contemplation whatsoever immediately results in orgasm in which feces shoot out through urethra and you die. After death, brain continues to spasm and controls certain voluntary muscle action causing torso to bend forward convulsively and neck muscles to contract until head actually works way up anal opening, at which point brain thinks body is still alive and causes mouth to attempt chewing its way back out of colon. Usually all activity stops about time navel is masticated from inside."

Leo was laughing so hard he rolled off his bed onto the floor, struggling to catch his breath. Thus encouraged, Dean continued.

"Number of times monkey would type Hamlet is so large that if other monkey typed one random letter for each complete Hamlet, it would also type Hamlet an SLN number of times."

When Leo began to catch his breath, he made a grand gesture while lying on the floor, and proclaimed, "Infinity!"

Dean tried to laugh, but aborted the attempt. "Large in terms of a number, but incapable of creating nausea when contemplated. Disqualified."

Leo made a retching noise.

Although the door to Leo's room was closed, they hadn't bothered to use the latch. When Leah opened the door, Leo was struggling up to his knees, intending to "vomit" all over Dean.

"What are y'all doing, anyway?" Leah asked, half a smile on her face.

They stopped, surprised, but then resumed laughing. Leah shut the door, but somehow her brief appearance had punctuated the day, ended the momentum with which the big numbers had blossomed from their minds. It was, in fact, the end of the SLN Society, which they later deemed to have been born, flourished, and died in a most satisfying manner.

—

At lunch, Leo had been staring blankly across the noisy cafeteria as he listened to Dean reading a poem by E. E. Cummings. He had finally become aware that Vince Agee, at a table full of large football players, was returning his gaze. Leo quickly looked away, and realizing he was out of time, hurried toward his locker, the route to which took him directly past the table where Vince Agee, he noticed with chagrin, was still looking at him.

"Nobles," Leo heard Vince say. Was he addressing him, or referring to him in conversation with his large friends? Leo decided it was the latter, and continued on.

After retrieving his algebra book for his next class, he hurried out of the locker bay and toward class. Vince Agee and Neal Fuller stood in the middle of the walkway facing him.

"Hey, Nobles," Agee snarled. Neal stood to the side, his huge forearms folded across his chest, his stance wide and threatening like a bouncer.

"Hey, Agee," Leo said.

"Why didn't you stop when I talked to you?"

"Didn't hear you, man. How you doing?" He thought of adding "Good game Friday," but remembered that Brownwood High had lost.

"I don't like being ignored, Nobles."

"Hey, I'm sorry. I didn't hear you." At this moment, Leo saw Dean walk out the door of the cafeteria toward the science wing classrooms. He also saw Dean look at him, quickly avert his eyes and hurry along. "Hey, Neal," Leo said. "What's new?"

Neal glanced at Agee and said nothing.

"Hey, Nobles," Agee said, and took a step toward him. "You better not be looking at me."

"Looking at you?"

"I'll beat the living shit out of you, Nobles. You get it?"

"I don't know what...."

"You get it, Nobles? You better say yes."

"Well, I get what you're saying, but...."

"Then shut the fuck up." He glanced at Neal and the two of them headed back to the cafeteria. Leo took a step toward algebra, realized his heart was pounding, stopped, felt a little dizzy. He glanced across the green to where his friend had passed by. Couldn't blame him, Leo thought. Wouldn't have done any good if he had come over. He was being smart. There was nothing he could have done except get his own ass in a sling. There was nothing to be done. He thought of Leah, took a deep breath, and went to class.

—

Leo wanted to seek Dean out, let him know that he understood, did not blame him for staying out of the altercation. He would not have been any help, and they both knew it, of course. It would have been easy for Leo to smooth over the incident. But he also realized it was an opportunity to let his relationship with Dean cool, to do what Leah had been telling him he'd better do. He avoided Dean in the coming days, and when Dean did approach him, tentatively, contrite and downcast, Leo was cold. He hated doing it, but he did it.

14

LEAH'S BUMBLEFOOTED FALCON DELIVERED EVERY insult in the pavement straight to the passenger and the driver. The Sunday morning traffic was light, the warm autumn day was light, Leah's heart must have been light. She looked on the verge of smiling, her hands draped over the wheel, wrists doing the steering. Leo was sleepy, out of bed in body only, but leaning against the door, admiring Leah. Dressed in wrinkled silver trousers, a white shirt, the blue tie a nod to propriety, he believed he was the only sophomore at Brownwood High School who went to church, and he was an atheist, though he kept meaning to think about it some more. Leah had insisted on church since last spring, just after her shopping spree. Leo believed she wanted to dress up every Sunday morning because she had some nice clothes.

Windows rolled down, spitty smell of oak and cottonwood turning to dust, drying, browning on the air gusting into their nostrils. This week Leah would turn twenty-five. Would the preacher have the information and announce it from the pulpit? Leo thought he'd heard Leah on the phone last week, someone called, sounded like it could be someone from church. Oh god, oh hell.

"You need to comb your hair before we go in."

He knew that. He didn't mind her telling him, though. He looked at her hair, holding itself in place even in the wind at thirty-five miles an hour. She had it poufed into a perfect sphere, large as a volleyball, her head fetchingly inserted at the lower front quadrant. And her eyes, blackened all around, like a raccoon, he thought, making her crazy pretty. And the wool pullover, the cones protruding therefrom....

"You looking at me?"

He looked away, wondered if he would have more control over the flow of his blood into specific tissue in his body if he drank coffee in the morning, woke up better, did a little moving around before heading out to places, school, church for god's sake, oh hell. He had brushed his teeth, at least. When would he need to shave? It was good that he didn't have to, could do it when he felt like it, didn't make much difference anyway. How long will that last? The facial hair looked a little darker now, almost light brown, no longer transparent like the snow that blew along this street last winter when Leah had smiled and touched his jism after he delivered it, and then touched her wetted finger to her tongue and then kissed him. So strange because what kind of a kiss had it been, lingering on his mouth but not for long, and then she was still smiling when she ended the kiss and left him to use the tissue by his bed. It had been their only kiss and he still thought about it, thought about it now going to church, oh hell.

"Oh, hell."

"Don't say that!" She punched him on the leg.

The small brick structure came into sight, that elderly couple with the '54 Lincoln making their way up the ten steps to the door to the sanctuary. Smile, Leo. It was all that was required. At least it was not a Baptist church. Leah would not consider Baptist, even though it was the family's denomination. She would not be yelled at by some preacher week after week, not be told she was bad, not hear about some supposed place where she would burn for eternity. So instead she'd found them a place where God was love.

First there were the smiles. That happened before the service started, while people were taking their seats. Leah sometimes spoke with someone, allowing Leo to fade back behind her, only occasionally required to participate in a pleasantry.

They made their way to the fourth pew from the front, right side. It was becoming their pew. The modest stained-glass windows along the sides of the sanctuary were embedded with leaden legends of early donors to the church, their names and epochs. Leo turned his head in feigned curiosity toward the nearest window and read *James Leach 1852 - 1919* and did the math, though he'd done it a number of times before. He felt little more than disdain for the whole church routine, but he knew there was a power in this place that couldn't be explained in physical terms, not by anything mental or emotional, and certainly not by anything religious, and he refused to call it spiritual.

Three times the congregation was required to stand and sing, and these times Leo begrudged and thought this was agony. *Why, oh, God, do we have to stand up when it would be so much easier and more comfortable to remain seated? Not a mystery—It's to make us wake up so we'll be conscious for the sermon.*

Leo had never heard a single one of the sermons, but pretended to listen, tried to keep a look on his face similar to the one he saw on Leah's, hers tilted up toward the pulpit, giving her chin a lovely curve slightly more acute than usual. Today she wore a charcoal flannel skirt, the fabric portending a wonderful warm cavity unseen above her knees, a warm place Leo had never been, though he knew well where it led, the warmest cavity of all, the woman cavity conjectured at length every day at lunch by his hormone-riddled classmates with their screaming pimples, contraband *Playboy* stashes, yodeling voices in flux. They named the girls in their class, and the junior and senior girls they would like to ball, or whose pussies they would like to eat. Endlessly they yearned out loud, as though saying it brought some relief, even though it made them seem to agonize even more. And Leo played along, but couldn't honestly sympathize. None of the high school girls were any prettier than Leah.

After the sermon, the congregation was bidden to rise and sing again, but Leo laced his fingers together, pressed the backs of his thumbs against his forehead, and leaned forward until his arms were touching the back of the pew in front of him. He closed his eyes, and in this posture of intense prayer he stayed throughout the closing hymn in spite of Leah's whispered command for him to stand up. He stayed in this posture also through the closing prayer, during which the congregation remained standing, and even through the postlude as the preacher proceeded down the center aisle to the doors where he would greet his parishioners as they exited.

Leah leaned down to him and whispered, "What are you doing?"

"Pray with me," he whispered back.

"Please get up," she whispered.

"I can't. Pray with me until everybody's gone."

The preacher apparently respected their need for prayer and walked on outside to wait in the humid autumn brilliance.

"He's gone outside," Leah murmured. "We're alone."

Relaxing, Leo turned around to check that the sanctuary was empty. "Talk to me about... I don't know... golf."

Leah was confused for a moment, glanced at the length of Leo's folded body, realized he had an erection. "Oh," she said. "Think about Mr. and Mrs. Abernethy and their Lincoln."

When they met the preacher on the front lawn, Leah asked him to remember her sister in his prayers, that Lulu was in failing health, must rest almost all the time, no thank you, it would be better if no one came to call. The preacher, it seemed to Leo, was over-filled with admiration for Leah and him because they had not been embarrassed to stay and pray after the service. And in fact, the preacher said he wished others would be less confined by traditions and follow their hearts to God in whatever ways God might lead them.

In the car, Leo said "Do me a favor and don't wear that skirt to church again."

"Are you serious?"

"Yes, I am."

Leah tossed back her head in a silent laugh—something she did when she was pleased with herself.

"*Shall we gather at the ri-ver...*" Leah sang. "That Nazi-looking couple," she said, "that always sits right in the middle on the third pew...."

"With the two little boys?"

"Two little poo-poo boys."

"What about em?"

"All the couples with children in there. The children are prettier than the parents, don't you think?"

"I don't know. I never thought about it."

"I know what the parents are thinking."

"Why? Because you can read their mind?"

"*Where bright angel feet have trah-od...* I just know. They think their children are the crowns of creation. They think they've evolved. They think their children are more evolved than they are."

Leo just sat. He followed her, didn't care much.

"You, Leo," she said to him. "*You* are the crown of creation."

"Who me? Not me."

"You are but you don't get it."

Leah drove not to the house, where Cord and Lulu were, but out to the city limits where the town-side bank of Pecan Bayou, *with its crystal tide forever flowing,* provided a municipal picnic area. The park was deserted, and Leah pulled up under a large pecan tree, which was in the process of dropping its delicious seed at the whim of the breezes. The green water—not crystalline at all, but muddy, unctuous—moved light detritus along its surface, mere feet in front of the car. Leah opened her purse and retrieved a small packet of tissues and, with a coy smile, placed the packet in Leo's hand, at the ready as it were. Wordlessly, Leo attempted to show with his slunk down posture not just sullen acquiescence, but the gratitude he felt even before she began.

15

SOME THINGS YOU CAN KNOW without being omniscient. They're a matter of record. You can look up the obituaries and see that Ina was just a few months preceded in death by her elder son Drew, who had been an embarrassment to the family because of his criminal ways. He was especially worrisome to Ina because he had caught her with the ice man and must have figured out that Leah was the ice man's daughter. The whole episode is unknown to me and always will be except for a vague reference or two, something about shame I will overhear and assume refers only to Drew's delinquency.

And it's a matter of record, if you could find a record, that by the time Leo was an upperclassman at Brownwood High, Leah was working a steady job at the new glove factory housed in a cluster of old barracks buildings in Camp Bowie. She worked in the office as secretary to the general manager. Cord was happy to receive part of her pay each week. He left her alone, and she never asked for more than her place on the couch.

The pecan trees in Brownwood were bare to the brown wood a year after Leah had driven to Riverside Park and serviced Leo's church-begotten urgency. She pulled the Falcon up to the front of the high school where Leo was waiting for her, standing alone at the curb as usual. His grades had improved—in fact he was making the honor roll and he was in the lead role in the junior class play, *Ah Wilderness!* He was friendly with the rest of the cast, but those relationships were contained within rehearsal periods. His close friendship with Dean was a memory.

He slammed the car door and dropped his books to the floorboard. Out of habit, he glanced at Leah to see how she was dressed. This warm, damp day, her clingy paisley skirt of thin jersey arrested his gaze at her thigh, and he was sure he saw the muscle in her leg tighten beneath the fabric as she stepped on the accelerator and pulled down the circular drive toward the exit.

"Drew died," she said.

"Uncle Drew? He did?"

Drew had been away from Brownwood for years, having moved to Cisco after finishing his jail time in 1958. In recent years he'd held a decent job in El Paso as a sales rep for Philip Morris, or so Lulu had claimed. Leo tried to remember the last time his uncle had visited, some years back.

"What was that he did jail time for," Leo said, "when I was little?"

Leah turned off the radio. "That was 1957. For stealing a tractor from a farm and trying to sell it. He met some guys in jail, and when they all got out they started doing more serious stuff. Burglarizing. I don't know what all."

"How old is he, anyway?" Leo asked.

"Forty-two," Leah said. "Was." She turned right onto Stephenville Avenue instead of the usual left toward home.

"What killed him?"

"You'll love this. He overdosed on some drug. Heroin I'm sure."

"Shit, man," Leo mumbled, trying to imagine. "Are you sad?"

"He was already grown up when I was born. I mean, he was seventeen. I remember him living at home, though, off and on, when I was little. He was gone all the time, wasn't like a brother. He didn't seem to like me. He was always mad."

"He got the bad genes, I guess."

"Yeah. Russell was always a sweetheart. Still is, if we ever hear from him." She drove them into the vast desolate area that had been a large Army base during World War II, Camp Bowie. She pulled onto a concrete road that no longer led anywhere, its expansion joints sprouting weeds as high as the car's hood. She stopped the car where weeds were dense.

"Ol' Drew seemed pretty nice to me," Leo said. "Last time he was here he invited me to come see him in El Paso."

"Well, he died in Nacogdoches." Leah turned in the seat to face him, doubled her right leg up under her. Leo noted the view she was flashing him, and met her unabashed eyes. He looked away, focused on the long earthworks of the water reservoir breaking the horizon a few hundred yards before them. Leah leaned toward him and touched his knee, then the inside of his thigh. He turned away from her, hunching up against the door, turned his head to look out the side window.

Some scissortails fluttered close by the car and shot up to perch on a dead wire running from a pole to some mysterious concrete structure from the camp days and started their familiar scratchy call.

"Let me," Leah whispered.

Not looking at her, he shook his head. "I don't want to." Then he added, "right now."

"But I do." Her voice was so soft, the way she did the little girl voice. Yet something in him was cringing, would not yield to her. Drew was dead, and though Leo hardly knew him, cared little about him, still he needed this moment to acknowledge something about the passing. "Let me," Leah said, her voice as soft as ever, but now it was a demand, not a request. But Leo would not.

—

As she drove them home, Leah was silent, leaving Leo with the sense that something in his relationship with Leah had changed, something had developed. He glanced at her profile several times, noting her set jaw, her placid countenance, her effortless concentration on the drive home. Were they going home? Apparently, yes. Was she angry? If so, was that bad, or did it mean she had relinquished something to him? Had he grown into some kind of power? Would he want that?

He let his gaze linger on Leah, first the perfect line of her nose, and the wisps of loose dark hair that fell down to her nostrils until she brushed them away with her hand. Then her smooth neck and then, inevitably it seemed to him, the luscious protrusion of her breasts. Though he willed against it, he followed the line of her body down to her lap, and on to the beautiful arching line of her thighs pressing through her skirt. He remembered dead Drew and forced himself to think of the man beginning to stink in his coffin.

And he wondered, *Is this what she wants me to know? That I can't refuse her? That I'm in love with her?*

—

Now the summer had baked away the pale green life April had spawned as Drew was breathing his foamy last, and August offered endless days of unbearable wet heat. Leo had wondered, that spring day, about his relationship with Leah, but nothing changed. He'd enjoyed her attentions later that very night.

Lounging on Leah's couch in the living room, they were alone in the house. Ina had phoned earlier and complained about a terrible headache and wanted Lulu to come see her. Lulu had walked over to her mother's an hour ago, and would be gone for a while.

Leo and Leah were contentedly swapping complaints about Lulu. "She's been talking to herself," Leo said, scratching left toes with right toes. "You hear it?"

"She does it in her sleep, too," Leah sighed. "She wakes me up all the time. I get scared thinking there's a burglar. She sounds odd, like a man, or a munchkin or something. And you can't understand what she's saying even though she's loud."

"Yesterday," Leo yawned, "she got up to go to the bathroom. I was sitting on my bed reading a book. She went in the bathroom, didn't close the door. I don't know what she did, but she didn't flush."

"Oh, yuck."

"She came out and looked in at me and said, 'You just better.' Then headed on back to bed."

"She's going nuts."

"At least she's getting out of bed more lately," Leo said.

Leah sat up straight, stretched. "She's on some kind of new medicine and I think it gets her going."

This was news to Leo. "Oh, so ho ho. That's why she's been kinda deranged. Going out in the yard...."

"...made her own lunch yesterday," Leah yawned.

"I wonder if the same medicine is making her talk to herself."

"Probably. I'll take some of it and see if it makes me talk to myself."

Leo glanced at her but she gave no indication as to whether she was serious. It was a heartless comment in a dull conversation. Leah abruptly went into Lulu and Cord's bedroom where the bottom drawer in the dresser had been assigned to her when she'd moved in. Leo heard the dresser drawer slide open. Leah appeared at the doorway, leaned there, her left arm stretched high up against the frame, her hip jutting and never quite coming to rest as her pelvis nestled, nestled. In her right hand she held a bit of pale tangerine softness, a brassiere Leo had seen once before when, stopped at a red light on their way home from school, she'd playfully maneuvered in front of him and let her sweater fall free so he could see.

"Whatcha got there?" he said, his voice as dead as the lawn outside.

She signaled her intentions with a smile. He was suddenly conscious of his posture, slumped far down on the couch, his head barely still propped up. His remaining in that position was all the acknowledgment Leah needed.

For her to take his hand in hers was unusual, and he enjoyed the softness of the palm of her hand on the back of his. She placed the inside surface of a bra cup into his palm. "Isn't that soft," she said.

"Nice," he said.

"That's the part my titties go in."

He closed his eyes, and her hand left his hand holding the bra as she unzipped him. By the time the telephone rang, she was moving the bra over his erection, letting the softness touch him.

"I better get it," she said, and she hurried into the kitchen where the phone was. He could hear only muffled bits of her voice, was not able to make out any words. When she came back, she was holding a box of tissues. He had not moved a muscle, had not even opened his eyes until he heard her coming back, but he'd lost his erection.

Leah sat back down, worked her hand up under his shirt and rubbed his stomach.

"Who was it?"

"I'll tell you later. Right now...." Without finishing her sentence, she unbuttoned her blouse and pressed her breast to Leo's mouth as she began touching him again. She moved back, left him wanting the breast. Placing him inside the tangerine bra, she grasped the cup and moved him. When he was breathing hard, she let the tangerine bra drop away, took him in her hand. She breathed into his ear. "That was Lulu. We have to go get her."

Leo barely managed to say "Yeah, all right," because he was about to explode, and Leah put her tongue into his ear.

He was in the moment beyond stopping, and Leah breathing hotly into his ear, "My mama's laying over there dead on the kitchen floor."

—

Lulu had not attended the dismal prayer service after Drew's cremation in Nacogdoches, Texas, in April, though Cord, Leo, and Leah all went. But along with the rest of the family, Lulu did attend Ina's funeral and the graveside service at Brownwood's

Greenleaf Cemetery. Throughout Leo's senior year, she continued to get out of bed almost every day. With the death of her mother, she seemed determined to take on life again, and told Leo she was proud of how well he was doing in school. Cord admonished Leo to help her, talk with her, try to keep her spirits up. Which Leo did, but with increasing pessimism because he never saw the mother he remembered from a few occasions in his childhood when she seemed truly happy and alive. She had insisted that what he'd tried to explain to her about his mind was a gift, but her understanding did not mature as he grew up, as far as he could tell. Her faith in him began to seem childish, and that made him feel childish for not abandoning the mystery of the strange aspect of himself that he could not explain. As the months passed after Ina's death, it seemed to Leo that whatever evil was in his mother kept consuming her and leaving her stunned.

16

AVE YOU EVER WONDERED ABOUT the dynamics between a father and the son he whips? What happens when the son starts growing up? Do they come to an agreement that the whippings will stop, the father will no longer be a physical threat but maybe some other kind of threat, or not a threat at all? Or does the son finally defend himself successfully, showing the father that the whippings will no longer be tolerated without violence in return? Cord did stop whipping Leo, but there was no stated or implied finality about it. I can tell you that the last whipping occurred when Leo was fourteen. If anything, Cord just stopped paying as much attention to Leo, and time passed, and kept passing, and that was it—there was a new understanding that whippings were probably a thing of the past now.

Maybe Cord was preoccupied with his own childhood baggage, or his failed marriage with Lulu, or his slowly failing health as he grew older. Or maybe he stopped paying attention because unconsciously he didn't want to know what was really going on in Leo's life. If he had wanted to know—especially if he'd suspected anything about Leo and Leah—it would have been hard for him to bring it into focus. Leo and Leah were good at obscuring their relationship. They had spent years perfecting the nuances of their camouflage, and Leo, it happened, had—or maybe had developed—a knack for acting. It wasn't until Leo's senior year was almost over that Lulu stumbled across his relationship with Leah.

Lulu had prepared the meal for May Day, and they were grateful, cautious because she sometimes began cooking and then forgot, went off and did something else, leaving meat to burn, pots of water to boil away, carrots peeled but uncut. Leo sometimes imagined that her absent-mindedness was the mist rising off the swamp of a vast anger rooted not just to the bottom of the swamp, but all the way to the center of the Earth, which was Hell. I know, he was an atheist, but that doesn't mean he couldn't use religious concepts as metaphors. But other times, he considered that real anger never erupted from his mother, that she was afflicted with a boredom as extensive as the cosmos, and nothing could amuse her or hold her attention, simply because nothing was important in the context of infinity.

Addled, Cord had said to her, and about her, on many occasions. He was seated at the head of the table, waiting with Leah and Leo, listening to the rattle of the big spoon against the pot of corn as Lulu scraped the margarine-drenched kernels into the dark blue serving bowl. She seemed well today, probably because of the new drug. The ham was on the table. The bread was stacked on a saucer at Cord's right hand. Boiled potatoes steamed, heaped on the pewter platter. Lulu had even remembered to set out glasses and the carton of buttermilk.

Lulu carried the corn to the table, the big spoon protruding from the bowl. "Let's see," she sighed, surveying the table, "I guess that's everything."

"It is. Sit down," Cord told her. And she did. Cord took a slice of the white bread and passed the saucer to Leo. Without a word, they served their plates, aware of an edginess amongst them. Leo glanced across the table at Leah, who met his eye. Cord saw the glance. "What's the matter with you two?"

Leo shook his head and cut into his ham. Leah cleared her throat.

"She's worked hard to cook us a meal," Cord grouched. "Can't somebody at least say thank you?" He glared at Leo.

"Thank you, Mother. This is good."

"It is good," Leah said, nodding.

"Shit," mumbled Cord, "bunch of ingrates."

"We said thank you," Leo muttered.

Cord tossed his fork onto his plate with a clatter. "She works all afternoon getting this ready and you two act like you deserve it." His gaze challenged them to argue. They knew this foul mood too well. All, including Lulu, dropped their gazes to their plates and made small motions with their forks.

"Well... *eat*, god damn it." He picked up his fork and jabbed it into a potato, hacking at it until he had a bite, which he jammed into his mouth, tasting nothing but his own indignation.

Leo habitually channeled his anger at Cord into pity. The man was put upon at his job, never advanced, even though he worked hard—his temper was part of that situation, no doubt. And it must have been frustrating to be married to a woman who'd been retreating for as long as Leo could remember. Tonight, though, Leo allowed himself a small roll of the eyes. *Daddy's an asshole, let's face it. We were all sitting here waiting, pulling for Mother, proud of her, waiting for a moment to offer real thanks, real gratitude.* That was all ruined now. He was an inconsiderate boor. Childish in his inability to restrain angry outbursts. Irrational. Completely self-centered. He hadn't seen the roll of Leo's eyes, or the smirk he was now maintaining. For reasons of his impending permanent exit from the household upon graduation from high school, Leo was blasé regarding Cord's state of mind. Unwise, he did not care. And with no intention other than to pique, he said, "Ham's kind of gristly. Maybe you didn't get it done, Mother."

There was just time for Leah to look up and say, "Oh God." Cord erupted, slamming his fist down on the table as he banished Leo to his room.

Kicking back his chair, Leo proclaimed, "Gladly. Who can eat with you acting like a crazy man. You're insane." He stalked out of the room and into his bedroom, not because it was where he'd been sent, but to pick up the book he'd been reading. Lulu crumpled into a keening posture, beseeching her husband as he bolted up from his chair, "Don't you hurt him."

Never having been confronted by his son like this before, Cord stormed after Leo and caught him at the bedroom door. He grabbed the boy's shoulder and spun him around. With a finger in Leo's face, he yelled, "Don't you ever bow up at me, boy."

"Grow up," Leo said evenly. And then he was on the floor, there was a sting on his chin and his ears were ringing. First, he wondered whether he'd been knocked unconscious or was simply put down so fast that he was unaware of the falling. *Cold cocked*, they called it. Hit without warning. He struggled to his feet. He saw a look of surprise and something that might have been shame on Cord's face, and he heard Lulu moaning. Grabbing his copy of *The Catcher in the Rye* from the windowsill, Leo brushed past his father, walked out the front door, made it to the corner and down the side street before the tears began streaming down his face.

Twilight was still fresh. He hoped nobody would see him crying. There was the mercy of a quiet neighborhood, and men already home, settled after long days at work, and no children outside playing. There was the further grace of remembering the space hidden behind hedges, a short, unused passageway between the old grocery and the firehouse—a secret place that he hadn't visited for years. The recess of earth and leaves he had long ago called his clubhouse was three blocks away.

He was reading the inexplicably comforting *The Catcher in the Rye* for the third time, until the light faded into deep dusk. Words of a New York City boy—a rich kid in a life unlike his own, making reference to places and mores Leo had never seen or heard of—and yet every page, every sentence, assuaged his own sense of isolation, offered him the promise of anonymity. And why should anonymity be so alluring? But it was. Leo wanted to ride on one of those subways in one of those crowds of people he'd never seen before and would never see again, and be unknown to all of them, and unknown to the crowds he would see the next day, and forever.

But as dusk gave up the last light, Leo felt lonely, and wished for someone who did know him, and whom he knew. He'd found a comfortable seat, the old stone steps to a doorway that had been bricked in long before Leo discovered this place. He heard a bird, a sparrow no doubt, rustling the low leaves of the dense hedge, and when it was quiet again, he said to himself, "I've got to start smoking cigarettes."

He denied the inevitability of leaving this hideout, the denial nothing but the first phase of leaving. He wondered what Cord would be like when he went home. Contrite? Possibly. Cord had been contrite on occasion. If contrition was a sign of weakness, then there could be an apology, for Cord was a weak son of a bitch.

It had been hours since he left the house. The neighborhood was quiet, the sparse streetlights dim. He pushed out of the bushes and strode toward downtown. He walked for hours, had no watch but figured it was past midnight. Tired after circling the large cemetery along the Braxtonville Highway, he began wending his way back toward the hideout.

Safe behind the bushes again, he sat on the brick steps and remained there, exhausted, dozing sporadically until dawn.

He was dreaming when Leah pushed through the hedge and startled him. "Aha! So there you are," she said, and sat down beside him. "I thought maybe you had gone to the bus station last night even though that didn't make any sense."

"No," he said, feeling a new, different pain in his jaw.

"When I woke up this morning, I thought of this place. You didn't stay in here all night, did you?"

"Walked around most of the time."

"What's that you're holding?" She took the book from his hand. He'd been clutching it all night, and the red from the book's cover material had transferred to his fingers. "Thought you read this last year."

"And the year before that, too," he said. "Where's Daddy? Home?"

"Still asleep when I left."

"God, if only it was September. If only I could get the hell out of this goddam town."

Leah giggled, flipped through the pages of the book.

"It's not funny, Leah. He might kill me or I might kill him before this summer's over."

"It's funny that every time you read this book you start saying 'goddam.' It's not 'goddam,' you know. It's God damn."

Leo stretched, stood up. "Weird dream. I'm hungry."

"Let's go eat."

"At home? I don't want to."

"I'll bring you something," Leah said, standing up. "You could go over to the park and wait for me."

"No. Bring it here."

She pushed through the hedges, distressing them with her maxi skirt. She returned wearing the same white cotton blouse but had changed from the skirt to bell bottom jeans. Leo shared the sweet rolls and the one can of Dr. Pepper with her.

When Leah stroked his head, he leaned into her breast, thinking he would cry some more. Instead, he drifted toward sleep, and Leah found them a comfortable position on the ground where sunlight had warmed the dead leaves. By increments, they shifted into reclining positions, and it was Leah's face that was buried now in Leo's breast. Facing each other, they intertwined their legs, Leah's toes reaching to her lanky nephew's mid-calf.

—

The noise Lulu made poking through the hedges woke them. Leah hadn't been sound asleep, though Leo had. She took a matter-of-fact posture as she sat up, grasped her knees to her chest and asked Lulu, "Is he still home or gone yet?"

Leo saw Lulu's uncontrollable eye darting, the good eye permanently registering the scene of the sleeping couple.

"Lulu, I said is Cord gone yet?"

Lulu backed out to the sidewalk, never having made it through the bush, saying, "He got up and went downtown to breakfast."

Emerging from the hideout, Leah was muttering, "I don't know how you found us here, anyway."

Leo then heard his mother say, "You told me."

"I was just offering him a little comfort and the poor thing fell asleep 'cause he was up all night crying."

"I should've seen it before," Lulu said, starting down the walk toward home.

"Seen what?"

"Let her go," Leo said, coming through the bushes, dusting himself off. "Hell with her. Hell with both of them."

Leo was through with his mother, through with his father. Yet even as he thought *good riddance,* he began to feel the vacancy where his mother had been, with parts of her yet clinging to him, and a large, cold emptiness that Cord had left scarred and damaged.

17

AT ABOUT 4:45 P.M. ONE DAY, while he's taking a walk for his health, Papa will pass through the metaphorical door from late middle age into the first moments of old age. And he will know it, right at the instant it happens. I will be in another part of the country, attending a seminar, and will never know about this interesting moment in Papa's life. I'm not sure when, if ever, I will notice Papa becoming old, and yet it will be clear to me, eventually, that it has happened somewhere along the line.

On the day Papa becomes an old man, he will have known for some time that those strange moments that began on the windowsill next to his childhood bed in the night-fragranced air, share some aspects of *deja vu,* namely the feeling of recognizing something unremembered. But he'll have experienced deja vu occasionally like anyone else, so he'll know the difference. *Deja vu* seems to hearken to a previous experience—Papa's "id leaks" were more like memories of a future that has no content yet.

—

Time travel is not possible in our universe in the same way that God is not possible. But this is because of a perception problem. In the same way we have to step aside from our "natural" perceptions in order to understand that God is possible, we need to step aside from our storytelling perceptions to see that time travel is possible. In the case of God, we must start by eliminating the anthropomorphizing of God in our mind, and proceed to pick through what is left of our concept and find the pure truth.

As for time travel, the analog of anthropomorphizing is the concept of storytelling, or *cause and effect*. Eliminate that concept, and you wreak havoc on how we understand existence in motion. But it's only by eliminating it that we can, again, pick through what is left of the concept, the difference between a story and time. If we can accomplish this, we find that it is pretty easy to "arrive" at different "points in time," and it has nothing to do with any machinery or physics per se.

God operates in a time-travel mode, not the storytelling mode we normally operate in. God and time travel are accomplished mentally. Prayer can be thought of as the attempt to bring the two into confluence. Thus we—some of us—pray about concerns that are in the past as well as in the future.

Here is a poem I wrote in third grade, called "Poem about Time."

The speed of light
is quite finite
The speed of time
we can't define

To us, light doesn't
seem to travel
While time's a sleeve
we perceive to unravel

We make the easy concept hard
and the hard one easy
Trying to switch this around
makes us feel queasy

Not everybody can be a great poet. These are difficult concepts. Papa said I would be better equipped to understand later, and that I should always write poems no matter how bad they are because it makes room in your brain for your mind to grow.

—

The Main Mall extended south below the Texas Tower, the university's architectural centerpiece. At the foot of the mall, Littlefield Fountain's waters roared, too turbulent to reflect the tower, noisy like the sea in a gale, like the buzz of freshman chatter arriving in a lecture hall. The goddess Columbia, standing in sexy bronze grandeur at the prow of the Ship, drove four monsters, half horse half fish, each ridden by finny mesomorphic mermen. In heroic scale, the monstrous sculpture was set in a concrete pool shaped like a giant lavabo, the arc of its front curve set in cannon and terminating at a back wall forty feet across.

This wall was surmountable from the mall side, and wide enough to sit atop. Jeanine leaned back against the marble stele rising beside Columbia. Her honey blonde hair flattened against the cold stone, she held her knees up to her chest and rested her chin on them, grasping her left wrist with her right hand. She peered into Leo's eyes as he spoke of the theater. Leo straddled the wall like a cowboy, leaning forward, bouncing the weight of his anxious upper body onto his arms, his hands flat down on the top of the wall. The crisp autumn roar of the fountain masked the sounds of university evening, the occasional sticker-privileged car or cruising campus cop motortrike revving past the mall, and tones of conversation, pedestrian pairs and trios returning to dorms from the undergraduate library or the stacks, conversation in the authoritative tones of completed reading, comprehension, ability to express, even if just to paraphrase. And chatter too, coed chatter about dorm life, college life, home towns, serious chatter, young men chattering, party chatter, Vietnam worry chatter, movies and music and sometimes dope and often sex, but Littlefield Fountain masked it from Leo and Jeanine. He brought up Maeterlinck, about whom he knew little, and Ibsen about whom he had already learned much. But as he talked, he was thinking how beautiful Jeanine was, how smooth and strong her slender dancer's legs appeared, and that in her hunkered position, in the brown velvet miniskirt she must be ruining on the marble, she was showing him her panties, and she must have known it but seemed not to care. After all, this was not high school any more. It was college, and the Mamas and the Papas and Jefferson Airplane, not to mention the Beatles. So Leo was enjoying it, unaware as yet that he was falling in love, and Jeanine was listening, tabula rasa because dance majors were not required to take dramatic criticism. She didn't much care about Maeterlinck, and the appreciative look she was giving Leo had much more to do with his smooth good looks and polite nature than with his grasp of Ibsen's use of symbolism.

They had both been cast in *Sergeant Musgrave's Dance*, which was a play and had no dance in it. The director, Dr. Aria Nichols, new acting teacher from New York State without tenure and anxious to impress the hiring board, had added eight War Dead to the cast list. Leo and Jeanine were both in those roles, no lines, should be easy credit.

They sat and talked for over an hour, then climbed off the wall and strolled up the mall toward the tower from atop of which, four summers ago, the madman Charles Whitman had murdered thirteen and maimed many more around the campus below. Afternoon light was fading. Jeanine needed to head back to the huge new Jester Dormitory for dinner. As they walked, she brushed up against him several times, pretty unsteady gait for a dancer, crashing into him like that. October was off to a nice start, Leo thought. Nice conversation, normal. She was from Houston. Not pretentious, either. Had an uncle home from Vietnam in a box, a real-life War Dead. They wondered if it would come up in rehearsal. Nichols wouldn't care, Jeanine suspected. Leo agreed that she was too interested in her own agenda to inquire of her students.

As he had when he'd arrived on campus, Leo felt dwarfed by the big buildings, especially the old-style ones like Garrison Hall, the granddaddy of the geology department. He wondered if his Houston friend felt it, too—the massive older buildings of yellow and brown bricks, built to last through the ages, looming over the greenways and pebbled concrete walks. Several times he glanced at Jeanine's profile, the long line of her neck exposed when she looked up at the old buildings, gawking a little, like him.

How had they ended up spending the late afternoon together, anyway? It had started in the Green Room when several War Dead, lounging in the thick cigarette smoke, were discussing Nichols' concept for the production, laid out for Acting 301 during the previous hour. Nichols was having an accurate replica of a Gatling gun constructed, and it would be trained on the audience at the climax of the play. Risky, considering Charles Whitman was still fresh in people's minds. Good stuff. Not in the script. And then coincidentally Jeanine and Leo headed for the student union at the same time, walked there together, and shared a booth in the Chuck Wagon as they had Cokes and french fries for mid-afternoon sustenance. Littlefield Fountain had been the culmination of an aimless walk around campus as they continued their conversation.

But when they reached Jester dorm, she was casual with him. She hardly glanced at him to say goodnight as she hurried to catch the busy elevator. "See you," and she was gone. He stood a few feet back as she squeezed into the crowded elevator car, gazing after her, suddenly wondering if he'd been kidding himself, and the chemistry was all in his mind.

As the elevator doors began to close, Jeanine turned around to face outward, and when she saw Leo still standing there, her sudden smile burned straight through to his heart.

He lingered for a few moments, nosing around Jester's main lobby, her lobby. They had Acting 301 together, and they would be rehearsing Musgrave for the next six weeks. He stood next to an island of sofas and love seats, taking in the aromas of carpet so new it was still off-gassing, upholstery still new, construction still new, piano, baby grand still new, and glass and steel and bricks—more bricks, he'd heard, than had ever been used before in a single construction project. It was all new, posh, gargantuan. She was from Houston, but she was not a snob. Far out.

He took his time walking back to his room in the little two-story house eight blocks west of campus. Far out, he practiced thinking several times on the way to his little room and his studious roommate, David.

When he reached the decaying Victorian and went inside, David looked up from his desk, lowering his reading glasses to look at Leo.

"You got a phone call," he said, holding up a piece of notebook paper.

"Oh, thanks," Leo said. Leah had called him about twice a week since he'd left. This would be the first time he hadn't been home to receive her call. She'd been arranging to move to Austin, was trying to tie up loose ends in Brownwood.

The phone was in the foyer at the foot of a steep staircase. This location afforded some privacy from David, but not necessarily from the boys upstairs.

"Hello?" Her voice had warmed over the years, had not hardened, yet had deepened in a subtle way Leo noticed on the phone.

"Hi. Me, here."

"Didn't come home today?"

"Been at the library."

"You have?" Did she suspect something already?

"I went by this fountain. Littlefield Fountain. You'll like it. It has these men with fins on their heads and all over them, riding half-horses half-fish."

"I've heard of it."

"How are you?" Too formal?

"I'm fine."

"Me too. Got cast in a play."

"Really?" Pleased. Good.

"Called *Sergeant Musgrave's Dance.*"

"A dance?"

"No, that's just the name of it."

"Who are you? Sergeant Musgrave?"

"No. I'm a Dead. All the Dead are war dead." Nothing. Wait. She giggled. Good.

In these conversations there were long silences in which Leo perceived sex—or some odd mental aspect of sex—taking place in the mind's background. For the first time, it made Leo uncomfortable.

"I'm dead, too. I'm quitting at the glove factory."

"Have you given notice?"

"No. Definitely by next summer, though."

"That's a long time." A long time to be with Jeanine!

"What's the matter?" she asked. *Because she felt something. She felt Jeanine, though she couldn't know what she felt. No, please no.* "I'm sick of that job. Can't wait to get out of there. What's the matter with you? What are you thinking about?"

"It's Maeterlinck," Leo said to her, and he knew this was a good diversion. "I've got to do a paper. It's hard. I can handle it, though."

"I'll let you go." They were quiet for a while before they hung up, which was how they always did it. But she knew, he was sure. She didn't know what she knew, but she knew.

Feigning a careless attitude, Leo walked out the front door, across the porch, and onto the sidewalk. For some time he roamed the neighborhood, worn old houses converted to student rentals. There had been no assignment about Maeterlinck.

—

"Hedge and ditch, dear. Up and over," one of Sergeant Musgrave's men instructed the prostitute.

It was all Leo and Jeanine could do to keep from laughing. The playwright was British. What did it mean? *Hedge and ditch, dear. Up and over.* They were required to stand downstage, dead and expressionless, as one of Sergeant Musgrave's men engaged in love for hire in the public house where the soldiers were putting up for the night. Earlier the prostitute had asked the Sergeant if he wanted drink with his food, and he had said No, just the cheese. Leo wondered if the cheese was supposed to be a substitute for a drink. Deceased and gazing expressionless into the empty auditorium, he was planning to use this absurdity later to make Jeanine laugh.

The set would be dominated by a central scaffold suggesting a gallows and serving as a platform for the Gatling gun. For rehearsals, the entire stage was bathed in bastard amber, the auditorium a black void punctuated by five red exit signs, two at the rear, two on a side, the other one out of Leo's sight line. He tried to concentrate on the lines, remember his cue to walk off left, dead and expressionless. He wanted to look stage right to see Jeanine where she was standing, dead and expressionless, with two other Dead. He resisted the temptation, had been called on it once already. Nichols could be nasty.

The soldier and the prostitute were making love. When Nichols jumped up on the stage to direct them more surgically, Leo risked looking across at Jeanine. She was already looking at him. They smiled at each other. Leo was sustained.

"Dead, take a break. Stay near your positions, please," the director ordered. Word on Nichols was that she was something of a hard-dick, even rumored to have made it with Lacy Firestone, a cute and fem acting major from out-of-state.

"Hedge and ditch, dear," Jeanine whispered, approaching Leo. They edged offstage behind the velvet black, out of the sight line.

"Do you have any idea what that means?" Leo asked her. He was disappointed that he couldn't see her more clearly, hoped his eyes would adjust to the offstage dark.

"It sounds like a steeple chase," Jeanine whispered, glancing toward the tableaux of lovemaking upstage.

"Whatever that is," Leo admitted his ignorance, something he would normally avoid, would have made a mental note, checked a dictionary or encyclopedia at the first opportunity. But Jeanine was standing close, and he looked at her and she was looking at him, her face tilted up toward his, as though they were about to kiss. Leo giggled, caught himself, checked upstage. Nichols was absorbed in the work, her hand flat on the small of the prostitute's back, she in an awkward position on the rehearsal pylon substituting for a bed.

Leo felt Jeanine's breath on his face, he was almost certain. It was like strange herbs, something he wanted to suck into his own lungs, yearned for it. Another Dead, Sam Wear, sidled over from somewhere to join them.

After a moment in which neither Jeanine nor Leo adjusted out of their somewhat intimate juxtaposition, Sam whispered, inches away, "Go ahead, Nichols, better demonstrate how to do it to her." Jeanine covered her mouth to stifle a giggle, poked Sam in the ribs.

Leo wanted to make Jeanine laugh like that. He wanted to be easy and funny like Sam Wear. He felt a pang of jealousy. He wanted Sam to go away. He wanted, in fact, everybody to go away and leave him alone with Jeanine. Alone in the theater, the cave, as William Saroyan had called it, with Jeanine his Queen and he her King, cave dwellers together.

They heard Nichols and the soldier and the prostitute laughing, though they hadn't heard anything that was being said. Nichols clapped her hands twice and announced, "Listen up, people, dead and alive, front and center please." She clapped twice again. "Front and center."

The entire cast assembled, taking seats in the first few rows. Nichols, leaning on the rail in front of the orchestra pit, was telling them the rehearsal was over, fifteen minutes early, because of something she had to do, and she was reminding them of the next rehearsal, tomorrow, and giving some notes about the play, and something specific about the Dead, her own conceit, something she wanted to work brilliantly, and the cast should bear with her on it. But Leo wasn't listening, because in the bustle to take seats front and center, somehow he had ended up not beside Jeanine but between Sam Wear and Kirk Sirois, one of Sergeant Musgrave's men. And worse, on the other side of Sam Wear was seated Jeanine. Leo suffered a pounding attack of jealousy, knew only at the edge of his consciousness that it was inappropriate. He forced himself to concentrate on Nichols. But Nichols was dismissing the group. The others were standing up, collecting personal items in a sudden chattering cacophony.

Jeanine hurried away before Leo was even standing. He was disoriented in his body, his legs somewhat numb. He'd had to stand still on stage too long, cut off the flow of blood somehow.

The crowd was thinning, exit doors clanking open and crashing shut as the cast hurried away, by couples and singles and groups. Leo stood up, remembered he had only his script to carry. A sweater? No, he'd earlier opted for the flannel shirt. *No, just the cheese.* He walked up the aisle, alone, toward the back of the house, not even sure those doors were unlocked. He realized that he was now a Dead and would never feel the part on stage as he did now. *Did I see her walking out with Sam Wear?*

He began pouring all his energy into blocking out the raging speculations. She'd never said anything to lead him to believe.... They were just standing there, no reason to think.... *Forget it. Think of homework. Intro to the Theater, Architecture section.*

Hogg Auditorium was cavernous, seating two thousand, ceiling forty feet up, a large balcony extending almost a third of the distance from the back wall to the stage. The plummet from the balcony rail, where the darkness was rich and velvety, was a fall toward the imaginary, the metal and fabric seats below merely part of the larger illusion. Leo saw a young man, himself, launch from this balcony edge of the world, plummeting from a high place into a dark eternal void, dropping endlessly in painful twisting somersaults and slow, fearful writhing, his hands clutching his face in the sure knowledge that there was nothing else to reach for. *Row W. Row X. Row Y. Row Z. Row AA. Row BB.* He pushed his gaze to the lobby doors, their brass push bars reflecting a dim line of the red exit light. *Row EE. Row FF. There are no vomitories in this theater. Vomitsam Wearvomit, one of the what? Two or three other straight males in the drama department and he's a damned Dead. Tall and good looking too. Vomitnichols castingvomit.*

Then he heard Jeanine behind him, halfway up the aisle, hurrying toward him with the notebooks and sweater she'd retrieved from backstage. "Leo?"

Turning around, suddenly weightless, he watched her approach. "Hey, I thought you'd left without me," he said, and to his ears, it sounded *cool enough.*

"I don't think you can get out that way," Jeanine said. She brushed past him and pushed on the bar. The door was locked. She moved back past Leo and turned to him, blocking his way back toward the front.

"I was afraid of that," he said, and when he tried to step to her side, she moved to block him, clasping the green spiral notebook to her chest, looking at him with her mouth set. Leo was confused. But only for a moment. *She's mad that I was leaving without her.* Not mad, just letting me know. Letting me know. All was calm, all was bright. She's waiting for me to say something. Not going to move until I say something.

"Hey Jeanine," he cozed, trying for sexy but failing.

"What?"

"Can I walk you home?"

She lowered the notebook to her side, freeing one hand with which she smoothed imaginary wrinkles from the sweater she had pulled on. "Sure," she said, and smiled at Leo. "That's better than nothing." She walked down the aisle and Leo caught up with her.

"Want to go to a movie with me this weekend?" he said.

"Twist my arm," she said, giving him her arm to twist.

18

LEO HAD NEVER SEEN SUCH a large, busy bus station. The ride from Austin to Houston had been both too long and too short, both tense and stupefying as Leo worried and Jeanine laughed off his concerns, held his sweaty hand, kissed his cheek. Leo had been hesitant—terrified in fact—when Jeanine invited him to her house for a short weekend in January. The new term was underway, the holidays done with, and although Jeanine's parents were too busy to make the drive, they paid for both bus tickets and the taxi ride to the house, so sorry they couldn't pick them up in the car, but would make up for it with a good dinner.

Through the window of the taxi, Leo could see the clouds blowing in from the gulf at visible speed as they exited 290 and took a long, straight two-lane, its pavement sun-bleached and smooth, a single ochre line painted down the middle and not much of a shoulder to pull onto, or cry on if this went badly. Palm trees lined a stretch of this road, the houses set far back. Leo noted large, well-maintained compounds in Spanish, Tudor, and modern designs set in vast landscapes of manicured grass and tropical shrubbery. After a mile or two, the driver made a right turn onto a quiet, more intimate neighborhood. A block in, the houses were on larger lots, sedate, traditional architecture now, set back behind walls, or obscured by dense foliage. Some of these residences had circular driveways accessing their front entrances. Farther on, there were fewer houses and more woodland. They crossed a bridge over a small lake, and Leo noticed, looking past Jeanine's beautiful—*Is that an aristocratic nose?*—profile, a golf course, one rough running right down to the lake's shore.

—

During the first course, there was a drink Mr. Licavoli laughed and called "fox mimosas." It tasted like orange juice mixed with ginger ale. The rack of lamb was served with mint jelly. Leo was unclear at first as to whether the lady serving them was a family member who would soon sit down with them, or was a servant. He didn't ask, but gleaned from the conversation that she was a live-in cook, and they referred to her with feigned respect by her first name.

"Would you like more tea, Leo?" Mrs. Licavoli asked. His glass was half full. He knew he could say no, I'm fine. But it needed to be broken, the elastic membrane separating him from this family, the sheet of thin skin, the drum head, *the hymen, her hymen, oh man....*

"No, just the cheese." He looked at Jeanine, who was supposed to get it. There was no cheese on the table.

No, just the cheese as though cheese was a substitute for drink, but she was stuffing her mouth with a forkful of mashed potatoes, and it was too long before she looked back at him, alerted by the silence, and said, "What?" Now Leo wondered what the taste in the mashed potatoes was, and his wondering filled the rest of the intolerable pause to overflowing.

"That's a line from *Sergeant Musgrave's Dance*," he told them. "I have yet to figure out what it means."

"Oh," Mrs. Licavoli said, puzzled.

"But I want to ask you about the mashed potatoes," Leo went on. "What makes them taste that way?"

"Oh," Mrs. Licavoli said again, still baffled. "I don't know what you mean."

"They taste so rich. It's good," he struggled on. "Delicious."

"Well, I think we put in olive oil," Mrs. Licavoli said.

"What you're tasting," said Mr. Licavoli, chewing a piece of lamb, "is truffle oil."

Leo nodded. Truffle oil. "It's good," he said. Silver candlesticks. Silver silverware. Cloth napkins that are soft. The hymen is intact, so intact, so intact. *Hedge and ditch, dear, up and over.* Suddenly he knew what that line meant. Musgrave's leftenant was about to mount the prostitute. *Hedge and ditch* referred to horses jumping over hedges and ditches, and the leftenant was using it as a metaphor for his anticipated fornicating.

"Well," said Mr. Licavoli, "I'm glad you like it."

"May I have some more salad?" inquired Jeanine of her mother. Jeanine's hippie peasant blouse, Leo realized, was not the affront to her parents he'd suspected, or hoped, it would be. It was a youthful style for their youthful daughter. Leo had tried to dress straight, straighter than he usually did anyway, and had ended up looking—or at least feeling—dishonest. At school, he'd been trying his best to acquire some hip clothing on his small budget.

The Licavolis were so in sync, so in the same groove. *Groovy. I am so separated from this.*

As she was handing the salad to her daughter, Mrs. Licavoli said to Leo, "I remember how I know about Brownwood now. There was a hurricane, Hurricane Carla, wasn't there? It flooded and was terrible. Hasn't been that many years ago, a decade maybe, you must remember it."

"I do, but that was Brownsville, down the coast, right across the Mexican border from Matamoros. Brownwood is up in the center of the state."

"Oh, I see. That was what I was thinking of, I'm sure."

Fine, so Mrs. Licavoli had never heard of Brownwood.

Still chewing the glob of lamb, making good progress on it, Mr. Licavoli mumbled, "Doris is not from Texas originally, Leo."

"We'll forgive her anyway," Leo said, smiled, took a bite of asparagus, wrong choice, because when he went on to say, "She's what we call a ring-tailed tooter," he unmouthed part of the asparagus into his lap. Only Jeanine admitted to seeing it happen, though they all did. She giggled, which helped a little, not much.

Dessert was strawberry shortcake, and when it arrived Leo dismissed his idea of calling it groovy, although he wanted to call something groovy because by now he'd stopped trying to break through, and was instead cherishing the hymen, wouldn't want to get too close to Mr. Licavoli for fear of catching his razor burn. This sudden change of intention came to Leo's rescue, charging out from somewhere between his brainstem and cerebellum when the asparagus charged out of his mouth. It allowed Leo to relax a little. This was hopeless. Hell with it. It wasn't, however, enough to allow the Licavolis to relax also.

Mr. Licavoli invited Leo to join him in the den. A fire was burning in a copious fireplace, but they didn't take the chairs facing it, which would have enabled Leo to stare into the flames. Instead, Mr. Licavoli sat on a leather couch and indicated for Leo a swivel chair, also leather, at a small roll top desk.

The fire crackled and popped behind a dense screen, out of sight. For a moment, Leo wondered if Mr. Licavoli was going to say anything. He wondered if it would be all right to get up and stand at the fire for a little while, a minute, to enjoy it. Leo thought of saying, *The fire is out of sight.* His hippie classmates would have understood that.

The problem with letting your daughter matriculate in the drama department of a university was that she'd meet men who were also matriculating in the drama department of that university. Most would be homosexuals, of course, but there would be some heterosexuals, and those would be the men she'd be likely to date. Leo wondered if Mr. Licavoli realized how loudly he was thinking.

"Doris is from New Jersey. In fact, that's where I met her. I tell you what, Leo, she may not know her Texas geography, but that girl is *magna cum laude* from Barnard."

Nodding enough to be seen, Leo said, "No kidding. What in?"

"*Magna cum laude.* I did pretty well in college, but got outa there without honors. Just happy to get out, do pretty well—better than pretty well, but no great honors. You ever been out to California?"

"No, I haven't. You went to school in California?"

"No. I have a brother in San Diego." Mr. Licavoli nodded his head, agreeing with himself. Then he looked over to Leo and explained, "He has a Ford dealership. Does real well. He's married, has two sons, they're a little younger than my kids. Wife's pretty. And John's a nice-looking fellow. He got all the looks. I got the brains, but there weren't that many brains to go around." He glanced at Leo with a tight smile. "No, I mean John's smart enough. He keeps the dealership afloat. Can't keep salesmen, but they're a dime a dozen so it doesn't matter much." Mr. Licavoli nodded to himself again, cleared his throat, nodded some more, tightened his lips.

"Car dealerships can be a real gold mine," Leo offered, proud of his innocuous but relevant thought.

"No, he drinks like a fish. Sooner or later the business is going down the tubes. His marriage is already on the rocks. A matter of time. I think they want to get the boys out of high school...."

Leo was nodding his sympathy. "Sorry to hear that."

"Now you know our son Jason is at Yale."

"Yes, Jeanine told me he's studying...."

"Graduate work in oceanography. He and Doris and I took a nice trip to Italy last year." Nodding and remembering, *not even bothering to ask me if I've been to Europe. Knows I haven't. Not really pompous. He's just already written me off.*

"So Jeanine didn't go with you to Italy?" Leo asked, knowing that she didn't. He was curious to see whether Mr. Licavoli remembered where Jeanine had been, why she didn't go.

Mr. Licavoli thought a moment. "No, now Jeanine was in Aspen with her friend Jessica and her family. They've been friends since kindergarten. I tried to get her interested in Florence, showed her a bunch of pictures, sweetened the deal, but she had her heart set on Aspen with Jessica. Jessica was going off to Sarah Lawrence, and they had to be together for one last fun time before college. You know how it is, uh, Leo."

"Sure."

"We've been friends with Jessica's family for years and years. They're artists."

"Artists. Really?"

"He has work hung in New York all the time. Gets big money for his stuff. I like it, but don't see how it's worth what people pay for it. The art market is funny, you know."

"I've heard."

"You know, speaking of California, after college I did some exploring. You know how it is. You want to garner some experiences before you dive headlong into business. I headed out to the Big Sur. I'll never forget. I had a '39 Buick convertible, beautiful creature. I drove that thing all along the coast. One time I stopped 'er right next to the beach. Rocky beach. Beautiful surf. Built me a fire up against some rocks, sat there all night listening to the surf, watching clouds float in from the ocean, watching the stars pop out from between the clouds. It was a beautiful moment in my life."

Who cares? Why are we not talking about me, checking me out, seeing if I'm worthy of Jeanine? It was plain enough—Mr. Licavoli was not interested in learning any more about Leo.

And Leo was, in a way, relieved by that. He knew well that he didn't have acceptable answers to the questions Mr. Licavoli *could* ask. *Yes, I'm on a full scholarship—based largely on financial need.* It was irksome that Mr. Licavoli was perceptive enough to realize it. He was not a stupid man. It seemed unfair.

After a while, when Mr. Licavoli was talking about his and his brother's shared interest in sports cars when they were teenagers, Leo did get up and go to the fireplace and watched through the screen as the logs burned. If any of Leo's gestures interested Mr. Licavoli at all, it was this one—the moving to the fireplace as if to ignore Mr.

Licavoli. Leo had stood up in an effort to stifle a yawn, but the attempt was unsuccessful, and he turned away in a last-ditch effort to hide it from his host. Mr. Licavoli finished his story about the Stutz Bearcat his brother had acquired for a pittance, and then he said good night and left Leo alone in the den.

Leo sat in a stuffed chair facing the fireplace, content, more or less, and wondering if he'd be embarrassed in some horrible way before leaving this household, imagining what might happen, what might be said, questions he might yet be asked. And if he was to be humiliated, how many times? He imagined one scenario after another—and *what line did you say your father is in?* but each time convinced himself, based on the evidence, that no one in this family would stoop to doing that on purpose, and even Mrs. Licavoli was poised enough not to do it accidentally. Part of Leo knew that they had written him off, but he allowed himself to long for the resumption of classes, when he would have Jeanine in the familiar element again. He saw himself buying a motorcycle and taking her away from this threatening—*let's try 'threateningly normal'*—family forever, realizing the absurdity even as the fantasy played out. Threatening family? It was a wonderful family, full of love, damn it. No threat to anyone except an intruder who might end up hurting one of its members.

The fire was burning down, crackling and falling in on itself. From down the hall, Leo heard Jeanine fussing around her mother, something about a corduroy coat, and a mumbled response from Mrs. Licavoli. A metallic clack and clang, like a pair of scissors dropping to the hardwood. Silence, and then Mrs. Licavoli laughing, and Jeanine complaining again. This was from a room he'd glanced into earlier, a hobby room, or a sewing room, right down the hall. He decided he would wait here for them to find him. He was prepared to spend the night in this chair if they didn't remember to come and get him—even though he'd already been shown his room upstairs. Of course, they thought he was still talking with Mr. Licavoli. Unless Mr. Licavoli had checked by with them. And who cared? If he could steal a hug, a kiss, be alone with Jeanine for even a few seconds tonight, he'd be fine. And back at school, it would be fine. It was a new age, was it not? Was it not the dawning of the Age of Aquarius? Was there not a war, a bad war, an unjustified war, and was society not being shaken to its foundations? *I could fall asleep in this chair. No one I trust has ever told me whether the world can change.*

Leo preferred to believe it could.

19

LEAH CHECKED ON LULU AT noon, then went into her room, which had been Leo's room until he'd gone away in September. Now it was February and she had not rearranged anything in the room—the stored boxes were still stacked against the wall—but now her things were in the dresser and the closet. It was much nicer having a room of her own, and she couldn't help daydreaming about fixing things up, maybe even changing the wallpaper, putting up some curtains. But she procrastinated. Daydreaming was one thing—actually doing it seemed... not daunting, but repugnant. She closed the door and took off her sweater, and stood in front of the mirror and held her breasts, imagining being able to suckle herself. She thought about hippies. She wished there'd been some hippies in Brownwood. She pulled her sweater back on, went to the chest of drawers, extracted a brassiere and went back to the mirror, watched herself put the brassiere on over her sweater. A laugh welled up inside of her and she squinted, clenched her teeth, squelched it.

Feeling her heartbeat in her ears, she pulled up the wool skirt she was wearing and removed her panties, smoothed the skirt back down. She went into the other bedroom and stood above Lulu until she opened her eyes, the right eye searching, then finding Leah.

"What are you doing, Leah?"

"Standing here."

"Why you wearing the bra on the outside?"

"I thought it might make you laugh."

Lulu didn't laugh. She looked toward the window with her seeing eye, the other one pointing toward the ceiling.

A brown prescription cylinder was open, the white plastic lid nowhere in sight. Leah picked it up and read the label—Thorazine. She dumped the contents into her hand. Six capsules. She replaced three of them and took the other three into her room, added them to a tray of other pills she'd pilfered from Lulu. Thorazine was only good for a few minutes before they made you sleep with no dreams. Still, they came in handy. Phenobarbital was better, wonderful for taking a walk, getting sleepy and dreamy, and getting back home hardly knowing who or where you are, and then going to sleep. Better than the best good dream. Hippies knew about other ones, but in Brownwood there were no hippies.

She opened the door, went back into Lulu's room. Lulu's eyes were closed. Leah crawled over Lulu and straddled her at the waist, waking her.

"Oh, get off, Leah. You're too big for that now." But Leah pretended to ride her like a horse, jarring the whole bed, making the springs squeak and the legs groan in a painful rhythm against the floor. "And take off that bra. You look ridiculous."

Instead, Leah leaned over and placed her cheek against her sister's, enjoying the stretching openness, and bedspread rubbing against the nakedness under her skirt. "Is he all right?" she whispered.

"He's fine," Lulu murmured. "Don't worry, he's smart and wise, too. He'll be fine. You need to leave him alone."

"Leave him alone? Why?"

"So he can grow, Leah. Let him grow away from us a little. You don't want him stuffed into a life the size of Brownwood, do you?"

Leah sat up, uncomfortable now, unprotected from the roughness of the bedspread. She crawled off the bed, went to the window and pushed aside the blinds, looked at Brownwood. "Sure don't want that." Something in Lulu's tone had alerted Leah. "Which-a-way would you like him to grow away from us?"

Lulu sighed. Another curious warning to Leah's ear.

And then Leah understood.

"You saying he has a girlfriend?"

Lulu sighed again.

No. Lulu couldn't know anything, because she never talked with Leo. He couldn't have told her anything about a girlfriend. And yet, Lulu was his mother. She always knew everything about him, at least on an intuitive level. Leah considered. And then she knew it was true, and there was no doubt about it. The phone calls were the proof.

The feeling she'd gotten in October when she'd called him. She would have to move to Austin, leave Lulu alone with Cord. She'd have to get to work on it right away. She'd been thinking about it anyway, almost. It shouldn't come as a surprise. It was a good idea. The hippies. The different clothes, the candles and the incense, the drugs and the world. The killing, thousands and thousands of men being killed, and for what? *They're growing their hair as long as women's and telling the government to go to hell. It's wonderful. Austin will be wonderful. Someday Lulu will die. Cord will never die.*

"If I were Leo, I'd come home for the summer and get a job, save up a little money for next year." She squinted at Lulu, leaned against the window frame, crushed the blinds with an alloy crackle.

"Well, you're not Leo," Lulu said, staring wall-eyed like a fetal serpent. "I always thought of you as the big person and Leo as the little person, and then I saw you both all wound around each other, rolling in the leaves. And then y'all were waking, pulling apart from each other."

"Oh, Lulu, good gosh, we just fell asleep like that...."

"...this sin, this waking...."

"You're crazy, Lulu, and everybody knows it...."

"...carnal knowledge is all dug into my mind...."

With effort, Leah kept quiet, hoping Lulu would calm down. She pitied Lulu's uneasy, long insulted brain, but her secret with Leo must remain secret. She would continue the denial.

"He's who I should have been," Leah said when Lulu's stare looked dead. She touched herself—it didn't matter, Lulu wouldn't look over and see anyway. "He started out with the same kind of intelligence and sensitivity I have. Until somebody beat it out of him."

"Cord came from poor backwoods people. It's not his fault."

"Oh Lulu, what difference does that make? Fault. Who cares. Nothing is anybody's fault. So what." Leah sat on the foot of the bed. "I wonder how I could ruin his life. I'm his daddy, so let's see. Oh, I know. I could beat him with a belt, calling him a worthless whelp and a sissy, and all through his childhood I could terrorize him with a violent temper, never show him any tenderness except when I was buzzing on a six pack."

"He's a smart boy. You'll see. He didn't get a full scholarship to the University of Texas by being a mess, you know."

"I know he's smart. But the only reason he got good grades in high school was because I made him."

"He has special talent, Leah."

"Well, he's going to start wondering why this special talent isn't coming through for him."

"How do you know it won't?"

"It doesn't work that way, Lulu. He's going to figure out, later on, that hard work is part of it after all, that hard work is not a sign of being untalented."

"I never said that!"

"Oh, calm down, Lulu. Lay back down. What's done is done." Leah caressed Lulu's forehead until she closed her eyes and settled back into the pillow. "I wish Mama would come back to life. She was the one who took care of him, not you." There was no tear on Lulu's face, but Leah could see the hurt and anger burning through from far out in the cosmos that Lulu's mind contained.

"He has a gift," Lulu whispered.

"What is the gift?"

"He understands God."

Leah pushed herself up from the bed, scratched an itchy spot on her scalp. "He's an atheist, Lulu. Has been since he was fifteen. We talk about things like that."

"That doesn't matter. He's been in touch with the spiritual since he was nine or ten years old, probably long before that even." Lulu opened her eyes as Leah turned to look at her. "It doesn't matter if he thinks he's an atheist, Leah. That's only to do with religion. Not important."

Leah was thinking again about some girl who had captured Leo's interest. "Yeah, not important," she said.

—

The next day, Leah stood in the living room, leaning against the front door, staring down at the dilapidated couch that for years had been her bed. She had found ways to sleep on it that were not too uncomfortable, now considered whether Leo's old bed was any better. It was, but not much. Two more nights, three, a week at most, and she would be in Austin with her own apartment, a car of some kind, and a job. These were not unreasonable expectations. She had a small bank account, her savings from working plus her paltry share from the sale of Ina's house. Lulu would have to get along without her now.

It was not a decision at all, but an inevitability. Her new life was real now. She pushed herself off the door and walked into the bedroom where Lulu was awake, sitting up, and looking at some documents.

"What's all that?" asked Leah.

"These are some papers from Kimball's," Lulu said. She had not worked at the cannery for over twelve years.

"Let's see." Leah sat on the bed next to Lulu and peered at the yellowing paper. It was a mimeographed list of safety rules for the factory. Leah glanced at the other papers spread on the bed. There was a tax form and a few other items. "Where'd all this come from?"

"The dresser drawer," Lulu said, turning her head to look at Leah in such a way that her eyes lined up together. She might have been normal in that instant, and Leah blinked with emotion. Lulu would have been such a lovely woman in her maturity.

The bottom dresser drawer was open. Leah started to reach over with her foot and push it to, but thought Lulu would benefit from doing it herself. "You be sure and put those papers back, Lulu. And close the drawer."

"I will."

"We can't lose that stuff. It's important."

Lulu again cocked her head to look at Leah, and gave her little sister a crooked, pleased smile. Leah had intended to tell her about leaving, but couldn't take away Lulu's moment of happiness, however deluded.

Two days later Leah told her, having waited until Lulu had taken a chlorpromazine and was already drifting. Cord was unaware of her plan and had shown open disdain for her purchase, the day before, of a yellow 1960 Plymouth with fins large enough to fly. The Falcon had bitten the dust months ago and Leah had been getting rides to work. She bought the Plymouth with a down payment consisting of very little money and an easy view up her skirt for the salesman while they negotiated credit terms. She had located the *Austin American-Statesman* at the library, but the issue was several days old. Still, she'd gleaned some want ads listing apartments and jobs.

"Moving?" Lulu could barely hold her eyes open, but the alarm was evident.

"Have to," Leah whispered, and she kissed Lulu on the lips. "We have to take care of Leo, don't we? Don't we?"

Lulu closed her worried eyes, and Leah sat with her, holding her hand, until the furrowed brow relaxed.

20

L EAH MOVED TO AUSTIN AND found an apartment north of campus. She knew about Jeanine, had ferreted it out of Leo the day she hit town, though they had not met, and Leo insisted they would not. Jeanine, on the other hand, knew only that Leah, an aunt, existed, but not that she had moved to Austin. Leo's room was more than a half hour's walk from Leah's apartment, and he didn't visit often. Leah found a job almost immediately, and was so busy organizing her life that for the first few weeks in Austin, she had little time for Leo. As she settled into her new life, she found that the Northland Mall, where she worked, was not a good place to meet hippies. Leo, meanwhile, was not inclined to introduce her into peripheral campus life. For a few weeks she enlisted a man at her job to take her to clubs downtown. He was uncomfortable at the hippie spots like the Vulcan Gas Company, but Leah loved it, and after some weeks, she connected with a hippie who was pleased to be seen with her, though he couldn't pay her way. By April, Leah considered herself hip, complete with wardrobe, apartment décor, and marijuana. But what she longed for was Leo's willing company.

—

Far out on the deep green waters of Lake Travis, motorboats buzzed and sailboats nodded in the spring breeze. Hippie Hollow was a remote cove on the east shore, with boulders lying just under the surface making the area too treacherous for boating, so it afforded swimmers a degree of privacy. Directions to Hippie Hollow were passed by word of mouth only. Jeanine had learned of it from her dance-mate Judy.

The hike down from the dirt road to the Hollow was rocky and steep. When Leo and Jeanine reached the boulders at the shoreline, they found no one around. They'd been ready to strip and skinny dip with throngs of naked hippies, but by themselves, they were embarrassed. They left their clothes on and climbed onto a boulder, water lapping at its sides, its top surface flat and the size of a small room. Lying next to each other, they held hands and squeezed their eyes shut against the glare. The midday air was moving and fresh, with the mossy scent of lake water. The only sounds were the intermittent nasal drones of distant motorboats and, barely distinguishable from those, cicadas buzzing somewhere back up the trail.

Jeanine had received a brand-new Camaro for Christmas, burnt orange with white upholstery—the UT colors. She had let Leo drive it while she navigated, with directions written for her by Judy, the hippie girl in her jazz dance class.

"This is the life," Leo said, breathing in the air.

"So peaceful," Jeanine said. "I wonder how often it's abandoned like this."

"I guess I'm a little disappointed. Kinda wanted to see you naked. Are you disappointed?"

"No."

"Far out." Leo squeezed her soft hand. "When I was little, you know, back in my childhood? I used to feel ecstasy once in a while."

"I'm pretty happy right now," she said, and turned on her side, gave Leo a long, wet kiss on his cheek, but pulled away when he offered his mouth.

"Oh, I don't know, Jeanine. Happy is good, of course, but...."

Jeanine sat up, wrapped her arms around her knees. Leo squinted up at her, loving the way wisps of her hair escaped the clips at her temples and waved in the zephyrs.

"My dad's a talker, hmm?" She gazed out across the lake.

"Oh yeah. I couldn't get a word in edgewise, and I was glad of it." They chuckled.

"Have you ever smoked grass?" she asked him.

"No. You?"

"No. I'm satisfied with happy. I mean, I had a happy childhood. I don't think I need ecstasy." She tilted her head back to sun her neck. "You think you'll try it?"

"I don't know. I might, but right now I don't want to mess myself up. I've heard of a lot of students dropping out because of it."

"I've heard that too."

"Why? Are you thinking of trying it?"

She took a deep breath, considering. "No, but I'm not ruling it out, you know."

"Don't do it without telling me first."

She looked at him. "Why?"

"So I could try to talk you out of it."

She laughed, stood up, stretched, did a plié, did another one.

Leo felt that her lissome body was the meat of the empyrean, the substance, and everything else was illusion, including himself and all the stars and other so-called matter. She was real, and he was near the reality, though he did not feel real himself.

"Man, I must love you," he said.

"Why?"

"You're so beautiful, Jeanine. In every way."

She did another plié. "Thanks. I have to go out with this guy my parents know. Did Dad tell you about Zack Constantin?"

Had he heard right? "What?"

"He said you would understand, and it sounded like he'd mentioned it to you when y'all were talking in the den."

"No. Who is this...?"

"This junior in the Business School. Some frat rat. I supposedly know him, but I don't remember him unless it's who I think it is. Anyway, my parents know his parents. You know how that goes."

Leo did not know how that went. He sat up. "What do you mean you have to go out with him?"

"Nothing. You know. Parents do these favors for other people's parents. I think this is some guy Dad knew in college or something, and then had some kind of business with for a while. They're friends, so this guy is his son."

Leo sat stupefied for a moment, feeling a jagged rift between what Jeanine was saying to him and what it meant. He heard her saying something about wishing they'd brought bathing suits, but he wasn't listening now. He was separating from the scene, the one where Jeanine was the only reality, and he'd been so near it just seconds ago. He lay back on the rock, looked up as she was arching her back, pointing her pretty nose skyward, taking in the air, enjoying the sunshine. Like a photograph now, her image lay flat on the plane of the observable. The truth would come into focus in a few days—that her loving parents had watchfully waited as Jeanine had her little infatuation with the poor boy, but enough was enough.

He would be still now, encapsulated, separate.

—

Carrying his note pad and a currently favored pen, Leo treated himself late the next afternoon to a small table at *Les Amis*, a hippie-style sidewalk cafe sprung up on an old parking lot west of campus, not far from his room. He began to work out the situation. Letting him drive her car had been an assuagement. Obviously—in retrospect—she'd known she was going to tell him about Zack Constantin.

The waitress approached his table with a pleasant "Hi there!" Their eyes met, he realized he knew her from somewhere, she smiled, pointed her pencil at him. "You're...."

"Leo. Leo Nobles? Drama Department. I saw your outdoor exhibit."

"That's right. How's the play coming along? You were dead or something."

"It's over. It went well. I'm alive again."

The art building was located across the street from the drama building, and Leo had stopped by her exhibit before Christmas break. She'd been tending her exhibit, giant Crackerjack prizes, and they'd talked for a while. She was a junior. Though she was hip and he was not, she'd made him feel at ease. *Far out.*

He ordered something called chamomile tea, admitting to himself, as the pretty artist chick took his order, that the hippie culture had its appeal. He liked that his table rocked on the uneven surface of the old parking lot, that the plywood roof overhead appeared flimsy, and that walls had been deemed unnecessary. The prices weren't cheap, but the menu was mysterious, and that interested him. What was bulgur? What was tabuli? Tahini sauce? Alfalfa sprouts?

Strange sitar music began issuing from several speakers that were mounted overhead on posts. Leo could see the wires leading into the speaker near him, down the pole disappearing into the pavement.

Sound Equipment

I had forgotten the artist lady.
*   I failed to recognize her—at first.*
*   Then she came near and I saw*
*   her light body and kind eyes*
and had to touch her again
and touching her made me light.

And light, I moved with her,
  in her manner,
  gliding over the walkways
  like Seurat's figures.
Only the most sensitive, precise
  unidirectional microphone
  created by science
  could detect our thunder,
  we were so distant.
Our thunder, though, was sharp
  and clear, as rendered
  through the mic's electronics,
  and all the spies and their
  companions marveled at it
  when they heard.

The chamomile he found relaxing, tasty, like drinking a liquid version of the smell of wildflowers. The hippie chick touched him on the arm when she delivered it, and he thought that was nice, although it brought Jeanine back to his mind. He'd thought of little but Jeanine all day. They had kissed last night as they parted at her dorm, after the outing at Hippie Hollow and then a movie called *The Strawberry Statement* at one of the movie houses on Guadalupe. But the kiss had not been right. It was not true. Or was it true and a goodbye kiss? He contemplated over chamomile.

People with long hair and heavy clothing, sitting at tables around him, conversed in whispers. Was this the way hippies talked? In quiet tones at wooden tables in open air cafes on parking lots?

He brooded for a long time. Mr. Licavoli had not approved of him. He'd been a nice man, but that's the way those kind of people were. Mrs. Licavoli had not liked him, because she could not figure out where Brownwood was. She was probably addicted to Valium, distressed over an abandoned career or something. The Camaro was a sudden, unexpected surprise for Jeanine. Freshmen were not allowed to have cars parked on campus, were they? Mr. Licavoli must have pulled some strings. The car was a bribe, of course. The date—dates, let's be realistic—with Zack Constantin were to get Jeanine off track with Leo, on track with someone else, a frat rat, diversion. It was a plan. It would work. Jeanine was gone. There was nothing he could do. In the back of his mind, he had wondered how Jeanine would ever have worked anyway. Mr. and Mrs. Licavoli in Brownwood, crowding into the living room. Meeting Cord? Nosing into the bedroom to say hello to Lulu. Oops, she's asleep right now. We'll try her later.

The chamomile soothed. He could almost have smiled if irony, defeat, sadness, and loss had been amusing. But none of it was, and he was beginning to realize the totality of his loss when the hippie chick returned with a chrome pot and asked if he wanted more hot water on his tea bag. He said sure, and glanced at her, tried to return her smile.

"So Leo," she said, and now he had to look at her. "I can't remember if you said you were an acting major or something else." Before he could answer, she spotted the pen and paper with Leo's scribbled poem on it. "Oh! Playwriting I bet. Can I read your poem?"

"Let me get you some dinner or something, after you get through. What time do you get off?" It was Leo's entire repertoire of pickup lines. He completely surprised himself, didn't even know he knew the lines, and would not have said them if he'd considered the idea first.

"I'm off in ten minutes. Want to hit Holiday House for a cheeseburger?"

"Yeah."

"Groovy."

"Way out," Leo said, and she laughed. "Yeah, far out," Leo recovered.

For the next ten minutes Leo panicked because he could not remember her name. He paid his bill at the register, returned to his seat, worried about a tip—no, I'm taking her to dinner—and still her name would not come to him. He tried to recall whether there were signatures on her sculptures. At the last second, as she came out of the kitchen area, another waitress saved him. *Night, John Quill. Hey, you on tomorrow?* And John Quill turned back and said, *Lunch shift.*

—

Leo's instinct to rebound was premature. Jonquil was a flower, so pretty, her millet hair and millet freckles so fresh, her curvy build hidden by the corduroy jumper she wore. And her manner was relaxed, not so hip once they started walking to the Holiday House at the south edge of campus. With the ease of an old favorite song, she told him he was handsome enough to be an actor if that's what he was going for. He said he didn't know, and before the silence grew uncomfortable, she began telling him about her home town, Liberty Hill, not far from Austin, such a country place, nice people but not her scene. She took his hand and told him where she lived now with some other heads, west of campus. Leo realized it was near his place, and he veered off the subject.

While they ate delicious cheeseburgers and grooved on the restaurant's large aquariums and tropical birds, Leo realized he was on track for Jonquil's pad and her bed, likely with some grass to relax with first. But it was too fast for him, too soon, and it scared him. He liked Jonquil, but something seemed wrong, and he lost his appetite and could not finish his burger. She ate some of his french fries and her eyes sparkled and laughed, but it was so pretty, so inviting, that his mind took a sharp turn and suddenly he panicked—he was too big. He would rupture her. *No, that's ridiculous!* His depression over Jeanine crushed down on him.

It was all he could do to walk Jonquil to her pad. Embarrassed, he refused to go inside with her. She laughed at first, then saw he was serious and smiled and said okay. He said he was in love with another girl, regretted saying it, and backed away from her, gave a little wave goodbye.

—

He couldn't go to his room. He had to walk, though he knew every step would pound his despair deeper into him. Jeanine was gone. *Would* be gone, something in him insisted, but what was the difference? Everything she'd said to him last night—every nuance of her words, examined now, indicated that she was breaking up with him. This was how nice people did it. She was nice. He loved her. But he'd lost her.

21

TWO WEEKS LATER A LONG, meandering walk took Leo across campus to Littlefield Dormitory, a freshman girls' residence with Victorian history, architecture, and traditions. He rested on a bench sometime between eleven and midnight in a tree's shadow cast by golden light from atop a lamppost. Since dusk he had wandered around campus, off campus, in and out of the library without ever stopping to sit down, let alone look at a book.

From the shadow, he was watching the couples kissing goodnight on the limestone terrace in front of the dorm. A low balustrade surrounded the terrace, and a few couples were sitting on it smooching.

The couples kept arriving, kissing goodnight, and then the boy left and the girl went inside the dorm. Only a few of the boys had the hippie look, and none of the girls. The girls could have been from Brownwood, and they looked pretty in the flattering pale golden lamplight.

He could not work up any envy. Rather, he thought the couples were embarrassing in their conformity, but he didn't mind spying on them. He had a roll of hard candies in his hand, one in his mouth, pineapple. He looked forward to the green one, too, the lime.

They kissed and they kissed. He told himself he did not care. Some kissed more passionately than others, lingered longer, stayed in an embrace, while other couples hugged and let go. A couple arrived, spoke briefly, and waved goodbye, no kiss. Leo smiled. More time passed, lights on the terrace blinked twice, a signal to the girls still lingering outside.

He took the next candy and it was the green one, the lime, second to the last in the roll. By the time he was finished with the final candy, a red one, the couples had disappeared, females into the dorm, and males into the dark lanes of campus. Curfew was midnight, long thoughts ago. When a campus copmobile came too close for comfort, Leo pushed himself up from the bench and meandered off in a direction that would not take him back to his room.

He walked out Guadalupe almost two miles, far past the edges of campus where the newer dormitories clustered and sparkled, cutting east into quiet residential neighborhoods. He passed an elementary school, quickening his pace to escape any ghosts that might have flown up from the school he'd attended in Brownwood. He arrived at the Elisabet Ney museum, a sandstone castle-like structure set on landscaped grounds. From a certain concrete bench at the side of the castle in a crape myrtle hell, he could see the two-storied apartment complex where Leah lived, incongruous among the frame houses along Avenue H.

He'd hastened the final breakup, which occurred today—yesterday now. It was not intentional, but in the two weeks since Hippie Hollow, he'd been unable to stop testing Jeanine, and she had failed every test. She had been amiable, even acted the "old" way, the way of love, when he would let her. But he'd been unable to stop questioning her about Zack Constantin. And she had been open about going out with him—first only two days after she'd announced his existence to Leo. Then, on the weekend, she'd turned down Leo when he asked her to a movie, citing a date with Zack—and then refusing to characterize her relationship with him as unwanted. "He's nice." It seemed to Leo there was not only a flavor of defiance in her tone, but also a defense of this frat rat, and all he stood for.

He rested on the cold concrete bench, his fingers working the tired flesh under his eye sockets in the wee hours. How long until dawn? He could see doors to three of the downstairs apartments, but not the door to Leah's, which was around to the side. He should have worn the lumber jack coat he'd picked up at the Army Navy Store, but instead had on a flannel-lined blue jean jacket, macho and fetching but not warm, too short, too open in the front. Ears were cold. When would she be awake? He'd walk to the edge of the museum grounds where he'd be able to see her windows. When there was light on, he would go to her. If daylight came first, he would go anyway. She might be on those pills. He'd knock loudly if necessary.

He stared at the museum. He had taken the tour once with Leah. Elisabet Ney had cremated her young son in the fireplace in her living room.

In the darkness, emotion boiled up into his throat. He sobbed, but managed to stop it. There was no explaining, no justice, no life possible, no light, no happiness, and none of that had ever been promised, so there was no reason to be surprised. There was no reason to feed the pain, nor to end it, nor to commit suicide, no reason for anything—nothing to do that would help, nothing to understand. Searching for at least some course of action, he could envision nothing but crawling into a stream, a gully becoming a river going to the sea, and letting it pull him along like so much detritus washed down by a random, mindless, destructive squall. The squall was gone. She'd been here, and now she was gone, and with her the wind, the rain, the bright smell of wet earth, the promise of green life and birth and growth, gone and gone and nothing, no action, nothing, nothing to do, no reason. No sound. No vision. No place. Not even the headlong dive into the abyss, no plummet to destruction that would at least end the sorrow. "Cursed," he muttered. "Cursed to survive. Oh my god...." He was cursed because he knew he would not kill himself. He'd even written a little poem about it earlier the previous morning as he sat in Eastwoods Park, cutting classes and grieving in anticipation of the inevitable breakup. He'd sat at a little stonework table in the cute little copse and stared at the varicolored paints spattered on its surface, stray marks left by an artist. In a whimsy, he had realized that an artist cannot die, cannot take his own life, but must keep returning to some small, paint-spattered table in some park, however obscure, and paint his pain onto a piece of paper or canvas until it was alleviated enough for him to go back to life for a while, for as long as he could stand it.

He knew he would never get over the pain of losing Jeanine. He would never stop grieving until his life ran out.

Twice during the night he walked to the edge of the grounds to see Leah's windows still dark. The breeze kicked up, and he wondered if that meant dawn was near, having heard one time that a breeze foretells sunup. Shivering, chilled through, he stood up and strolled around the perimeter of the grounds. The castle loomed from every vantage point, its upper level a small chamber just large enough to sleep in, or sit and read or draw, inviting, like a tower prison cell, where time stood still, grief was forever fresh and blinding. A vague memory, or something less, flashed through his mind, enticing but ephemeral, and then it was gone. It was one of those fragments of dream or vision from long ago, one of the places he used to "remember" as a child even though it was somewhere in the future, this little art museum "back here" in his college days.... "Bull crap," he muttered. "It's just a game I play." But his cynicism was unconvincing. He knew this kind of time travel was real, and it was easy to visit the old concept of it, and then he wondered if there may be some small comfort in it, but he didn't find any. "Cold," he complained, frowning at the ground as he hurried along, stiff and clammy. There was no light in the sky, but he walked on around the block and crossed the street to Leah's apartment.

It took repeated rounds of knocking to rouse her, but finally a light came on. He saw her check out the window from behind a heavy curtain that moved at her touch like a miniature of the one in Hogg Auditorium. She opened the door wide and stood before him in flannel pajamas. Her eyes were so wide, so blue even in the dim light that it amazed him. He forgot for a moment why he was here. And her hair. It was no longer poufed up like a balloon, but long and straight and parted in the middle. She had hippie hair now. Was that why her eyes looked so big? Why were her eyes so wide open? What was that look on her face? Was she so surprised to see him? Or was it almost a smile?

—

Even though I can tell you every detail of what Leah did, and what her thoughts were at any given time, I can't explain her to you. Whether that's a failure of omniscience or of my descriptive abilities is moot. I can step inside her, *be* her for a while, but I suspect I'm no closer to illuminating her.

When the knocking began to encroach on her dream, she saw it as Milton hammering on the cast iron housing of an electric motor. He was in his workshop, but in her dream it was not the little enclosed porch on the house in Brownwood, but a stone cell atop a clock tower, and the electric motor was transmogrifying into clockworks when she awakened. It was the middle of the night and someone was pounding on her door.

She knew, as soon as she saw him standing there. "Come on in. It's five o'clock in the morning. What are you doing up so early?" She closed the door behind him. He crossed the small living room in two lanky strides and slumped into the couch.

She didn't rush to him, didn't start in with concern and consolation. There was no hurry now. She went to the tiny kitchen, an area separated by a breakfast bar, and put on a pot of coffee. He looked exhausted, sitting there with his legs splayed, his furtive gaze dull underneath his eyelids. He was hers, and she reacquainted herself with the ecstasy of knowing it, as she shoveled an extra measure of coffee into the pot. Strong coffee for Leo.

When the percolator's comforting *tup-tup-tupping* sound began, she ambled back to the living room, sat on the couch with Leo. "Is anything wrong?" she asked, watching his face go yellow with pain, watching him struggle to hide it. "You want to crash on the couch?"

He rolled his head from side to side to indicate "no," too distressed even to speak. She restrained herself from touching him—waited, instead, near his side but not touching, letting him develop and understand his need gradually.

"What does it smell like in here?" he said.

"Nothing. What do you mean?"

"I've smelled that before. Like perfume but soft and dry."

"Oh, I know what you smell. Patchouli. It's incense I burned last night." She left him, went into the bedroom, giving the beads hanging in the doorway a good slap to make them rattle because it pleased her. They were louder than the perking from the coffeepot. She returned, rattling the beads again, a packet of incense in her hand. "It smells wonderful even before you burn it." She pulled out a joss stick and handed it to him. He held it across the top of his lip and breathed it in. "You like it?"

"It's like honeysuckle and wisteria through a rusty window screen," he said, and she could tell he meant something, and she hoped it had nothing to do with Jeanine. But there was no worry. Jeanine was gone, or he wouldn't be here.

Leah knew the sound of her percolator. It was almost ready. She opened a cabinet and took two cups. But why were they green, these dishes she'd bought before leaving Brownwood? She never should have bought dishes before she moved. She should have bought some in Austin. And she bought the wrong ones. But they would do for now, and it didn't matter, because it was just an everyday detail, not wrong, not a sin, not a sin, and not a sin, like Milton had said. Her nipples were erect. The coffee was done. She poured the two cups. They both took it black. She carried the cups, no saucers, to the couch.

"Don't spill."

"Thanks," he said, pulling himself up straight to take the cup, then hunching over, grateful for the hotness. "Thanks for letting me in."

"Sure," she said in a small voice. No hurry. No need to encourage him. No question of getting what she wanted. A little waiting was required. Enjoy your cup of coffee. It's good. Strong. Caffeine was false and that's what she loved about it—a quality that you would resent in a person, but in a cup of liquid, so right, so false, so right, strength that is not there but is there until the coffee wears off.

Milton had liked coffee but he'd put sugar and half and half in his. He was always cast in the role of Noah in her mind. He was always a character in the stories he told her, but he was mostly Noah, rounding up lots of animals and putting them in a big boat, and she didn't call him Daddy because Ina called him Milton and she didn't call Ina Mama like Drew and Russell did, nor did she call her Ina, like Milton did. She called her Ma. Ina made Lulu wall-eyed. Milton put her on his lap and told her it was not a sin.

"Sorry I came so early. I waited in the park over there by the castle but I didn't know what time it was."

"It's okay."

"Kind of cold out there."

Leah sipped her coffee. Good, strong. Go inside Leah. "Good coffee," she said, leaving him again, putting her cup on the breakfast bar and going into the bathroom.

Dark eyes. Skin pale. Puffy lips. She looked good, looked fine in the mirror. Sat on the commode and peed. Sounded like the bell for school's out at the elves' school. She flushed, pulled up her panties then the bottoms. Brush teeth? Soon, not now. After coffee.

Leo sat on the couch hunched forward now, his face in his hands, his fingertips gouging his eyes. "Want more coffee?" she asked him, going for another cup herself. He didn't answer. With quiet, gray magic, she said, "She was a beautiful girl."

Leo was as still as Elisabet Ney's statues.

Leah took a small sip of coffee, and savored it and the balance between stillness and surrender that she saw in Leo. Then, more quietly still, she said to him, "I'm sorry," and it was that easy. He began weeping.

She uttered words of comfort, a motherly sense of practicality. *You've been up all night. Why don't you stretch out on the couch for a while.... Better yet, go lay on the bed.... Here, let's get these clothes off you.... Goodness, how long have you been wearing this shirt?*

And when he seemed to be drying up, she offered condolence again, reminding him of his loss, bringing him back to tears until he was in her bed, in his underwear, the soft bedspread pulled over him.

"I know how you're hurting. It hurts me, too, seeing you in this much pain. I hate that I can't do anything for you. I don't think anything will ever help." Her voice quivered, showing that she, too, was about to cry, his pain so strong that it extended to her. And then she was on the bed next to him, saying *I'm so sorry, so sorry, nobody will ever replace her, nobody can, nobody ever will...* and she slipped under the bedspread and caressed his head, letting the hair find the crevices between her fingers. He shook his sad, tear-inflamed head back and forth.

"Leah, you can't comfort me like this. I can't... it's too...."

"I know. I know. There's only one comfort for you, and that's Jeanine."

The name stung him each time she said it. He sobbed again.

"Jeanine," Leah whispered, "is the only one that could help."

Leah waited in the dark, covered, silent, and felt the remaining sobs ebb from Leo's long, tired body.

"Yes," Leo said. "Only Jeanine."

Whispering, her wet lips touching Leo's ear, Leah asked, "Did you ever have her, Leo?"

She felt him choking back his tears, and his voice quivered. "No."

For Leah, the world fell back into order. "Here," she said, turning onto her back. "Do this. It's a small thing, but it'll help. I know it will."

"What are you talking about?"

"Get on top of me, like I was Jeanine."

"No...."

"Not to *do* anything, Leo. Close your eyes and pretend for a little bit. Just get on me."

"No, I couldn't pretend, Leah. It wouldn't work. It doesn't feel right."

"Just give it a try. Here...."

He acquiesced, grateful for her warmth, but uneasy with the unfamiliar posture of love-making with her body. It had always been only her hand.

"Now, close your eyes. Think of Jeanine."

He closed his eyes, and Leah closed her own eyes. If he was thinking of Jeanine, it would be only in flashes and fragments.

Her warmth mingled with his. "That's it, Leo. I know I'm not her, we know it. But you can get lost in the fantasy. Hold her."

But it was not *her* he was holding, was it?

"That's good," she said, and after so many years, at last she gave him not a hand, but her warmth and wetness.

"But...."

"You won't hurt me, Leo. Go in," she whispered, and their mouths opened with pleasure when he did.

—

"You weren't her," he said later, when it was done. His eyes open, he watched the orange glow of a lava lamp reflecting off the pillowcase. "You were you," he murmured, and he realized it sounded anything but the accusation he'd intended it to be.

"I'll take care of you, Leo," she whispered. "I really will."

—

Believe me, there is no need to die.
Rather, you may come to this small,
paint-spattered artist's table
in this small park,
and with your sharp knife
cut open the flesh under which
you keep that little box.
Take it out and review the contents,
which are you,
barely recognizable,
squinting in the light,
your homunculus.
He will be fine.

22

D URING THE SUMMER OF 1971, Leo tucked his Jeanine pain into his bowels as far from his heart as he could, and tried to exhaust himself beyond emotion in a summer job doing maintenance work for an Austin real estate entrepreneur. Leo learned swimming pool maintenance, helped re-carpet some apartments, painted the undersides of sun decks on swank motels, even helped tear down a small wooden building to make room for a new structure.

And he immersed himself in reading. He was interested in the existentialists and the absurdists, had read dozens of plays and novels by Beckett, Handke, Sartre, Camus, Jarry, Artaud, Genet, then Brecht, then more Ibsen, whose work he'd studied freshman year. He might finish off a night with an essay or two from Martin Esslin about the literature of theater. Exhausted from the day's often brutally tiring work, he nevertheless needed his reading in order to find enough peace for sleep.

And still, in his dreams, Jeanine would sometimes appear, not always as herself, but in some obvious metaphor. She was a deer in one dream, beautiful in a woodland. He watched her, awestruck, until she noticed him, and then she darted into the trees and was gone.

The University Interscholastic League was the source of Leo's scholarship grant. Thanks to the drama coach at Brownwood High School, the League had taken notice of Leo's sudden ascension, once he was involved in the Thespians Club, from his perennial academic failure to straight-A report cards. Maybe the seeds of his growth had been planted by Dean, who introduced him to reading. Possibly he was motivated by the sweet taste of self-esteem upon receiving his first A on his report card, regardless that it was not through his own effort, but because Leah had done his homework for an entire grading period. Whatever led him to it, he found sanctuary in study, and stayed there. Occupying his mind with learning blocked out everything else, except the demands of his libido, and those were met neatly by his aunt.

Because his theater work in high school was the genesis of his scholarship grant, he chose Drama as his major at the university, but the liberal arts courses outside the Drama Department provided most of the sanctuary he found in study.

His Tuesday-Thursday Philosophy in Literature 303 lecture course, an elective he took along with ninety other undergrads in his sophomore year, first semester, animated Leo. He found an easy rapport with Dr. Gottschalk, who of course was unaware that Leo's immersion in the class coincided with the young man's ongoing heartbreak dodge. Gottschalk called on Leo often.

"Do you see a problem with any of that, Mr. Nobles? A contradiction lurking somewhere? A dead end? In the logic?" The discussion was based on some reading, weeks ago, in Theodore Dreiser that Leo was dredging up again, to the universal chagrin of the other students.

"I do."

"And this would be chocolate thinking? I see you thinking, Mr. Nobles," the professor goaded, "but I don't hear you answering. You say you see a contradiction. I'm wondering if this would be some of your chocolate-inspired insight."

"It would," Leo said. "The problem is not so much in anything I'm thinking or saying. It goes beyond that to this whole class. And beyond that to the course itself. And beyond that to literature. And beyond that, also. It needs a larger context." Several other students cleared their throats audibly.

"I see. And what is this 'larger context,' Mr. Nobles? Larger than humanity?"

The air in the lecture hall gelled, and one student sniggered and then shut up. Leo felt all eyes and ears tuned to him, but it was chocolate thinking, and his only awareness of the present moment was an irrelevancy that happened to pop into his mind—there were no windows in the room. But his chocolate thinking was working on The Larger Context, hell, yes larger than humanity—larger than the universe.

"The Shingaru," he whispered.

Gottschalk cocked his ear toward Leo. "The singing? I'm sorry?" The class sniggered.

"The Shingaru," Leo said, and the class stilled.

It was not Gottschalk, but the girl with red hair who finally spoke. Without turning to look at Leo, but instead looking at Gottschalk as if it were he she was addressing, she said, "What is the Shingaru?"

"The Truth about the Shingaru," Leo said, "is that when you think about life, or humanity, or the world, or our world, your perception is limited. There's no context that's large enough to put your thoughts into properly, because your thoughts are nothing. They're not even nothing. They're a parody of nothingness."

Professor Gottschalk had been enjoying his repartee with Leo Nobles since the beginning of the term, especially because the young man seemed impervious to common classroom decorum. For the first few weeks of the semester, Nobles had made so much noise unwrapping Hershey bars that Gottschalk banned them from his classroom. Nobles then announced that consuming chocolate was essential to his achieving deeper insights, was his only hedge against debilitating anguish, and that without it, he could no longer be expected to participate in discussions. He complied with the rule, though, and continued to participate anyway.

"Really. A parody of nothingness. I guess I'll need some chocolate to understand that one." The class chuckled. "I'm afraid I'm unfamiliar with the Shingaru, Mr. Nobles. Can you briefly explain?"

"No. I just made it up. I'll never mention them again."

"Fine, then. So you need a context beyond literature and real life. Beyond the universe. To where?"

"Ultimately, back to life," Leo answered. "Life doesn't cooperate with literature. In a practical sense, it's pointless to study literature because literature doesn't represent anything. And if it doesn't represent anything, it needs to be something in and of itself. But it isn't, because it purports to represent the real world, in one way or another, even when it's just trying to say that life is absurd."

"You don't think life is absurd?"

"That has nothing to do with it. Life might be absurd or it might not. If it's absurd to you, then you make sense of it that way. If it's an adventure to you, you create adventure stories. If you're Dreiser, you think it makes sense if you describe it down to its dirty details. My point is, regardless of the sense writers have tried to make out of it, in the end, life doesn't make any sense at all. Events unfold willy-nilly. Ultimately, literature categorizes our existence in this way or that—absurd, sublime, you name it—to try and help us deal with it, I guess. But literature is always, *always* artificial by its very definition."

The class burst into applause, which Leo welcomed, though he knew it represented a complaint about the latest reading assignment, the first hundred pages of *Ulysses*.

"We'd better define some terms here," Gottschalk said, unable not to look straight at Leo. "You talk about 'events' and 'life' as though they're the same. Events, or, let's say the universe, is not the same as life, or, let's say, humanity. Right?"

"Yeah," Leo said.

"Humanity might be considered a subset of all things that exist."

"Right."

"So when you talk about events unfolding willy-nilly, to me that smacks of determinism, or the lack thereof. Not sure where you come down on that."

Leo took a deep breath and closed his eyes. "Aside from the fact that predestiny is both undeniable, and completely meaningless and irrelevant," he said, "I think what matters is that people—real ones, I'm talking about here—people can do things that are.... Let's use one of our terms here—people can do heroic things." Now he was looking at Gottschalk.

By this time, the rest of the class was lost, but still enjoying the show.

"So you believe in the concept of a hero."

"I said I was using a literary term, but I'm referring to real people, not literature."

"Then let me ask you, Mr. Nobles. Do you think *in literature* there can be heroes?"

"This is a very hard question to answer, and I can't think deeply without chocolate." The class erupted in laughter along with Professor Gottschalk.

"What's you're off-the-cuff answer, then? No deep thought required or requested."

Leo thought for a moment. The girl with the red hair and expensive silk blouses and tartan skirts and rich, thin body, and hose, sheer ones, and always the blue leather notebook, turned to look back at Leo, pushing into him that fragrance she always wore, that morning dew with porridge and books and bed linens and wildflowers. She had been a focus of esthetic interest to Leo all term, and this was the first time she had ever looked at him. "That humans are good," Leo said, "and that there's a normalcy inherent in them, regardless of how perverted they may become because of factors environmental or otherwise. And that no matter how perverted they become, their goodness and normalcy are always at the base of their nature." He met the red-haired girl's eyes and she didn't look away. "And finally, that there is never a time in a human life when the good and normal nature could not surface, given an opportunity and the person's will." She smiled at him and turned back around in her seat.

"That sounds pretty stock to me," Gottschalk said.

"It is. And off-the-cuff. I don't know if I believe it, and I couldn't say it has any significance even if it is true. There's a level of truth beyond this kind of thinking, and without chocolate I can't break through to it." A gentle reprise of laughter smattered from the class. "Even with chocolate I don't know that I can make sense of anything beyond what I just rattled off."

Gottschalk smiled. "How about we leave aside the distinction between literature and the real world. Do you believe this goodness, this normalcy as you call it, can emerge at any time? Class?"

But it was Leo who answered the professor, as though the class were not even there. "If the character has been perverted from an early age, and his course through life has driven him more in the direction of his perversion," Leo stood up at his seat and thought for a moment, gaining the quiet, full attention of everyone in the lecture hall. "...and he's become comfortable in his perversion, and while in this state, which is mature now, he falls into circumstances that require the emergence of the normalcy and good nature at the base of his humanity, and for this to happen requires an act of will from him—then do you think the normalcy and good nature will in fact emerge?"

"That's what I'm asking you, Mr. Nobles."

"The answer is yes... if he exercises the will to make it happen. In which case, he is a hero."

"Is that chocolate thinking, Mr. Nobles?"

"No. It's standard issue. Chocolate is...." he stopped and looked at the windowless wall.

Softly, Gottschalk urged, "Let's have chocolate, Mr. Nobles."

Someone in the back of the room started softly, *chocolate, chocolate, chocolate...* and another student joined the chant, then another.

But before any more could join in, Leo quieted them, saying, "What if the normalcy and good nature that do emerge through his strong act of will are not clearly illustrative? What if his action looks to everybody else like insanity? What if it looks hurtful and dangerous, for example? Then we need to look deeper and wonder what his action means, whether it really represents normalcy. Who knows what normalcy looks like when it emerges from a deep place where it's been hunkered down since early childhood, or the womb, even."

"Then we need to go deep into the fudge, don't we Mr. Nobles?"

"Yep, because we have no point of reference for judging his heroism, or even whether or not it is heroism, in which case we have to abandon logic and rely on how it made us feel when he did what he did. And finally—the icing, dark brown and double—we might need to give up our need to label his action, and that would be abandoning our concept of literature, wouldn't it."

"You'd like to think so."

"No. I'd rather play by the rules." Leo sat down and there was quiet in the hall.

"Horseshit, you would, Mr. Nobles. You believe in literature and you, yourself, are a practitioner of it."

—

Leo climbed the stairs to the third floor of Parlin Hall, one of the 1920s vintage brick structures lining the vast Main Mall. On Gottschalk's office door, which was closed, he found posted a variety of items cut out from papers and magazines. One was a cartoon showing a medieval knight in full armor mounted on a huge armored steed. The knight held his lance downward, its sharp point poised above the heart of a peasant who lay supine on the rocky ground. The peasant, showing a solicitous smile, was saying to the knight, "Tell me more about this Christianity of yours." Leo smiled and knocked on the door.

"Come, it's open, and bring your chocolate with you."

Gottschalk's cramped and cluttered office had a warm light going for it, the wall space crammed with odd bookshelves and file cabinets, and otherwise sweetened with posters from faraway places and, Leo noted, some touches of psychedelia too. Unlike other professors' offices Leo had visited, this one had no cloying smells of tobacco, untended carnal off-gassing or other unpleasantness. In fact, it smelled faintly of the aftershave Gottschalk was probably wearing.

"What's up? What's new? What can I do for you?" Gottschalk said, kicking his chair back and throwing his heels to the edge of his desk as Leo took the other chair.

"Nothing, I guess. Any problems with me? Class work all right?"

The syllabus required one student/professor meeting, with an optional second during the semester. This was Leo's first.

"Leo, you're great," Gottschalk said with a smile. "What the hell are you majoring in, anyway?"

"I started out with a drama major. Probably going to go with that. No specialty yet." Gottschalk pursed his lips, nodded, touched all his fingertips together and let the resulting spiders do push-ups against each other.

"Dramatic literature maybe? Is that a major?"

"I'm interested in the drama, partly because it's not real literature, but also because it is literature. Theater history is good if I want to go academic. But, you know, I don't know, I'm pulled by the art of theater."

"Pretty strongly?"

"Yeah. The whole art as collaboration thing. It resonates for me."

"I could see that, yeah, now that you mention it. It would."

"So the next question becomes, what am I going to do with a degree in theater?"

"I was going to ask first what kind of degree are we talking here?"

"BFA."

"Are you feeling any leanings at all? Playwriting? Acting? Directing? Scene design?"

"Dance, actually." Leo watched Gottschalk avert his eyes, put a serious look on his face, and nod as though considering what to say next. "I'm bullshitting, Professor."

Gottschalk took a moment before he smiled and looked at Leo, who smiled back. Then, an unintended ambiguity occurred to both of them at the same time. *Bullshitting about dance, or bullshitting about theater?*

Leo clarified, "I couldn't dance if you held a gun to my head."

"I imagine few could, very convincingly," Gottschalk replied, and they laughed.

"I might go theater history, or I might go directing, both are majors. Not acting. I took that last year and acted in a play and it's not for me, career-wise."

"What part did you play?"

"A dead soldier."

"Sounds... challenging?"

"I did meet a girl who broke my heart. Don't have to worry about her now. She transferred to Trinity. So anyway, I have to take all the theater classes and that's good, all the tech courses, all the design stuff, costuming, makeup, more acting, you learn everything. Haven't ruled out educational theater either."

Leo noticed a framed photo on Professor Gottschalk's desk. Gottschalk's foot was going to knock it off the desk if he wasn't careful. "What's in the picture?" Leo asked, partly as an excuse to reach for it and save it from falling. "Ah! Wife and children?"

"Yep. That's a pretty recent shot. Oren is three there and he just turned four. Lexy is six. That picture is, what? Six, eight months ago. Good picture though."

Leo uttered an approval, but he was thinking Gottschalk had never struck him as a fatherly man. It was unsettling to see that the man was fatherly. No, he was a father, not the same thing. Where was this discomfort originating? Was it some kind of attraction? And then, somewhere a little below consciousness, Leo realized he had felt this kind of chagrin—was it yearning?—before, with other men. And the shadow of this realization did break the surface into consciousness.

"I love literature, but teaching—it's just a job, Leo. I'm kind of.... Let's see, I want to level with you here. What the hell. My advice to you is give some serious thinking to whether you want to teach, and if it's not your passion, fuck it. Go do what you want to do instead."

"Sounds like sage advice."

"Well, look, what the hell...." Gottschalk was struggling, wanting to be open, Leo could tell, not wanting to hurt, wanting to help, but unsure. "Let me talk about my course for a minute. That's what we're supposed to be doing anyway, right? Look, you have an admirable knack for the concepts involved in this course. You contribute to the class better than any other student I've had in the eight years I've been doing this. Your papers are... I want to say, they're not brilliant in the technical sense because you're too inexperienced for that, but they are brilliant nevertheless. I'm going to confess to you something.... Have I been drinking? No? Okay, I guess I'm in a confessional mood. I spent three god damn hours in the stacks trying to disprove the originality of your paper, what was it called? *Levels of Judgment in Art.*"

"*Judgment Levels for Art,* actually."

"Okay. Not sure which title I like better, but anyway. I don't really give a shit, in terms of your grade or even my opinion of you, whether it was completely original or not, but I am very damn curious. I couldn't find anything at all that you might have derived it from. Is it original or what?"

"All I can tell you is I made it up. I assume I've been influenced by all kinds of reading, but I guess I did synthesize it all by myself."

Gottschalk stared at Leo for a moment, his mouth lax. "I mean, Leo, it's not the most profound postulate I've ever read. It's not a breakthrough in literary or art criticism. But damn, man, it's pretty good for a sophomore. I mean, you even broke it down into temporal forms and non-temporal forms. It's more than pretty good. I was a little blown away by it."

"Thanks very much. I did think it came together pretty well. I worked on it all night one night. Got all bent out of shape about the concepts, know what I mean? I appreciate that you appreciated it."

"Gave it an A+."

"I know, I noticed."

"I haven't seen a *senior* come up with thoughts like that and be able to synthesize them into anything that made sense like you did."

"I appreciate it."

Art, Leo had surmised, could be judged on any of four levels. The class discussion during the previous week had been about the definition of "art," but no paper had been required. Leo had done it on his own, turned it in without regard to any requirement or grade, and Gottschalk had graded it and included the A+ in Leo's average, which was close to A+ anyway. The fourth level of judgment, the lowest, was about whether the subject art meets the judge's—e.g., a potential buyer—personal taste requirements, a subjective judgment, not defensible. Above that, at the third level, the criterion was whether the work of art embodied some benefit for individuals. Would it make money, appreciate in value, match the furniture, have a palliative effect...? Level three judgments would likely be made, asserted Leo, by entities, such as corporate granting bodies, looking to impress the public. The penultimate level, Leo named "The Level of Good and Evil." Arts Councils might typically use this judgment level in deciding grants and residencies. "Good" art would benefit mankind by expanding human perception and perhaps in other ways. Finally, the highest level at which art can be judged, Leo wrote, is "Realization of the Artist's Vision." This would place the artist himself in the judge's chair, and leave open the question of the artist's self-awareness, perspicacity, and honesty.

"I love that you put Duchamp's Dadaist criterion at the top of the hierarchy," Gottschalk said. "And that it makes sense. You might even conceivably stir up a little controversy there." He took his feet off the desk and stood up, took a few steps in the cramped office, looked at a poster. "This is a blow up of a photo I took in Manali with the Himalayas looming in the background," he said.

"Nice."

"Look, Leo, there's one thing...."

"Build me up just to shoot me down. Damn."

"No, nothing like that. It's something I feel about you and I want to do what's best, if I can. And of course who the hell ever knows? But the thing is, you deserve— and need, you damn well need a good mentor at this university." Gottschalk sighed as though he had confessed something, sat back down in his chair, picked up the picture of his family, looked at it—but barely—and put it down. Was it guilt that Leo saw on Gottschalk's furrowed brow, the brow he was now rubbing in a palsied sort of way, closing his eyes tight at the same time?

"Yeah, you're probably right about that," Leo said. "I mean, a mentor's definitely something to think about. I've heard that before, you know. It's what we call 'wisdom' in the business." *He's saying he's not the guy for me, isn't he.*

"Hey Leo," Gottschalk pulled open the top drawer of his desk and retrieved a foil wrapped lump. "Chocolate-covered cherries." He held it out to Leo, who took it.

"Thanks."

"Not your favorite."

"Not my *favorite*, but I dig the hell out of em."

"Don't rule out playwriting."

"Good chocolate cherry, thanks," chewing and tilting to keep from dripping the runny part. "Okay, I'll tell you something. This is my feeling, okay? In your lit class, I don't think I'm doing any deep thinking or understanding anything in particular. I'm just trying to entertain the troops."

"And you certainly do sometimes."

"I've noticed I have a sort of talent for composing ideas on my feet, verbally. You think it's possible to think by talking?"

"I think some people do all their thinking by talking."

"To me, it's a *theatrical* ability, something that would be useful in public life—politics, selling, show biz."

"Interesting take on the situation."

"No, let me tell you. I've thought about this. Not much, but some. The ideas I form, like in class, themselves tend to sound pretty good, but ultimately they don't mean much to me. Not sure what that says, but I wouldn't mention it if I didn't feel it strongly, you know? I enjoy the reading I dig up at the stacks and the AC for doing the assignments. I like to pursue lines of inquiry begun in literature class even after the assignment is over and done with. I guarantee you I'll keep doing it even after the semester ends. They throw me out of the Academic Center two or three times a week because it's closing and I'm still there. But with every passing week, I focus my attention more on theater studies. I'm into it like it's my true major field of study, not only on paper but in my soul, if you know what I mean. I've started to love theater, and my feelings for it are growing.

Unless there's some kind of self-deception going on that would be mind-boggling to contemplate, I mean seriously, I think I'm a theater person."

Thus, Leo relieved Gottschalk of mentor duty. But had he done it on purpose? Leo didn't know. Father.

23

AT THE BEGINNING I MENTIONED the names of some of my loves. I'll meet Esbeidy in middle school and go bonkers for her because she lets me kiss her. No, to be honest, she kisses me first, and then lets me kiss her daily between algebra and gym for some weeks. Diane Morgan will be my college love, University of North Carolina at Chapel Hill, but that's a long and all-too-familiar kind of story. Johnny Bishop's story is the one I need to tell you now.

In 1958, long before I was born, eleven-year-old Johnny Bishop, who would grow up to become a pharmacist, walked into Sneed's Grocery, a tiny stucco building tucked between two houses on a dusty residential street in Lucern, Gateway to the Foothills of North Carolina, home of the Lucern High School Lions, Pride of the Piedmont. The complaint of the screen door behind him almost masked his demand, "packa Kents nuh Snicker."

Roger Sneed let the front legs of his rickety chair find their place on the scrubbed wooden floor, sized up the kid, whom he'd seen riding his bicycle up and down the street almost daily for the past few months.

"That okay with your daddy?" he asked.

"Yeah," Johnny said, pulling a dollar bill from his jeans pocket.

"Forty cents," Roger said, ringing it up on the ornate cash register.

"Booka matches."

Roger tossed a book onto the counter. Johnny waited for his change, then opened the cigarettes and patted one out, lit it, inhaled it and tried to indicate pleasure and relief. "Anks," Johnny said, and Roger nodded, closing his eyes for a moment in acknowledgement.

Although it was Johnny's first cigarette, there was an element of truth in his mock addiction. Addiction, in essence, was in his body, his personality, his soul—to be a smoker, and to find other addictions as well. Addiction was the animus in Johnny Bishop, but his salvation would be a woman's love, and that would be his ruin, too.

His mother was always at home, father never there, always working, both of them were heavy smokers. His mother kept a bottle of vodka hidden but Johnny knew all about it, and he had plans for it. He had many times picked up an open pack of cigarettes left on the coffee table and held it to his nose to breathe in the creamy acrid smell of raw tobacco. Already he associated that smell with hidden, delicious moments.

Johnny first thought of checking the medicine cabinet when Garry Modesett bragged, in the lunchroom, that he "got drunk" with aspirins and caffeinated soda pop. The idea that there might be something entertaining in his own bathroom stuck with Johnny all afternoon. His mother was already smashed when he got home at three, so it was easy for him to rummage, unnoticed, through the medicine cabinet.

He knew what the Benzedrine pills were, and the brown plastic prescription bottle was brimming full. He dumped half a dozen tablets into his hand and replaced the bottle. Stepping to the lavatory, he tossed one of the pills into his mouth and washed it down, then reconsidered and took a second one, pocketing the other four.

He had no appetite at six o'clock, the bennies in full force, but he knew he had to be at the table for supper.

"Anything happen at school today?" his father asked.

Johnny put a glob of mashed potatoes into his mouth. It sat there like so much wallpaper paste. His father did not expect an answer, just an acknowledgement. He nodded. He tried to make the nodding help him swallow, or at least chew. After some time, he did swallow, and he needed iced tea, lots of it, so he drank the whole glass. "We had a pretty interesting science class today."

His mother stopped chewing the piece of fried cube steak in her mouth. His father looked at him, then at his wife, then back at Johnny.

Johnny had never offered up a whole sentence before—not that his parents could recall, anyway.

"What was interesting about it?" Johnny's father said.

"It was about these little animals that can grow a new head. Planaria. You can cut off their heads and the heads will grow new tails and the tails will grow new heads."

"I kind of doubt that, Johnny," his mother slurred.

"No, it's true. You can even split their head down the middle and each half will grow into a whole head."

"Then it would have two heads," his father said.

"They do," Johnny insisted. "We did an experiment... well, I was in the group that did the experiment, but I didn't do my part... but they did their reports today and they showed these Planaria...."

"You didn't do your part?" his father said.

"Because I was absent that day."

"He was," his mother said, poking at a piece of meat.

"No problem, I get to make it up. But they had the Planaria, and you could see the ones that grew new heads and the ones that grew new tails, they were labeled. It was like, well, it was not like a lizard growing a new tail, regeneration, but it's the same thing in a different way. I'd like to do an experiment with lizards, but you'd have to be very careful because if you cut off the tail too far up, you can injure the subject, you can even kill it." Johnny could not stop talking, even though he tried. "It can get infected and the experiment is useless and you've hurt a little creature, which scientists do all the time but they're used to it and it's part of the scientific method."

"Eat," his mother said

Johnny forked up a yam, held it an inch above his plate as he went on, "I'll tell you an experiment I'd hate to see, but they do it because it helps understand trauma to the head. They take a monkey, strap him into a chair so he can't move, can't move his head or anything, can't move at all, just has to sit there looking straight ahead. They take this five-pound steel ball that's attached to a meter-long rod, a meter's like a yard... well, you can change the length of the rod, it's adjustable, because the other end of the rod is over the head of the monkey." *Why can't I stop talking?* Johnny wondered. "You get the length of the rod the way you want it and put where it swings just right, the longer the rod, the farther the five-pound ball has to swoop down to the monkey's forehead. The ball is held out, straight out or maybe higher, depending on how hard you want it to hit the monkey's forehead. When you let the ball go, it swings down and hits the monkey. I think that's horrible. But it lets the scientists see what happens to the monkey, so they don't have to just guess. So when people are in head-on collisions, they won't get to the hospital for however long, and doctors wouldn't know what happens right when you get smashed into the windshield. And stuff like that."

His father looked at him. "What the hell...?"

"Maybe when Rand Burke got hit on his motorcycle if they had more knowledge like that then he might not be in a wheelchair drooling right now. He was a nice quiet kid and everybody thought he was dumb but then later I found out he was making straight A's all the time. All I knew about him was he had that Honda 50 which I wanted one like, and he had those guinea hens in his yard we'd always hear and say 'what the heck is *that?*' and then remember it was the guineas. He told me one time they were the best watchdogs you can own, they make a big racket any time something comes around that they don't know. Too bad they all got eaten by a red-tailed hawk that liked the way chicken tasted."

"Fine, blabbermouth. How about you liking the way some of that chicken fried steak tastes," his father said.

It was not possible. He knew he would never be able to chew up anything, let alone swallow. "Can I have some more tea?"

His mother frowned. "You've had too much tea already. Listen at you talking a mile a minute. I've never heard you talk that much. Didn't even know you could talk like that. And quit bouncing your leg up and down."

"Anyway, I ought to go see Rand. I wonder where he is. At home, you think? I wonder if they still live over there. He might understand everything going on around him and just not be able to say anything. I ought to try getting through to him and letting him try to give me some kind of signal, even if he can't blink once for yes and twice for no, or the other way around, he might be able to do something else. Maybe you could hook him up to some kind of sensor sort of like a lie detector so you could tell if he was thinking yes or no even though you couldn't see anything from the outside. They already have all kinds of things like that, I mean, EGKs and EGGs and stuff. I think someday they'll be able to show your dreams on a screen like a movie. I don't think it'll be in my lifetime, but if you get right down to it, I can't see any reason why it's not possible. Maybe not for a long time, but it could happen in the future."

It would never occur to either of Johnny's parents that his logorrhea was drug-induced. Their amazement was dulled in their own drug-fuzzed minds, and forgotten before the meal was over and they each started the next round of Vodka and tonics. Johnny, however, did make note of the strange effect his mother's pills had on him. Several days later, when he stuck his hand into his pocket looking for a penny to put in the gum ball machine at the barber shop, he felt the other four pills and remembered that there was a *feeling* that went along with the talking. It was a good feeling, now that he thought about it. He'd been unable to sleep the night of the pills and the talking, and found that very disturbing, but that *feeling*—now that was something worth going after again.

—

By the time Johnny was in eighth grade in 1962, he'd discovered several other interesting medications in the medicine cabinet. By noting the correct spellings of the medications and then discreetly checking them at the library in a reference book called the PDR, he'd been able to determine that Luminal was Phenobarbital, that it was sure to be fun, and that Talwin was something like a synthetic form of morphine and would be more than entertaining at certain doses.

He learned to get high on Friday night or Saturday so that his head cleared in time for Monday morning school. His grades were erratic, but he managed to pass his subjects with relative ease, taking advantage of his natural intelligence and ability to judge when the time came to bear down. He had a knack for discerning soft spots in teachers, knew when to play them for sympathy and when to try and impress them with a term project. He knew he was regarded as an underachiever, and he used that image to his advantage whenever he could.

As a sophomore at Lucern High School, he worked the sympathy routine too hard on Miss Georgia Fredericks, his English teacher. She took a genuine and intense interest in Johnny when he wrote an essay with the cryptic title, "Nec." Trying on the guise of a depressed youth—inspired by an article he'd read in *Life* magazine—Johnny wrote this essay about death, having found the prefix "nec-" by accident when he looked up "necrophilia" in the dictionary after reading an issue of *Sexology* magazine loaned to him by a friend. *"Death is quiet, even in the midst of the battlefield... death is clean, even when brought on by disease... death is painless, even when preceded by long and painful suffering...."* Miss Fredericks was impressed, and marched headlong to the rescue of this thin, under-parented young man.

She retrieved his health records, report cards, and discipline files going as far back as first grade. She studied them. She detained him after school, to his chagrin, and interviewed him extensively. She gained insight, judged him to be a clever manipulator, a smart kid, a smoker—though he first fooled her into believing the smell had come from his household—and well worth a helping hand, deserving of some helpful directives and the encouragement he would need in order to change his direction.

Johnny preferred to meet with Miss Fredericks during the school day, but when he began his junior year, his class schedule made it impossible. Their first official meeting, 3:45 p.m. on a Tuesday afternoon in late September, took place in the classroom, just as their meetings had last year, but when Johnny walked into the room, he found Miss Fredericks sitting at a student desk near the back of the room.

"Hey, Johnny, come in," she greeted him.

He'd just been enjoying the clack of his hard soles in the echoing hallway, and winced at the sound of his first hard step onto the wooden classroom floor. It was obnoxious. Miss Fredericks didn't seem to notice, but he softened his gait. Rather than take the desk next to her, he leaned against the wall, resting his buttocks against the window sill.

"How's your schedule going?" she asked him.

He nodded, pursed his lips like a wise man. "No complaints. Mr. Byrd is going to be hard because he can't put together a complete sentence, but algebra comes sort of naturally to me, anyway, so I'll get by. Everything else is fine if I study."

"Any problems in that department?"

Johnny sucked air through clenched teeth. "You know."

"You want to sit down?"

"That's okay."

"Here," she said, getting up. "I thought it might feel less formal if I wasn't at my desk and you in the hot seat, you know?"

"It doesn't bother me."

She was in high heels, Johnny noted, and they clunked across the wood, taking her toward the display table, a folding lunchroom table she used for distributing things and displaying exemplary work. Johnny had enjoyed her class and thought she was a good teacher. She wore a fetching tweedy skirt that fell over rather slim hips. The appreciation he felt for these details was unfamiliar. Due to her age, he had never seen her as an attractive woman, but today he noticed that she was. This was no cause for alarm, no cause for anything, just something he noticed.

Miss Fredericks, he knew, was unmarried, in her early forties, bland by anybody's standards Johnny thought, just well-dressed and well-churched. He had learned a lot about her last year. He also knew she had succeeded in influencing him. He had begun applying himself to his school work and his grades showed it. It hadn't registered on him so much last year, but when she sought him out this year, a note to his home room teacher having put the process into motion, he gave the matter additional thought. She wanted to continue to advise him. She could and had already seen through his disguises and ruses, supported his better efforts, and praised him for them. He was letting himself drift toward achievement. His grades had improved. They could continue to improve. Over the summer, he'd begun to think about the future, although by August he'd convinced himself that Miss Fredericks had been a fluke and the chlordiazepoxide in his mother's purse was of more immediate interest.

They each took a seat at the table, and Miss Fredericks positioned her hands on the table and laced her fingers together, leaned forward, smiled at Johnny. He'd already kicked his chair sideways so he could lean one arm on the table and prop an ankle on a knee, and not have to look straight at the face that is not ugly, not ugly at all, kind of pretty for an older woman. And before she said anything else, he just had time to form a thought. Don't take this good thing and let it skid off the road. Don't be an idiot.

"I've typed up a chart for us to work with," she was saying now.

"A chart?"

"We're going to meet every third week, and I've already put the dates on the chart. Here, might as well get it so we can talk about it." She unclenched her hands, placed her palms on the table and pushed herself up—not all that attractive, come on—hurried to her desk and got the chart out of the top drawer. "There are two copies," she was saying as she returned to the table, "one for you and one for me."

She placed the piece of paper in front of Johnny. There were a lot of lines, boxes they were, and quite a list down the left side, and dates across the top. He read a ways down the column.

"Rest?" he said.

"We're going to rate how well you're getting your sleep. See? 'Food—nourishment.' How good the food is you're getting? 'Food—schedule.' How regular...."

"Yeah, I get it." He ran his finger down the list. "Leisure—inquisitive?"

"We're going to keep an eye on what you spend your time doing. When you're on your own time, and let's say you've done whatever homework, you've taken care of whatever home life obligations, well then, what do you do?"

Get high, he thought, managing not to smirk.

"Do you, for example, read a book? That would score pretty well in that box. But a higher score might be if you read a book because you've read something else that led you to that author, or you like that author because you've already read another of his books. Maybe Mr. Byrd introduced an idea in algebra class and you wondered where it came from, who thought of it, and you looked it up and discovered some mathematician who was interesting, and you were interested enough to find out more about him, his life, what else he had thought of. That kind of thing would get you a high number in the inquisitive box."

He felt her looking at him as he stared at the sheet. His eyes focused on another word down the list, "social—affection.'" He released a laugh, a short, hoarse, embarrassed exclamation. Then he looked at Miss Fredericks and smiled. "You really went all out with this."

She might have reached across the table and put her hand on his arm, and there was a moment he thought she would. But she leaned back, separated her deprived body from his young one, and said with a nod and a smile, "I want this to work, Johnny."

When Miss Fredericks continued to concern herself with Johnny even the next year, when he was a senior, he made a conscious decision to do his best for her. He never let her discover his occasional use of drugs, didn't believe she needed to know. He graduated in the top quarter of his class, barely, and with Miss Fredericks' help, he was able to apply for, and receive, financial aid for college. Blue Ridge University in Morganton accepted his application. He majored in Pharmacy, graduated in 1970, having been extremely careful in his drug use, cutting it down to almost nothing for fear of the dire consequences if caught.

Once he graduated, however, and landed his first job at a drugstore chain in Cadbury, over in the foothills of Callan County, he relaxed quickly and helped himself to small quantities of the stock. Because it was a large volume pharmacy, and he was not greedy, he managed to keep himself in all the pills he required, with little chance of being caught. He liked several uppers and downers, and a favorite was the synthetic morphine called Talwin, which, at high enough dosage, induced the euphoric sensation of champagne bubbles coursing through his body tissues.

Johnny also began to take notice of a strange social movement among his cohort nationwide. At first the hippies were of marginal interest to him, with their long hair and costumes and free love. Then he noted their close association with recreational drug use. Although he wasn't interested in pursuing the hippie lifestyle, he was paying attention when, one day in May of 1972, a hippie walked into the pharmacy to fill a prescription for an antibiotic. Curious, Johnny struck up a conversation with the young man, and tried to induce the hippie to talk about illicit drugs.

The hippie was Greg Jones. He didn't solicit drugs, and was far from the kind of creature Johnny had seen described in magazines and on television. This hippie was just a college student, home for the weekend from Raleigh. He lived down the road in Cannon Shoals, probably never smoked a reefer in his life—nor had Johnny, for that matter. But for some reason, the two men hit it off—Johnny genuinely interested in the counterculture represented symbolically in the young man's clothing and long hair, and the young man interested in choices of professions. Majoring in biology, Greg Jones hadn't ruled out a career in medicine.

Johnny took a break and the two men had sodas at the snack bar on the other side of the store. Greg Jones was, it turned out, part of a special subset of hippies called Jesus Freaks. His Savior's birth was being celebrated that weekend. He invited Johnny to join him at his church in Cannon Shoals, less than fifty miles down the road, for the Christmas pageant on Sunday. On a whim, Johnny did just that.

24

J ANET MABRY WAS THE VIRGIN Mary. Great with child, she made her way
from the door of the vestibule to the choir loft, enroute with Joseph to pay taxes to
Caesar. Stopping in front of the communion table, Joseph asked an innkeeper for
a place that he and his pregnant wife might spend the night. Since there was no room
in the inn, Joseph and Mary ended up over by the pulpit, where a wooden manger full
of hay was surrounded by sheep and other unidentifiable animals, all of whom stood on
their hind legs and tended to glance out toward their parents, one sheep conspicuously
picking its nose with a fore hoof.

Johnny was hardly aware of anything but Mary, and when she pushed back the
hood of her robe, revealing long, flowing brown hair, giving it a quick little shampoo
commercial shake to straighten it, his heart raced with admiration. He sat about halfway
to the back, the same hillside from which the shepherds, standing in the center aisle,
watched in awe as the golden-gelled Leko spotlight shined down on them from afar.
But he paid no attention to the shepherds when they started following the star, nor
when the angels popped up from behind the choir loft's modesty rail. Janet Mabry was
the most beautiful girl he had ever beheld. That he might have said no to hippie Greg's
invitation to this church was beyond contemplation.

"You're gonna introduce me to Mary," Johnny whispered to Greg, who sat next to
him on the pew, enthralled with the story unfolding before them.

"Janet? Yeah, sure. She's too young for you, though. High school."

"Still like to meet her," Johnny whispered.

"You will. Oh, far out! Look, they have a real baby Jesus."

Johnny nodded his pretended appreciation of the newborn six-month-old now held by a miraculously slimmed Mary. The baby was being very good, cooing, looking around. Charmed giggles rose up from the multitudes.

He met her in the Fellowship Hall in the church basement after the program. The fluorescent lighting in the room defeated the warm incandescence from the multicolored lights on the Christmas tree, but there remained a friendliness in the atmosphere, as though, Johnny thought, all these people were related to each other, all brothers and sisters and parents and grandparents in one big family. Friendly man after friendly woman after friendly old codger after friendly old biddy approached him to say hello, welcome, oh you're Greg's friend from Cadbury, Greg's in college you know—excuse his long hair. But Janet remained out of reach, now standing near the Christmas tree, now gone from the room, now back over there, standing behind the table filling cups with hot cider.

Johnny had been waiting agonizing minutes while Greg talked to the preacher. He watched them from a position against the wall, and knew the moment they were finished. "You're going to introduce me to Janet now, right?"

"Yeah, sure. Gotta figure out where she is...."

"She's over there serving apple juice," Johnny said, placing his hand behind Greg's arm and guiding him in Janet's direction.

The acoustics in the Fellowship Hall were lively, the happy crowd chatter a homogeneous roar punctuated with someone's unchecked laughter, the clatter of a dropped saucer. When they reached Janet, Greg leaned across the table and yelled, "Janet, this is my friend Johnny Bishop. He wanted to meet you."

He was staring into her eyes, his mouth unclosed, a half-smile of awe evident on his face, as though he were the first mortal to have laid eyes on the mother of God. Her church social smile, upon meeting his eyes, changed subtly but certainly—there was an extra instant of eye contact before she looked away. And that was enough.

"I'll let you two talk," Greg yelled. "I gotta go talk to Anna Bachman." And he disappeared back into the crowd.

Janet seemed disinclined to work hard at making a conversation with Johnny. He was afraid she would retreat into serving hot cider. She did say "Nice to meet you," and reached for a cup, the ladle at the ready in her other hand.

"Could I take you out? Maybe to dinner or something?"

At first he thought she hadn't heard. Then she gave him the delayed reaction, a look of mock consternation that said *What? Are you crazy?*

But then she said, "I guess. Why don't you call me?" Ancient Mrs. Parsons materialized, standing there wanting another cup of cider. "Greg can give you the number."

A little girl with bright red, curly hair asked for cider. Four years old. Janet hesitated. "Get your mommy to get it for you, Gail. It's hot. Where's your mommy?" The little girl twisted herself without moving her feet and pointed, pouting, to her mother standing in the middle of the room talking with another woman. "Go tell her to get it for you, Gail." Gail bolted toward her mother, and Johnny watched, amused. Gail changed her mind en route and ran, instead, toward two other children who were playing under a table, using the tablecloth as a tent.

Gail misjudged herself in some physical, four-year-old's way, and did not stop in time when she reached the table. Her mouth was at the exact level of the tabletop, and the edge of the table came together hard with her upper lip, and she was down, red hair sprawling. Johnny gasped, along with the few other witnesses, and then Gail was screaming. Her mother appeared and picked her up. Her father showed up from the other side of the room. They hurried off toward the kitchen, or bathrooms, with the bawling child.

Johnny looked at Janet. She was looking at the door through which the emergency had just exited. But when it was happening, she'd been admiring Johnny's profile.

—

By springtime, Johnny was a regular fixture at Grace Methodist of Cannon Shoals, and at the Mabry's Sunday dinner table. The Mabrys thought the very best of Johnny, and as long as there were no alarming signs, they trusted him with their daughter.

The drive from Cadbury to Cannon Shoals, Johnny discovered, made dating expensive and inconvenient. Janet was well worth it, but he found he couldn't go to see her every night as he would have liked.

Spending much more time longing for her than being with her, Johnny called Janet on the phone every evening. When she was not at home, he spoke with her mother or father, cheerfully maintaining their faith in him.

When Janet graduated high school, Johnny was at the ceremony. Wearing a suit, he sat with Mr. and Mrs. Mabry in the Piedmont Pavilion, a colosseum-like auditorium in the nearby city of Hickory. Noting Mr. Mabry's broad smile when Janet walked across the stage, still only seventeen, to accept her diploma and high scholastic honors, he whispered, "You must be bursting with pride." Mr. Mabry grasped Johnny's hand and squeezed it, and Johnny said, "I feel exactly the same way." He made sure Mrs. Mabry heard him as well, and turned to catch her tearful smile as she nodded her agreement.

The four of them had dinner at Baldwin's, the nicest restaurant in Hickory. Johnny began to panic when it seemed that he would not be able to get Janet alone that night. He had something very special he wanted to discuss with her.

As Mr. Mabry was carefully examining the check, he said, "I suppose you two want to go join your friends. Don't worry, we understand. We won't be offended."

"Just please get her home not too late, Johnny," Mrs. Mabry added, smiling.

—

Janet's friends, with whom Johnny rarely socialized, were already back in Cannon Shoals getting drunk, some of them at a party, others parked in cars. Johnny did his best not to appear in a hurry to bid Mr. and Mrs. Mabry good night.

"You did a good job," Janet said as they reached Johnny's car.

"At what, Sweetie?"

"Acting normal, like you weren't dying to get me alone so you could...," but he was already holding her, and pressed his lips to hers, before he even opened the car door for her.

They drove back toward Cannon Shoals and stopped at the far corner of the parking lot for the auto raceway. For a moment, Johnny draped both his hands over the steering wheel and stared toward a distant security light. "You know I ache for you every day."

"You do?" She moved over to him and rested her head on his shoulder. "I miss you too. Wish it wasn't quite so far to Cadbury."

"Mmm hmm. Me too. I want to marry you."

Janet was still. There was no mistaking what he'd said. And once she ran it through her mind again, she knew that he was serious. "You do?"

"Oh, yeah, Sweetie. I really do. I love you so much I can't even put it into words." He took her hand in both of his and held it in her lap. "Do you feel the same way? Would you want to?"

The truth was that Janet had been so busy being an excellent student and active in her community and church, that she had not thought about getting married. "I do feel that way about you, Johnny. I really do."

"Will you marry me?"

"Well, yes. I'm not too sure about when, exactly. Can you wait a little?"

"All I hear is the 'yes' part. That's all I needed to hear." He turned full toward her and embraced her harder than he ever had. They kissed until their passion threatened to explode, and he reluctantly drove her home.

—

Johnny opened the pharmacy for business the next day. Graduation had been on a Wednesday, and Thursdays were always slow at the pharmacy, so Johnny worked the counter himself. As he was powering up the cash register, it occurred to him for the first time that he should have had a ring to give Janet last night. He would buy one right away and give it to her, make a special occasion of it, of course. He probably didn't even need to apologize for getting it out of sequence, but he thought maybe he would, anyway.

Somehow, his engagement seemed tentative. Maybe it had to do with the missing engagement ring—easily corrected. They had not discussed a time frame, and he began to worry that Janet might want to start college first, or even finish college first. He glanced toward the secure area where the vault for drugs of abuse were locked up. He usually did not work the combination until he needed to for a customer with a prescription. He considered opening it now, even though Thursday was the least busy day.

Janet slept late that morning. It had been past one o'clock when she'd arrived home, secretly delighted to see that her parents, for the first time, had not waited up for her. She'd been dreaming she was in sixth grade, the year after which she was double promoted to eighth grade. She opened her eyes and the dream faded quickly. She thought about Johnny's proposal, and her acceptance, and telling her parents about it, even though this morning something about it seemed, somehow, tentative.

—

Janet entered NCCT, the teacher's college at Oak Hollow, North Carolina, in the fall. Oak Hollow was too far from Callan County to commute, so Johnny and Janet had to see each other less often, but the situation helped Janet concentrate on her studies and didn't seem to diminish their relationship.

Johnny found some solace in his loneliness through the judicious use of drugs.

Morning phenobarbital taken with coffee eased him through entire Sundays without leaving him sleepless at night. And he had friends, not exactly hippies, whose hair was fairly long and who came from the surrounding rural areas. These friends came and went, and they included men with guitars, men on motorcycles, men with sexy fat girlfriends, men with quiet girlfriends, girls with girlfriends, one woman who showed him a gun she kept in her pocket. These people, Johnny soon learned, often had ready access to locally grown marijuana. They convinced him to trade pharmaceuticals for it—small quantities. He was as careful as ever. Thus, Johnny tried and learned to appreciate smoking something other than his beloved tobacco. Still, he was always cautious, never got stoned during or before work so that he always appeared normal to his co-workers.

—

Janet's first summer vacation from college, she traveled to London with a group of student teachers. It was a five-week theater tour, and Johnny had convinced Mr. and Mrs. Mabry to let him drive to Charlotte to meet the midmorning arrival of her flight, pick her up and deliver her back home to them.

When Janet stepped through the arrivals gate, she caught Johnny's eye in an instant. Her face lit up, and the smile that had first enchanted him recaptured his heart and gave him relief, for the moment, from the loneliness and suspicions he'd been harboring in Janet's five-week absence. They rushed to embrace, and Janet whispered in his ear, "Hi," which was their secret signal of affection.

"Hi," he whispered into the fragrant warmth of her hair.

—

He drove her back to Cannon Shoals and the waiting arms of her parents. He had to get back to Cadbury so he didn't stay for lunch, but returned to Cannon Shoals on Sunday, attended church with the Mabrys, and after lunch at a favored barbecue joint, Janet and Johnny finally got away for a walk.

They were strolling hand in hand along the broad curve of a blacktop road that wound through a weedy edge of town and the rusting remnants of an old sawmill.

"What did you see in London?" he asked her.

"Well, we went to this one show called *The Norman Conquests*. It was good."

"Sounds like one I would like."

"Mmm, it's not what it sounds like. Let's see, *The Mousetrap* was one. It was raining like crazy when we got out."

Johnny stopped and stepped to face Janet, wrapped her in his arms. "I would have kept you nice and warm just like this."

She cooed and fitted herself into his embrace. "That would have been nice."

"What else?"

"*Canterbury Tales.*"

"No, Sweetie. Whisper it into my ear."

She stood on tiptoes and whispered, "*Pajama Game.*"

"Tell me about it."

"It was good."

"Tell me a lot about it." She laughed, knowing he loved her warm breath in his ear. "Tell me every detail."

She glanced down the road toward town to make sure no cars were approaching. "Well," she breathed into his ear, "it had a nude scene in it."

He jerked away and looked at her. "Really?"

She stretched back up to his ear and breathed, "*No Sex Please, We're British.*"

"That's a play? Seriously?"

"Yes, it is," Janet said, resuming their walk. "It was so funny I almost died."

After a while, they could see they were approaching an old cemetery surrounded by an ornate iron fence. "I missed you so much," he said.

"I missed you, too."

"I thought... I mean, I was afraid you were going to... I mean, I knew better, but...."

"What, Johnny!" she laughed.

"That you were going to fall in love with that English guy."

"What English guy? The whole group was women."

"That cousin of one of the girls."

"What are you talking about? You mean Loretta's cousin that went to dinner with us that one time?" She laughed. "How in the world did you get that idea?"

"I don't know. I'm just telling you. I guess I got jealous."

"Oh Johnny. That's silly."

"I know. But that day I got your card and you said you met Loretta's cousin and he was very nice, I had to take a long walk and I thought about what I would do if you broke up with me."

"He was nothing for you to worry about, believe me."

"Look, the cemetery has a nice bench. Want to go in there and sit?"

"Okay." They entered the cemetery through a gate in the iron fence and walked toward the bench. "So, what would you do if I broke up with you, Johnny?" They sat.

"Die. End up buried in a place like this."

"Don't worry. I'm not going to leave you." She kissed him to seal the promise.

25

AFTER FINISHING SOPHOMORE YEAR, JANET took a summer job as a reading coach at Cannon Shoals Elementary. The children she worked with were the ones who needed summer school in order to pass to the next grade. The work was trying, the children did not wish to be there, and Janet sympathized with them. She herself felt the call of the shade trees, the summer breezes, books she wanted to read but hadn't quite enough time.

She missed Johnny. He'd given her a diamond ring the first time he'd seen her after proposing. It was not an expensive ring, but she wore it proudly. The ring helped dissolve the feeling of impermanence that sometimes crept into her. It gave her an anchor for long-term planning, and helped to make waiting through four years of college before marrying seem feasible.

When she doubted that she could wait until after graduating to marry Johnny, she asked her father to speak again about the advantages of waiting, and he always sounded wise, and his reasons made sense. She asked her mother the same questions, and her mother's sympathy was warm and helpful. And the ring on her finger, the anchor, was helpful, too.

Her senior year, Janet moved into Cosper dormitory and gained a new roommate, Shelley. Shelley was a hippie, at least in her fashion choices, and projected an attitude toward Janet that seemed condescending, especially about their respective love lives. Shelley openly spoke about having sex with one man after another, it seemed to Janet. And when Janet revealed that she and her fiancé Johnny were "waiting," Shelley's silent disapprobation was at first insulting and then disturbing. Had the old small-town, pre-hippy era mores actually survived intact in her and Johnny's long engagement? Or was Shelley right? Even Maryanne, her roommate last year, had laughed, thinking Janet was kidding at first. Janet had become defensive and summarily informed Maryanne that the wedding was already set for the June after her graduation, and that she was glad her moral values would be intact on that day. Even to her, it sounded sanctimonious and rang hollow, but she believed it. And she believed it now, but she would not say so to Shelley.

—

While his love for Janet never wavered, the years were long for Johnny, the months were long, and the weeks. The days grew very long, sometimes excruciatingly, and Johnny found that he needed relief from the incessant longing for Janet that distracted him to the point that he made several mistakes filling prescriptions—one of them potentially serious, though he caught them all in time. He was grateful for the friends he was making, and liked visiting them out in the country. He felt comfortable around their poverty, their drug use, the transience of most of them, and also for the stability of Inez and Jason, who never came into town and always seemed to be home, and Porky, who might show up to visit Johnny any time, at work or his apartment.

At a few minutes past six, having shut down the pharmacy at the end of a remarkably warm weekday in the February of Janet's final semester at NCCT, Johnny came out of the store, glanced around the lot and saw Porky leaning against the kiosk near the parking lot entrance and walked toward him. Porky leaned off the kiosk and waited, finishing his cigarette.

"*El Porko*, peace, brother. What's happening?"

"Where's your car, man?" Porky did not have a car himself, and it was a mystery how he went from place to place.

"Follow me." Johnny reached Porky, they gave each other the solidarity handshake, and Johnny led the way to his car parked not in its usual spot.

"Let me get something to eat before we head out," Porky said.

"Groovy. I'm hungry too. What's good? You like Dixie Burger?"

"You got anything at your place?"

"Might have some peanut butter and jelly. Actually pear preserves Janet's mom made. Glad to make us some sandwiches."

"Far out."

At Johnny's apartment, Porky washed down two sandwiches with the end of a carton of milk. "My cousin's blowing in tonight," Porky said.

"Yeah? Where from?"

Porky laughed. "Who the fuck knows! He's got this far out station wagon and he's been going all over the country, man. I don't know if he'll really show up. If he does, he's supposed to have some ungodly grass from Mexico."

"With paraquat all over it."

"No, man. He's been dealing ever since he was born, man. You'll dig Santana. He knows what he's doing."

"His name's Santana?"

"That's who he's been ever since 'Evil Ways' came out. Don't try to call him anything else, man."

"Far out."

Johnny drove them into the Brushy mountains, rugged foothills just outside Cadbury where Porky's sister and her old man—and presumably Porky, sometimes—lived in two small trailer houses and a utility building, all conjoined. They arrived at the end of the rutted dirt road at dusk. Pulling into the clearing lit by a coal oil lantern hanging from a tree branch, Johnny noticed there were several people there he didn't recognize, not an unusual occurrence. Tonight there were two men with long hair, one with cropped hair wearing a necklace of bear claws, and a short woman in a muumuu. They were all drinking beer in front of the compound, and seemed unconcerned about—certainly did not acknowledge—the arrival of Johnny's familiar car. Porky's sister Inez emerged from the utility building's door and gave Porky the peace sign. She then gave Johnny a hug and a kiss on the mouth.

"Johnny, peace man," she said in her low, breathy voice. "Unbelievable how warm it is. Introduce yourself around." She pointed at the short woman and said, "That's Breeze. You'll love her. She's so out of sight."

Breeze looked up at Johnny and smiled. She had a sweet, baby face, and at first glance in the dim light Johnny thought she must not be over thirteen years old. But she was much older than that, in her mid-twenties, which became apparent as Johnny viewed her from various angles as the evening progressed.

Santana, the man with the longest hair, it turned out, had indeed brought a new supply of weed, and the evening passed quietly as the group partook of the green bounty. Inez's old man, Jason, came outside, acknowledged Johnny briefly with a hand bump, and smoked without ever saying a word, his silence a sort of trademark he cultivated. Johnny had heard him speak only twice in the several months he'd been coming out here.

"Man, this stuff is righteous," Porky said as he approached Johnny and sat on the ground next to him.

Santana heard and added, "Damn straight, man."

Johnny had never been so high, and found it difficult to speak, so he nodded his head, then smiled first at Porky and then at Santana.

Santana nodded large and chuckled. "Fuck yeah, man." He had just finished rolling another joint, and lit it up, then passed it to Porky, who toked and offered it to Johnny.

Johnny held up his hand and shook his head, still smiling, but Porky said, "Oh man, come on, you gotta reach the next level with this stuff. While you have the chance." He poked Johnny's shoulder gently, and it was enough to persuade him.

When Johnny finally stopped watching the beautiful movies that appeared on the inside of his eyelids, he was surprised to find that the lantern was off and everyone had gone inside, where there were no lights. Everyone except Breeze. She was dozing with her head in his lap, and now he remembered that she had taken that position about the time he was starting to watch the lid movies.

"Breeze," he said, his voice seeming to come from somewhere other than his mouth.

"Mmm," she said, and she slowly sat up.

"I'm too stoned to drive."

"Come on, let's sleep in the station wagon. It makes a bed in the back."

Everything they said seemed to take a long time. It also took a long time for them to open the tailgate of the station wagon and turn the seats down, but as Breeze had promised, it made into a bed. As they crawled onto the lumpy bedding, Breeze said, "Hey, man, wanna ball me?"

Balling Breeze was, Johnny decided a few days later, not something he should feel so guilty about. Everywhere he looked—television, magazines, newspapers—he saw a world that had passed him by. He felt unduly timid, and knew that his contemporaries would have been laughing at his virginity if he'd revealed it to anyone. With all that in mind, he balled Breeze several more times in the following couple of weeks. Then one day she was gone, as was Santana and one of the other men at the compound, but Inez assured Johnny that Breeze was coming back. Just not sure when.

—

Janet graduated near the top of her class. With her bachelor's degree and teaching credential in hand, she had little problem securing a job at Cannon Shoals Middle School. Johnny, meanwhile, accepted a position in the pharmacy in downtown Cannon Shoals. Their life was well planned and prepared for. Mr. Mabry had found the little house on Althea Street and fronted the down payment for Janet.

—

The Mabrys lived in a modest two-story frame house with three bedrooms— one more than needed for the family that never conceived the second child they had requested from their Methodist God. Janet was partial to the swing bench on the front porch, and loved to sit in it with Mr. Mabry and talk.

"Let's just go over the next few weeks very generally and see how things stand," Mr. Mabry said to her. "I know you and Mama have it all organized, but I can't remember anything for five minutes, it seems like. It would help me."

"Okay," she said, marking her place in *The Other Side of Midnight*.

"You don't mind?"

"I like going over it. Okay, I start helping out with summer school a week from Wednesday." She had volunteered for this at Cannon Shoals Elementary during spring break before she graduated from NCCT.

"No pay, right?"

"No pay. And that's good, because that way they're lucky to get me and can't complain when I take off for my honeymoon."

"Now, do they know you're going to do that?"

"Miss Gresham knows it, and that's good enough. She coordinates all the volunteers."

"And then the wedding is June what? Twentieth?"

"Right."

"Small, you said."

She saw him looking far out into the yard or beyond it. "Daddy, it's going to be kind of lopsided as it is. Johnny has no family."

"That's what your mother told me."

"None that might come, anyway. I don't want it to look like he's some kind of, I don't know...."

"No, 'course not."

"And then, I guess we'll go somewhere for a honeymoon."

"But he has friends over in Cadbury, doesn't he? Wouldn't he invite some of them?"

"Yes, he does have friends." Janet stood up, setting her father to swinging as she pushed away from the seat. "I don't know, he might invite some of them."

"Well, see, hon, that's what I was wondering about. The way you kind of move away when we mention Johnny's friends."

"I don't 'move away,' Daddy. I just don't really care whether he invites anybody or not. I don't want a lot of people. I want small. I don't see what's wrong with that."

"Nothing. Nothing wrong. It seems like you used to want a big fairy-tale wedding, I was trying to remember."

"When I was a little girl, Daddy."

She sat on the front steps and rested her head in her hands. Mr. Mabry sat down beside her.

"It's all fine, Daddy."

"I know."

"Sometimes I think it's a little too fine."

"What do you mean?"

"Well, sometime this last year, senior year, I don't know, I got to thinking, probably because when I switched over to the Cosper Dorm, remember I got a new roomie?"

"Shelley, yeah?"

"Shelley... she had a way of saying things that, I don't know...."

"What? Got you thinking?"

"When I told her about me and Johnny, she acted like it was weird."

"I don't see anything weird about it. Your mother and I did something pretty similar."

"I know. But things are different now. Social mores have changed, Daddy. It's hard to talk about."

"No, I know what you're talking about. I'm not completely isolated, hon. I figure you and Johnny were not the way your mother and I were. People can't wait now, and I don't really blame them. Not really. It's a different world from what we lived in."

Janet shook her head slowly and looked at her father. "No."

"No, what?"

"Johnny and I never... had relations. We never have."

"Oh. Well...," and he smiled, pleased.

"Daddy, that's what Shelley made me feel weird about."

"Well, that's her problem, not yours."

"No, it's mine. So I tell myself it doesn't matter. We hardly ever saw each other, over the last four years, for one thing. And I know we love each other. I know that, if I know nothing else about anything."

They sat beside each other and watched a neighbor's cat cross their lawn, stop and look at them, then disappear beneath a rhododendron.

"I'd just say," Mr. Mabry gathered his thoughts, "that you and Johnny may have one aspect of your relationship that is, for this brief moment in the nineteen seventies, considered old fashioned. I don't think that's a problem, and I don't think it will ever be a problem, and I think it's actually a good thing."

Janet leaned her head on his shoulder and held his arm. "Thank you, Daddy."

"And your Mr. Bishop," he continued, "whom I have always liked, is a bit higher in my estimation than he was a few minutes ago."

—

Johnny Bishop had been in charge of the pharmacy in Cadbury for five years, answerable to no one except the drugstore owner, Mr. Dewayne Mask, who treated Johnny almost like a partner, if not a son. Now that Johnny was marrying a girl over in Cannon Shoals, and she was to be teaching at Cannon Shoals Elementary, and her parents had made the down payment on a house for her and Johnny, it followed that Johnny would need to relocate to Cannon Shoals. As Janet's plans worked out seamlessly, so Johnny's parallel plans with her seemed almost charmed in their facility. A pharmacist's position opened up in March at the drugstore in downtown Cannon Shoals. Johnny had already applied there, and he secured the job with no complications and a glowing letter of recommendation from Mr. Mask. Even his start date was optimal—he would make the move just after the honeymoon.

—

Janet was awake early on Sunday morning, anxious for Johnny's arrival in time for church, where Reverend Chastain would announce the couple's wedding plans for the benefit of the few in the congregation who didn't already know. Johnny would stay overnight, maybe even a few nights as he did some minor repair work on the house on Althea, a turn of the century bungalow that had lain vacant for some months and was priced to sell when Mr. Mabry suggested it to Janet and offered to help with the purchase.

Downstairs, still in her pajamas, Janet made coffee in the trusty old percolator and was enjoying her second cup when she heard Johnny's car stop in front of the house. He was much earlier than she was expecting. She hurried to the front door and opened it. Johnny was sitting in the car, his hands on the wheel, staring straight ahead. She waited a few moments, then decided to hurry upstairs and start getting dressed, thinking Johnny must be waiting because it was so early.

In her Sunday dress, a light blue jersey with a paisley design, she went back to the front door and looked out. Johnny was still in the car, his hands still on the wheel, but now with his forehead also leaning on the wheel. Janet hurried out to the car and knocked on the passenger side window. He didn't move. She opened the door.

"Johnny?" He looked at her, and she felt a thrill of horror when she saw his expression. She quickly got into the car and took his face in her hands. "Johnny, what's the matter?"

He stared at her and almost imperceptibly shook his head. The interior of the car reeked of cigarette smoke, and butts overflowed from the open ashtray and littered the floorboard. From the front porch Mrs. Mabry called out, "Y'all come on in, for goodness sake. We're all up. Johnny, come have a cup of coffee. Have you had breakfast? We didn't think you'd be here until after ten. Janet? Y'all come on in."

Janet heard the front door of the house close. "Johnny, you're scaring me. You look awful. Has something happened?"

"I'm sorry," he said, his voice slurred. "I've been up all night."

"You look like it. Are you all right? Why were you up all night?"

"Trying to decide."

Janet waited for more, but there was no more. "Decide what, Johnny?"

He looked at her, and she saw his eyes wet and glassy, yet he was not crying. And suddenly tears formed in her own eyes. "Have you changed your mind? Please don't tell me you've changed your mind." A huge tear rolled down her face.

"I didn't mean to," he said, and looked away, out the window, which was rolled up even though it was a warm morning. "I have to marry Breeze."

"What? Did you say you have to marry Breeze?"

He looked at her. "I have to marry her. I don't want to, but I have to."

"No you don't, Johnny. Why do you? Is she a girl you got pregnant?"

"Yes."

"And her name is Breeze?" Janet tried to stop the quivering in her voice. "But, you don't really have to, do you? Doesn't she know you love me? Didn't you tell her you love me, Johnny?"

Johnny nodded, and nodded again. "Yeah, I told her. It doesn't make any difference. She's nice, but she wants me to marry her. And the thing is, Santana's in jail. And if I don't, she's going to make it where I'll never work again." He slumped against the steering wheel and closed his eyes.

"Why? What do you mean? Who's Santana?"

His eyes closed, his mouth barely able to form the words, Johnny said, "I have to do the right thing."

"We can work this out," Janet said, but he didn't respond. She shook him, called his name, but he was hardly even conscious.

She got out of the car and began walking down the sidewalk. She heard the front door open and her mother call out like broken glass from the porch, but she kept walking, glad she had chosen flats instead of high heels. She thought there must be a way to work the situation out, this being the 1970's, people being enlightened. She began to devise scenarios for how things might be made satisfactory in the long run. After a while, she saw Grace Methodist where she would not be attending today after all, walked past its leering facade, walked past downtown on the back street, walked past Cannon Shoals Elementary, and she turned down Althea Street and walked past the little house where she would be living, and making the mortgage payments. And by then, she was not sure things would work out with Johnny. She was not so sure things had ever really been right with Johnny, even though she loved him so very much.

26

CONCRETE WALKS CRISSCROSSED THE GRASSY quad before the asylum's somber facade. I sometimes think this place must be one that Papa had a vision about when he was little. The building was brick, not red but a fecal ocher. Four stories high, it loomed, even though he was sitting two hundred or more feet from the building. He counted twenty-two windows across the front on each of the upper stories. Too wide, too massive and filled not with innocuous bureaucrats or friendly clergymen or cartographers with cups of coffee going cold, but with people caught in the web of death without the mercy of the spider's poison. This was not the infamous State Hospital with its shock treatments and lobotomies. This was the Texas State Care Facility, another public institution, one for people who needed—or whose families wanted—minimal or no medical treatment. It was subsidized by both state and federal funding, and had the good will associated with one of its founders, Stephen F. Austin.

Leo had watched Cord roll Lulu into the place, considered too frail to walk, though she could still take a few faltering steps if persuaded. He had filled out some forms and signed them, though none of it was his doing, and none of it was his responsibility. A man in silver poplin with a name badge had poured Leo part of an orange soda into a paper cup too small for the whole can. Leo had said some words of comfort to his mother, but had not seen the room to which the man in silver poplin pushed her in the wheelchair, the dejected Cord tagging behind. Leo was to visit her in the room at another time soon. For now, only Cord had gone with her to the room.

Daddy doesn't know where I am—probably confused because I stormed out. He'll look for me when he's done inside.

Leah had not come along, had said yesterday she did not want to see Lulu and Cord arrive from Brownwood in their stupid car, did not want to see the hospital just east of the Austin airport, wanted nothing to do with it. She was asleep, was up most of the night, high on some drug Brian brought to her. Brian H. Brian the Hippie. Brian the Harmless, of Moscow, Idaho, so he says, but can't say why he's in Austin. Leah likes him because he epitomizes—her word. Brian E. Brian the Epitomizer. He brought her something he called Purple Double Dome. Leah was interested in these drug names she thought were wonderful. Leo had heard Pink Lipstick, Windowpane, Orange Sunshine, and some others all within the last couple of weeks while sitting at his desk trying to study. And not just from Brian the Epitomizer, but also from Leah talking on the phone to Hippie(s) the Unknown. Living with her was free, as she paid the rent. She worked at Northland Mall in the management office, doing payroll, screening applicants for security and maintenance positions. She liked nine to five. Leo, meanwhile, was able to concentrate on his studies.

And living with Leah was interesting. One night, Leah was on LSD and she announced that her mind had separated from her body, which she commenced referring to as her robot. For two days she spoke of her robot and her mind as separate entities. "My robot says it's hungry." "I've lost part of my robot," she said, and then, looking at her hand, "Oh, there it is, on the end of its arm."

When not at work, she lived in varying states of consciousness, but always returned to an awareness of Leo's libido. Her skillful hand was there, like magic, when he needed it, which was often. And so was her whole body, which crawled into his bed from time to time and warmed him when he was cold and went around him for release and relief and melting into her soft white flesh, after which she laughed and guaranteed him that he was free as long as she was too. He thought it was just hippie talk. "Freedom" needed context to give it meaning, and he had none.

Leo stood up, the bench too hard, the view of the asylum too depressing. He wiped perspiration from around his lips, noting that the air was dead still and muggy. He wondered what was taking his father so long. Saying goodbye?

Yesterday Leo had finished his paper on Max Frisch. The playwright had been one of Leo's recent drugs of choice, along with Gunter Grass, and before that, the Stanislavski acting method. Although his grades had plummeted after he lost Jeanine, and he'd been placed on scholastic probation for a semester, Leo had rallied and scored close to a four-point average since then, immersing himself in his studies, insulating himself from the crazy Leah life around him.

He visualized Leah sitting on another bench a hundred feet away, along one of the diagonal sidewalks. He imagined Leah next year, 1974, when he would graduate and need to make decisions. It would be difficult because although he had no normal feelings for Leah–feelings like he'd had for Jeanine—he knew well that he had formidable, unnamable ones.

His mother must have been settled into her room by now. All she had said to him today was, "They won't hurt you," and then, before they'd entered the big building before him, "Don't worry, they won't hurt you." She must have been repeating what someone had said to her, but it was maddening to hear her say it.

—

We called it lazy eye but that's not what it is. Lazy eye is something else. What she is, she's wall-eyed. It's exotropia, the divergent strabismus. If you're cross-eyed, that's esotropia—still strabismus, but the convergent kind. There are six tiny muscles around the eye, and....

Yes, an injury. She was seven years old. An accidental blow to the face. A measure of discipline, actually, but not intentionally injurious.

Things were different back then.

Her mother, yes. That'll be meaningful to you as you work with her, won't it.

No? Not working with her?

Maintenance care only.

A downward spiral, Leo thought. He wondered now if the brain deterioration could be another result of the blow from the water hose. Could the story, told to him long ago by Leah, have been untrue, or exaggerated? Had Lulu really made some reference to the male member that enraged his Granny, incited her to lash out with the hose? Might it have been instead that his mother was *born* with exotropic strabismus? Maybe. But the story had the ring of truth, and was too sad to be invented. An innocent remark by a seven-year-old girl, and an innocent reaction by an innocent, overwrought mother. And what about the personality Lulu was said—by both Russell and Drew—to have exhibited up until the blow, and for many years afterward albeit in decreasing radiance? Could she really have made people fall in love, just by being in their presence?

A puff of moist air disturbed the heavy stillness, and within a minute or two there was an obnoxious gusty wind. Leo took himself for a walk around the perimeter of the

grounds. Ugly place, even if the grass was healthy and well kept. Building made of bricks
of dried cat shit. The clouds were banking and darkening. Leo considered returning to
the lobby, but remembered the awful light and the disturbing smell of paint and lemon-
scented cleanser, and the frightening impulse to hit the registrar, that asshole.

Penises. Why wasn't Leah here?

He reached the far bench again, considered sitting, but just then Cord emerged
from the building, hunched over to light a cigarette, then surveyed the expanse of lawn.
Seeing Leo, he started out across the grass, ignoring the nearby sidewalk. Leo stood and
waited, thinking how like an old man his father walked, and yet how fast.

"She's settled in," Cord said, and they continued toward the parking lot at a pace
Leo considered too brisk for comfort.

"Say anything?" Leo asked. Cord shook his head no.

Cord unlocked the car, saying "She went straight to the window and looked out.
Didn't stop looking out. I told her everything, and she seemed to hear me."

"You told her I'd be here every week."

"No. Your name seemed to get her upset. Just come on and see what happens."

"What about you, Daddy? You going to make the drive once in a while?"

Cord started the car and backed out of the space. "I'll get down when I can."

On the way back to Leah's apartment, Cord was silent, smoked two cigarettes. He
drove past the apartment complex.

"You missed the apartment."

"I know." He passed the Elisabet Ney museum, drove several blocks into a residential
neighborhood, pulled over at the curb and turned off the engine.

"Why are we here? What are we doing, Daddy?"

"This ain't right."

"What? She has to be taken care of and you can't do it yourself."

"You and Leah, I'm talking about."

Leo looked at his father and his father looked him square in the eye. How did he
know it wasn't right? It was true, but how did he know? Leo decided to say nothing, but
the silence lengthened. So. Cord was going to wait.

"What, me staying with her? What's wrong with that? Saves a lot of money."

Cord flicked his cigarette out the window, sending it skidding across the pavement,
throwing off sparks. Leo could see it from the passenger seat, out the front. It still gave
off smoke, still had some fire.

Cord could trap you and not say anything, bring up the subject but leave you to do the talking. He'd done it before, once when he suspected Leo had taken the saw to the edge of the front steps. By saying nothing, Cord had elicited a confession. He had then taken Leo to the bathroom and whipped him to *get my money's worth, you worthless little whelp. Do you know how much it's gonna cost to replace that damn board?*

"There's nothing wrong, Daddy. I'm saving a lot of money by staying with her."

"Staying with her?" Cord snapped. Leo had not expected him to say anything, at least for a while. "Staying with her, or fucking her?"

Leo thought fast. The best he could come up with was to perform a quiet, solicitous nod, then say, "Is that what you think?"

Leo was slumped in the seat, his knees pressing into the dashboard. He could watch his father, who stared through the windshield, pursed his lips, exhaled through his nostrils. In a moment he pulled the pack of Winstons out of his shirt pocket, fingered around in it. It was empty. He wadded it, let it fall to the seat beside him. "Look in the glove box there and see if there's another pack of cigarettes, will you?"

Leo pulled himself up to get his knees off the dash, opened the glove compartment, found two packs of Winstons, handed one to his father, slammed the metal door shut. As Cord popped the pack of smokes hard onto the dash before opening it, Leo rolled down his window, leaned his elbow out, settled back to hear whatever was coming, more impatient and annoyed than worried.

When Cord had a cigarette lit and had satisfied his lungs with the first deep pull, he said, "I tried to do what I was supposed to do."

Leo looked at him. "Putting her away, you mean? We all know it had to be done."

"I don't mean that. I tried to provide. I worked, paid for things. I paid for everything."

In the ensuing silence, Leo formulated his response, *Yeah, you did that, and not one thing more other than terrorize all of us and beat the shit out of me once in a while.* But he said, "Well, you did support us, Daddy. Thanks."

"You're doing good in college, ain't you?"

"I am."

"Good."

"I study my ass off."

"That's good."

"I just live with Leah. That's all." He could hear his own lie, the different timbre in his voice so obvious. He wondered if Cord could hear it, too.

"You're lying, Leo. No point in it. I want to tell you to quit her. I'm telling you to quit her."

"But...."

"Leo," he cut his son off. "I'm telling you what to do. I don't want to hear what you have to say. I ain't stupid, I know you don't have to do what I say."

"I know you're not stupid."

"So I'm telling you what to do, and you hear what I'm saying."

Cord smoked his cigarette. Leo considered getting out of the stifling car and walking the few blocks back to the apartment. But he stayed. There was something unsaid, something beyond the situation with Leah, and beyond anything he and his father had ever talked about. It was not time to fight, not time to reminisce, not time to try for a connection. But it was time for something, so he waited to see what it would be.

When Cord flicked the cigarette out, this time way across the street, out of sight, he put his hand on the ignition key, but then let it go. "I want to tell you something else, Leo," he said.

"I'm listening."

"I have feelings, too," Cord said, and his voice shook on the last word. Without thinking, Leo turned to look at him. He was not crying, not about to cry, but his voice, that one word, *too*, had betrayed strong emotion.

"Yeah, I know you do, Daddy." He had intended a sympathetic tone, but it sounded, to him anyway, cold and dismissive. "I know you do," he tried again.

Cord started the car, drove around the block and back down the street to Leah's apartment. He pulled up at the curb and left the motor running.

"You coming in?" Leo said.

"No."

"You driving straight back to Brownwood?"

"Yeah, I am."

Leo let himself out of the car, closed the door, leaned back in. "Okay. Be careful on the road."

Cord nodded, looked at Leo, nodded again. Leo gave the car a slap on the roof and backed a step away. There was a moment then. Should he say something like *I hear what you're saying, Daddy,* or should he let it go? Cord pulled away.

It was the last Leo would ever see or hear from his father.

—

Lulu remained at The Texas State Care Facility for over six years. Leo visited her weekly without fail while he remained in Austin. It was a routine that became increasingly abhorrent to him as his mother sank ever deeper into the confusion of her synesthesia. But Leo and his aunt had long moved far away from Austin in 1980.

The afternoon was lasting longer than the satisfaction of her lunch. There was something in her stomach but it was not food and it was not hunger. It was more like a picture forming out of colored particles converging from other parts of her digestive system, and from her other organs, heart and liver, kidneys and spleen. It was a picture of summer green in morning yellow sunlight, a doorway darkened by the touch of children's grimy hands and play and climbing in trees, brothers, and wetting and then growing out of that. The particles of color carried flavor. Certain green particles were the lime of hard candy, certain oranges were oranges and others, more toward the yellow, were pineapple. She stood in this picture, her own face tanner than the other children, cream with a touch of coffee, her hair still baby blonde, cornbread, and curled around her sweaty brow. Expectant clear eyes, undamaged, darting about for life, insect life, cat life, shadow life in the morning sunshine. She wore a linen dress of some faded purple, not grape, no longer grape, and she stood near the door, panting. She had run through the weeds, knocking dew to the ground and her bare feet.

But then she was on the ghost bus riding to Kimball's, and all that was left of the colors was the powdery white green of the oxidized bus paint washed down the side of the lumbering, wheezing vehicle, and the buses went out sometime in the fifties. Her stomach churned a little, and on the bus there was a man, older, squat and nose-haired, wearing a nice straw hat and a seedy tweed jacket. He had blue eyes, pale, clear and bright, gazing out the window, watching beige Brownwood pass by, as he must have done for a long time. She smiled at him before he looked at her, so that it was an invitation, not a response. He saw her and tilted his head, a polite nod, and a smile in return, and the smile and its kindness and wisdom traveled to her and brushed past her clean blouse and pregnant figure and on out the bus window and into time and through time and then she was now again, her stomach tight with its emptiness and the thirst in her mouth.

Neon color flashed like the signs in the soda fountain where she sat on the stool at the end of the counter, where there was a coolness, almost uncomfortable, a draft from the door when it opened and other teenagers came and went chattering and chitchatting. The light was too sweet, or was that the soda, or the ice cream? The coral feeling of her shyness surmounted by the unconquerable intuition—when she was approached, she made people see each other without fear, even, it often seemed, when she herself could not focus on them. The young man was in uniform and the war was over. The color of the uniform faded until all was gray, out of focus, both eyes, not just the one.

And out of the gray, once again she found *now* in the room to which she had never become accustomed. The one where lately Vander came and went.

Standing in the room—rather, just outside the room, on the other side—Cord abused her but it was dark blue, spotted with dark, and it lumped and curdled and shrank somewhat through time. She was considerably insulated from it by her skin and a layer that used to be fatty tissue. He was gone, was he not? Not gone, but outside, abusive, unpleasant, angry, and a reminder of pain. He grew hair, and his hair wicked out a measure of his meanness, but he did not go away.

He was also kind. He never wanted to hurt. He wanted to be loved. He didn't know about the cushion of kind consideration. It had been stripped from him by his mother. He had been gone for a long time, and all that was left was the dark blueness wicking on the other side.

Her connection with Leah was not a secret. It was not a mystery. It flooded into her room like silver grains of wheat from her skin, dissolving the walls and scattering into the invisibility beyond until it reached everything and everything's colors, making everything shine. Everything—though not everybody—knew that her love for Leo flowed into and through Leah. Leah became purity and she became everything when she was born, and Leah became transparent to the light and color of love when Leo was born. She knew that Leah had passed through Leo many times, and passed through him now. She sensed this through her stomach and skin, and the picture of Leo and Leah together in the green leaves had melded with everything and she sensed this because she was the way for people to meld. This, along with everything, swirled and all colors mixed to form one silver shining.

But the silver shining faded and her room returned, walls and all. She heard a mild boxy thud from somewhere in the hallway. The sheen on her walls was the homogenized and smeared-out remains of the presence that used to reside in her body, the one she tried to have Leo destroy when she worked at Kimball's. If she could or wanted to scrape it all off the walls, it would form itself into a dead, rotted and dried up small dark mass.

It was dehydrating into an unrecognizable lump, small and tumbling across the floor, rolling under her bed where it stopped, present, still. How did it get that way?

The walls were naked now. The light from the window was naked. Her stomach ached a little, not much, in an unfamiliar way. She heard an attendant talking, as though on a phone, one-sided, somewhere down the hall, muffled through the walls. Leo was far away, pursuing a job up in Chicago. How long had he been gone? Something told her the length of time was not a detail worth trying to figure out. Cord had been gone a long time—ever since she'd been brought here. Leah, too, was far away, with Leo, or chasing after him—she was not sure which, and that didn't much matter. Drew had died eleven years ago. A time detail known. How inexplicable! Russell was far away. Where? She had only vague colors for an answer there. Vander, the new attendant, had faded into her mind, and she had seen in him the stuttering loneliness of the redhead, and wished for him some nice companion, someone gentle.

There was weakness now, only now was it complete, and it spoke to her. With all guilt erased, she heard her little words from long ago and recaptured the little vision of a penis—small and dangling in front of little Drew and little Russell when they took a bath. Then the ringer washer hose, chalky blue and brown and black, approached her from a place above the door to her room, and though her weakness was complete, the beater startled her so much that she tried to turn her head to see its slow, menacing, rubbery advancement. She could not move, and for fifteen or twenty minutes, she lay on her bed watching its approach with the peripheral vision in her injured left eye. Then someone turned the knob on her door and pushed the door in so that it stood open, but the person, maybe Vander, did not enter the room. She was contemplating this when the beater touched her face and the gritty red pain stopped her heart.

27

I 'VE SEEN MY PAPA GET mad a few times. He is not like Mike Draper's dad who gets mad and throws things and hits Mike and kicks down the door. Mike has described his dad's rampages in detail to me because he seems to feel he can confide in me, and I take that as a compliment. Papa has only been mad in my presence two or three times that I remember, and he will let you know he is mad but then he will storm off and disappear and not come back until he cools down.

He has explained to me that while it looked like he was mad at me and Mama, he was just feeling frustrated with his company, the community theater here in Oak Hollow. The actor playing Biff threatened to quit a week before opening, and Papa came home and acted mad at me and Mama for wanting pizza delivered. He told me about transference of anger from its real source to a more convenient target, and that makes sense. But then I asked him about where he goes when he is mad, and that made him stop, stare, and then laugh. And then we talked about places. We discussed the different ways your whereabouts can affect your mental state, and it was a fun discussion. I suddenly remembered a poem I'd written a long time ago—well, a long time for me, which means a few months ago, and don't panic, I'm not going to share it here—and I ran to find it and show Papa.

This poem was about finding places where I can observe but not be observed, where I can think in a way that's not possible otherwise. My mind gets calm, I let go of logical thinking and let *mystical* thinking come in. I come to a grokking of God and time, which I've discussed earlier, usually based on what Papa has told me and I've already processed logically. The logical process, applied to abstractions like God and time travel, leaves untidy loose ends, but the loose ends get tied up neatly when you apply mystical thinking. It's like the problem of untying a knot in a string without letting go of the ends. It can't be done until you add another dimension of space, and then it's easy as pie. Mystical thinking is like adding another dimension to logic.

Papa told me about a place he used to know, back in Brownwood, Texas, that was just the kind of place I was writing about in my poem, and even better. His place was hidden behind bushes and backed up to an old fire station building with bricked-in doors. I could relate to that, and I am planning to someday go and find that place if they haven't torn it all down. I don't understand, at this early age, why he hid from his father. I never knew him, but Papa says he was the product of his upbringing, like we all are.

—

The Plum Hill community, fifty miles to the north and west of Texas' dead center, was a handful of small homesteads spread over several square miles, watered by windmills sucking from an aquifer a hundred feet down. Though the land was flat, few neighbors were within sight of each other, and only Williamson's Store, on the highway, sold supplies. In 1931, neither the store nor most of the hardscrabble farmers had yet felt the full impact of the Depression—their poverty was older than the crash.

"Your head looks like Shep," Alzon told his little brother Cord. "You better go in Shep's house."

Shep lived in an accidental space between the old rock foundation and a later addition to the house that extended back about four feet to something that was probably rock. Shep was getting old, and was of no use, but the Nobles tolerated him because he never killed the chickens.

Cord was taking half handfuls of millet from a lard bucket and slinging a russet dusty arc into the barnyard dirt. The chickens followed him, pecking up the seed, unhurried, well fed. He felt a fresh glob of chicken shit ooze up between his toes and cursed his own carelessness, cocking his elbow up and looking past his arm at the offended bare foot.

His brother, who was idly heckling Cord, squealed with laughter and forgot his plan to shove Cord into Shep's house. They heard their mother pushing at the back door—right near Shep's house—and Cord grabbed a half fistful of millet as Alzon ran off and disappeared into the scrubby grove of peach trees.

"Cord," she called in her nasal voice. "Ain't you through yet?"

"Feedin' the chickens."

"Hurry up. I need them eggs if you want cornbread for supper." She stood on the back step for a moment, her hands on her square, stone hips, looking at her younger son. He glanced at her, feeling, out of habit, the degradation of her sneering look of disapproval, a mild shaking of her head from side to side before she jerked the door open and went back inside. He tossed the remaining millet directly from the bucket into the thickest bunch of pecking fowl, trying to hit them, but barely perturbing them.

Shep startled him, coming up from behind and sticking his wet nose to Cord's besmirched foot. "Git away, dog. No good old dog."

He tossed the lard bucket at the tow sack of millet hanging outside the barn door under the shed roof. He was supposed to put it inside the sack. He picked it up, remembered the eggs, kept the lard bucket for collecting them. He hated going into the chicken coop. There was no point in trying not to step in the chicken shit when you went into the chicken coop.

He pulled the hens off their nests with savage disregard and purloined the warm fresh eggs, deriving some satisfaction from the chickens' hysterical protests. "Shut up if you know what's good for you," he muttered to them all. Six eggs today. Mom won't complain about that. One more than yesterday.

Straw and dust and down glued to roosts with chicken shit. Wooden box nests were slick where the hens polished them with breast feathers and tails. Thick dusty dry millety moldy smell in the chicken coop, he hated it here. One time his brother snuck up and latched him in. It was not too hard to reach the latch and unhook it with a stick he found in the straw. But he hated it. He was careful never to let his brother know how much he hated it. His brother loved to shove him into places, lock him into places. Mom never made Alzon do any work except to go to Williamson's Store for groceries once in a while, and one time go to Cleburne with Otis Efron in the truck, before Otis Efron and his family left the county.

If he ever tries to get my pocket knife, I'll stick him with it.

Half an inch was broken off the tip of the long blade. It had been like that when he acquired it. The short blade was complete, and he kept it sharp as a razor with the whet rock in the kitchen. He carved sticks with it whenever he wasn't doing a chore. He made toys from the flesh of the scrubby trees all around his life. He made buzzbobs from the mesquite bean pods. He used the straight willow branches around the tank to make an Indian bow, stringing it with a hemp strand from a tow sack, and he made the arrows from smaller branches and carved the tips sharp and feathered them with chicken feathers cut straight with his blade. He tried to kill horny toads with this weapon, and sometimes did, but not the green striped lizards because they were too fast. He had made a toy from a rattlesnake's rattle after killing the slinking beast with a hoe he was using to weed the peach orchard.

After leaving the eggs on the wash stand in the kitchen, he found a piece of dry-rotted wood, yellow as mustard, lying in the gully. It was light and crumbly like a loaf of old bread. He carried it down the gully, past a garden where melons were swelling, to a place where some overhanging willows gave the place a shaded, peaceful look. He tossed the piece of wood into the sand and was about to piss on it, see how much liquid it would soak up, but as his flow was about to begin, he turned and wet instead a tangle of twigs that the last rain had washed up. He picked up the spongy piece of wood again and carved from it one breast, the breast of a woman, with a nipple as he imagined it would be, pointed like the stamen of a bull nettle flower. He spent an hour down in the gully, out of sight, smoothing his breast. Then he lowered his face to it and parted lips to suckle it, but he did not touch it. On impulse, he stabbed it with his knife, slashing at it, cutting his work into nondescript pieces in a matter of a few seconds.

28

ORD JOINED THE CIVILIAN CONSERVATION Corps on December 2, 1935. Alzon was already in the corps, and had shipped out to Montana. Cord made no request to join his brother. He signed his name to a form he had not read. He'd heard all he needed to know about the CCC from a man talking with Mr. Williamson at the store.

Why did she act so mean to me? Like I was trying to get away with something? Why did she think I didn't like her until I really didn't? Why did she stand at the back door like that and spit into the dirt before she talked to me? She liked Shep better than she liked me. And she didn't like Shep, wanted him to wander off and disappear. Didn't have it in her to kill him, though. Kept feeding him. Kept feeding me, but gave Alzon the middle biscuit, and a hot one before supper and don't tell Cord, but I heard her say it.

Cord received thirty dollars at the end of his first full month digging mud out of Longhorn Caverns, working with over 200 other men to turn the cave and grounds into a tourist attraction. He banked half of it with the paymaster, kept the rest to spend during the following month, and did not spend all of it. He sent nothing home to his mother. She heard nothing from him until the beginning of World War II when he let her know he was joining the Marine Corps.

—

Hip to hip with other Marines, Cord felt diesel exhaust from the amphibious landing craft wafting past his face in the stiff breeze. Whatever was on Wallis Island,

Cord figured, would beat hell out of the weeks aboard ship. His thoughts drifted to the bus he'd boarded, short months ago, in Maypearl, Texas, where he'd ended up after his stint in the CCC. He remembered the thin girl who'd sat across the aisle from him and smiled at him once. He'd tried to decide whether or not she was pretty, and decided she was, but then she was gone into the dusty streets of some Texas town and he'd continued his journey toward Fort Worth to join the Corps.

The diesel exhaust, the pacific rolling waves, and the noise of the engine were making others sick, but not Cord. He'd learned to smoke in the CCC, and knew how to stay above nausea.

A few hundred yards out from shore, the pilot laughed, a short, high report, hee-hee-hee. Several of the men stood up to take a look toward the beach, where brown-skinned men, women, and children stood naked, regarding the approaching boats. They disappeared into the jungle just before the first barge landed.

On the beach, the men slapped at the swarming *u-namu*—mosquitos. Black thunderheads were rolling overhead from beyond the jungle. Before two more LCs landed, rain began to fall, but it did nothing to chase away the *u-namu*.

—

The Japs, the men learned, were nowhere near Wallis, but could attack unexpectedly. The sergeant warned against touching the natives, especially the children, lest they contract yaws, a disease with terrifying symptoms the sergeant described in detail.

The Marines, it seemed to Cord, had an easy time of it while the Seabees worked around the clock constructing concrete bases for howitzers and eight-inch guns. He had to sit in daily assemblies and listen to information about their mission. His attention drifted, but he was sure he was getting the important parts. The gun positions were located in the jungle, well-hidden about two hundred yards apart. He would be part of a detail manning one of the positions. There would be a mess tent back in the jungle.

Cord found plenty of time to look around the jungle and the beach. He discovered that there were pigs on the island, no other animals except some birds—he had hoped to see monkeys. The natives, Polynesians, were brown skinned people, darker than the Hawaiians he'd seen in pictures, but they were not black like Africans. Each family lived in a *fale,* one room constructed of coconut palm leaves woven and interlocked both for the walls and the roof, with an open space for a doorway.

Cord and three other men, Woodie, Benfer and Horseman—who, Cord noted, had a long, horse-like face—were positioned in the jungle on a gentle slope a quarter mile in from Gahi Bay. All four were in their twenties, all from the South. They manned an 80-mm mortar with a three-mile range, rotating their watch in six-hour shifts. The only daily connection the men had to the rest of the company was at the mess tent farther back in the jungle. There, Cord would find a spot to eat alone and spoke little with men from other posts. What was happening on other parts of the seven-mile long island, he didn't know.

Seven weeks into Wallis, Cord returned to the mortar position minutes before his guard duty began, an hour of daylight left, to find the post deserted. By now, the trail to the mess tent was well worn, but other lesser trails also led away from the mortar position. One led to the latrine, another to a bluff the men preferred to piss over, and yet another to a small clearing about thirty feet down the slope that Horseman and Benfer had groomed as a place to play cards and invent schemes. Cord checked all these destinations when he arrived at the post, but Woodie, Horseman, and Benfer were all missing. Concerned, but with no walkie talkie, and knowing his orders, Cord took his entire six-hour watch.

Afterward he followed the trail back to the mess tent, now worried that he'd made the wrong decision in keeping his watch instead of reporting the men missing. The tent was dark and quiet.

"Anybody here?" Cord called out. He heard a chair creak and then the sound of shoes shuffling on the soft dirt floor.

"Who is that?" a hoarse voice came from the darkness.

"Nobles, sir."

"Don't 'sir' me, asshole. What the hell are you doing here?" A battery powered lantern came on and Cord saw Sergeant Potter's face glowing over it.

"Benfer and Horseman and Woodie all gone missing."

"Missing? Where'd they go to?"

"Don't know. They's just gone."

"Shit. Where you think they went?"

"I don't know. Benfer and Horseman always cooking something up, no telling."

"But Woodie's gone, too?"

"Yeah."

"Shit."

Cord could tell Potter had been asleep on his watch and was now trying to orient himself. Potter was old, seemed to be in his forties, and had a likable lax attitude.

"You want me to go back and man the position, or...."

"Shut up, Nobles. I gotta think a minute."

Cord straddled a bench and watched Potter fumble around near the stove, pouring himself some coffee.

"Shit," Potter mumbled. "You better go look for them son of a bitches. Where you think they went?"

"I don't have no idea."

"Well what was they talking about today?"

"Talking about making liquor out of coconuts and talking about going swimming."

"Swimming in the ocean?"

"No, in that crater."

"Shit, they fell in that god damn crater and drowned. You know where it is?"

"I seen it once."

"Well, shit, what time is it?"

"One hundred hours."

"Go look at that crater and holler out for em."

"That thing's a damn mile away," Cord protested.

"Well, I thought you said you could find it. Can you or not?"

"I probably can."

"Go look for em and get back here before light, you understand?"

Cord took the battery powered lantern with him. He knew the general direction of the volcano crater, but it was through dense jungle unmarked and not navigable except by sensing the shallow slope of the terrain.

—

He found Woodie, Benfer, and Horseman marooned on a small rock jutting out of the freshwater lake in the volcano's cauldron about thirty feet out. Cord made his way down the steep, vine-snarled bank, and communicating across the water mostly with Horseman, learned they had been waiting for daylight before attempting to escape the crater. Benfer had been hit hard by a large electric eel and they hadn't been able to get him off the rock onto which they dragged him out of the water. Benfer was in pain and disoriented.

Cord swam out to the rock to demonstrate that the eels were not present in this part of the lake. "You can see the damn things glowing in the dark," he told them. "They all out there in the middle, not around the edges." Eventually he convinced Woodie and Horseman to swim to shore, and he dragged Benfer through the water, threatening to drown him if he didn't at least dog-paddle.

Benfer was sick, barely able to get through the jungle, but by first light Cord had led the men down to headquarters where they deposited Benfer at the infirmary, much to the annoyance of the personnel there.

—

Lieutenant Horton, a tanned, thin young man from Arizona whose small blond head looked like it would bald before he turned thirty, sent for Cord two days later. Cord was sure he would face some sort of reprimand or punishment regarding the volcano incident.

"At ease, for god's sake," Horton told him. "Sit down. Relax."

The lieutenant's tent was outfitted with native art. Mounted at the peak of the tent's rear wall, hung two *hele,* long metal knives the French had provided the natives in past decades, with their long blades crisscrossed. Cord was impressed.

Horton offered Cord a cigarette and lit it for him, and one for himself too. He eyed Cord and said, "Iletefoso tells me *Kotu kote tagata poto lahi aupito ite faahiga ote folau ite vau.* Is that the truth?"

"I don't know, sir. What does that mean?"

"It means my native man thinks you're pretty damn good in the jungle," Horton said.

"No sir."

"Bull*shit.* How'd you know how to get out there to that damn crater and back?"

"I don't know. I guess...." Cord trailed off.

Horton took a long drag on his cigarette. "Nobody else coulda found that fuckin' thing in the daytime, let alone middle of the night. Where you from anyway?"

"Texas."

"They have jungles in Texas?"

"No sir."

"What do they have in Texas?"

"Buncha prickly pears and mesquite trees."

"Sounds kinda like Arizona. I'm from Arizona. Ever been out there?"

"No, sir."

"How you likin' Wallis?"

"Fine, I guess."

"Yeah? You must be baggin' you some of that gook poontang."

"No, sir."

"I'll tell you what, Nobles, I got word that we got a Jap here on Wallis, radioing reports. How 'bout that?"

"I don't know."

"Well, I do know. We have to nail his yella ass. He was here long time before we got here, probably living with the gooks, probably has a buncha half-gook kids with some gook poontang by now. I don't know. I been asking around and nobody thinks they've seen any half-gook half-Jap looking gook children. You haven't, have you?"

Cord thought. "What would they look like?"

Horton laughed. "Hell if I know." He sat up, put his feet on the native mat that covered the floor. "Look Nobles, we're supposed to find this Jap and get him and his radio. He'll likely be in a *fale* somewhere on the island, and I bet his radio'll be hidden in there, too. He might look pretty much like a gook. These gooks are not any darker than a Jap, anyway."

Cord nodded, not knowing what to say, not knowing why he was here.

Horton stubbed out his smoke. "So, how about you lead a detail around the jungle and find some of these gooks. Look in their *fale* and see what you see."

"What if I was to find him?"

"Well, arrest the son of a bitch if you can, or else shoot him. Command'd rather have him to interrogate than to have him dead, but I guess you do whatever you have to. I'd have to guess he's got some kind of weapon on him, don't know what, though."

Cord needed to put out his cigarette and Horton saw this, handed him the ash tray, a yellow and brown striped clam shell. "You take this on, Nobles, we'd have to make you a corporal first so you can lead this detail."

Cord felt the blood in his temples. *A promotion.* He had never even considered such a possibility. He expelled a single short sound.

"What's so funny?" asked Horton. "How about it then, Corporal? Give you about three or four men. Not Horseman and Benfer and them. Buncha idiots. They're gonna get court-martialed for abandoning their post, you know that? Benfer is anyway. It was his watch. Who you want?"

"I don't know."

"Don't worry about it. I'll give you some good men."

Two days later Cord was promoted to Corporal. The strange tide of emotion returned to his head, trickled and then flooded all through his body, changing the way he walked, unfamiliar to himself, confusing but pleasant, more cigarettes than usual, appetite somewhat suppressed, his thinking no clearer than usual, but taking mysterious twists and turns. He thought a piece of gook poontang might not be a bad idea, and then mentally explored how that might come about. For all the bullshit talk he'd heard from Benfer and Horseman and in the mess tent, he couldn't recall anyone ever describing how they arranged to do it.

On his last day assigned to the mortar position, Cord blew cigarette smoke onto his forearms.

Wiley Woodie looked up from his book. "What the fuck are you doing, Nobles?"

"Puttin' smoke on me. Keeps the damn *unamoos* off."

Woodie gazed at Cord for a moment, bemused. "That works?"

"I don't know. It might."

Woodie snorted and returned to his book.

Horseman was on watch, out of earshot. Benfer was in the stockade. Cord had decided that if anybody would bag some poontang, it would be someone like Woodie, a smart guy. "You must like that book a lot," Cord said.

Woodie didn't look up, but pumped his hand up and down a few times.

Cord paced around the small clearing, glanced up to the mortar.

"It's not too hard to get that gook poontang," Cord offered carefully. Woodie ignored him. Feeling even more awkward, Cord added, "If you want it, you can sure get it."

Woodie put down his book. "Nobles, what do you want? Advice?"

"I'm listening," Cord said.

"Listen good, then, Corporal sir," Woodie said. "Go fuck yourself. Probably the best lay you're ever gonna get."

—

Cord and his detail went out every day for weeks, poking around the jungle, looking into every *fale* they came across. With rain falling and the sun shining at the same time, Cord and his men were four miles from HQ one morning, following the beach and making forays into the jungle any time they found footprints across the sand, smoke rising from the forest, a fresh pile of fish offal, or other evidence.

"Smoke," said the kid they called Punky, a dark, short mesomorphic Bostonian. He pointed to a spot in the jungle where white smoke rose from the foliage.

They moved down the beach, but no trail into the jungle was apparent. Wet and complaining about it, the four men chose a more circuitous route toward the smoke. Once they were uphill of it, they edged along the ridge of the gentle slope. As Cord had suspected, they came across a trail.

"Take this trail back down," Cord whispered, "and we'll hit the *fale*. This ain't like them other set ups. Trail shoulda gone down, not up. Let's see if this ain't that old Jap living here. We'll cut on down the trail a little ways, but then let's spread out and me and Punky'll come up to the front and Corcoran you and Buford get stationed right behind the hut in case he tries to bust out that way. Let's check them rifles now before we go."

It was a good plan, better than necessary. The Jap, an old man wearing a lavalava, was finishing a meal of roasted fish. They found his radio in a hole under the floor mat.

—

Cord returned to his mortar position, and Sergeant Potter, inexplicably annoyed, ordered him to have Horseman and Benfer dig a latrine in a designated area some two-hundred feet from the mess tent.

Horseman was on watch, so Cord conveyed the orders first to Woodie.

"That son of a bitch," Woodie spat. "He's pissed off because those clowns couldn't make that coconut liquor. *Shit.*"

Woodie trudged up to tell Horseman, and Cord heard Horseman swearing and threatening to cut off Potter's nuts.

Heavy with trepidation, Cord joined Woodie and Horseman. They were smoking, sitting in front of the mortar on a rock where there was a clear vista of the ocean below.

"Hey, Corporal sir," Horseman said in a friendly tone. "We just getting ready to dig you a latrine. Planning it all out now."

"Then we're gonna kiss your ass," Woodie added, flicking his butt into the vegetation below.

"I'll show you where Potter wants it dug tomorrow," Cord said. He left the men sitting there, took a little walk into the jungle.

With a new man, Hauptman, on watch the next afternoon, Cord reported to Potter with Woodie and Horseman in tow. Woodie said he was too sick to dig, and Potter threatened him with the stockade. Horseman acquiesced along with Woodie. Cord stayed at the mess tent, checking on the men's progress every half hour.

At first, Horseman made a show of working when Cord approached, and Woodie lit a cigarette and said he was taking a momentary break. But then all pretense of work stopped, and Cord found himself caught between the men and Potter, who was swearing loudly about the situation and emphasizing that it was Cord's responsibility to make these men obey orders.

On his fourth trip out to the latrine site, Cord found Woodie and Horseman lying on the ground, hands locked behind their heads, puffing cigarettes. No work had been done in the last half hour.

"You men," Cord said. "I see what's going on."

"You do?" inquired Woodie. "You mean, you just now figuring out that we're digging a latrine?"

"No," Cord's steady voice belied his anger. "Naw, I see you're both goofin' off."

"What?" Horseman said, oozing incredulity.

"So, I tell you what," Cord said, "Y'all get off your lazy asses right now and dig that latrine, and that way I won't have to kick your lazy asses all the way down to that... that...." He meant to say stockade, but couldn't remember the word.

Horseman laughed, comfortable, not bothering to look at Cord. Woodie decided to play it indignant, but never got the chance, because he was the first man Cord grabbed. Taken by surprise, Woodie found himself up, and then aloft, and then hard on the ground where the few shovel marks had marred the designated site of the latrine. He landed on a shovel, the blade of which pressed into his ribs.

Horseman just had time to sit up. Cord had his shirt at the collar and smashed his fist into Horseman's elongated face, knocking him straight back to the ground. Woodie was holding his side, moaning in pain, when Cord approached him, picked up the shovel and held it high over his head. Woodie looked up, his eyes widening.

"No, don't hit me."

His shaking voice full of rage, Cord replied, "Then get your god damn ass up and dig this latrine."

"I'm digging," Woodie cried out. "Shit, I'm digging." Favoring the pain in his ribs, he picked up the other shovel.

Cord moved to Horseman who struggled to his knees, stunned but conscious. Cord threw the shovel hard at the ground in front of Horseman. It bounced once and hit Horseman on the thigh. "Shit!"

Cord moved behind him, placed his foot square on the kneeling man's back and shoved him, sprawling him to the very ground that needed digging. Face purple, Cord growled, "Y'all give me any more shit I'll come back out here and I swear to god I'll split your heads open." The men were petrified. *"Git to work."*

They began shoveling.

Cord stalked away, back to the mess tent, where Potter was brewing some coffee.

—

Benfer and Horseman were cowards, and even Cord, with his limited acumen, had gathered that they joined the Marines to avoid unpleasant consequences for actions involving, in Benfer's case, bootlegging, and in Horseman's, a fourteen-year-old girl. As for Woodie, Cord knew little about his past. None of the three were Marine material, that was clear. Cord's sudden display of tyranny, however, was not enough for Potter. He had no intention of letting the matter drop, and Cord became convinced that the money he'd advanced for the failed brewery enterprise was the cause.

When Potter took Cord out to inspect the latrine after Woodie and Horseman were back at their gun position, he spit into it and proclaimed they had dug it running east and west and that it had to run north and south. Cord would have to make the men dig the latrine again the next day.

—

By the time the Marines had occupied Wallis for six months, with no action, Cord had rotated away from Horseman, Woodie, and Hauptman, though he sometimes ran into Woodie in the mess tent and found that he could talk with him.

"You still trying to get some gook poontang, Nobles?"

Cord had not even thought on the subject for months. "No. You can't get it without getting yaws, too."

"If you're stupid, that's true," Woodie said, and scooped up a spoonful of chili, chewed thoughtfully.

"Why? What about if you're smart?"

"There's a lot of us getting plenty of it. Not getting no god damn yaws neither. You just have to know how."

"How do you do it, then?"

Woodie shook his head. "No. We some of us worked pretty hard to figure this out. There's a lot of valuable details that if command gets ahold of, we're all going to be beating the meat again."

Valuable. Cord figured this meant it would cost money. "How valuable?" he asked.

"We've let a few guys in the club for forty dollars," Woodie said, and took the last bite of his chili, chasing it down with a crust of white bread. "Don't get no ideas, though, Nobles. You're not club material."

"Why not?"

"You're too god damn dumb. First time some officer asks you about it, you'll tell everything you know."

"I'm not too god damn dumb, Woodie. I don't need y'all's help. Not for no forty dollars I don't."

Woodie pulled out his pack of cigarettes and offered one to Cord.

"Thanks."

"Well, Nobles, if you change your mind, let me know. I'm not going to charge you shit. We don't charge anything anymore. But you have to take an oath not to tell anybody about it unless you consult with the rest of us first."

"Who's the rest of you?"

"Can't tell you that until you already had you some gook tail so you'd be as guilty as the rest of us."

—

Cord spotted Woodie, Horseman, and some other men eight days later outside HQ near a Quonset hut used for supply storage. As he approached, Woodie saw him and stepped away from the group to intercept him.

"Hey Nobles, we're trying to have a private meeting here."

Cord looked at the men, knew Horseman and recognized two others, didn't know the other two. "This your poontang club?"

Woodie made a show of looking around furtively, placed his hand on Cord's shoulder and whispered, "Shut the fuck up, Nobles. What the hell's wrong with you?" At a distance from the Quonset hut, Woodie stopped under a pandanus tree and faced Cord. "Look, we were discussing you. Horseman was saying you have a big mouth and we couldn't let you in. I was telling the guys you know how to keep quiet. I just about had them convinced. The question is, are you willing to keep this to yourself if we let you in?"

"If I was in, I'd keep my mouth shut," Cord said, unsure. "*If* I wanted in," he added.

Woodie looked him in the eye. "Well, do you want in or not?"

Cord turned away, took out a cigarette and lit it, squinted back at Woodie. "If what you was saying is true, no money involved, and them girls is pretty, then I do want in."

Woodie smiled broadly. "Oh, they're pretty all right, but you ain't going to care one bit about that. And like I said, this is not a business. It's a way to get some social interaction with the natives."

—

Another week passed, then several more days. Woodie had told Cord he would come get him when they had a *fafine* for him, and not to be beating off in the meantime because there was no telling when the time might come. The time came at midnight, as Cord was finishing his guard duty at the mortar position. Horseman was waiting at the tent, smoking a cigarette.

"Nobles, I hope you ain't been flogging your log up on that lookout."

"No. Why?"

"Why you think? Come on with me to the club house. Time for a little R and R."

Cord followed Horseman into the jungle, tired but excited. Horseman led them to a spot sheltered by an outcropping of volcanic rock overhanging a depression in which Woodie and another man were huddled outside a structure the size of an outhouse cobbled together from some corrugated tin, canvas, and planks of scrap wood. The scene was lit by a weak electric lantern.

"Where's that gook poontang?"

"In the boudoir," Woodie indicated the structure with a sweeping gesture, then turned toward it, "Y'all ready in there?"

Cord heard a male voice answer *Ready.*

"That ain't no gook," Cord said.

"They in there holding her, that's all," Woodie explained.

"I ain't doing no rape," Cord said. "They'll throw y'all in the stockade and kick you out of the corps."

"Shit, Nobles, just go in there. It ain't rape. She's the one wanted to do this. You'll see. The thing is, she's shy and won't let us see her."

"What do you mean?"

"See, these gook women, they don't have no morals against doing it, but it's against their religion for the man to see them. So what we got here, is you go in there, and them guys will guide you in the dark to a hole in that piece of canvas that protects you from yaws. And on the other side of that hole, the prettiest little fafine, about nineteen years old, Nobles, is on her hands and knees with that poontang pushed right up to that hole, waiting for you."

Just dying for you to satisfy her, the voice from within the boudoir added.

"Go on, Nobles," Woodie winked. "We ain't got all night."

Cord pushed aside the canvas covering the narrow ingress and found himself in a tiny, humid, reeking cavity in total darkness. From the movement there, he realized there were two men. One of them urged him to drop his pants and get to his knees. He quickly became so excited that he began demanding, "Give 'er here. Where is she? Give 'er here!" One of the men laughed, told him to calm down, and helped him find the hole in the canvas. The poontang on the other side shifted, guided by prods from the two men until Cord found what he wanted. She accepted him in a bucking, violent way, it seemed to Cord, and she squealed and grunted with what must have been lust during his assault. She grunted and squealed, not like a girl Cord might have imagined, but with animal lust, squealing, grunting, bucking, until Cord was satisfied.

—

The Japs never came within a thousand miles of Wallis. Eleven months after landing at Wallis, Cord shipped out with the other Marines, destined for New Caledonia. In the landing craft, on the way out to the transport ship, he saw swine rooting in the surf. He never saw action, and when the war was over, he was shipped to San Francisco, a city much too cold for Cord. He was glad to be out of the Marine Corps, had no use for it ever again, and never felt the least bit faithful to it.

29

EVEN THOUGH I HAVEN'T ACQUIRED my raging teenage hormones yet, I'm thinking about Joyce Heffernan all the time. I'm wondering if what I feel is love without the physical part of it. But that seems incorrect because there actually is a physical part to it. When I think about her, I go off into a daydream, and I want to hug her and kiss her. I don't know what sex will feel like exactly, but I think I have part of it going for me already. Papa has told me that you do have these feelings at my age, and that I'm normal.

It's possible I could grow up and marry Joyce. It's not likely, I guess, because so much will happen before I grow up. Indeed, I can tell you that I will not marry her. But I would like it if it did work out, because she is so nice, and I think marrying a nice person would make life better. My parents are both nice and they seem to have a good life. Papa told me life can be happy even if your earlier life was bad. He said that would be a Hollywood ending, and contrary to conventional wisdom, Hollywood endings can happen in real life.

Joyce sits two rows up from me and one row over. I can see her hair and usually the side of her face. It's probably good that I can't see her eyes, because they are somewhat sleepy looking and for some reason that makes her even prettier. I don't think I could get much work done at school if I could see her from the front all the time. One time she wore a dress to school and I liked that. The main time you see girls my age in dresses is when they're in a play and it's their costume.

When Joyce was absent a long time, I learned something about time passing. She was gone way too long for the "death in the family" excuse, and Mama and I speculated that something else was going on.

Mom would sometimes ask me after school if Joyce was still absent, and that made me aware of the time passing. I was getting more and more worried about Joyce. But then, after a few weeks, I was thinking about her less and less. Then suddenly, after about a month, I started worrying about her all over again.

The problem was that her parents were divorcing and having fights. Social Services finally stepped in and put Joyce back into school. Now I'm trying to see if she acts any different, but I'm also trying not to let it affect the way I act with her. Not that we interact much anyway, but I observe her.

Can a ten-year-old be in love? What would it mean at this age? I asked Papa. He assured me that love is subjective, and that the answer to the first question is yes. As for the second question, he suspects the differences between a ten-year-old's being in love and a twenty-something's is mostly a matter of degrees. The younger lover would be operating with a lesser degree of physical attraction—although not so much less as you might think. The older lover would be encumbered by more life experience, meaning a degree of cynicism brought to the emotional mix, although a ten-year-old could be just as capable of jealousy and other insecurities.

Though I don't know it now, I will have forgotten all about Joyce by the time I finish high school. I'll have been infatuated with Karen Caldclieu and then Esbeidy Goetz, and fallen in love with the latter at age seventeen. A decade or so later, I'll have completed two university degrees and have a pregnant wife—not Esbeidy. I won't have gone into rocketry or any other science, and I will have felt pangs of regret about that sometimes. But I'll also know that my true talent and calling is in the liberal arts. For this I will good-naturedly blame my parents, and much later, when they are almost no longer able to prepare the whole Thanksgiving dinner for all of us, we'll joke about it together. Right, I won't be without my regrets and complaints, but I'll be fine with myself and my life.

Just to clarify, my omniscience is not a function of my life in linear time. If you ask me, in the distant future on the day I die, what Papa's relationship with his aunt Leah was, I will not know what you are talking about. Papa will never have discussed it with me beyond a few mentions of her in regards to their growing up together for a time. I'll have seen a couple or three faded color photos of her, so I'll know she was pretty, but I won't have an inkling there was ever anything special between her and Papa.

—

In his senior year at the University of Texas, Leo managed to pull his GPA up enough that he was accepted at Southwest Texas State to pursue an MFA in Theater Production. With that degree in hand, he was able to find temporary teaching positions and residencies in a string of high schools and community colleges. Leah attached herself to him, took on the heavy lifting of sending out Leo's resume and researching job opportunities for both of them, and they moved as a couple from town to town, job to job. In1984 Leo finally found a permanent position at Lanier High School in suburban Chicago, and he moved there without Leah, announcing to her that this was the time for them to part ways. The principal at Lanier, Mr. McQuain, was at his mother's funeral when the hiring board signed Leo on. Though he said nothing, McQuain felt slighted because he had not signed off on Leo Nobles before the hire became official.

The students assembling in the auditorium were the troupe Leo would guide through the new semester. Most had chosen the Thespian Club enthusiastically, but there were always a few other kids who had been unmotivated in choosing an elective, but shunned study hall, and would end up in the Thespian Club, resentful and sullen.

He sat on a high stool, down center stage. He'd placed a work light up left and dimmed it to half, just for the drama of the light atop the stark black pole. He had lit himself with bastard amber and lavender from the catwalk and an even mix from the foots. He watched the students filing in, seniors and juniors confident, jaded, cool, and sophomores more tentative, eligible for the first time because Freshmen were required to take Study Hall. Watching them, he was being watched, and that was his intention. Otherwise he would have been sitting down front facing the stage instead of on the stage, posing in the light. It would be their first little lesson from him, unspoken. Take the focus if you want the focus. This was Leo's third year teaching at Lanier.

The bell rang, the group seated already, quiet, studying Leo. He was studying them. How many male, how many female? About even. How many blacks? Only one, a female. Always a shortage of blacks for some reason. Going to do the Athol Fugard this year anyway. How many altogether? About twenty-five.

Geneve appeared at the top of the aisle, entering from the senior wing and creating in Leo the false impression that she was a senior, an impression he'd have trouble correcting.

"Come in. You're late." He waved her down the aisle. Geneve's apparition stunned Leo, and that surprised him. He had seen plenty of pretty high school girls. Why was this one special? How was she special? He made himself take his eyes off her and look again at the group. He'd forgotten what he was about to say. He found himself mute. He pretended to be waiting for the girl to take a seat, but the truth was he was speechless. She was gorgeous.

"At the downstage left corner of the apron, there's a clipboard on the floor. It has a piece of paper on it. There are lines on the paper. Please pass that down. I need everyone to print your first name, last name, class and homeroom teacher's name, all on one line. What is your name, sir?"

"Kirk Johnson."

"I'm Leo Nobles, but you can call me by my nickname, Mr. Nobles." Good, a gentle laugh from all. "Kirk, since you're closest to that downstage left corner of the apron, would you grab the clipboard and fill in your information and pass it on." Learn by doing. None of the kids knew what an apron was, or what downstage left meant. But they were already learning.

As soon as the clipboard was progressing down the front row, Leo allowed himself to glance at Geneve, who was seated on the third row by herself, the first and second rows being more or less filled. She was looking at him and when she didn't look away, all he could do was give her a smile, which she didn't return, and still didn't look away.

"Once you've signed the clip board, go ahead and take out a piece of paper, put your name on it, and write me a letter. I want to know your interests, what you know and/ or think about theater, what you think about Ronald Reagan," he scored a gentle laugh here, all was well, "what you think about the Bears," no reaction at all, good, Leo wasn't much interested in sports himself, "any opinions you have about plays, particularly any you'd like to be involved in, because we will be doing a one-act play as well as many scenes from other sources."

—

Weeks passed, adds and drops ended, the roll stabilized. The new Thespians learned *up, down, left, right, plaster line, apron,* and dozens of other terms. It was a good group, some scholars, some talent, and even a couple or three males who could pass for masculine. Geneve took notes using a cartridge fountain pen, which for some reason, Leo felt, made her more interesting, deeper.

No fool, Leo was careful to hide his fascination with Geneve. He did have the opportunity to feast his eyes on her when she recited her monologue from *Barefoot in the Park.* He caught himself formulating the opinion that her presentation revealed the tip of a huge iceberg of acting talent.

What horseshit! Leo stopped himself, again, from inventing reasons, excuses, to act as though she was any different from the other babies he taught. She was different by virtue of her physical beauty, a chance of birth, nothing to do with her individual worth or her personality. She was a B student, beautiful student, bored student. B cups, tasty laceful. The same ingenuousness and awkward, tactless manner he found so beguiling in her, he would have disdained in every other girl in his tutelage because none of them were such dreams to look upon.

Still he couldn't resist subtracting her age from his, 33 minus 17 is 16. *She was born when I was about her age. When I'm fifty she'll be what... 34. When I'm 49 she'll be 33. Can that be right?*

Pamela Peterson, the black girl, approached him from the wing. "Mr. Nobles, we need to talk," she stated. As usual, her tone indicated she was calling him to the carpet. It no longer alarmed him.

"What's happening, Pam?"

"I don't see how we can do *Sizwe Bonzie is Dead* with white actors."

"Really? What's your take on it?"

"I talked with Mom and Dad about it last night and they agree. They think you're trying to make a statement that won't be made, and so do I."

"You mean, a statement other than what the play is saying?"

"By using white actors, yeah."

Leo put down the clipboard he'd been holding, hopped down off the stage and plopped onto a first row chair. Pamela dropped to the stage floor, dangled her legs off the apron.

"I didn't have a statement in mind, Pam," Leo said. "Other than the playwright's message. I did think about what kind of impression it would make, using white actors, but I didn't think it would make a statement, you know?"

"Well, maybe it does, is what I'm saying."

Leo nodded. "You know what? You're right. It might make a statement to some people. Maybe a lot of people. I don't even want to think about what it might say to some people. Let's don't do it."

Pamela stopped swinging her legs and her mouth dropped open. "But we're in rehearsal already. I was just...."

"No, you're right," Leo said. At the weekly teachers meeting in which Leo had announced his choice of *Sizwe Bonzi* for the one act play, there had been some discussion and a consensual, if not enthusiastic, approval among the faculty, most of whom didn't know the play anyway. But it was McQuain's silence, his looking away as though uninvolved, that Leo now remembered. He'd gone away from that meeting with some niggling trepidation. "If you and your parents have a problem, Pam, then others might, too. Probably would."

"I wasn't saying we have a problem with it, exactly."

"Well, you were saying something, Pam."

She started swinging her legs again.

"Down front," Leo shouted, startling Pamela. Then, to her, "Go backstage and round everybody up."

I guess she thinks I'm going to embarrass her, make it look like she's the reason I'm canceling the production. Only two weeks into rehearsal. The actors are abysmal. Pam has a good point, too.

Leo announced the cancellation of *Sizwe Bonzie is Dead* at the next teachers meeting. He asked McQuain directly for his reaction. The principal—appeased, Leo suspected—accepted Leo's reasoning regarding rumblings of discontent from unidentified black sources they both knew to be the Petersons. He was amenable also to excusing Leo's original misjudgment, well-intentioned as it had been. *Sizwe* was dead, William Saroyan's *The Cave Dwellers* would be cut to one-act length forthwith.

Days later Leo was in Cicero, waiting in the car to pick up Leah at her job in the squat, re-faced Merchants Mart Building, now housing *Mejía Servicios Financieros* and the candy wholesaler where Leah worked. He wondered about some subconscious motive he might have harbored in changing the play. Geneve was not involved in *Sizwe* except as a house crew member. She was cast in *Cave*, however, as The Girl. And he knew that he'd manipulated the casting of that part, even though he'd involved the whole company in the casting process. Geneve had a rather modest bust, he reasoned to himself at the time, which could be bound, no problem, so she could play the girl. Hardest to overlook was her substantial height. Pamela Peterson, a tiny girl, would have been more convincing, and in this case her race would have scored a point for color-blindness without affecting the meaning of the play.

In the Pontiac Astre station wagon's still, interior air, with a good ten minutes wait ahead of him, he fell into a detached consciousness. He had become comfortable with

Leah. Where his struggle—which he had sometimes regarded as a moral one—had resided, he now sensed a stale, fetid, and fatigued animus that he habitually avoided. This private infatuation with an untouchable schoolgirl was some perverse attempt at distancing himself from that scary animus—scary because it would not die unless he did, too.

"Watch out," Leo murmured to himself as he relived Geneve delivering her line, "I've come back for my man, if he'll have me."

"Things are not the way they should be, are they?" Leo said to the steering wheel. He thought of Cord, the missing father, and was wondering if he was alive, the heavy smoker, sixty-five now, and if alive, where he might be. And then he saw Leah emerging from the refurbished old building where she worked as order processor.

—

Leo had named Pamela Peterson Student Director. She had accepted the honor and taken on the job with enthusiasm. But now, three weeks into rehearsal and two weeks from opening, she sat on the third row sulking as Leo had seized the reins and was directing the play himself. When Leo interrupted the scene to give The Duke a direction, Geneve broke character and shifted her weight to one leg, jutting the opposite hip.

"Remember you're a boxer, an ex-champ of the ring," Leo told Robbie Ferguson. "Those boxing skills, all you know, they're useless when you're dealing with a little girl. You have to reach way down inside and find some gentleness, and it's hard for you."

"It *is* hard," Robbie said, and a few stage hands chuckled.

"But we need to see the struggle. And remember what we learned about indicating."

"Not to do it," said Robbie by rote.

"Find it inside," Leo told him. "When you find it, it'll find its way out. Don't try to act it. Just find it."

Geneve took a deep, audible breath, something close to a sigh.

Robbie jutted his jaw, glanced at his impatient partner, the one who never seemed to get any direction but *indicated* having to put up with the ineptitude of the other actors. "Maybe I could find something deep inside if Geneve looked a little more like a girl instead of a star."

Leo checked himself, aware that Geneve had been affecting the look of an actress more and more as the weeks of rehearsal had gone by. She wore a loose white men's shirt, untucked, tails falling to her knees. Her pants were black and tapered to a tight fit at the ankles. "What," she said to Leo, who was looking her over.

"Fine," Leo said to Robbie. He jumped up onto the stage, approached Geneve, giving her an appraising frown. "What if we tuck in the shirt, leave it baggy but not out. Would that help?"

"I don't know," Robbie murmured. "Would that affect her *attitude?*"

Leo let the comment die. Geneve was already tucking in the shirt.

"No," Leo said. "Not all the way in. Leave it baggy. Here...." and he stood behind her and tucked the shirttail in for her, leaving it baggy, not seeing the tickled faces Geneve was mugging at the others until a half dozen Thespians broke out laughing.

McQuain was standing unseen at the back of the auditorium, having arrived just when Leo began tucking in Geneve's shirt.

Leo, embarrassed by the laughter, turned red and snapped, "Come on. What the hell is so funny?" Geneve, to break the sudden dark silence, turned around to Leo and ran her hands up around his neck, saying "Nothin' honey," and another round of laughter erupted.

McQuain slipped out of the auditorium, but the movement caught Robbie's eye. "Mr. Nobles," he said, "did you know McQuain was back there watching?"

Leo looked out to the auditorium.

"No, he left just now," Robbie said.

After a pause so brief that no one noticed it, Leo said, "So, let's take it from your last line, Duke. And remember, dealing with this little girl is like you're an alligator trying to arrange flowers in a vase. You don't have the skills, don't have the background, never had to try before. Get it?"

30

LANIER WAS STILL NEWISH, BUILT in the seventies. McQuain's office retained the smell of paint, the same smell that mixed with the noxious ones in the cafeteria, and the chemical ones in the restrooms, and the sweaty, pulpy, metallic, contraband ones in the locker bays. McQuain had chosen diplomas and one framed photo of himself in high school football gear—less helmet—as adornment for his walls. No plants, no aquarium—not even lingering aroma of the privilege of pipe smoke. He was a clean machine, Leo noted, sitting uncomfortably in the chair in front of McQuain's cherrywood desk.

In the light from the window it was hard to discern colors. The sky had clouded over. Why did the principal's office have a view of the student parking lot?

Leo stared into the spot of light reflecting off the polished brass base of the piano lamp on the desk. All of the world, as allowed by the window to the outside, was concentrated onto the convex surface into a spot the size and shape of the little snail shells Leo used to find in the dirt along the underpinning of the house, in the hidden area on the side of the unliked neighbor, where he was not supposed to play. He would be punished.

"You could fight it," McQuain said. "You would go to the school board first, I think. Next would be a lawsuit."

"What would you do in my place?"

"It would depend on what I wanted. If I wanted to save face, I wouldn't fight the dismissal, because fighting it would have the opposite effect. Bring it out in public. As it stands now, you and I can work together on keeping the terms of dismissal worded in a way that might even let you go to another school, start over. The other thing you might want is to try and prove you didn't do what you did, have a clean record, so to speak. But that gets back to a big public airing. Depends on what's most important to you."

"Or I could find the people who reacted the way they did and try to talk some sense into them. I didn't do anything wrong."

McQuain was still and silent for several moments before he heaved a great sigh. "Well," he said, "you're talking to the one who saw what happened. You can talk all the sense you want to into me, it's not going to change what I saw." He shifted in his chair, pushing it backward, hiking his ankle to his knee, pulled down a sock and scratched. "Look, Leo, I can't get into personalities and I certainly can't mention the names of any students or their parents. Let me say this. I'm not unaware that a seventeen-year-old girl can emanate sexual signals in a big way. The teens are when a woman is supposed to breed, in nature—if we weren't civilized, you know. The cloud of phemorones around some of those young women are like thunderheads. Doesn't take much imagination to see them extending all the way down the hall, all the way out into the parking lot." He pulled his sock back up, uncrossed the legs, leaned a little toward Leo. "I understand this, and I know it takes extraordinary discipline, as a teacher, as a person in a position of power and privilege. It takes a particular kind of strength to put that cloud of phemorones out of your mind. You don't mind me using that kind of figurative language, do you?"

Leo had been staring at his own feet. *Phemorones? This guy is a high school principal, for god's sake!* He looked up and saw McQuain staring at him, wide-eyed, waiting for a reply. It had been a plea for commiseration, Leo realized. Obscure, muffled, oblique, yes, but the man is asking me to commiserate. He wants me *with* him in the face of the temptation. Laughable, under the circumstances. Embarrassing under any.

"Figurative language?" Leo said. "I don't think it's... I don't think you really mean it figuratively, do you?"

McQuain leaned back in his chair, locked his hands behind his head. "Phemorones are real, of course."

He is firing me unilaterally. He would love it if I fought it—get the whole school board in on it. He would also love it if I cowered and slunk away and disappeared. He's loving this no matter what I do. He hates me because he has always known that guys like me try and succeed to get what guys like him, the lumpy jocks, cannot. He may not know this, may not have a clue. He seems to think he's doing his righteous duty. But he is so hot for all the teenage pussy in this place, and his heat is so deeply buried and inaccessible that it can only come out this way—fire the drama teacher because he was putting his hands on the babe and she was giggling. Giggling. That's what he saw. I was putting my hands down her ridiculous pegs and she was giggling and he hates me because he can't do that. He never has been able to, never will be able to, and he has put himself in the position of watching the clouds of pheromones—phemorones!—smelling them every day of his life, and righteously holding himself back, holding himself back, holding himself back.

I don't have a chance here.

"I guess there is one other alternative," McQuain said, taking Leo by surprise.

"What would that be?"

He breathed again, this time not so much a sigh, not so much resignation, but a contemplation. He seemed to be asking himself if this new possible alternative was even worth mentioning.

"Taking into account that you're not married…. That's right, isn't it? You're not married, are you?"

"No. I live with my aunt."

"Live with your aunt, that's right," McQuain nodded, remembering the earlier conversation, the initial interview or whatever.

"She happened to land a job in this area a few months after I came, so as an expedient…."

"No, that's fine," McQuain interrupted. "This shouldn't be touchy. Let me just say it. If you convinced me you were not interested, sexually, in that type of person who is represented here as the victim of your… aggression…." He trailed off, but then continued. "Look, Leo, I can't mention any names of students in this conversation. You understand that, right?"

"Yes, I get that."

"If you came out with the argument, as I was saying, that you have no interest in…."

"…girls…."

McQuain nodded. "You get the idea. The parent would not even need to sit down and talk with you. He'd accept it and it would all go away. That would blow the case against you. But it would blow, let's say, everything else, too. You have plenty of legal protection in that area. You would keep your job here, with nothing more than a mild verbal reprimand for laying your hands on a student."

Leo was not sure whether to dignify the suggestion with a response, but also didn't want to let it ripen in the mortifying air of this office and begin to look like an option. "I'm not gay, McQuain."

"I more or less felt I should air that option. Had nothing to do with my conception of you. I never thought you were gay or even considered it, but it was a possibility, and I wasn't sure I wouldn't have been remiss. Well, fine. That was the only other thing. Leo, I'm sorry for this."

"Okay. Are we done here?"

"Stay," McQuain said, "please, if you don't mind."

Leo checked his feelings and surprised himself. He didn't mind staying. He was in no hurry. He wasn't sure what he was feeling about McQuain. Pity? Improbable. Anger? More likely. And yet what was this sense of relief? How did that make any sense? He was going to have to think about what was to happen next. That was daunting, so why the relief?

"I want to say, Leo, it's been a hard decision, a very hard thing for me to do."

Squirm if you like, McQuain. I don't mind. But what do you want from me?

"Hard decision?" Leo said, inviting McQuain to squirm a bit more if he felt the need. McQuain, small but mesomorphic with a bulbous head, a thin mustache covering the wormy line of his upper lip, placed his fingertips together and gazed leftward and downward toward the floor.

"Well, deciding between firing you or letting you resign at the end of the term."

Trying not to slip into sarcasm, but having a difficult time under the circumstances, Leo said, "I guess that must have been tough. I guess."

"Well look, Leo," and McQuain shifted forward in his chair, an appeal for attention in case Leo was tuning him out. "I was thinking it could be more like letting you quit at the end of the term, but then I find out the word is out. The word is out among the parents. I mean, it was inevitable, I guess, but I was hoping the kids'd have some fun with it and it'd stay here at school. But that doesn't happen. That's not the way it goes, Leo. This is a small community, not Chicago. Did you think this was Chicago? Because it's not. Nothing stays here, it all goes home. I mean fast. You know that. Don't you know that?"

"I guess so," Leo felt he was being generous to let McQuain rave on, and yet he himself still felt no particular inclination to get up and walk out.

"Physical contact with even the hint of sexual meaning is absolutely unacceptable. That is spelled out in the contract," McQuain proclaimed, and leaned back now in his chair, projecting a sense of finality and regret.

"Sexual contact? *What?*"

"I saw what was happening, Leo. I was standing at the back of the auditorium."

"Then you know that what you saw was nothing. Unless you somehow got the wrong impression because you missed the context."

"No, I saw the context. I'm chagrined to be firing you because you're a talented drama teacher." Here he looked Leo in the eye. "I think, in fact, you could do well in Chicago, you wouldn't even have to move. Or New York. Directing, acting. But teaching? In a small town like this...." He shook his head and looked at the polished cherrywood of his desk top.

Leo considered for a moment. "Which parent has gotten involved?"

"I can't talk about that."

But Leo was pretty sure someone had exerted pressure, not merely a complaint, but a demand with clout behind it. Would it be Geneve's father, whom he had not met but disliked because Geneve had so freely let her contempt for him be known? It didn't matter. Leo was fired. Two weeks' notice, officially, but with permission to leave now, and a strong suggestion to do so. Leo stood up, felt the blood leave his head, the room go a little dark, not enough to cause him to pass out. He waited for his vision to clear. "You know, McQuain, you're a fucking ignorant jock. You have no business being in this office. You're not doing your job."

"Okay, Leo, don't make things...."

"I wonder if you even realize you're a closet homosexual."

"Great. I'm striking these comments from my memory because I understand how you must...."

"No, don't do that. Remember what I'm telling you. You're in the principal's chair because you're too damn dumb to actually teach anything. You're exactly the kind of stupid bubba we used to make fun of when I was in high school."

"All right, Leo. Get out of here before you say something I can't overlook."

"I am out of here. Fuck you, McQuain."

As Leo turned to make his exit, McQuain added, "Good luck ever teaching again, Mr. Nobles."

To which Leo tossed a middle finger over his shoulder, back toward McQuain.

—

His routine was to take the city bus home after school unless rehearsals went late, in which case sometimes he had Leah pick him up in the car. Today he would walk, the route mostly along Nasali Avenue, the wide, straight throughway that ran from the south side of Chicago all the way down past Chicago Heights and Forest Park. As bland a landscape as America had to offer, it would afford Leo the long contemplation he needed, the chance to find the distance to the ground. At first, he couldn't. At a curb, he came close to falling down. His back hurt. Twenty minutes into the walk, he pulled himself into an erect posture, and after a while he fell into a safe rhythm, his feet reaching the ground right where the ground started.

I feel disdain, cynicism? Yes, and superiority that is actually nothing more than a way of insulating myself from my real reaction of anger, outrage at the injustice. If I really felt superior, I would have defended myself, told McQuain where to get off, to go ahead, try and make me leave, see what all I might bring out about him and his pheromones. Phemorones, for God's sake. The guy is a joke, and I cowered. I cowered and then I cracked, self-destructed. I never let the real situation even touch me. I sat there all superior. What is going on? What am I?

Leo tried to rethink what had happened since he first saw Geneve walk into the auditorium, but it was all fragments. How obvious had his attraction been? Had there been gossip? Had he been blind to the hints Geneve dropped about her father, his new wife, the unhappy circumstance of his bribing Geneve with the promise of a car? He'd had too many after-rehearsal conversations with her–that he saw now. What had her father wanted but for her to do well and accept her stepmother? What was Geneve really after? *Did she sacrifice me to get it?* His thoughts wandered back to the event in question. *Had* he groped Geneve? Had his attraction to her overwhelmed his will, over-ridden his self-control? His hands found what they wanted, a nice warm feel of Geneve's luscious buns. So was it worth it?

There I go, working my ass off to somehow twist things around so I am to blame. The only crime I'm guilty of is not kicking McQuain's ass, if I was going to be fired anyway. Tell the son of a bitch off. Phemorones. You stupid dickhead.

Leo hated himself. As he passed into areas with gaps between buildings, the afternoon sun threw punches, made him perspire. He quickened his pace, lost control of his thoughts, which wandered to the bathroom, the cool green floor, the waiting for the all-powerful man who would whip him, bringing blinding tears, unbearable pain, inscrutable humiliation that would wrap itself around his skeleton and infest his body.

He was walking home from school. Yes, with two friends, Fred, a new boy who was

easy to talk to, and Naomi, who lived two blocks on down the street. It must have been
fourth grade, or if not, then third. The three of them had lingered on the playground at
school for a quarter hour, talking, playing, bonding the tenuous way children sometimes
do. His heart sank when he saw Cord waiting in the front yard for him, the grave look
on his face, the working of his mouth, and then the lurch forward toward the three
children, Fred and Naomi still smiling and chatting—until they saw Leo's father grab
him by the neck and sling him into the yard, yelling "Where the hell have you been? Get
in that house and get in the bathroom." On the ground, the palm of his hand skinned
and burning, Leo felt, more than saw, his father turn on the stunned pair stopped in their
tracks and staring in horror. "What the hell are y'all looking at? Get your ass home."

Had Leo forgotten that he had something important to do right after school? Some
commitment with his father? If so, he couldn't remember it now. That whipping itself
blended with memories of other whippings. Now awakened was the humiliation he
felt in front of his friends. The next day, Fred had attempted to smooth it over. "My dad
gets mad, too," he told Leo. But there were no more walks home together, and although
Leo did sometimes linger at school before going home, neither Fred nor Naomi walked
him home again.

An hour into his walk home, tired, Leo slowed his pace, asked himself why he
was thinking about fourth grade. Of course, McQuain, the authority figure, with the
fearsome power of punishment. *Yes, yes, yes, I have a problem with that. The effect is
so ingrained that merely understanding it changes nothing. I'm forever an emotional
cripple around policemen, bureaucrats, anybody I perceive to have authority over me. I
can kid myself all I want, but I'm powerless because of who I am. Is this how I should
be feeling at age 33? No.*

When he reached the apartment, Leah was waiting for him.

"I was getting worried," she said, letting the door close as he fell across the room
onto the lumpy sofa they'd bought second-hand.

"I walked home. Needed some walking time to deal with a bad situation."

Leah sat beside him. "What happened?"

"Got fired." He was prepared to tell the whole story, had worked it out over the
past hour, would tell her the truth, why not? But she just sat there. He glanced at her,
waiting for the questions to start. Her eyelashes somehow stood out, her perfect profile,
downcast, sad at the news, although her current job at a marketing firm was paying
well and there was no financial panic due to this news. Five years ago, he had sent out

resumes and took the job here partly because it was far away from Texas, from Leah and her charms. She had followed him within five months, and when she showed up at his door, he was glad to see her, embraced her, couldn't wait to get her clothes off her. It had been at the beginning of a long weekend, and they had screwed themselves raw. As the months passed, though, Leo had secretly reconnected to his need for independence, and he knew, now, that Geneve had been part of that dynamic. Leah never asked for any commitment from him. She seemed rather to avoid any discussion of his having left her, and just seemed happy to be with him.

After a while, Leah gently placed her hand on Leo's lap. "You loved that job."

"I'm sad. Tomorrow we should talk about what to do now. You're off tomorrow?"

"Yep." She stood up, went to the kitchen. Their apartment was the ground floor of a wooden two story pre-war duplex, cold in winter, hot in summer, but located on a nice quiet tree-lined street two blocks off Nasali. "Let's make some hamburgers and drink some beer," she said. "I'll do the cooking."

Leo watched her shapely figure disappear into the kitchen, felt a surge of gratitude up from his gut, took in a sharp breath to stay the tears. He wanted to jump her, take her down to the kitchen floor and smother her with kisses, cover her small body with his lengthy one, and push himself inside her.

Seven weeks later they took an apartment in Knoxville, Tennessee, and for the next few years they followed jobs, mostly temporary, mostly around the southern Appalachian region.

31

THEY ENDED UP IN SPRINGDALE, North Carolina, where Leo, at Leah's urging, dropped his resume off at the Arts Council, leading eventually to the gig in Callan County as visiting dramaturge under the auspices of the state's Arts for All program. Janet, the lovely fifth-grade teacher in whose classroom Leo tried for five days to inspire ten-year-olds, was impressed, and Leo fell off the dewy brink of death and into love, he was pretty sure. But Janet disappeared.

Leo stayed in Cannon Shoals for several more hours that night. He walked around Janet's neighborhood, a sense of guilt annoying him. He knew he had nothing to hide, could be seen by police or anybody else, and why not? He didn't even *know* the pharmacist, if that's what was working on him, and he wasn't sure. Tired of walking, he drove to the barbecue joint and lingered over a glass of tea and a piece of pie. Then he drove past Janet's house again. Nothing had changed. He cruised through downtown, hit the Interstate down to the next exit, wound his way along a twisting, desolate stretch of blacktop back to town, and drove by Janet's again. It was past eleven. He didn't know who her friends were, and it was too late to try and ask anyone. He took the highway back to Springdale for an uneventful weekend with Leah.

—

When he arrived at his room in Cadbury on Monday morning, having driven out of Springdale at 5:30 a.m., he still had time for a cup of coffee downtown before heading to Walkerton Middle School, located at the opposite end of the county, twenty-five miles from Cannon Shoals. Two weeks—three more schools—and Leo's residency in Callan County would be completed. As he sipped his coffee in the metallic cafe, and then drove to Walkerton, his thoughts returned again and again to Janet. Only when he was dealing with the middle-schoolers did he escape his troubled yearning.

His day at Walkerton ended early, the last of his classes over at 1:45. He drove straight back to Cadbury, used the phone in the house to try Janet again. There was no answer. He took a long walk, found a public library where he read newspapers and browsed through book shelves until six o'clock closing. In downtown Cadbury, he found a vegetarian restaurant on the second floor of an old brownstone. The Bagh End was quiet, with comfortable seating in worn, unmatched tables and chairs, two young couples in the place, and a group of three middle-aged men chatting at an art deco dining table. Leo sat at a tiny table next to a window looking down on the quiet back street.

A smiling young woman brought him a menu, said "Hello," and lit the funky guttered candle on his table. Leo smiled back and thought she looked something like Janet, which caused him to stare. "I'll be right back," the woman said.

Full of spicy food—tabouli, some sort of pan-grilled eggplant and mushrooms, coarse whole-grain bread, and herbal tea—Leo went to bed as soon as he made it back to his room at just past ten o'clock.

At about midnight, he awoke from a dream. The pretty teacher was standing closer to him than she needed to be. Her coy, almost sly smile, told him she knew she was standing too close—and he leaned to her and kissed her.

Waking from the dream, he stared into the dark and filled in the real-life counterparts—him and Janet, of course.

He did not venture to Cannon Shoals that week, but tried to phone Janet each day when she should have been home. There was never an answer.

Although his work days were short at Walkerton, he found that filling his afternoons was easy and he was tired early. He went back to the Bagh End for dinner twice more, but the original waitress, whom he liked, was not there. Every night that week his dream recurred. It was cast with different actors, but always fit the same scenario. He would wake, feeling a longing to bring his dream into reality.

—

By Friday afternoon, Leo had covered the middle school—two days—and high school—two days—and now had finished at Walkerton Elementary. He was standing in the front office, filling out residency assessment forms and chatting with the principal, Mrs. Richardson, who was saying she'd heard good reports about Leo this week.

"It's been an outstanding experience for me," Leo said. "I'm humbled by the creativity and energy in these kids."

"Energy for sure," Mrs. Richardson chuckled, and then a lady breezed into the office with a huge, exaggerated sigh.

"I have to go to Cannon Shoals Monday so forget about the field trip," she blurted, directing her words toward Mrs. Richardson and the woman at the secretary's desk behind the file cabinet.

The secretary answered her. "Cannon Shoals? Wait a minute. I thought we had you through Wednesday."

"You did, now you don't, unless you want to talk to Ruth about it, and Mr. Gryder."

Leo was staring through the assessment form, his attention fastened to the adjoining conversation.

"Did she say what happened?" the secretary asked.

"The drama teacher up and took off, several days, no notice, no idea when she's coming back."

"So why can't they get a sub?"

"I don't know. Gryder wants me there so it doesn't look so bad for that drama teacher, if you ask me. But what do I know? Life as a floater, I tell you. I was kind of looking forward to the zoo trip."

So—she was a floating substitute. Leo had heard of this system the county had cooked up to keep several people on payroll while saving the expense of hiring substitutes.

He arrived back at his room in Cadbury around three o'clock. Leah would expect him for dinner. It would be possible, he reasoned, to make a trip to Cannon Shoals and still make it back to Springdale by dinnertime. But Leo tried Janet's number several times, only to hear it ring and ring. He was convinced now that she did not want to see him anymore.

32

AFTER FINISHING HIS RESIDENCY IN Callan County, Leo settled back into the sub rosa routine of living with Leah. Springdale was known for mild summers, the higher, cooler air of the mountains buffering it from the lowlands heat. Vacationers sought the relief and the mountain rusticity, the camping and woodsy hiking, waterfalls and streams, vistas, smoky foods, sighting bears and deer and wild turkeys and strange little creatures unseen at lower elevations. Leo knew all this and tried to participate, to occupy himself and take his thoughts into the present, away from the woman he'd met last spring. He told Leah he was embarking on an exercise program. He would take long walks every day. With Leah working in temporary positions and no job of his own, Leo found it easy enough to schedule walks, but he discovered that the warm weather and exercise began to wring the energy from his body. Where was the "energizing effect" he'd expected? He found himself watching the concrete blur toward his alternating shoes, his thoughts spiraling backward to his childhood or, sometimes, into fantasies of doom.

He tried concentrating on domestic tasks, sweeping the floor, doing the dishes, laundry, occasionally wiping off the woodwork or getting serious about the bathroom. He phoned the landlord when the apartment needed a repair.

By July, he'd retreated even from these meager household chores. While Leah went to her job, Leo spent many mornings and early afternoons in his underwear, lounging on the couch, drinking coffee, reading, and drifting into daydreams about Janet. He was nurturing a psychological scab over her memory. It could never have been—it never was, he told himself. More than once when Leah was home for lunch, Leo thought he saw her reading his mind, and would try to distract her with the minutiae of his morning. *The newspapers were askew in the vending trap at the convenience store. I told that strange skinny man next door that his boxelder tree looked like it was about to fall.* Meanwhile, he developed the habit of walking to the convenience store once his day was underway, and in doing so, he acquired a father named Sid Koff.

On a stagnant, glaring mid-morning in October, he walked toward coffee, annoyed that he had caught a cold. The passing sidewalk, concrete scored into squares, the summer decay pasted to pavement, and the haze conspired to bring him back to the sidewalks of childhood, when the cracks were committed to memory. The air was warm, and the sun was white through fog that had lifted only in the last half hour to reveal dark clouds rolling over the sharp hills to the south. It was a Monday, and Leo acknowledged his privilege—that no one knew or cared exactly where he was. Anonymity was possible in Springdale, and desirable. He needed to be nameless in order to dismiss his preoccupations. With a little effort, he quietened his mind, walking on the broken, eroded sidewalk through the South, this America, and by stepping apart from himself, he stepped into the moment, arriving from another somewhere, somewhen.

Though his nose was clogged, he smelled the pungent creosote on a telephone pole as he passed it. The damp houses, the ragged lawns and fallen leaves, the trees hoarding their sap against the coming winter, the flawed fences, unsure shrubbery, and the frayed matrix of wires overhead—everything came into view, and he floated through it all like a neighborhood cat, old, comfortable and needless. What would it be like, he wondered, to walk through all of life in such a state, aware of everything of the moment, and heedless of everything that had already receded and all that was yet to come, smelling the creosote instead.

He swam in the ether of time, in places remembered on the smell of wisteria and honeysuckle and dusty rusty musty screen wire. It seemed entirely probable that walking along this cracked sidewalk was a moment he had remembered long ago. Here was a window, a glimpse backward, a moment he could say, *Ah, here I am, arrived through linear time at this place. Unlike before, I possess the complete history of what has happened up to now.*

And here he contemplated the *real* issues. If he wanted to, he could walk away from Leah. It was about wanting, and the heaviness of wanting, the weight compacting him, keeping itself camouflaged and disguised, the idea slippery like a restless child. Wanting. But *what?* And if wanting, then why not *driven?* Why the yearning for something unknown? Was it love he wanted? If it was, why was there no drive to find it? Because one doesn't find love—it finds one. But other than love, wasn't there something to life?

No, Leo thought. *Love is all there is.* If you tried to think of wanting something separate from love—a career goal, a power, a satisfaction—your desire was contained, and you with it, separated from life, because separated from love.

He felt the time banking in front of him, pushed ahead like sound waves before a projectile. He could contemplate the mystery of want, and love, and life, until he burst, not through the sound barrier, but the time barrier, back into real time, preoccupations, goals, his immediate goal, the convenience store. Coffee for money, meaning civilization and its illusions. Somehow, before he returned to real time, he had to know that it was not all lost, not all hopeless. He needed to grasp and hold that, have it in his hand not just in his dream, but also when he awakened.

—

All men were potentially Leo's father. He had no real model against which to judge paternal authenticity. In his adult life he had sensed two or three men, other than Cord, to have been his father. Sometime after his college days he had recognized his yearning. Most men, it seemed to Leo, resisted being father to anyone except, sometimes, their own children. In Springdale, Leo acquired a father named Sid Koff. An incipient alcoholic in his early twenties—Leo's junior by a couple of decades—Sid was working toward a divinity degree at Springdale-Pidgeon Methodist Seminary. Mornings, he also manned the convenience store Leo frequented.

On this soulless Monday sometime after Halloween, with a sore throat and stuffy nose, no job prospects and his efforts to find work merely token lately, Leo walked the several blocks to the convenience store, enshrouded in his history. He kept thinking of the creosote, wondering for some reason if it might somehow be or contain a cure for his cold, his itchy, runny nose.

"Leo, coffee," Sid said as Leo walked into the fluorescence. Leo poured his own, black, took a booth near the cash register.

"Have a burrito," Sid said. His bright tone told Leo he was into the Colt 45 already, and it was ten o'clock.

Leo shook his head, but Sid took a burrito out of the refrigerated case and placed it in the microwave. "Not for me," Leo said, reaching for a napkin, in a hurry to blow his nose into it.

"I'll eat it," Sid said.

"Do they pay you here, or just let you eat?"

"That's the question, isn't it," Sid said, watching the invisible heat penetrating the burrito. When the machine beeped and quieted, Sid took the paper-wrapped morsel out and leaned back against the counter. "Look outside at that gray movie. What a lousy scene. Who wouldn't want to eat a burrito and have a beer? Look out there, Leo."

Leo regarded the gloom out the window through one of the few spaces not covered with an advertisement of some kind. From somewhere in the store, an oldies station issued static and Beatles. Leo sipped his coffee while his catarrh gently wept.

"Leo, look out there," Sid commanded. "There's lightning."

Leo looked again, stared for some seconds, and saw lightning, too distant for thunder.

"You should hang around today and watch people come in for ice cream," Sid said. "You think I'm kidding. It rains, they come in for ice cream. I've observed it."

The electricity failed. The store plunged into a darkness that alarmed Leo because the coffee he was staring into disappeared into the blackness around it until his eyes began to adjust.

"Aw man," Sid said. "Awww maaa-yan," he said, imitating the soft local drawl. He'd once told Leo he was from Michigan, once told him he was from Chicago. "I can't stay open without electricity." He made his way around the counter to the front door and locked it.

"Take your time with the coffee, Leo. Who knows, maybe the electricity'll come back on and I won't have to close." He disappeared toward the large refrigerated vaults of beverages at the back of the store, returned a minute later and sat down in the booth with Leo. He had opened a fresh quart of Colt 45.

"Don't you need this job?" Leo said, wiping his nose with a napkin.

"That's not the point, Leosito. What do you think life is, anyway?"

Leo saw that his host was waiting for an answer. "I guess it's a period we go through from the time we're removed from the rest of the universe until we get put back," Leo said, more than satisfied with his use of the passive voice on his seminarian friend. He took another throat-soothing swallow of his warm coffee.

A car pulled up to the front of the store, its headlights cutting through a misty rain that had begun to fall.

"We're closed," Sid muttered. He took a huge gulp of the malt liquor and sent its odor toward Leo with a quiet but substantial belch. "I'm thinking about that," he said. "Let me think about that."

Leo watched Sid take additional pulls on the bottle and shake his head. Leo felt his eyes and then himself adjust, the store's usual glaring reality suspended. He looked around in the natural dark, half expecting to see a piece of real wood or an animal of some kind. He heard the distant buzz of the idling engine in the car outside, saw a jagged line of light move across the back wall as the car backed out of the parking space and pulled away. Leo sipped his coffee.

Sid drank from the bottle until it was empty. "Awww maaa-yan," he said.

"What?"

"I mean, haven't you ever been in love, Leo?"

"I'm in love now," Leo said, feeling reckless. Then he laughed. "How about you?"

Sid burped. "I'm in love with your mother."

Leo felt a shock, almost physical, but it burst apart, crumbled into something else, unsettled. Sid had thrown a northern style insult at him, cheap and easy. He was drunk and just joking. *He's never even seen my mother.* He was a kid when she died. Was he even born when she died?

But the joke insinuated itself into Leo's coffee-drenched, rhinovirus-fatigued brain such that Sid pegged his position as Leo's father. Who would love your mother? Your father, of course. Offhand remark, offhand result. But there it was.

"I'll tell you what to do," Sid said. "This'll help you, Leo."

"Tell me."

"You might be right about that, what you said." His words were beginning to slur a bit. "Yeah, this is all just waiting to get back to God."

"I didn't say God," Leo said.

"You know what I mean, though. So, I'll tell you what to do. Stop thinking about that and do it."

"Do what?"

"You know, whatever."

"I don't know, Sid. What?"

"*Whatever*," Sid said, some impatience rising.

"Well, I'll think about it."

Sid looked angry. "Don't think about it. Thinking is nothing, you jerk." He unfolded himself from the booth, grabbed the empty Colt 45 bottle, and stalked off toward the back of the store.

The fluorescent light flickered, giving Leo a sudden headache. Too much coffee. Coffee too strong, cups too big. Price too high.

In the light he could see that Sid had left the key stuck in the keyhole, with the other keys on the ring fanning out below it. Leo slid out of the booth, without a word and without paying for his coffee, went to the door and turned the key to unlock it. He walked out into the drizzle, marveling at how his daddy had spoken to him. *Our Daddy who art in heaven.*

He took the short route home, walking on streets paved too long ago, through his neighborhood of small houses, cramped yards unevenly kept, back street homes, but homes for people who don't know. They don't know *something* or else they would live elsewhere, in the house across the street, or in another town, or at least they would put their bed in the other bedroom, or even just move the furniture around a little. They don't know the desperation of their tenuous existence outside the universe they are touching with their skin, and to which they might return any day, any hour, with or without notice, but no choice. *What did He mean, stop thinking about that and do it?*

The mist was collecting on the outside surface of his haircut. He felt the weight but did not touch it because he knew doing so would break the surface tension and send cold drops down to his scalp.

He had forgotten to pick up a newspaper, but he would not go back to the convenience store. His business there was finished for now. He hurried toward his home.

—

The following Friday dawned with headache-inducing low cloud cover. Leah was beginning a supposedly long-term temp job and Leo dragged himself, sore head, full blown cold and all, from the bed at the same time Leah rose. He put the coffee on, made her some breakfast. He felt it was the least he could do, get her off to a decent start on the new assignment, give her a chance to impress, and it might lead to something better. A few times, these temp jobs had turned into full time.

Finishing the perfectly fried egg, Leah patted her mouth with a napkin. Leo had already retreated with his cup to the couch. "Thank you, Leo," Leah said.

"*No problema,*" he managed through his pre-caffeine haze. Watching her apply lipstick, he was anxious for Leah to get gone, leave him alone in his misery. She was dressed now, attractive, sexy as she walked out the door.

The mail arrived around noon. There was a letter from the North Carolina Arts Council. Leo had applied for a residency in Yancy County a few weeks earlier. Tossing the junk mail on the coffee table, he fell into the couch and tore open the letter. Funding for the North Carolina Arts-for-All program had been slashed in half by the legislature in Raleigh, and although there had been a tentative plan to send him to Yancy County to do another residency.... He was still unemployed, but now again with no prospects.

———

By October Leah was having to hustle hard for temp jobs. She registered at a second agency to up her chances, not letting either agency know about the other, a risky but necessary scheme. It was Sunday, and Leah was to start a new temp job in the morning. About dusk, the steam pipes clanked, the first evening the thermostat had kicked the heat on, and then came the waxy, comfortable smell of heat burning the accrete dust off the radiators. Leah sat at the kitchen table reading the newspaper, and Leo, on the couch, had finished reading Ken Follett's *Night Over Water* and was leafing back through it to re-read short passages.

The phone rang on the end table next to Leo, and he picked it up.

"Hello."

"*Can you come see me?*" It sounded like she had the phone very close to her mouth, lips touching it, the proximity muffling and amplifying her voice. Husky, hoarse, it did not sound like Janet, but he knew it was, and his heart pounded, his face flushed.

"Well, not right now," he said, summoning all his will to try and sound offhanded. He prayed that Janet would ask him next if he could talk freely, but she proceeded as though she assumed he could.

"*I may lose my job,*" she said. "*Probably not, but I don't know. I felt like talking to somebody. You don't mind, do you?*"

"No, of course not. It's nice to hear from you." *Surely* she'd understand that he couldn't talk.

Leah looked up from the paper, a signal for Leo to indicate who was on the phone, but he gave her a quick shake of the head, frown, pursed lips to indicate it was nothing.

"I was gone for almost three weeks," Janet said, and then there was silence. *"Did you try to call me?"*

"Yes, uh-huh," he said, nodding to some unseen bureaucrat or salesman. Seconds passed. Leo struggled to appear bored, unconcerned, but his panic mounted. How had she obtained his phone number? *It was on all the residency forms, and how hard would it be for her to get those out of Gryder's office? Not very. And besides, we're in the phone book under my name.* He pretended to listen to someone rambling on and on.

Seconds dragged by. He could hear Janet breathing. Was she crying? Was she stifling tears? Time crept, an eternity of silence broken only by Janet's unsteady breathing. Leo tried clearing his throat, not knowing what it would communicate, except that he was there.

There was a click, and nothing. How long before the dial tone would come on, or that awful signal that a phone is off the hook?

"I will," Leo said into the phone. "I sure will. I'll send it tomorrow. Good hearing from you. Yep, bye." He hung up. Not glancing at Leah, he headed for the bathroom to gather his wits. "That was one of the Callan County teachers I worked with last spring," he said.

He stood in front of the commode until he produced some urine, letting it fall as loudly into the middle of the water as possible.

Trying for nonchalance, he started talking before he was even back in the living room. "There's some possible opening for a drama teacher in Round Oak."

"Which is where?"

"Way east. If I'm interested, I should send my resume." He fell onto the couch, indicating his indifference.

"I like your enthusiasm."

"We'd have to move there," he said. *We?*

"So, what is it? Round Oak? Never heard of it. But maybe it's nice."

"It's a tiny country community she said. Not near anything except some big corporation, I forgot what she said. There's money there, but not for education. I'll have to find it on the map. But I'm not taking it, anyway."

"You're not? You didn't say that to them."

"Well, I wasn't going to burn the bridge, but...."

"How tiny?"

"Twenty-five miles from the nearest town. All tobacco farmers everywhere except the town which is families that work at whatever it is, some big company I've never heard of."

"Wouldn't work," Leah said.

"I know."

It was possible that she did buy it. Probably not. Why had he given so many details? What if she checked up on it, found there was no Round Oak? Or that there is one but it's in the piedmont, nowhere near the coast.

The tiring prospect of continuing to cover up who the call was from brought him to the edge of confessing, then to a sense of defeat that made everything irrelevant. Nothing was possible, and if he lost Leah, then he would have nothing. But he would not lose Leah. He would never lose her, even if he tried. Unfaithfulness to her might change a dynamic for a while. It might be unpleasant—it might not be. But nothing mattered.

In this state of mind for the next few hours, Leo moved restlessly from living room to kitchen area to bedroom and back to living room, his motion contrasting the way Leah sat on the couch absorbed in an Us and then Vanity Fair. He tried to light on the comfortable chair, and as always, became annoyed that it was not near the window because the radiator was in the way. But he sat as long as he could, staring at pages of a book he had already finished.

Sometime after ten, Leah placed her magazine on the couch. "You know when you came home from Callan County that last day...." she said.

"What?"

"And you were supposed to be here, I mean, I thought you would be here early that day if anything, and you were so late getting back."

"I don't remember."

"Yeah, I can't remember either what it was that held you up that day," she said. "You told me, but I don't remember now."

"Me, neither."

"I'm guessing that this phone call tonight was from the same person that made you late that night."

Leo said nothing. That she was correct was clear. How sure she was didn't matter.

Leah stood, stretched, and took a deep breath. "Let's hit the sack. Aren't you tired?"

Leo caught himself staring at the electrical outlet above the baseboard where the living room merged into the kitchen area. He felt the moisture on his eyeballs evaporating, blinked, and then felt Leah's hand caress his shoulder.

"Yeah," he said, "kinda tired," and he could not blink for a moment or pull his gaze away from the rectangle of plastic.

After a moment, Leah went into the bedroom. Leo tarried in the bathroom, having disrobed at the easy chair, leaving his pants and shirt draped on its back, still clean enough for tomorrow. If she was truly tired, she would be asleep, would she not?

Janet, he now realized—her face, her voice, her eyes, her laugh, the warm scent—it had all been running through his mind for hours now, and for months.

When he did crawl into bed, Leah draped her hand over his stomach. He turned away, and she moved up close behind him, reached around and began touching him.

"Not sure I feel up to it," he said, hoping he sounded tired.

"Really," she murmured. "I know. Why don't you tell me about it."

He feared, already, that he was found out and Leah was beyond any doubting. "Tell you about what?"

"Whatever," she said, stroking him through his shorts, so gently. "We have all night."

Leo was never conscious of the way Leah did what she did to him. All he knew was that she could arouse him easily, and if there was something she wanted from him, he would give it to her.

He told her all about Janet, that they had had sex—though he kept secret that it had been on the sidewalk—that it was meaningful for him. And he assured Leah that he would not be getting in touch with Janet any more.

"You don't know that, Leo. You don't know for sure what you're going to do, or how you feel about her. Time will tell," she said, and soon fell asleep holding Leo's hand in hers, neglecting his hard yearning now, leaving it to subside on its own, unfulfilled.

—

Leah's ghost stayed in the apartment longer than usual after she left for the new temp job the next morning. Leo dressed more slowly than usual, too, planning his morning outing to the convenience store. Knowing that Janet would be at school now, maybe even in Gryder's office trying to save her job, he could not phone during the day. And the times when he could phone her would generally coincide with the times Leah would be home. Something should work out, though, even if he had to use a pay phone somewhere. The real question was whether he had the right to call her. Wasn't he in a committed relationship? Moreover, was he in possession of his own life?

Leo was about to head for coffee at the convenience store when he began to imagine Sid's thoughts, setting him in a small kitchen—probably a fairly accurate envisagement—on a recent evening, say last night. Leo took off his sweater and searched for a pen and paper. This time there was no poem, just some prose.

"You have no choice but to believe everything I tell you. I've made it easy on you, so you should be grateful. You should thank Me for the South, the slow talkers and iced tea drinkers and those who smile and nod, the strangers who should fear you and do not. You should be thankful that you need not wonder, need not choose to believe in Me, but have Me in your heart and your mind and even in your body at times. Drink, and remember Me as often as you do it. Go to school and learn, of course, but know that you are learning only for the benefit of those who live here on Earth, not for those who have passed on and not for those who are yet to live, and not for yourself. You have nothing more to learn that is for your benefit, as you already have true knowledge of Me. Work, and make a living, and know that all you do and all you earn belong to Me, just as you belong to Me, and as all people and all their livings belong to Me, even if you alone know this fully. But don't worry about your work, or making your living, as these labors are merely to keep you alive. Anything beyond comfortable quarters and enough to eat is misguided, wasted effort. For you, I have chosen a path of enlightenment, and everything will be revealed to you when it is time.

"Yes, drink more wine, but remember, this cheap wine leaves you with a headache, and is full of tannin or other acids that, in moderation, may be helpful due to the antioxidant content, but in excess, cannot but harm you. Nothing beats vodka or gin, for their spirits are more pure."

"Yes, God, yes, but the liquor store is closed, and I have a class in the morning and then I have to be at work at ten at the convenience store, and besides I can't afford any more booze."

"No One is telling you to go out and buy booze tonight. I was speaking in general terms, instructing you to stay away from the cheap red stuff."

"Thank you, God. Thank you."

"This do in remembrance of Me."

"I sure will."

33

PAPA TOLD ME THAT RELIGIONS are paradigms for understanding spirituality, but that they don't usually work that way in real life. Religions tend to usurp your spirituality instead of putting you in touch with it. You may know there's something beyond your physical and mental existence, but your religion is, if anything, obscuring it, so you reach out—search your soul, so to speak—and all you find is morality, and you find it in religion! Well, morality can relate to the spirit, but only as something that comes out of the spirit. You don't somehow impose morality into or onto the spiritual aspect of yourself. Religions try to do just that, however, so again, religion stands between you and your spiritual nature. I will come to understand this—barely—when I am in my early fifties, during a conversation with my daughter in which I try to explain what Papa said to me when I was a kid.

Satisfied with the little piece he'd written about Sid's conversation with God, Leo went for coffee. Sid was off that day, so Leo was unable to chat with him, though he had wanted to. When Leo left the convenience store a brisk wind had kicked up, and was blowing the iffy drizzle and mist in odd directions. He wanted the thunder and lightning and rain to come on, get it over with, but the electricity had passed by Springdale, lost in the hills now. He would need to make his own storm. Back in the apartment, as he ran a towel through his hair and hard across his face, he imagined the storm out in the hills, and yearned for it. *I'm the rain man, who threw away all that was not his own body, and pulled himself under the water swelling the gullies. Who opened his eyes under the rushing mud, and felt the sticks and sand abrading his eyeballs and washing away the protective, lubricating tears.*

Leo stood in the doorway of the bedroom, looking out through the tiny hallway and into the living room where his reading chair crouched near the phone. He worked his fingers into the towel to find the dampness that had come from his hair. The caffeine began to betray him, as always, the energy clotting into twinges in his stomach. He could see the phone. He heard his own heartbeat, felt heavy, suspended, undecided, and yet it was decided. God the Father had commanded him, had He not?

He phoned Leah at work, asked her to come home for lunch, and hung up when she asked why.

—

Leah banged open the front door, startling Leo as he was sitting in the easy chair reading. He looked up to see her face twisted in fear.

"Leo," she said, "what is it?"

"Take your coat off and sit down," he said. "Calm down. I thought we'd have lunch together."

She stood still, staring at him for a few seconds. "Are you sure?"

"I made us some pimento cheese sandwiches," he said, getting up to help her with her coat. She turned her back to him as she unbuttoned the heavy black woolen coat. He watched her arms slide from the satin lined sleeves, and felt the rush of warmth as it carried her familiar scent to his face.

She turned to him, searching his eyes for the truth. He hurried into the bedroom to toss her coat onto the bed.

She was right behind him.

"What is it, Leo?" she said, blocking his exit from the room. "You're scaring me."

He wanted to push right past her, but was afraid to brush up against her, afraid of what he knew she could do with him. Shaking, feeling perspiration break out in his armpits, he sat on the edge of the bed.

And then, when he looked up at her, he saw that she knew. Neither of them needed to speak, and she knew he was planning to see Janet. She knew, even though they'd never discussed Janet beyond that night she'd phoned.

Leo tried to steady himself as he looked up at Leah's pain. Her dark eyes were watery, her lipsticked mouth was open just enough to show the even, white teeth working up and down, wordless.

And then her face went cold and still, and Leo realized, when she looked away, that he had not stopped looking at her, had not averted his eyes. He had won.

Leah went to the small chest of drawers they shared. She opened the top drawer and pulled out a prescription bottle. It was the chlorpromazine she often used for sleeping, and sometimes used in the daytime on weekends in smaller doses for retreating from all cares.

"What are you going to do? Go down there to that town?" Leah said, taking the cap off the bottle.

"Let's eat some sandwiches," Leo said. "And don't forget, you have to go back to work after lunch."

Leah considered this, replaced the cap on the bottle without removing any pills. She put the bottle back in the drawer. Leo looked at her broad, high butt and, as always, felt the tiny electric spark in his sleeping penis that would wake it up. But he ignored the spark this time. His head ached, and his heart felt like it was tearing itself open, and he knew it would all be fine if instead he did not ignore the spark, if he would once again follow the spark back out of his body and into the universe.

But he held on, stayed in his body, and ate pimento cheese sandwiches with Leah before she returned to her temp job.

They'd been making do with one car, which Leah used for getting to and from work. Leo called the bus station to find out what it would take, in money and time, to get to Cannon Shoals.

The bus was to leave Springdale at six-thirty. Leah would be home around six. He would be out of the apartment well before then, the walk to the bus station a good half hour at least.

He chose clothing and toiletries, packing nothing extraneous into his brown canvas bag with leather handles strapped around it. He opened the drawer where he kept his underwear. There, mixed in among his shorts and T-shirts, was a lilac brassiere. The unexpected sight of Leah's undergarment stopped him cold. Was it just the usual mix-up? Or had she placed it there when she'd gone back into the bedroom to retrieve her coat, knowing he would see it at just this moment of packing to leave?

Leo stood poised over the open drawer, breathing through his mouth. He felt himself about to drool, closed his mouth. Thus back in motion, he reached for the brassiere and extricated it from his underwear. He brought it to his face, pressed the soft inner lining to his nose and inhaled its fragrance. A sudden discomfort, a need for adjustment at his crotch, and his hand found its way there to twiddle the limp appendage unstuck, re-nestle it, and unthinking, he let his hand stay there to comfort the piece of flesh. And when he realized what he was feeling, and that he was a prisoner, that even if he took the bus to Cannon Shoals, no matter how far he made it, he would be pulled back here, and soon, before the bonds even began to weaken.

He looked up and saw himself in the mirror above the chest of drawers. The brassiere in the mirror was somehow even more appealing than the one he held against his face. The man in the mirror holding it was also more appealing than the one looking at him. Leo wanted to be him.

"Leo," Leo said, and the man raised his eyebrows back at Leo, "you're trapped." He let the brassiere, still lingering in his hand, slide down his chest and stomach to his crotch, where he pressed it close to himself. He turned away from the mirror and stepped over to the bed, resigned, no longer hurried as he had been while packing. He flopped onto the bed and brought the brassiere back to his face, let it rest there on its own, peeked out from under it and saw the familiar crack in the wallpaper at the corner of the ceiling.

"No, you're not trapped," said the man in the mirror. Leo heard him distinctly, his voice coming from where the reflection of the bed would be in the mirror world. Leo was not alarmed, knew it was his imagination, even though he'd never before experienced something this vivid.

"I'm not trapped?" Leo said.

"Not at all. Think about what your old Dad said."

"My dad?"

"With a capital D. Sid Koff."

"Ah, Sid Koff," Leo said, and smiled. "What was it he did say?"

"He said you've always laughed at existentialism. That you only *act like* you are what you do. That you *think* you are what you think. That you're *afraid* that you are what you fear."

"He said that?"

"That you *feel* like you are what you feel."

"I'm sure of it," Leo said, and took the cup of the brassiere with his teeth, working it with his lips until he had a piece of it in his mouth, sucked on it, made the spot wet.

"You could simply...."

"What?"

"I said you could simply do it, Leo. Don't forget your houseshoes. You know how you hate not having them when you rise in the morning."

"My houseshoes," Leo said, and the brassiere slipped out of his mouth and fell on the pillow beside his ear.

Packing his suitcase, he wondered whether to leave the lilac brassiere on the pillow for Leah to find, a sort of message. He did leave it there, hoping the wet spot on it would not dry before she came home, and that she would feel it, smell of it and know the scent of his saliva, and she would know what had happened, even though there would be no words for it.

34

CANNON SHOALS HAD NO BUS station per se, but a drop-off outside a barbecue joint at the far south end of downtown. Leo was hungry, but with less than a hundred dollars to last him indefinitely, he had to be frugal. He walked away, avoiding the pungent smell of barbecue and the dust and exhaust from the bus as it pulled away.

The route to Janet's house took him right through downtown. He stopped in front of the pharmacy and peered in the window. The store was closed at that hour, but it was in business, still a pharmacy, some of the displays rearranged by the new operator, but much of it unchanged.

He wore a stocking cap pulled down against the chill. By the time he'd reached the end of the main business section, several cars had passed him head on, and he had turned his face away. Realizing he was skulking out of habit, he straightened himself up, head held high. He was walking, after all, toward himself. Once he reached the darker side streets, after ten minutes walking past little mysteries in small houses lit white and yellow from within, he turned onto Janet's street and saw her house, several windows lit, a block and a half away. Across from it stood the pharmacist's house, dark.

As he came closer, he saw a *For Sale* sign in front of the pharmacist's house, and noticed that the yard had not been cleared of its autumn leaves.

Pushing through growing apprehension, he made it as far as Janet's front walk. But there he stopped, paralyzed by the idea that she might have company. There were many lights on inside the house, it seemed now. Wouldn't it be prudent to wait a moment and watch and listen for evidence of visitors?

A car turned onto the street. To avoid looking suspicious, he walked toward the front porch, and by the time the car had passed, he was standing at the front door. The handle of his suitcase was beginning to cut into his hand, but he held onto it, feeling that it anchored him to the air, and that it would be presumptuous to set it down. He knocked.

The porch light came on and Janet opened the door. When she recognized him, her eyes widened a bit and she said, "Oh, no." Her hand went to her mouth.

"I know it's rude," he said.

"Well, come in," she said, and unlatched the screen.

Inside, Leo was first struck by the familiar freshness of the air in the house, a sweet presence he had registered when there before, now tugging him back through the intervening time.

Janet left him in the living room while she turned out lights in two other rooms. She reappeared from the direction of the kitchen, stood in the doorway looking at him.

"Why don't you put your suitcase down," she said. He did. He saw a book, open and face down on the lamp table next to the couch.

"You were reading."

"A movie star biography. Let me take your coat and cap."

He took them off and handed them to her, feeling the sudden chilly evaporation of his exposed perspiration. He worried that his hair would look misshapen. Janet tossed his things onto a wooden chair in the corner of the room. "You know where the bathroom is if you need it," she said.

He stood there looking at her, helpless, struck again by her quiet beauty. She was avoiding his look, but when he didn't move or speak, she looked at him and smiled.

"Please go comb your hair," she said. "Would you like something? I was thinking about something hot."

He felt heavy, tired. "Yes," he said, "if it's easy, no trouble. Some coffee or tea."

"I'll have some too," she said.

Leo went to the bathroom, pleased that he knew where it was. Once there, he began to feel more than pleased—elated, even through his weariness. He combed his hair. The man in the mirror watched him, mimicking him but half-heartedly. He smirked a bit more than Leo did, grinned while Leo merely smiled. He whispered "Easy, see?" Leo shook his head back and forth. *It's not so easy as the man in the mirror would have me believe.* But as Leo shook his head no, the man squinted his eyes and nodded.

Leo looked away, noticed the wallpaper, a rose floral design on deep green background. He touched the lip of the ancient, claw-footed bathtub, let the coldness there enter his fingers. He took a small step to feel the cushion of the deep green rug that hugged the commode. He wanted to stay here in this tiny sanctuary forever, and that was why he hurried out, back to the living room.

He sat on the couch.

"Coffee'll be ready in a few minutes," Janet said, coming into the room. She sat on the couch next to him, holding a dishtowel.

Letting her hands drop onto her lap, the towel wrapped around one hand, she took a deep breath. "I'm surprised," she said, and let a sharp, single note of laughter escape before composing herself again.

"I'm sorry I showed up without...."

"Don't apologize," she said. "I'm glad to see you. Very glad." She stood up and moved to the window, peering out into the blackness before turning toward Leo. "It can't be like it might have been," she said.

"Oh, I understand that," Leo said, but he was lying. "No, actually I don't understand anything. Not even why I'm here, except that I... my strong feelings for you. And a sense of... I don't know."

"Could you try and be a little more vague?" she said, and smiled at her joke.

"It would be hard for me to tell you," he said, "although I could, given some time, I mean, tell you how important. How important, you know, it is. You are. To me."

"And you came here to try and tell me?"

"That would be part of it," he said, "but I came here...." He leaned forward on the couch, placed his face into his weary hands.

"You're not going to cry, are you?" she said.

"No," he said, the word muffled against the heels of his hands. Idiotic words and phrases whirled though his mind, some of them phosphenes on his eyelids. The utter hopelessness of his disorganization crushed against his upper back, pushing him down. He was tired. He could not tell her anything. Yet he had to tell her something. He let his hands fall away, sat up straight, looked at her.

"I want to live here, with you," he said.

Beyond her silence there was the sound of the coffeemaker sputtering in the kitchen. She stood up and left the room. Leo heard her rattling cups, opening and closing the refrigerator, clinking spoons. She returned, handed him his cup of coffee, sat down in the easy chair across from him.

"No, you can't," she said.

The words numbed him. A monster stirred inside him, a delighted monster who relished the idea of his death and torturing him for a good while beforehand. Leo recognized the monster's heat, its smell, and once he sensed it, he recognized its spoor, and knew it was everywhere and there was nowhere he could turn to get away from it. He sat there shifting his mind, ready to succumb to the dumb beast he would follow back home, to his childhood, to his thinnest claim to humanity, to Leah.

But then Janet was sitting beside him, her hands wrapped around one of his, the strong electric connection between them established again. He looked at her face and saw it full of concern and fear. "Leo," she whispered, "I didn't mean that as a death sentence. You look like the judge just pronounced that you'd be hung at dawn."

"I'm sorry. I'm tired."

"Tired? I don't think I've ever in my life seen somebody so affected by something I said. I wasn't prepared for it. You're not feeling sick, are you?"

"No, just exhausted. I better go. I'll find a motel room."

"It's just there seems to be so much we need to talk about," she said. "Before we talk about something like living together. See, I'm, I guess, old fashioned in a lot of ways."

"I know," Leo said. "I was wrong to say what I said. I didn't know where else to start."

"Why don't you tell me what else you have in mind. Here, let's drink some of this coffee." Now she took both of Leo's chilled and rigid hands in her warm ones. She rubbed them for a moment, then guided him to the coffee cup. Together they administered the first sip of coffee. The taste, the warmth, sent a spasm of comfort through his body. Janet returned to her easy chair and sipped from her cup.

"The truth is, Janet, I don't have anything else in mind. I have very little money, no way of getting any more at the moment. I have no car, either."

"No car? But how...?"

"I took the bus, walked over here from the bus stop downtown. What I have in this suitcase, that's it."

They sipped their coffees.

"And your wife—is it Leah?—you had a fight with her or what?"

The monster, now reclining, eyes closed, snorted, sounded almost like a chuckle, a threat. He could not explain Leah at this moment. "Leah and I don't belong together. There's a horror story there. I can't tell it to you now, but I will have to tell it to you. I realize that. I will have to tell it to you. It could destroy me, but there's no avoiding it."

"But you didn't hurt her, did you?"

"Well, I may have hurt her psychologically, but no, nothing like physical abuse. No."

"Does she know where you've gone?"

"I imagine she'll be able to guess, Janet."

"Have you told her about us?"

"The night you called, she was sitting there. She's... well, perceptive. And she can read me like a book, if you know what I mean."

"Yes, I get it."

"She doesn't know your name, but if you're wondering whether she could find you, yes, if she decided to. She knows you're someone I met in this county while I was doing my residency. She would go to Cadbury first, but it wouldn't take her long to find me."

"Leo, does she know that we...?"

Leo gazed into Janet's eyes and smiled. "Not specifically about the sidewalk, but yeah."

"Do you think she'll come here?"

Leo hadn't let himself think about this. Now he did, taking a long pull of coffee. "I left her once before, a long time ago. We lived in Texas at that time. She followed me all the way to Chicago."

Janet peered down into her cup. She sniffed, looked over to the window.

"But as I said, that was a long time ago. And it was different then. I didn't have the resolve I have now."

"You left her to be with another woman?"

"There had been another woman, but that was over with. I went to Chicago to take a job I'd lined up. Teaching drama. I told Leah not to come, but she did."

"And she knew about the other woman?"

"She knew, yes. She knew I was... in pain, over the other woman. She came to comfort me, in a way."

"That's strange."

"I'm getting this out of sequence, too. She tried to comfort me before we ever left Texas. But then she followed me, but it was a while later that that happened. I was still in college."

"Oh. I didn't realize this was so long ago. You do go way back with Leah."

Leo let the fading heat in his cup seep into his hands, pressing his palms and fingers around the stoneware. He wondered if he could go any further now with his story, or if he had gone too far already.

"More coffee?"

"Yes. It's good."

When Janet came back with refills for them both, she said, "You must have known it was possible I would say you couldn't stay here. What were you planning to do then?"

"No, you're wrong. Thank you," he said, taking the hot coffee. "I didn't even know I was going to propose staying here. I threw some things in a suitcase... no, that's not right. I packed carefully, to maximize my ability to stay away, to enhance the chances of staying away from her forever. I phoned the bus company so I'd be at the bus station on time, with a ticket to Cannon Shoals. And I came here. That's it."

"Pretty adventurous."

"Yeah."

He thought Janet looked rather prim, sitting up, straight back, to drink her coffee. He realized he was slumping, had sunk into the cushions behind him.

"You realize...." she hesitated. "No, maybe you don't realize the clear picture you're painting. Leah obviously has a strong hold on you, Leo. You had to sneak away like a criminal, and you're terrified right now. I get the feeling it has more to do with her personality than with yours. Of course, I already know you, and don't know her. But you are connected with her, you know. Hopping on a bus and riding down the road a piece to see your girlfriend on the side doesn't change that. You know that, don't you?"

Leo took a deep breath. "I haven't even begun to tell you. Yes, I am afraid of her. But the connection... I have severed it."

Janet set her cup on the lamp table. "I think you want me to help you sever it, Leo. I don't think the deed is done yet, and I think you need my assistance."

She relaxed back into the big chair. Leo blew across the surface of his coffee, sipped the delicious, revivifying brew, feeling that he had said much, made much progress, and had not lied except by omission. "I can't deny it categorically, Janet, but to my way of thinking, the help I need from you is to go on, go forward. Leah might come, might try to repossess me. It might be unpleasant. But that is not about you, and you don't need to be involved in it."

Janet extended her arms onto the armrests, splayed her fingers and clawed at the upholstery like a purring cat.

Leo met her gaze and tried to smile. "I'm loaded with great offers tonight, huh?"

Janet's wan smile betrayed her understanding. Leo had come without a plan, but begging nevertheless, and he had come burdened, trouble to follow, trouble in his soul and in his past.

"Well, I have a suggestion," Janet said. "It's close to nine o'clock now. Too late to go looking for a motel. You can stay here tonight. I think we can be discreet. I've got school tomorrow, but I know of a place you might be able to stay. Would you mind living in a trailer house?"

"No, I wouldn't mind."

"It's one of those little silver, kind of round things. Shaped like a bean. Not much bigger than one, either. It's been sitting there empty for a while, but last time somebody was there, it was hooked up to gas and water and electricity, and I know it has a septic tank. I don't know what the situation is now, but I could check on it for you. Or you could check on it yourself."

"You know the owner?"

"Meredith Milner, a teacher at school."

"Meredith? Not *Meredith*."

"You know her?"

"Nosy gossip, ugly as pooting in church?"

Janet laughed. "Yes, that's her. But the trailer is outside of town, somewhere near where she lives. I forget how she came by it, some story. But she won't bother you, I don't think."

The idea was so alien, so mind boggling, that Leo couldn't help laughing a little.

"Well, think about it anyway. Just an idea," Janet said.

He wanted to keep his presence in town quiet, but even without Meredith's mouth, it seemed inevitable that word would get out anyway. In a sense, renting Meredith's trailer would be the best way to blend in. Meredith would be certain to thrive on the gossip, and soon it would be old news, Janet's boyfriend, the artist in residence from last term. *Oh sure, I ought to know, he's renting that old Airstream trailer of mine.*

They finished their coffee and went to the kitchen where Janet took the remains of a roast chicken out of the refrigerator, pulled the succulent flesh off the bones with her fingers and made thick sandwiches. Leo gobbled down his food, inspired as much by Janet's slapdash and hearty preparation method as by his hunger. He hadn't realized how famished he was until he learned he would be staying in Janet's house tonight. He begged her for a second sandwich, which she had him make for himself, and he consumed it before she had finished her one.

Barely past ten o'clock, Leo followed Janet through the house as she turned off the few lamps that still burned, and they ended in her bedroom.

"Yes," she said. "I want you to sleep with me. Would've said so before but just now made up my mind."

"Sleep, yes," Leo replied, the caffeine notwithstanding. "May I take a shower?"

"I'm afraid not," Janet said, and she pulled off her sweater. Beneath it she wore a utilitarian brassiere. She smiled and said, "But you can take a bath. I don't have a shower."

"A bath would be nice. Relaxing." He wanted to ask her if she would join him. He thought she might expect him to suggest it. It would fit the image he believed he had created the night they were together. But he was too tired. It would have been bravado, and he wanted not to be false.

He bathed. The old-fashioned tub was too small for two anyway. Having taken his suitcase into the bathroom with him, he was able to dress in his pajamas and house shoes before he returned to the bedroom.

Janet was lying on her back on the bed, the covers drawn up around her chin. Her fingers held the edge of the covers on each side of her face. She looked up at Leo, her pale eyes rounder than ever, as he walked around the bed to the other side and slipped under the covers beside her.

It was a regular full bed, unfamiliar, smaller than the queen size he and Leah had shared for years. He noted that Janet was naked under the covers. He turned on his side to face her.

"Janet," he said, "may we sleep together tonight without...."

She turned on her side to face him. "Of course we can," she whispered. She caressed his cheek with her warm palm for a moment and looked into his tired eyes, but did not kiss him. She rolled over to reach the bedside lamp and turned it off. They slept.

35

LEO STAYED IN BED THE next morning until Janet was gone to work. They exchanged a few words, planning the day, and she kissed him on the lips before leaving the house. Still weary and sore from carrying the suitcase, he'd planned to sleep another hour, but as soon as Janet was gone, he couldn't sleep any more. He shaved, dressed, and left the house, setting out on foot toward the grocery store.

The day was hazy, the sky bright white, the air thick and warm. He walked the mile or so to the Circle J, a supermarket near the interstate. There he strolled down every aisle, looking for items he hoped would be useful to Janet. It would be a sort of house guest's gift, practical, including a dozen eggs—he'd seen she was down to one egg— frozen orange juice, her brand of coffee, some canned tuna, a box of crackers. These items he would put away in the kitchen for her to find.

On the way back, Leo took an unfamiliar route, cutting away from the street through several vacant lots, emerging at the side of a graveyard surrounded by a mossy rock wall topped with wrought iron spearhead pickets. Beyond the cemetery stood locust trees, prehistoric-looking against the rusting corrugated tin walls of an abandoned sawmill. Leo negotiated weeds encroaching along the sidewalk, separated from the cemetery by honeysuckled pig wire fencing.

The orange juice would be melting, he knew, but Leo veered into the graveyard through an open gateway. The first graves he encountered were marked with smaller, more ancient and rustic stones. He walked toward the fancier monuments he saw farther on. Once he'd crossed a path marked with stepping stones, he could see the front fence several hundred feet ahead. It was made of the wrought iron spears but lacked the rock wall at its base, and so the passing cars would be able to see in. Why did he care? He castigated himself for his paranoia.

He was pleased to find, among some of the older, more ornate gravestones, a marble bench well out of sight of any passing traffic. Paranoid or not, there he sat, shaded from the glare of the sky by a gnarled fruit tree—he guessed it was a persimmon—his plastic bag of groceries beside him. He listened for the voice of God, which had always seemed close at hand to him when he was alone in a graveyard. The voice of God was no more than the peaceful proximity of dead people. It may not have been a voice at all, but whatever it was, it whispered and soothed Leo, and that was enough.

He sat and watched some sparrows fluttering under a bush. He read a few names and dates he could see from where he sat, imagined what Cannon Shoals would have been like in 1922, in 1938, between 1916 and 1919 when Thomas Milford Allgood succumbed to some disease or accident.

It was money that brought him back to the present. In 1922 or 1938 the money in his pocket would have been a substantial amount. In 1991 it was not. He would need income. But rather than contemplate the matter now, he sprang from the bench—it was getting uncomfortable anyway—grabbed the groceries and headed on toward Janet's house.

Exhilarated and hopeful, he thought about money again, this time practically. By the time he made it back to the house, he had imagined himself a cheerful grocery bagger at Circle J, an assistant-manager at a hamburger or fried chicken franchise, even a handyman scaring up yard work. People did these jobs. He would judge nothing, out of hand, as being too menial for him. After all, how much rent would Meredith charge for living in the tiny silver trailer, considering the gossip fodder he and Janet would supply her? And how happily he would comply with that!

Janet hadn't been able to tell him for sure whether she would come home for lunch. Just past noon, he heard her car pull up in front of the house. Leo opened the front door.

"Hi there," she said, closing the car door behind her. "Had a good morning?"

"Feeling anxious, you know," Leo said. "Found a pleasant graveyard and spent a few minutes there contemplating."

Janet smiled, coming up the walk, looking like a model on a runway, Leo thought, the way she walked.

"I talked to Meredith this morning," Janet said as they went inside. "Don't sit down. We need to go. I didn't tell her who was interested, but I asked about the trailer. She'll meet us over there in a few minutes."

Leo's mouth dropped open.

"If you want to," Janet added.

"Yes," Leo managed. "Yes, absolutely."

"Let's go then," she said.

Leo followed her out the door and to her car, feeling swept along, enjoying it even if it frightened him.

"You know how she is," Janet was saying as she started the car. "She's dying of curiosity. I let her know that it was somebody she knew."

"She won't be disappointed, then," Leo said. "You know, she made sly comments about you and me."

"Oh, I'm not surprised."

"Not worried either?"

She glanced at Leo and smiled. "Why should I be?"

The drive took less than five minutes. On the way, Leo told her about the conversation he'd had with Meredith. About how everybody loves Janet.

"How could she have known anything that... that soon?"

Janet laughed. "I hate to tell you, Leo, she wasn't referring to you."

"But...."

"Think about it. She didn't have a clue. Still doesn't. She will in a minute, though." Janet slowed and made a turn onto a road that appeared to head into open country.

"So Meredith thinks that, in general, everybody loves you?"

"She was referring to Mr. Gryder, Leo."

"Mr. Gryder. The principal?"

"He thinks nobody knows, but day after day, week after week, month after month.... People notice details, like the way people talk to each other, how they end up in the same place at the same time more than once, little things like that. It's called gossip."

"Mainly administered by Meredith?"

"She's a huge gossip, but I think it originates from the main office where they see who he's on the phone with, when he locks his door, when he leaves his office, that kind of thing."

The trailer—a space ship, Leo thought—squatted all alone in the middle of a grassy lot off an access road running parallel to the interstate a quarter mile back. They'd passed some storage units and a horse barn before arriving, but those were out of sight, around the curve. Beyond the lot, willows along a slimy creek masked whatever was beyond.

Meredith was already there, standing beside her car at the side of the trailer. Janet stopped just off the road, and she and Leo walked as Meredith squinted, watching them approach.

Leo offered a polite smile and waved as they reached Meredith.

"I knew it," Meredith said. Then she let out a thin shriek which broke apart into manic giggling as she looked back and forth between Leo and Janet. She sobered and reached for the trailer's door lever.

Pulling open the door, she said, "It's hooked up to everything, but I have to get everything turned on. City water because there used to be a real house here. The gas is propane, tank back there, and it's almost full, so you can cook already. You have to use the stove for heat, but believe me, it's puh-lenty."

Inside, the place was neat and clean, but stale, and cramped with three people.

"Stand back," Meredith commanded. She turned a metal handle similar to the one on the door. A Murphy bed folded down, taking up almost all the floor space.

"Voilà!" Meredith said, gesturing toward the bed and again looking back and forth between Leo and Janet.

"Great," Leo said. Meredith lifted and locked the bed back to its stowed position. The bottom of the bed, now a wall, was decorated with a bland—someone had thought "sensible"—design in plastic contact paper.

"Notice the wonderful, horrible, plaid curtains," Meredith deadpanned, gesturing toward the tiny window. It was an apt description of the tiny swatch of red plaid. "So whatcha going to be doing in Cannon Shoals?" she cooed.

Leo caught Janet's glance. "Don't know," he smiled. "How much you want for this crate?"

"You want to rent it or buy it?"

"Just rent it."

"Oh, I don't know. How much you want to pay?"

How much do I want to pay? Leo had never negotiated rent. Always there had been a set price. Janet came to his rescue.

"How about free and he keeps the lot clean and mowed."

Meredith again looked back and forth between Leo and Janet. "I don't know. No," she said, "I'd have to get something."

"Well," Leo said, "I'll be struggling at first, trying to find work. I'd like you to give me the best deal you feel you can. Maybe later I could do better."

"At which point you'll be out of here like a shot," Meredith said. "But that's understandable." She turned to the little kitchen area, barging between Leo and Janet. Suddenly she launched into baby talk full of mock affection. "Here's your little refrigerator." The half-size appliance fit underneath the only counter space. She opened it. "See? Plenty of room for a quart of milk and one weenie." She closed it. "And here's the stove. Two—count em—*two* burners. Oh, I just thought of something. Here's the sink, but we need to make sure the septic system is working. It was all right last time it was in use, but it's been known to fill up. The shower and commode, believe it or not, are in that corner." She pointed to the back corner where a plastic accordion partition masked the bathroom area. "Oh, well," Meredith spun around in a full circle, then held up one finger. "Free if you'll mow the lot once in a while."

Leo was stunned. "Really?"

"Hundred dollar deposit, though, against damage," Meredith said, the idea apparently just popping into her head.

Janet said to Leo, "You can do that."

Leo looked doubtful. "Well, I'll have to...."

"Oh, forget it," Meredith said. "Just don't tear anything up. This crate needs to be used or it's going to corrode away and nobody'll ever have any fun." With that, she was back outside. The sky was clearing now, the sun blasting through thinning clouds. Leo followed Janet out. Meredith was saying, "I should visit y'all sometimes."

"Meredith," Janet said, no mirth in her voice, "don't jump to any conclusions. You've been wrong about a lot of things, you know."

Leo took Meredith's hand in both of his. "I'm very grateful, Meredith. You should know the situation, so I'll tell you."

"No," she protested. "It's none of my business."

"I've left my wife, and want to start new here. I approached Janet for help in finding a place. That's all."

The lies soured on Leo's tongue before he'd finished uttering them. Janet and Meredith looked at him and he imagined their disgust at his cowardice.

Meredith broke the silence, babbling about having the electricity and water turned on. For the first time Leo noticed the power lines stretching to the trailer from the line of poles along the road. Meredith speculated that both electricity and water might be on by the end of the day, with luck.

"There shouldn't be any deposits if I keep everything in my name," Meredith said. "Your only obligation would be to pay the utility bills."

"Fine, perfect."

Meredith looked up at the wires connected to the trailer. "That one's the phone line. You can get your own phone service, okay?"

"Of course."

"So. You can take possession of the place now. No written agreement. Informal."

"Thank you, Meredith," Leo said, and shook her hand again.

"One question, though."

"Certainly."

"What exactly is a crate?"

Leo smiled. "An obsolete piece of argot."

Meredith looked at the trailer. "Well, it sure is that." She turned and headed for her car. "Can't cover for you if you're late for fifth period, Janet."

"I'll be there." Janet lingered with Leo as Meredith sped away. When she was out of sight, Leo and Janet embraced each other.

"God, Leo, you're crunching me," she said.

"It's fantastic," he said. It was all he could do to ease his embrace a little so she could breathe. "It's peaceful, isolated, very pleasant, don't you think? Thank you," he whispered, and he could not let her go.

36

THEY'D NEGLECTED TO BRING LEO'S suitcase. Janet drove him back to her house to pick it up, and returned him to the trailer before speeding off, several minutes late for her class. Leo knew that teachers were discouraged from leaving school for lunch even if they didn't have lunch duty. A teacher's tardiness could create chaos in fifth period.

Leo was grateful, had not wanted to spend the afternoon at Janet's house, nor to walk his heavy suitcase all the way to the trailer. Relishing the feeling of proprietorship, and of asylum, he carried his suitcase into the trailer. A bentwood chair stood near the tiny window with the plaid curtain. There he sat, craving a cup of coffee, but finding an intense peacefulness in the silence, and letting the entire wash of new feelings drift over him until he simply smiled.

Janet arrived a few minutes after four o'clock. By then he had unpacked his suitcase and found niches for his things. On a whim, he picked a bouquet of interesting weeds, arranged it in a jelly glass he found in the kitchen cabinet, and placed it on the drop-down table.

"Knock, knock," she called, opening the car door. Leo was already standing in the open doorway.

"Come in."

"How's it going?" she said, lifting a grocery bag from the floorboard.

"Had my interior decorator take a look," Leo said. "He's done wonders already."

She came inside. "Oh, look at your little, uh, bouquet."

"My own work, that one."

"I brought you a couple of items." She began pulling items out of the bag. "Utility candles. You have electricity?"

"Not yet."

"And here's some matches. I think it was pretty optimistic to think the utilities would be on today. Paper plates and utensils. Loaf of bread. I hope you like chicken salad, store bought. I'll make you some that's good one of these days, but this is edible. Jar of pickles...."

"You shouldn't have done all this. I'll pay for it."

"No. Small housewarming gift, that's all." She peered into the bag. "And what's this? Small jar of instant coffee. You'll have to find a coffee pot soon, but this'll tide you over."

"If I had water, I'd heat some up right now. The propane works."

"I didn't think of a bottle of water," Janet said. "We'll run you back to the store. Let's wait and see what else you might need first."

She crumpled the empty paper bag. "Oh, that's dumb, why did I do that?" she said. "You can use this bag for trash." Sitting on the built-in bench at the table, she started smoothing the bag, moving the dried arrangement aside to make room.

Leo placed the coffee jar on the few square inches of counter surface near the stove burners. He heard the paper bag rip.

"Oh, good *night*," she said to herself.

Leo turned, stood behind her in the confined space, placed his hands on her shoulders, tentatively massaging.

"Yes, oh god yes," her voice a whisper on the last word. Her head fell back, her slender neck limp, and she slumped, turning sideways on the bench and sliding against the wall until she rested into the corner. Leo had to step around her now, and he placed his hands on her shoulders again, this time from the front.

"Rough day?" he said.

"Oh, you know. It's always draining. You go on adrenaline or something. Caffeine. I don't know what. You can't not give them all you've got, and they need a lot. You find the energy somewhere."

Leo nodded, smiled, felt awkward standing there. He squeezed in next to her, facing her, massaging her shoulders all the while, watching as her eyes seemed to move behind the closed lids. He stopped massaging, cupped her head in his hands, feeling the tender lines of her ears with his fingers. She opened her eyes and sat up, running her hands up his arms to his shoulders, and they were together.

It was a warm and comfortable kiss, but their positions on the bench were awkward, and reflected some deeper awkwardness in Leo, which he tried to ignore. They shifted, sat side by side, leaned their elbows on the table.

"Do you remember a little boy in my class named Jamil?" she said.

"I don't remember any of the kids. All told, I stood in front of over two thousand of them during the residency."

"Two thousand?"

"I have the exact number the arts council gave me. Could be a typo. I had no idea I'd been with that many, but I covered eleven schools all told, so, you know. Can't remember faces or names. Oh, I guess a few kids who stood out do come to mind— their faces, vaguely, and personalities, but not their names."

"Jamil wouldn't have stood out. He was like any other little boy, a pretty decent student, but I don't think he was taking drama by choice."

"You don't have him again this year?"

"No. The kids only take a year of drama. I guess I've seen him in the halls pretty much every day, but I get tired of trying to smile and speak to every kid who's had my course."

"You understand me, then," he said.

But this was not her point. "This afternoon he stopped me in the hallway between classes. 'Miss Mabry,' he says, tiny little voice. He was blocking my way. I almost fell over him. He was smiling up at me. I couldn't remember his name. I say, 'How are you,' all smiles. 'Guess what,' he says. I say, 'What?' He says, 'I love you.' This was so sincere and happy, not some dare he'd taken or anything like that."

Leo took Janet's hand and squeezed it in his own. She acknowledged with a smile, and continued. "It took me almost until last bell to remember his name, but I did. Jamil."

"What did you say to him when he said he loved you?"

"Oh, I knelt down and looked at him on his level and said, 'I love you too.' I thought he might give me a hug but he just smiled and walked off. Seemed gratified, I guess. Turned around and waved and said 'Bye.'"

"Made your day, huh?"

"It did, but it made me wonder about his mother," Janet said.

Leo nodded. "I see what you mean."

"Is your mother living, Leo?"

"No." He sensed that Janet wanted more of an answer. "I barely had her. A few days, now and then, but mostly she was ill."

They made a shopping list.

—

When they returned from shopping, the water had been turned on. There was still no electricity, so they lit several of the utility candles, stuck them to the metal top on the stove. The night was warm, the trailer stuffy, so they left the door open. Not a single car passed by all evening. They felt private even with the door open. Leo sat on the doorstep and Janet sat just inside on the bentwood chair. They watched clouds move in the orange light over the town. Leo several times leaned his head back against Janet's knees. She still wore her pantyhose and he moved his head back and forth feeling the material snag a hair on his head once, unable to get it to do so again.

"Will my being here make any trouble for you?" he asked her.

"I thought about that," she said. "There's no point being secretive, that's for sure. I mean, we started at the top of the gossip pyramid with Meredith." She put the chair back in the corner, squeezed in next to Leo at the doorway. "No trouble, no. Even old maid school teachers are allowed to have a boyfriend."

"Even if the principal has a crush on you?"

"He might be jealous, but he has no right, and he wouldn't do anything to hurt me even if he could. He was a hippie in the sixties, no secret. Formed his political views then. He's married, has kids, straight as an arrow, but in his heart, I know he still believes in sex, drugs and rock 'n' roll."

They chuckled together, then sat for minutes watching the day darken toward twilight and dusk. Suddenly Leo laughed, and so did Janet. Leo said, "Were you ever a hippie?"

"No," she said. "Far from it. I never graduated from being a church girl, except to stop going to church. Were you a hippie?"

"No. It was all I could do to use some of the lingo and try to dress in style a little bit. It might have saved my life if I had been a hippie, gone all the way. But I wasn't. It was all around me, but I shunned it. Vehemently, in retrospect."

"Vehemently."

"Yep." He found this confession easy as long as he reserved the fact that Leah's will had been at the core of his rejection of the counterculture. Leah, not he himself, had seen the danger—not to Leo's well-being as he'd thought at the time, but to her continued possession of him.

"That's a funny thing to say," Janet mused.

"What is?"

"Might've saved your life. You haven't lost your life, you know."

Leo had to consider that, contrary to what he had believed for years, it was possible he had not lost his life. "Maybe you're right. I did feel I had stepped back from the dewy brink of death, not too long ago, making love on a sidewalk with a beautiful girl."

"'Dewy brink of death' sounds like a quote from something." Janet stood up and Leo heard her go into the bathroom, struggle with the accordion partition, succeed. When she came back, she said, "I'm staying with you tonight. If that's not a problem."

"Excellent," Leo said. He stood up, stretched, leaned against the door frame. A breeze ruffled the plaid curtain at the open window.

"It's not stuffy in here now," Janet noted.

"Kinda nice," Leo agreed.

The light inside the trailer was getting dim, even with the candles. He found the handle that locked the bed in its upright position and turned it. He jiggled it until it released the bed. Janet helped him spread the cheap soft blanket they'd found at the discount store and tucked it around the thin mattress. There were no sheets or pillows, but they did have a second blanket for cover.

Janet extinguished two candles, leaving lit only one at the center of the stove top—enough light, Leo thought, to warm his soul. He sat on the narrow bed. "Not comfortable," he warned.

"Doesn't matter."

"Well," he said. He started unbuttoning his shirt. Janet watched him. When he pulled down his trousers, it seemed to remind her where she was. Removing her sweater and wool skirt, she searched for a space for them, folded and laid them on the seat of the bentwood chair. She sat on the edge of the bed.

"You're right. Not too comfortable. Kind of hard." She removed her pantyhose, shivered, and stretched out on the bed. Leo stretched out beside her, careful not to bump, found himself pressed against the wall to make room for her. A moment later she was sitting up again, reaching into the shopping bag where the other blanket was still in its packaging. She ripped through the plastic and thrashed about, kicking at the blanket and working with her hands to get it unfolded and over both of them, Leo laughing at her manic method. A moment later they were under the blanket, facing each other. He had one arm draped over her, the other one smashed and going numb under his own body.

"This can be improved upon," Janet said, and she turned onto her back. Leo did the same. They held hands.

But that was all he could do. *I get it. I see what's going on. The excitement turns in on itself, beats itself down. It's a cringing sexuality, impotence. It's too laden with the excrement of demons, excrement of Leah, excrement of the possibility that tomorrow some tiny turn will induce chaos and cascades of changes that will funnel me back to Leah and the loss of life I've been so sure was done until lately, the last week or so, the last day or so, the last hour or so.*

And yet he trusted Janet. He trusted her because she had lived across the street from the pharmacist, who had killed himself when they made love on the sidewalk. The pharmacist had witnessed it. And she had disappeared afterward. This was not a matter of feelings, not a question of loyalty, and had nothing to do with tomorrow or looming chaos. It was only tonight, only the tiniest ticking moments lining up, "here we come," the moments said, and then saying goodbye, "away we go", the moments said. Tonight he could trust Janet, trust that it was her, her body, her mind, lying beside him. It was the most precious of all things, this holding hands, being next to each other.

"Where are you?" she said.

"I'm here," he said.

"You keep renewing your grip on my hand."

"Oh." He realized he was gripping her hard, and eased off a little. "Guess the real question is where is here?"

"That's easy," she said. "In your little space ship."

She was referring, he recognized, to an improvisation he had had her class do.

"Will you tell me something?" he said.

"Maybe."

"Will you tell me how the pharmacist ended up living across the street from you?"

Janet let go of his hand and sat up on the bed. Leo regretted his question immediately. But then she lay back down beside him.

"Well, I bought my house after college. Mom and Dad helped me buy it. Johnny and I had already set a date for our wedding in late June, so it was right on us. One fine day Johnny drove over from Cadbury on Friday afternoon as usual, but this time he came to me all hangdog and teary. He'd knocked up this girl in Cadbury and was going to marry her. He had a sort of stuffy, self-righteous side to him. There was nothing I could say to change his mind. And I tried... so hard."

Leo listened to her breathing, heard it fast and deep, then shallow, and gradually it slowed.

"See, he'd been in Cannon Shoals a lot, of course, and it turned out there was this opening at the pharmacy downtown. Suddenly Johnny and this girl were my neighbors, fine upstanding citizens, newcomers in Cannon Shoals, the pharmacist and his little round wife. They bought the house across the street from me. I don't know what Johnny thought about that, but it was probably the only house available to them. An old couple used to live there and one of them died and the other one—who knows?—went off to a rest home I guess."

"Sounds too coincidental to me."

"To everybody else, too. And me, too. But probably it was the only house in town they could afford."

"So you avoided each other, or what? I mean, this girl was pregnant?"

"Funny, but the months of her pregnancy all seem like one day to me. Guess I was in a daze. I'd see her once in a while, but we never spoke. I don't know if she even knew who I was."

"Could be he bought that house to put her right in your face, hoping you would confront her and mess up the marriage so he could eventually get you back. It would be your fault. He'd be morally okay."

"Hmm. I never thought of that. I doubt it. He wasn't that Machiavellian. Anyway, she looked sort of dumpy to me, but maybe that's because she was pregnant. One day she had the baby and somehow I was aware of it—someone I knew told me. Sure enough, I happened to be out in my yard when she and Johnny brought the baby home from the hospital. I saw them carry it inside. I just kept raking up the leaves from the cherry tree. And then, about a week or two later, she took the baby and left him. 'Ran off,' as they say around here. And that's the way things stood for all these years."

"But you didn't talk to him? You didn't get back together?"

"I was hurt. He was ashamed. That's the way it was, and that's the way it stayed."

"But didn't he at least try to talk to you?"

"When we first ran into each other after his wife left—this was at the grocery store—we said hello and then I stood there. I think if he'd asked my forgiveness and told me he wanted me back, I would have given myself to him completely. I think. Who knows? But he was scared and proud and, judging from the way he acted at least, morally superior. He made small talk. And after that, I also made small talk, and that's all we ever did, from then on, whenever we happened to run into each other, which wasn't often. In a town this small, you learn where and when to do errands so that you don't run into a certain individual. In the last ten years, I've probably run into Johnny Bishop three or four times if that."

The candle flickered in a freshening breeze wafting through the window. Leo took Janet's hand in his, but she slipped out of it a minute later and held it on her stomach with her other hand. Leo stared into the dull yellow candle light reflected on the painted metal ceiling and saw the pharmacist's house in the early moments of the dawn, dark windows where he thought he saw a curtain move.

Ordinary and ecstatic, we fornicated,
        Southland mucous (songbird rhythm in
        myxoDixian mode)
        smooth rubbing,
        her tender thighs wringing mine,
        we were voracious,
panted and grinned like wicked,
ancient blue-faced heathens,
while the yellow morning sun salved and
healed like the tongue of God
on my leprous soul.

        And then she lay crying in gentle relief,
        damping the grass at her cheek,
        her clotted hair like dollops of butterscotch.

        And done copulating, I held the grin on my face,
        our humicubation a blessing,
        blessed, oh God,
        found myself a pace back from the dewy
        brink of death.

        Death I needed yesterday.

The last of my youth had long ago drained away
and left my face wooden,
my body a papier-mâché sculpture
stuffed with ashes of dead rage,
the fire of my love cooled,
killed,
cold in me,
and black like burned letters.

The sun glimmered through the elms and splotched
 the yard with warmth,
and us fornicators with forgiveness.
Great baby blue morning glories gazed
down from the white trellis,
 dumbly giving up our long night.

37

AS HIS FIRST WEEK IN the trailer passed, Leo came to believe that Meredith was not, after all, the small mean ugly troll he had imagined her to be, but eccentric, morbidly curious, and no doubt frustrated with her own life. She had helped Leo settle in, and paid for some repairs and improvements to the trailer, saying she needed the work done anyway. He was beginning to like her a little—until she drove up to the trailer in her car, delivering Leah to his doorstep.

It was Saturday, about noon, a bright, cold, still day. Janet was in Cadbury, at the dentist.

Leo, framed in his trailer doorway, watched as Leah's shapely, denim-clad legs descended from the car, followed by her palpable heat of belly and wetness of mouth. Meredith emerged from the driver's side and leaned on top of the car, watching the reunion.

"So, Leo," Leah said. "I found you." This was the beginning of her *Say Out Loud Who I Am To You* act. He'd played his part in it before. In the presence of strangers or new acquaintances, she would leave the definition of their relationship to him. Would he act as though she were his wife? She did this in situations that would test how he preferred for others to perceive their relationship. She preferred to be presented as his wife, and when he did so, she would reward him later.

He wondered what, if anything, Leah had said to Meredith. It was a safe bet that Leah would have let Meredith go on believing she was his wife.

"Leah," he said, not trying to hide his dismay. "You found me, all right."

"Thanks to your friend here," Leah said, shooting a toothy smile back at Meredith.

Meredith looked apologetic, Leo thought. Not good enough, but to her credit at least. "She knew where you were," Meredith said. "I just gave her a ride out here."

"Thanks, Meredith," Leo said, attempting to dismiss her. She lingered a moment before getting into her car.

"I've got some errands," she said from inside the car. "Can I come back for you in half an hour, Leah?"

"No, don't do that. I'll wait for Janet." Leah smiled at Meredith, who then drove away.

Leo felt the weight of his enslavement sink out of the air, from another dimension, suffocating him. Life in Leah's world was simple, he realized, nothing like the complexity he was hewing with Janet. With Leah, it was simple, easy, and desolate in spite of the ecstasies that had marked his pathway through it.

Seconds passed, each one counted, released, lost forever. By the time Leah spoke again, Janet was a memory.

"What will I need to do to get you out of this kidney bean and get you home, Leo?"

He knew he had to sound easy if he were to have any effect at all, and that he would not be able to sound easy for more than a few words.

"You'll need to kill me," he said. He didn't intend to smile, but it was necessary to do so to keep from sobbing, so he did.

Leah saw right through it. "What's she done to you? Tried to make you feel small in this tiny place?"

This struck Leo as absurd and he thought Leah must be desperate to try such a ploy. Was she underestimating his resolve to escape from her? He tried to think how he could take advantage of her miscalculation. He could not think of a way.

"Am I going to have to stand here, or could I at least come in and sit down?"

"I didn't invite you here, Mother," he said.

"Oh, *Mother*," she said.

The word had come, unplanned, from somewhere deep inside, dug out with the sharp edge of his desperation. Why? He didn't know, but it seemed meet and right.

"I didn't want you here," he said. "I would have written to you or called when I got settled. I left you the car, the money, the apartment."

"The car's broken. I took the bus. Like you did."

"What did you tell Meredith?"

Leah would not say. She stood there looking at Leo, cocking her head from side to side curiously, in a way that Leo always had found fetching. He gazed at her face, assessed its beauty, and it was beautiful, even as she was aging. He found himself then looking at her body, and it was pretty, too. Fuller these days, but still shapely. She wore snug blue jeans and jogging shoes that looked like fresh marshmallows. Her baggy sweatshirt covered the modest bulge of her stomach. At 47, she looked no more than a well-preserved 35 by any standard.

When he looked back at her face, she was watching him. She whispered something. He could not hear it, but she smiled when she said it.

"What?" he said.

"Come on," she said, just above a whisper.

"Come on where?" he said, the petulance in his voice annoying him, reminding him, horrifying him, claiming that he was still the slave, the little boy, and lost.

"You have a phone?"

"Yes," he said.

"You call the taxi, then, and we'll get right over to the bus station. Get your things. I noticed you took that old brown suitcase. Pack it up quick."

He found strength, unfamiliar, clean, potent. How much of it there might be, he couldn't tell, but for now it was there if he thought of Janet.

"No," he said, disappointed that it was the little boy, now acting naughty.

"You want Janet to find me here with you?"

"No, I want you to go away," he said, and the words sounded not only like a child, but like an echo from some distance.

Leah moved toward him, the first step she'd taken since getting out of the car. A betrayal of relief washed through him. If she touched him, he would go with her and life would return to normal. She took one step toward him, two steps, and he tried to speak but couldn't.

Peace. The peace we know and long for in death. Only fools think there is life. The rocks know, the stars know, even the fish know that it all exists forever and only for an instant. What a strange invention our minds have had to concoct so that we may think about thinking. We require that there be time, yet time's only a parody of nothingness.

He backed into the trailer and slammed the door in Leah's face. It may have been because he was not ready, she had forced him a moment too soon, misjudged his vulnerability. His hand went to the sliding rectangle of metal at eye level and pushed it into the hasp. He had not used it until now. She was locked out—he was locked in.

He heard the door latch work, looked down and saw it turning. It was not a fixture that would lock, so it turned all the way and unfastened the catch, but the bolt kept the door from opening.

"Leo," he heard her saying, "I hope you're not going to leave me standing here." He crouched behind the door, his eyes squeezed shut, holding his breath until he thought he would pass out.

"Leo, I'm tired," she said, using a tone of slight, restrained annoyance.

Then there was silence for a long time. He hunkered there, listening but hearing nothing more. When he looked at his watch it was almost one o'clock. He crouched there, his breathing shallow, for an hour. Leah was waiting, if not for Leo to come with her, then for Janet to arrive. But Janet would be at home now, back from the dentist, grading papers until dinnertime. He crept on hands and knees the several feet to where the phone was mounted under the little window.

He dialed Janet's number. It rang a long time, six or seven rings.

"Hello?" It was Meredith's voice. He started to hang up, but didn't.

"Let me speak with Janet, please," he said.

"Hold on, Leo," she said.

Too many seconds went by.

"Hello," Janet said. She was distant, soft, a fire down to its last light in a cold rain.

"Come," he said, all he could utter before choking back the desperate emotion.

She was silent.

"Please," he whispered.

"It's not what I thought," she said, her voice so kind that he couldn't bear it. "I can't. It's not what I thought."

She hung up.

Leo sat on the cool plastic flooring, put the palms of his hands down on it, felt the exchange of heat and cold. He leaned back against the wall underneath the window, let his head rest backward and loll to the side. If only he had told her everything. But no, it would have changed nothing. And now she knew. How small the space looked, and how surprising that was. He would have thought it would look bigger from lower down.

Ah, now, this is better. Nothing more to be done. He crawled back to the door, crouched there, closed his eyes and looked into the void for something that was not there, held his breath, convinced for one moment that something had been there, but he had blown it away with his breath, like a speck of down. He opened his eyes, raised himself up to his knees, reached high over his head to the bolt and slid it back. He glanced at his watch and saw it was half past two. He pushed open the door and stood on his knees, framed there in the doorway.

Leah had found a five-gallon drum somewhere and was sitting on it in the spot where Meredith had stopped the car.

38

FOR A LONG TIME, PAPA supposed The Wanderer was dead, killed in Vietnam. He made me curious, but he wouldn't tell me much about The Wanderer, except that he was a high school friend. He expects to see him one of these days and catch up on everything. I asked him when, and he said when the time is right.

The Wanderer remained a missing person. Papa learned that he was alive, but they never connected, not even by phone, mail, or Internet, and Papa never did and never will know what happened to him.

But another missing person, Papa's father, will show up in 2011. I never saw him, knew him only as Cord Nobles. On March 20, 2011, at age 93, he is going to send word through a woman named Carrick that he is alive and not well in Australia. This woman Carrick will locate Papa on the Internet and email him at the address he uses at the theater. She will only say that *if* she has the right Leo Nobles, she would like to let him know that his father is in a hospital in western Australia and is not expected to live another week. "Sorry to be so vague," she'll write, and for a while, Papa will send reply emails asking for more information, but then, after about three weeks, the email address will go bad. Papa will do a lot of Internet searching but come up with nothing.

—

Waiting for Cord with the rest of them, Leah was upside down on the couch, her legs up the back, and her head hanging off the edge of the seat, her little butt nestling in the angle where pocket change might disappear. Ina sat next to her, glancing involuntarily at her little girl's blueberry eyes. Milton, anticipating the arrival of Lulu's young suitor, stood leaning on the door frame, his posture tentative.

Lulu slumped in the chair pretending to be bored, but she always paid attention to the people around her. She might not remember where a conversation had taken place, but recalled the exact words and inflection used. Had Russell commented about the fried egg while he was at the breakfast table, or was it in the kitchen, standing at the stove? "This egg has lace on it, like Mama's pillow case." Russell's concern, she understood, was that Drew had not come home for three or four days, and that Mama was worried about him.

Lulu also knew the colors of words, sentiments, actions, even ideas. Russell's offhand, yet pretty words about a lacy egg and pillowcase were the orangish color of the sandstone edging around the front walk. That was the opposite color—a smudgy teal blue—of Mama's hurting Drew with her comments about the way he dressed. Lulu always tried to be present when Mama and Drew were together, because the colors of sandstone and teal were prettier that way, and the textures were smoother.

Lulu liked that Cord was tall, because walking next to him made her feel more like a little girl, and she could let the violet come into her. Now that school was out for the summer, she no longer met him at The Mug after school, and it had been several days since they'd been together. He would be coming to the house today, for the first time. Even Drew would be here to meet him. It wouldn't be the first time a boy came to see Lulu, but this time she was interested, and they all sensed that.

Milton's ocher mood stained the toothpick he chewed. "Where'd you say he lives?"

"He's living downtown in the hotel," Lulu said. "He found work at the grain elevator. He didn't tell them he was an ex-Marine until the man asked, and then they hired him on the spot."

"Lagerfeld," Milton mumbled.

"And another man, the foreman, told Cord about a house for sale, a nice little place not too far out, on McKavett Street. Five thousand."

Ina laughed.

"Why?" Lulu looked at her mother. "Is that a lot of money or not a lot?"

"Depends on the house. Seems like he sure has told you plenty in a few days." Ina caught her daughter's eye and smiled.

Milton sniffed. Ina told Leah to be still and put her feet down, she would ruin the back of the couch scraping it that way.

"McKavett Street's right down there towards town, right past Knox," Milton said. "Stone's throw." He cleared his throat, looked toward the kitchen. "Well, I wonder where he is."

"He has to walk all the way out here," Lulu said.

"What, no car?" Milton shuffled over to the window. Russell and Drew were talking on the front steps, and the conspiratorial tones of their voices, though not their words, drifted into the room. Milton went into the dining room. Ina and Lulu glanced at each other. He was heading for the bottle he kept in his workshop.

Ina took a deep, resigned breath and stroked Leah's dark, shiny hair. Lulu felt the deep gray wash of emotion that often came over her when she saw her mother touching Leah. And almost as though Leah could sense Lulu's possessiveness, she climbed away from Ina and scurried across the room, laughing, burying her face in Lulu's lap.

—

When Cord came walking up the long street toward the house, Drew called out, "Here comes Cord." Ina had gone to the kitchen to look after the potatoes boiling in the pot. Leah had fallen asleep on the couch. Lulu went to the front door and opened it. Drew and Russell looked somehow intimidating, sitting with their legs spread and heads hung like a couple of rubes.

"Y'all stand up," Lulu said, not a command, but a soft request she knew they would find irresistible. They watched the awkward approach.

"Hi Cord."

"Hi Lulu." He took off his felt hat and nodded to her.

—

The living room was crowded with all of them there.

Lulu wished Milton would sit down because he looked unsteady, even with the support of the door frame. When it appeared that Ina and Milton had begun interrogating Cord, Drew snorted disapprovingly and returned to the front steps. Russell followed him quickly.

"Well, let them go," Ina said. "But after the South Pacific, did you go back to see your mother?"

"I went back after the war." Cord licked his lips, felt in his shirt pocket for cigarettes but he was out. "Went back to the place. She wasn't any different."

"Just for a visit, though," Ina prompted.

"I stayed one night. Had to make a bed out of some quilts."

"What happened to your old bed?" Lulu asked.

"She made me and Alzon's room into some kind of other room. I never did figure out what she was doing with it. It was full of stuff." Lulu appreciated the way he had honestly told them how he perceived his childhood, Ina and Milton nodding their understanding. Cord looked at Lulu. "You want to go outside?"

"Okee dokee."

"I'll call ya'll when supper's ready," Ina said.

"We'll be in the yard, Mama."

They stepped out to the backyard and Lulu ran her finger along the painted wall.

"Well, you do have a nice family, Lulu," Cord said, feeling his shirt pocket again, this time with acute need.

"Sorry Leah was such a little wiggle worm. She can't sit still. She's going to be starting school in the fall."

"That's a pretty little girl," Cord said. It sounded like he had wanted to say it for some time.

"Everybody knows it, too. She's the prettiest thing in this town."

"Except you," Cord said. Lulu smiled at him.

"Then what did you do? After you visited your mama."

"Had to get a job. Went to Cleburne and got on with the cattle auction but that's not full time. Worked for a farmer a while and that give me a place to stay too. Then I got on with the highway department and about burned up."

"Why?"

"Laying pavement in the summer. Got to be a hundred and fifty out there. We was out close to Snyder. Couldn't even keep water cold enough to drink in the afternoon."

"I hope you didn't do that for very long," Lulu prompted Cord.

"Made it through the summer, but they was heading out to the gulf and I didn't want to go that far. I didn't do nothing for a few months there. I had some saved, so I could get away with it for a little bit."

They strolled down to the creek and Cord searched for a flat rock to try and skip on the trickle of water.

"We had a gully out back," he said. "Didn't have no water in it except when it rained, and then when it stopped raining, the gully'd dry up again."

"This one dries up sometimes," Lulu said. "Not most of the time, though. Drew and Russell used to get crawdads out of it."

"They did?"

"They used to sell them and make a lot of money for back in those days."

"Crawdads. I never even seen one."

"Cord, I need to go inside and sit down."

Cord was looking at the water hoping to spot a crawdad.

"Cord," she said.

He turned to look at her. "Oh, you need to sit down?"

She was already turning toward the house. Cord followed her, still thinking about the crawdads.

Drew came around the house as Cord was reaching for the screen door. "Hey Cord, come on and meet a friend of mine."

"Go on, Cord," Lulu said. "I need to go in and sit down for a minute anyway."

"Come on around the house. He's in the front yard."

Cord was unsure. Lulu pulled open the screen door and hurried into the house, as much to ease Cord's dilemma as to meet her own need.

Ina was mashing potatoes. The rich smell of meatloaf thickened the warm kitchen air. "You doing all right, Lulu?"

"I need to sit down for a minute." She hurried into the living room and found Milton peering out the window.

"That god damn Joe Bob. I told Drew not to have him coming around here. Look at that pile of junk he's driving now."

"Dad, I need to sit down for a minute."

Milton cursed under his breath and headed for the kitchen.

They all understood that sometimes Lulu needed to be left alone. They didn't understand that she was not feeling ill, not upset, not dizzy or confused. It was simply that too many textures, too many colors, too many flavors had converged upon her in too short a time. They rarely hurt, confused or sickened her. Usually they tickled, soothed and uplifted—but in so doing, they demanded her attention. At these times, she needed to sit down and sort them out, the green from the blue before they became too intermingled, detach the cool satiny from the rusty wet before they ruined each other.

Often Lulu found that when she was done sorting, she felt a calm that invited her to do sorting of a different kind, the "sorting out" of situations in her life. She would think about how to bring up a grade at school, or what she would wear that day. And sometimes she would consider more important matters, such as how to help Drew stop straying from a decent, productive existence.

When she was calm, having set aside the color of sandstone, she considered Cord. From the couch, she could hear the young male voices laughing and swearing out at the curb. It might be that Cord was well accepted by her family already, and they had not yet eaten supper.

—

The summer had thickened into the buzz of cicadas, Cord had become a regular visitor, and had taken Lulu to a movie once in a borrowed car. Lulu took one of the wooden chairs from the corner of the kitchen and placed it on the front porch, sat in it, waiting for Cord. She gazed down the road and noticed the air changed colors from time to time. She understood this as the undecided nature of her relationship with Cord. He had walked from across town now a dozen times or more, a long, long walk, a major expression of his feelings for her. He would not be able to tell her anything in words, she was beginning to realize. He would not be able to demonstrate physically, such as with a kiss. But he walked the miles to her house every time he had an opportunity. He told her about his days, the work he was doing, the place he was living. And last time he was at the house, they'd gone down to the creek and he had seen, finally, a crawdad, but had been preoccupied with something else. He had been negotiating recently for the little house on McKavett Street.

The sun was still high. It would be a while before he'd get there. She began to wonder why she was already sitting and waiting. It was silly. She caught herself trying to see out of her 'other' eye, the one her brain had learned to ignore. She would do something else. She would talk to her mother. That was what she was neglecting by sitting in front of the house.

She found Ina in the kitchen sorting through some tomatoes Milton had brought home from the dairy, a gift from the owner. For a moment, the room forgot to issue its smells, and Lulu was waiting for them when Ina spoke without looking away from her task.

"Cord coming today?"

"He is. He finishes work at four today."

"Past four now, isn't it?"

"It takes an hour to get here from town. I wish we didn't live so far out."

"We'll need to eat this one an hour ago," Ina said, setting aside the over-ripe fruit.

Lulu needed the kitchen smells and they were not there. She picked up the tomato and put it to her nose. "It smells fine. Just soft."

"Reach under there and get me that basket. The half-peck."

Lulu found the basket and handed it to her mother. "Mama, is there anything I'm supposed to do?"

Ina carefully began filling the basket with tomatoes, the least ripe at the bottom. "Supper's not for a while."

"No," Lulu said, "I mean about Cord."

"Well, he likes you, that's for sure. Seems like he'd get himself a bicycle at least if he's going to keep coming all the way out here all the time. And he took you to that movie." Ina finally stopped fussing with the basket and looked at Lulu. "Does he act like he likes you a lot?"

"No. He talks about his work day and things that aren't interesting."

Ina laughed. "He's nervous."

"Well, am I supposed to make him less nervous or something?"

"You just be a good girl and if you get too bored with him, let him know. He's too old for you, you know. He shouldn't have gone into the Mug in the first place. That place is for kids your age. What was he doing across the street from the school?"

"Coming from the bus station, he said, just out of the Marines."

"How come you were in there, anyway? You never went in there before, did you?"

"Mary Helen and them invited me to come with them."

"Well, Cord's kind of backward, it seems to me. Does he ever talk about his mother and brother? Didn't he say he went to see them after the war?"

"He wasn't happy growing up."

"Well, that's not a very good sign. He's probably got a mean streak in him."

"Not that I can see."

"He wouldn't show it to you. Not yet."

"He was in the South Pacific in the Marines."

"I know. Did he kill Japs?"

"He said he never saw any action. Just sat out in the jungle and watched the ocean all night. He said he captured a Jap spy, though, on the island."

"What island was it?"

"Wallis Island."

"Never heard of it."

"He didn't like the Marines much."

"What rank was he?"

"I don't know. I'll ask him."

"Well, it won't hurt being a veteran when he goes to buy a house."

Lulu placed the ripe tomato on top of the others in the basket. "That's what he was telling me yesterday, Mama. He's been talking to them, trying to get a good price."

Ina opened the cabinet where they kept dried goods. "These tomatoes might be good with some butter beans, you think? And some cornbread tonight?"

"About that little house—he said he was looking at it like it was a pretty girl."

"You know what I think, Lulu? I think he's got things all planned out already."

Lulu looked at Ina and saw a tired little smirk that was an attempt to hide something real. Except for the detail of whether she would make it through her senior year at Brownwood High School, Lulu knew now what her future held.

39

IN 1939, WHEN MY GRANDMOTHER Lulu was just seven years old, she and her brothers Drew and Russell were playing in the kitchen. Ina was doing some housework in another room while the ringer washer filled with hot water in the kitchen. The children were not misbehaving—Lulu was hiding under a pile of dirty laundry and the boys were pretending to look for her, though they knew where she was because of her giggling. The boys were fond of their little sister, but enjoyed teasing her.

Ina may have been especially harried that morning. Also, the ice man had not shown up as he had promised. When Ina walked into the kitchen and discovered that the washing machine tub had overfilled, her anger spilled over to the boys just because they were underfoot. She burned her hand taking the hose out of the tub, and at that moment, Lulu jumped up laughing from beneath the laundry pile, scattering clothes. Ina had the hot water hose, now disconnected, in her hand, and in anger swung it at Lulu, hitting her face and traumatizing two of the tiny muscles controlling her left eye movement. One of the muscles never recovered, and Lulu grew up wall-eyed. This was the great source of guilt Ina lived with from then on. No one was ever sure if this same injury caused the malaise Lulu suffered later in life, or had anything to do with her synesthesia.

—

Leo stared out the parallelogram window at the trashy outskirts of Mortfordton blurring past. They were halfway back to Springdale and although Leah had invited him into a conversation about possibly moving into a house she'd heard about, he had not said a word. A stretch of construction on the Interstate slowed the bus to a wheezing crawl. Leo exhaled audibly, his lips flapping like a horse. Leah placed a comforting hand on his thigh.

"I'm going to enclose myself in a clay shell and pupate for a while," Leo said.

"Like a dirt dauber," she said after a while.

"Dirt dauber," Leo said, nodding.

Back in Springdale at dusk with a gusty cold wind picking up, they reached the apartment after dark. Entering first, Leo noted the close, stale odor the apartment acquired when left unventilated even for a few hours.

Swinging the door wide open, dropping his suitcase just inside the room, Leo went straight to the living room window, the one that didn't stick, and pushed it up to let in air, even though the apartment was cold. Leah was taking her time climbing the stairs. He went through the bedroom to the bathroom, tossing his coat on the bed.

It was a nice touch, typical of Leah, he thought, to have left the lilac brassiere on the pillow where he had put it. Even as he hurried to relieve himself, he had to smile in acknowledgment of her message back to him, the picture kind of message, too complex for words.

Hanging his coat in the closet, he heard Leah close the front door. "Me, too," she said, and hurried into the bathroom.

She left the door open. Leo watched as her blue jeans came flying out the door. He picked them up, folded them and placed them on the dresser. He heard her forceful stream, her quiet sigh of relief. He sat on his side of the bed.

Light in the bedroom was dim and golden, coming from a small electric wall sconce, an art deco piece that had survived remodeling efforts through the decades. Into this light source Leo stared and began to figure which gel color matched the amber light that escaped through the translucent milky glass of the shade. "Bastard amber," he mumbled.

Leah continued undressing as she came out of the bathroom. "Cold in here," she said.

"Heat'll kick on," Leo said, turning to see her as she pulled back the covers on the bed. She was naked.

Switching off the light, he went to the bed and picked up the lilac brassiere. Leah watched in the glow of the streetlight outside, the unabashed spectator, the audience, as Leo held the delicate item in both hands for a moment before putting it back in the dresser drawer. He undressed and crawled into bed where Leah was waiting.

At forty-seven Leah still had great firmness in her breasts, and Leo allowed himself an appreciative glance at them in the dim light when he lifted and adjusted the covers. There was no hurry, of course. Everything was determined now. He waited until he'd established his warmth, spread it a little outward toward the edge of the bed, let it mingle with Leah's. She lay still, on her back, not the position she usually preferred. It was not routine. Leo knew he was to wait until she turned toward him.

His eyes became accustomed to the dark, and in the cold gloom he could see her eyelashes in silhouette. She lay there with her eyes open, blinking only at great intervals, and this he watched, and thought how beautiful she was.

Finally, she arched her back as if to readjust to a more comfortable position. He strained to see whether her new position was opening to him, or shutting him off. It was hard to tell, as she was still on her back.

He shrunk down under the covers and let his warm hand find her belly. She didn't pull away, so he knew now he could proceed. Letting his fingers brush the tender flesh at the bottoms of her breasts, he pulled at her gently, and she responded, turning on her side to face him. Like a hungry infant he was at her breast, giving her all the sounds as well as real suction, taking first the nipple, then as much of the breast into his mouth as he could, sucking and swallowing in great noisy gulps, cups of it at a time, quarts of it.

Her arm now fell across his waist, and her fingers caressed his buttocks.

Together they inched their bellies toward each other. Leo found Leah's mouth with his own, and he sucked her tongue into his mouth. When she took his tongue into her mouth, he extended it as far down her throat as he could. Their bellies touched. She slid her hands around him and, clasping them at the small of his back, held him to her as she rolled onto her back, her knees making mountains of the blankets, the soles of her feet finding and caressing the backs of his knees. In the rustling of the covers as they rolled, he smelled her pungent, all-day sex, and he was desperate for it.

When he was poised at her wetness, Leah was suddenly still.

"When I spread my legs for you," she whispered hoarsely, "it burns pleasure into me, nasty into my sex, Leo, my woman's place, my heart, Leo... my mother's heart, into my brain, the middle of my brain. It's evil, Leo."

He was about to say no, *it is not evil*, but she continued, as though in a trance, "It's hot like the fire in hell, Leo. It's so evil that it destroys evil with evil's own fire."

She had never spoken such words before. Leo might have lost himself to wondering had she not then laughed, deep, with gusto, and then pushed herself around him, plunging him deep into her, doing all the work, and then beginning to whisper, "...

evil...evil...evil..." until they were both lost in it, and she was no longer doing all the work, her breathing a whispered "evil, hivil, hiivil, hiii, hiii, hiii" in rhythm with him. She began to vocalize "hiii, hiii, hiii" out loud. Leo opened his eyes for a moment, not losing the rhythm, held his head back to look at her face. Her mouth was gaping wide and her tongue was protruding, straining out and down her chin. "Hiii, hiii, hiii," with every thrust of her hips, her brow wrinkled with ecstasy.

He was sure they reached climax at the same moment, and strangely, he fell asleep at that moment—or so it seemed, as he never was aware of rolling off her or making any adjustment. He was sure, when he woke up before dawn, that the same odd thing had happened to Leah, because he'd met her, the moment after their orgasms, the two of them naked together in an ecstatic, burning-place he knew to be hell.

40

L EAH FOUND ANOTHER TEMP JOB, this time at a bank, nine to five. All it required was her presence and her voice on the phone. She read magazines. Leo was up with her in the morning as usual, set two bowls, filled his with raisin bran, set the box and other choices so she could reach them. She drank tea, so Leo did the same, not worth it to make a pot of coffee, would get coffee later at the convenience store.

Alone with the breakfast dishes and the tea bags—one cent each by the hundred, store bargain brand—Leo set the box on the shelf in the tiny pantry. He felt the box catch on something sticky. He had soapy water in the little pan, stainless steel, brown crusty bottom, what was it, layers of burnt foods, sterilized by the flame. The morning routine stayed a blur always. She was gone, looking good, he was in his jeans and t-shirt and sneakers, no socks. Today he would dress in decent clothing, not lounge around all day depressing himself, but get out and run some neglected errands.

He turned on the radio. It was tuned to NPR, the only station he could stand, but he didn't want to hear about the war. Kuwait. He was sorry, but didn't want to hear about it. Local weather. Thirty-one degrees. Going up to mid-forties. Oil wells burning in Kuwait, the sky black, how much of it would drift around the world to Springdale? Any of it? He turned off the radio.

It was brown outside, a dirty gray brown coldness that worked on him even inside the apartment. He put his cup in the sink, dropped the spent tea bag into the trash can, the kind with a top that opened with a foot pedal, but the pedal was broken. He always had to lift the lid by hand. It didn't matter. He should wash the cup. He should wash

Leah's cup, too, and the bowls. But these were not tasks he would perform now. Now, he would go into the living room and sit on the couch.

Here I am, arrived in 1991. I believe I might have come back here from later, although how would I know? Now that I'm here, I've never been to the future. I was there only later. But here I am now. What a strange time this was. Or will be. I am not required to do anything.

He sank into the comfortable cushions, began to catalog his chores. He sat a long time, but kept forgetting to finish the list of chores. Wash the dishes. Make the bed. But what was foremost? What mattered? He was supposed to think about getting a job.

—

Oh, my God, no, Janet! You thought I was sleeping with my mother? She told you that? Oh, my God! No wonder you acted the way you did. He sat in the booth at the convenience store, musings he knew to be imbecilic wafting through his head, steam from his coffee wafting across his face. *Oh, God, that's horrible. And here I would let go with a sharp laugh, but cut it short. I mean, I'm so sorry. But I see how you would have bought that. Leah is quite a bit older than me.*

But would it work to say she's been struggling for years with psychological problems, and sometimes she tells people I'm her son. Or we could try.... She's been struggling with psychological problems. That's the source of my guilt, you see, because on the one hand, it's a nightmare trying to live with her, and on the other, I did marry her for better or for worse.

No lie, no matter how elaborate, could change the truth. And yet, Leo asked himself, had he not lived his entire life isolated by a wall of lies, a wall he'd patched and repainted so many times that it looked almost perfect? Why not just keep lying?

"You don't listen to me. You don't listen to a word I say," God the Father called to Leo from behind the counter.

"What is it, Sid?" Leo's voice was murky and cold.

"You may have seconds. It's your choice. You ain't gotta ast yo momma."

"No mothers!" Leo exclaimed, bringing his fist down on the Formica with stagy violence, his imitation of a Northern street punk.

"Yah, yah," Sid laughed, thrusting his fist three times into the air above his head. "No mothers. You got it. I cut you bad you talk about my motha." He punched a button on the cash register and it sprang open with a ping. Leo heard him break open a roll of coins and dump them into the drawer. "Here's your brain," Sid said, holding up another roll of coins. Leo glanced up in acknowledgment. "And here's your brain on drugs," he said, and broke the roll open and emptied it into the drawer like an egg into a frying pan. "Hee hee hee," he sang, and slammed the cash register shut.

"Sid," Leo said, "what's the best drug? What's the most awesome one of all?"

"How should I know? What do I look like, a junkie?"

Leo stood up and glanced around to make sure there was no one else in the store. "You going to tell me you never tried anything?"

"What do I look like to you? A fff...," and he too glanced around to make sure they were alone "...ucking hippie?"

"No."

"You don't need drugs," Sid said, already holding the coffee pot ready to pour for Leo. "Alcohol is all anybody needs. Everything else is un-American. Except coke if you're in show biz. Caffeine, here you go." Leo placed his Styrofoam cup on the counter, and Sid filled it.

"What's your favorite drink?" Leo asked him. "Colt 45?"

Sid leaned his elbow on the counter, placed his chin in his hand. "No, man. Pernod."

"Pernod." Leo wasn't sure he would be able to find that. "Um... What's your second favorite?"

"Gin."

———

Light from the street lamp made a trapezoid of amber, too distant, red shifted, on the wall beside the refrigerator. He was up, two-thirty in the morning, out of some bad dream of thirst—worse than thirst, a mouth full of some horror of chocolate gone sour and rank and impossible to spit out, big globs impossible even to dig out with his fingers. He made for the sink, found a glass in the dish drainer, filled it from the tap, sipped at first, then sucked it in and swished in his cheeks and swallowed.

She lay unconscious, on some drug. They had gone to bed early and done it. He'd banged her hard, wanting the panting sound she sometimes gave out when his fervor was unchecked. She had done that, panted, vocalizing in pinched short husky squeaks, *hiii, hiii.* Awake, he put down the empty glass and felt his way to the couch in the living room. The darkness gave way to phosphenes and mild hallucinations, patterns on the walls that he knew were not there.

His mind cleared. It might have been noon, except for the lingering feeling from the thirsty dream, and the dark. Something had gone before. He had been about to be hanged for the crime, and had not known what to wear. Did one dress up for the gallows, wear a jacket and tie for such an important event? He was in his boyhood room, and there were all the cardboard boxes, and some of them had his clothes in them. Torn blue jeans. A faded bleeding Madras shirt. Sneakers. Nothing appropriate to wear. And then he'd begun to think, *Why should I care? They're executing me. Why should I even worry about what I'm wearing?* And then a billowing white cloud came into the room, filled it with whiteness through which he could not see. It made him forget about his impending execution, but it did not remove the feeling of his having been convicted, and the sense of doom.

I'm thirty-nine. There was a time I thought I would have accomplished something by this age. Dean would think I should have. I wonder where Dean is now. I should look him up. Tomorrow, I'll try to find him. Probably killed in Vietnam. Lost sight of him even before we were out of high school. How can things like that happen?

He knew how. Dean had skipped across the atmosphere of Leah and Leo, dangerously close to the pull of their gravity. Leo had been obliged to send him back off into space, and by the time they graduated, they no longer even spoke to each other.

Someone told him once that witches conjure and pray to the devil at two o'clock in the morning. It was back in the days when he and Leah went to church, and once or twice, to Sunday School. A woman spoke of waking up between two and three a.m. out of dreams, and a man in the class cautioned her. *Witches may be at work on you. What kind of dreams?* She wouldn't say. She was a widow, not very old. Sex dreams, safe bet. She called them "disturbing."

Shame. Guilt. Humiliation. *During the day, I'm in a comfort zone of denial. Only at night, the truth creeps in. I'll never achieve anything, will I.* He was not required to achieve anything, and therefore he wouldn't. Leah didn't require it, nor did his mother or his father, the ones who lived inside him and were of some importance. Certainly, the two actual people required nothing of him, since they were gone. He required nothing of himself. He was adrift, hungry but adrift. He pulled himself up and made for the refrigerator.

The appliance light hurt his eyes. He could not imagine why he had opened the door to the cold and unappealing food there. But he was hungry, so he took the milk and poured some into the glass he'd used. The milk was good for his soul. By the time he put away the carton and placed the glass in the sink, he was getting drowsy again. He crept back to the bedroom, crawled in next to Leah, felt himself aroused by her stuporous, fetal presence, pictured himself rolling her onto her back, pushing her legs apart and climbing aboard. Bang her again, unconscious. She wouldn't care, wouldn't know. He grew drowsy thinking about this. Cord, standing at the back fence, opened his pocket knife, whittled a little folk toy and offered it to Leo.

Forget it. You hurt me. It was out of anger, but not a case of losing control. No, you planned it, and you gave me time on the bathroom floor to contemplate what was about to happen. You made sure I dreaded it, feared it for an hour or so while I sat confined in humiliation. And you made sure it hurt me badly. Physical pain, I found, comes home to stay. It's not forgotten. It's not assuaged with times of smiles, times of friendliness, happy six-pack hour or two, a quarter tossed my way. And as for any physical comforting, there were no hugs, no kisses, not even an occasional pat on the back or shoulder rub. There was no fatherly affection of playful sparring, no roughhousing, no games. And if there had been, it wouldn't have mitigated the effects of the beatings.

Do you think I failed to connect anger and pain with hatred? Was there supposed to be some way I finally matured and figured out that the beatings were not administered out of hate for me? And how long was that maturation supposed to take? And in the meantime, were the emotional effects of those beatings supposed to hang inside me, in abeyance, with no adverse effects?

I was a child. A child sees his father as the authority. If the father calls the child worthless and makes him feel hated and drives it all home with physical pain and humiliation, can the child feel other than worthless and humiliated?

Did you expect me to grow up, my personality formed, and suddenly have a different personality? Are you stupid? Yes, I think you are. Can I forgive you for doing this to me?

What difference does it make if I forgive you? The point is that I am already who I am, worthless and humiliated, and forgiveness will change nothing. Sure, you are forgiven. Take all the forgiveness you want. Enjoy it. Knock yourself out.

—

The liquor store did have Pernod, but it was so expensive Leo decided not to buy it.

He found a large selection of gins, picked up a cheap pint bottle, still not sure if he was buying it for himself or for Sid. He even considered buying two bottles, but felt that would be extravagant, and to get drunk himself would delay the decision he wanted to make.

Walking away from the liquor store, along the busy boulevard back toward his neighborhood, Leo jammed the brown paper bag into his coat pocket.

She'll know if I'm drunk, of course. He trudged up a long, shallow incline. "Question is," he said aloud, and then thought, *whether I have the strength without it.*

"But I do have," he said. "Don't I?" he said out loud, and there was no one in sight, so he challenged himself just as loudly again, "Don't I? Isn't that the point?"

Rather than cut back into the neighborhood lanes, he braved the whizzing traffic on the boulevard and walked toward the convenience store, his thoughts returning to the painful whippings Cord had administered, the hate that flowed from Cord and into the little boy, the thick leather belt channeling. Having worked with children in school settings, he'd bothered to educate himself about the cycle of abuse that continued when whipped children became parents themselves. If whipping was not a sign of love and discipline, then how might a whipped person live with the anger? Answer: They wouldn't be able to, so they would instead defend the practice of whipping. The worse their abuse, the more deeply they would have to bury their anger until it could find release on their own children.

No. I'll live with the anger. I will not bury it, ever, to be unleashed on some innocent.

There were several customers lined up at the cash register. Leo waited, pretending to look at the canned goods. When those customers were finishing their purchases, new ones came in. It was maddening. Any other time, the place would have been empty. He moved to the booths and sat down.

"There he is," Sid called to Leo as he was ringing up a purchase. By the time all the customers were gone, Leo was absorbed in his thoughts and didn't realize the time had come. Sid was standing over him, saying "Leo, I thought of a drug for you. It's called Thorazine. It'll cure what ails you. They give it to nut cases to knock em out. I had this girlfriend once in Chicago, she had some and when she'd take it, that was it for twenty-four hours. Twenty-four hours, man. She tried to give me some one time. Forget it, man. Forget her."

"I know about Thorazine," Leo said. "I brought you a present." He pulled the bag out of his pocket and proffered it.

Without looking into the bag, Sid brightened, took it and said, "Swiss-Up, man, thanks, my favorite, my very favorite." He slipped the bag off the bottle and frowned. "What is this? Lane's Gin? Never heard of it. What'd it cost, ninety-nine cents?" He laughed. "Just kidding. Here." He tried to hand it back.

"Don't you want it?"

"What, you're giving it to me?"

"Yeah," Leo said.

"What for?"

"An offering," Leo said without thinking. "For Christmas," he added.

"Christmas? Man, it's not even Thanksgiving yet. Besides, I don't celebrate Christmas. But I'll take it, anyway, and thanks. Have a cup of coffee on me."

"No, thanks," Leo said, climbing out of the booth. "I gotta get home."

So God said there was no Christmas, Leo surmised. It was invented by mankind, then. Very little was real. Civilization was nothing but something men made up and women bought into. Or the other way around. Morality, same thing. So what did matter? What was real?

Sex.

Leo walked along a street where the pavement was crumbling at the edges, the asphalt eroded into clods that settled into dirt when the rainwater washed down toward the river beyond the big cemetery at the west side of town. He noted the entropy. Though he felt sad, he questioned that too. If sadness was not real, then could happiness be? Then he realized that these questions were themselves not especially tangible, and not very helpful. And again he remembered the one thing that did matter because it was real.

41

LEAH ALWAYS KEPT A SUPPLY of Thorazine, somehow garnering prescriptions for it for as many years as he could remember. She didn't take it regularly, but would empty a bottle over a period of some months. Leo found it amusing that God the Father was indeed all-knowing, else why would He mention that particular drug? It was of course up to the mortal, Leo, to interpret the exact meaning of God's words.

Leah arrived home from her temp job just after five o'clock. She exploded into the apartment as she sometimes did, full of energy and motion. Leo sat in the easy chair with a book, pretending to read.

"Lyle the supervisor said he wants me to work permanently. I have to apply and go through all the motions, but if I want it, he says it's mine." She was throwing her coat and scarf all over the room, it seemed, stirring up gusts of wind.

"Do you want it?" Leo asked, looking up.

"I think so," she said, still catching her breath, and flew into the kitchenette where she jerked open the refrigerator. "It would be security for us. You could do whatever you like and not have to worry."

"If I knew what I wanted to do," Leo said.

"Act in some plays at CTS. I'd love to see you in a good role again."

"I know I don't want to do any acting," Leo said, and without warning, God the Father made His presence known. Leo felt unprepared, but he had to go on with it now. "I know what I want to do," he said. "As a matter of fact."

Leah breezed over to the couch, munching on a piece of cheddar, imitating a mouse, trying to look cute. "You do? What?"

"You won't like it, I'm sure," Leo said.

"Yes I will," she said, nibbling and smiling.

"I'm going back to Cannon Shoals. Going back to Janet." He had the courage to look at her when he said it, and he saw the breath go out of her, but he kept talking with hardly a pause. "I know this is hard, but Mother, you've got to step back from everything—like I've done the last few days—and see everything in perspective. We both have to deny what's been going on so that I can...."

Leah dropped the piece of cheese onto the couch, her eyes rolled back in her head, and she fell to her side, then rolled off onto the floor, imitating a seizure. It was the second time Leo had called her "Mother," and though he wasn't sure why, he felt it was a powerful weapon against her.

"I've made up my mind, I'm afraid," he said. "You can try to destroy me, go and tell Janet everything if there's anything left you didn't tell her. Destroy Janet and me, destroy most of me. But that would make me disappear from you forever and become a monster somewhere. You'd never find me. Never."

Leah appeared to relax, her eyes seemed to focus, staring at the ceiling. Leo was still sitting in the easy chair, his book, a worn old paperback copy of Genet's *Miracle of the Rose*, on his lap face down.

He had said it. Now they both felt the silence like pressure underwater. Said it, yes, but had he *done* it? After a while, a quarter hour or so, he picked up his book and tried to read, but he couldn't. He kept looking at Leah, trying to guess what she would say when she finally spoke. He hoped it would be about her new job offer, an immediate sign of denial and yet a harbinger of some kind of acceptance. He went so far as to hope she would start making plans for living alone.

Another quarter hour passed. By now he was worried because Leah had not stopped staring at the ceiling, her infrequent blinks his only reassurance that she had not lapsed into some sort of death.

Finally, Leo placed the book on the lamp table and started to get up, but when he moved, Leah shot her hand straight up into the air. Leo froze, watched her. She turned her head and locked her gaze on his eyes.

He refused to look away. "You said yourself, the other night, that it was evil," he said, his voice raspy and unclear.

"Yes," she whispered. "Sinful and wicked. But I've needed it. Haven't you?"

He kept his gaze on her. "No. Whatever I may have wanted, I can't say it's been what

I needed." Leah looked away. "You've been selfish, Leah," he said, hoping to increase the power he felt rising in him. "You've used me. Do you see that?"

"Yes," she said, and she sat up, leaned back against the front of the couch.

A moment later, she pulled her knees up to her chin and leaned on them, looking at Leo.

"You're showing me the view up your skirt, aren't you," Leo said.

"Am I?"

"It's obvious."

"Are you going to tell me it doesn't do anything for you?"

"No, because that would be a lie. The question is whether I can resist it, isn't it."

"And do you think you can?"

Leo hesitated, showing Leah that his answer would not be unconsidered or merely argumentative, but would be firm. "Yes, I think I've resolved to resist you from now on."

"Well, I don't blame you," she said. "I have been selfish. I've wanted my own pleasure, my own womanhood. That's what you've given me. But have I given you your manhood, Leo? Have I?"

"No, I'm afraid you haven't."

She crawled across the floor on her hands and knees and sat at his feet. His heart pounded with what he believed to be apprehension and not sexual arousal. He was happy with the situation.

"I've been selfish," she said, more to herself than to him. She lay her head in his lap for a moment, then looked up at him. "I can be generous."

"Yeah. I'm not going to argue with you there." He took her face in his hands. "It doesn't matter, Leah. I've made up my mind."

She tried to kiss him, but he let go of her face and turned away, hoping she would see that there would be no more confrontation.

Leah went up on her knees and buried her face in Leo's lap.

"Leah," he said, "it's no use. If I have to physically push you away from me, I'm more than capable of doing it, and I will."

"But I think I can be generous," she whispered toward his lap. "I've been selfish, and I think I can give you fulfillment. I don't think any woman can fulfill you like I can."

"No," he said, and tried to get up, but she threw all her weight onto his lap, kissing the fabric of his trousers, her hand finding the zipper. "It won't work, Leah," he said in a calm voice.

But it was working already, and he was fascinated with it. The feeling of power, which he'd resolved to protect and nourish and increase, was now increasing indeed. He let his gaze fall on Leah's head, the dark hair a moving mass in his lap.

The evil worked itself up and ecstatically erupted out of him and into something, not the air, not the earth, not the stars. It was Leah. Without knowing why, Leo screamed "No."

He sat still, devoid. Leah, without trying to embrace him, rose up and put her face even with his. When he looked at her, she pursed her lips, inclined her head back, opened her mouth. Inside it he saw the mixture of saliva and his mucous ejaculate, and he stared at it. She tilted her head back a bit further, swallowed, licked her lips.

"You see," she said. "I took it all inside me, and I'll digest it, and it'll be gone. And you're free of me."

Leo shook his head side to side, but that was all.

"You can use me, and I'll never use you. You're free." She was speaking like a mouse, so he could barely hear her. "You're free." She lay her head on his knee. "You can go to Janet now. You can do anything."

But he was not free. He was lost. He had reached the dewy brink of death again, and there was no way to turn back.

42

PEOPLE DON'T HAVE CHOICES IN some matters, Leo thought, remembering Dean Warburton, The Wanderer. He envisioned Dean alone in a rented room on a back street in some windswept city in the Midwest, drinking wine, pretending to write his memoirs.

The humid cold made it hard for Leo to reconsider old attitudes. Chocolate was no help. He had tried it. Laughable. Schoolboy crap. Two weeks before Christmas, it was too rainy even for December. Several days of wet weather had given the apartment an unpleasant odor, as though releasing old tobacco smoke and body odors from the wallpaper. Leo changed clothes in the middle of the day, sure he smelled the apartment on himself.

He sat in the easy chair reading passages from Anais Nin's *Delta of Venus,* a volume he'd stolen from Dean in high school because it had affected him so much that he never wanted to be without it. He found himself unmoved by the writing now. He picked up one of the *Frederick's of Hollywood* catalogs Leah had been receiving in the mail for a while.

As usual, he'd slept late, pulled himself out of bed in time to prepare lunch for Leah. He heard her high heels clacking up the stairwell, and went to the door to open it for her.

"Yucky, yucky, yucky out there," she complained. She threw off her coat, letting it fall onto the couch. "Anything to eat? I'm starving."

"Got tomato soup already hot," he said, and indicated the table, where bowls were set for two.

"Sounds good," she said, and went to the sink where she washed her hands. Leo sat again in the easy chair and picked up the book. "Not eating with me?" Leah said.

"Not hungry," he said, nosing into the book.

He heard Leah filling her bowl from the pot, opening the refrigerator for something to drink, pouring, moving the chair. Staring blindly at the page, he concentrated on the sounds Leah was making. Their behavior, he realized, had evolved into a routine in the several weeks since the evening of the fellatio. As always, Leah tended to be a little bossy, reminding him about his errands as she left for work each morning. She did take the regular job she'd been offered, and since then she'd asked Leo several times to consider auditioning for the spring production of *Fiddler on the Roof* at CTS. He could not imagine himself in any role in the play.

Days would pass that almost seemed the same old way between them, but attitudes were new and different. It was up to Leo now to initiate their rituals, whereas before it had almost always been Leah who sent the first signal.

They developed certain understandings. He would not start anything during lunch, since Leah did have to go back to work, and time was short.

"Try not to leave such a mess this time," Leo said, not looking up. He wasn't sure why he said it, but little castigations like that had been serving as openers to their rituals. It might have been that he didn't want her to leave a mess on the table, but no. He was testing to see if she would play.

"I'm sorry," she said, a bad little girl. So, she would play if he wanted to. Not that he would make her late for work. He would let it drop, of course. Interesting, though. He heard her push the chair back, take her dishes to the sink, wash everything. He noted that she dried and put away, too—she was going overboard. "Don't make yourself late, Leah. I was just kidding."

There were other sounds in the kitchenette he didn't recognize. He looked up when he heard Leah pad over to him and stand in front of him. She had taken off her dress and high heels. As soon as he looked at her, she went down to the floor in front of him. She still wore her pantyhose over her panties, and her bra.

"No, really, Leah. You don't have time."

She scooped her bra up over her breasts, pulled it off over her head without unhooking it. She looked at him with big puppy dog eyes, and cupped her hands under her breasts, offering them up to him. He didn't even try to resist, just held *Delta of Venus* out of the way. She left him exhausted in the chair as she retrieved her garments, put them on, and was out the door.

It was an abbreviated version of their typical evening ritual. His gentlest criticism

elicited an apology followed by some small thoughtful favor. Her contrition would
grow throughout the evening. By bedtime she would take a posture at his feet, having
scurried around the cold apartment fetching his book, his pajamas, whatever he seemed
to require. Sometimes this ritual culminated while he sat in his easy chair, other times
they went to bed for it.

Other rituals materialized, and Leo let his fascination overcome the sense of dread
and profligacy that descended on him like a swarm of gnats. He swatted at the self-
recrimination with long walks, caffeine, occasionally alcohol, oversleeping. He even
tried masturbation once, thinking it would fortify him against Leah's next seduction,
but it was stupid, because there was no ecstasy in it—it only proved to him again that
Leah was his ecstasy. Like an addict escaping the craving by feeding it, he could escape
from her only by giving himself to her. As the weeks went by, more and more he found
himself waiting anxiously for her in the afternoon, imagining how she would look as
she took off her coat, turned to face him, and began something new this time.

"I want me some gook pussy," he said one night. He'd been thinking of Cord,
had been in a dark mood all afternoon. Leah registered his bile, disappeared into the
bathroom for a while. Leo could hear all the bathroom noises as he stewed in his
melancholy. Leah emerged naked, and slowly coaxed Leo out of his clothes. On the bed,
she draped her luxurious, freshly clean hair across his genitals until she saw him respond.

"Him want some gook pussy?" By now she had conceived of what that might
mean—certainly Leo had no idea. "Gook poossy? Gik pissy?" She flipped herself over,
jutting her bottom up by flexing her knees and lifting herself from the middle. Leo
went up on his knees and assessed her pretty little cloven beach ball of a bottom. She
wiggled it back and forth for him. She moved under his touch as he maneuvered himself
between her ankles. "...me sim gook pissy...," he whispered. *Ook ook* she said and
wiggled what he was asking for. He pulled her knees apart a little and she responded
mm hmm ook ook ook say him want him sim gook pissy and wiggled some more and
backed a few inches into him. When he pushed it there she hunched forward so he was
too far up so he hunched down to get it at the right hole but she moved again and *she
wants it there she wants it in her bottom oh* and he pulled her apart more and put it
there and she sounded *mmm ook ook mmm hmmm ook ook ook ook ook* and she was
moving with it and he tried but it was too tight.

Then she broke the spell and ran into the bathroom and returned with a squirt
bottle of baby oil and she started it all over again. Very quickly they got back to it and

neither of them cared about the oil on the sheets just pour plenty on and let it run down her crack all over that thing, and he got excited and rammed it past the sphincter and she screamed and went flat down on the bed. It scared him but she caught her breath and started *ook ook ook ook ook ook ook ook* moving with it and she pulled her knees up under her and he started helping and it went in by tiny increments until he got it in mostly all the way trying to control it but then she was laughing and *ook ook ook ook ook ook* and he thought it was hurting her and she kept laughing and that made him hurt her more until he was done, and it was more than they knew was possible, so they lay in each other's arms and kissed until their mouths were sore.

—

She disappeared into the bedroom some evenings and emerged in outfits he had never seen, made up in ways he had never imagined. These were prompts, the accoutrements—some of them from *Fredericks*—made possible by her steady paychecks, and she let him go with it where he might, as he let her go with it where she might.

—

He heard the clack of her heels descending the staircase, and the distant sound of the front door closing. The car was running fine these days, and he listened for its engine starting. He heard her drive away. And then he heard his blood coursing through his veins, and the sound of the cosmic radiation he knew to be penetrating him all the time. The more he listened, the more he heard his own soul sleeping, snoring, struggling for breath, soul apnea, unable or unwilling to awaken. This was, in fact, the way he lived. This relationship with his young aunt—was it not about as good as he could hope for? Why, then, did his soul sleep and snore, as though to try and escape awareness? He did have a soul, didn't he? It was asleep, was it not? *Delta of Venus* should be a fun read, should it not? Then why was it not?

The automatic, insular nature of their life together was so extreme that Christmas came and went in their household with no celebration, no tree, no ornaments, no gifts—scant mention of the holiday, though they were both aware of it. People would learn to leave you alone if you politely ignored them. The old year, 1991, passed into 1992, noted only in Leah's brief recounting of the office party at her job.

43

T HE FIRST SATURDAY IN FEBRUARY, after breakfast, Leo noticed Leah
taking two chlorpromazine tablets. Her usual dosage was one tablet—rarely
he'd seen her take two. She lay down on the bed in her terrycloth robe.

Leo suspected it was a sort of invitation to him. Things she had said—nothing
specific, but certain questions about his desires, and his having done things to her in that
condition before—led him to believe she was inviting him to take her while she was
unconscious. If so, he was unsure whether it appealed to him, and if it did, whether he
could live with knowing that about himself. He also wondered what Leah expected to
gain other than a long sleep.

Half an hour later, settled on the couch, he heard Leah moan. He went to the
bedroom door.

"Leo...," she slurred.

"What. I'm right here."

"Wait 'til I'm slee...."

"What?"

"...do me. Bad."

"What? Do you bad?"

She loosened the sash on her robe, pulled the robe open a few inches, moved her
legs apart a bit more than they already were. Leo could see a smile spread across the
lower part of her face, grotesque in its slack.

He paced around the apartment for a while, sat in the kitchen, pondered for the
thousandth time whether there wouldn't be some way to move the easy chair over by the

window. No, because of the radiator. Outside it was well below freezing. A light wind was shaking the brittle trees. The sky was blotched with ugly gray clouds moving gracelessly eastward. He stood at the window, watching these torn shapes in the sky, wishing for more coffee, finding the prospect slightly nauseating. He went to the pot anyway, found it empty but for a few drops. On an impulse, he put on his hat, coat, and gloves.

His plan, formulated as he descended the stairs, was to walk for a while, end up at the convenience store to have some coffee. But the air was so cold, the day so raw that he walked straight to the store, and was glad to get inside.

Sid Koff was not there. At the cash register stood a lovely young woman, a college student, Leo guessed, who smiled at him as he passed her on the way to the coffee pot. She had thin lips, a thin nose, thin black hair that was long, well below her shoulders, with one cerise streak and one chartreuse.

"Sid off today?" he said, trying to separate a Styrofoam cup from the stack.

"He never works on Saturday," she said.

"Ah, yes," he said, though it was news to him. He paid for the coffee and sat in a booth, where he tried to take his time, but drank fast, needing the warmth.

Several customers came and went, some just paying for gasoline from the pumps outside. When he was finished with the coffee, his hands were still cold. He stood up as the girl finished ringing up a gasoline purchase. The customer hurried out and Leo was following when the girl's voice—thin—stopped him.

"You know where the Unitarian Church is at?" she said.

"No," he said.

"All the way back down Poindexter," she said with a generous gesture over her shoulder. "All the way to Bennett Avenue. That red brick thing that looks like an old timey schoolhouse. You know."

"Oh, yes," Leo said. He remembered now that building was the Unitarian Church, but couldn't fathom why she was telling him this. "Thanks," he said, and she smiled and nodded. "You are a very beautiful girl," Leo said, "or woman, whatever you like."

She looked at him and tried for a smile, but he had frightened her. She glanced toward the back room. "Sorry," Leo said, and hurried out the door, feeling foolish, wondering why he was so edgy.

He turned down Poindexter. "I think I'll walk to the Unitarian Church in the old school building," he said in a conversational tone to the cold air in front of his face, his breath a cloud before him. If he claimed that he was going, he reasoned, then he would go. He wondered if another customer—there had been several in the store—had asked for directions, and she'd confused Leo with that person. But no, she had flat asked him if he knew where the Unitarian Church was at. The girl was telling him where to find Sid. Had he seemed so interested? Or was this an act of God?

The tall sycamores along each side of Poindexter began to sway back and forth with the rhythm of Leo's walking. He stopped and stood, because the trees were making him dizzy. He vowed to cut back on his caffeine consumption. When he walked on, the trees, separate from the sedate houses, began to sway again, and then they began a low moaning and crackling like frozen, dead limbs falling. The cold air made Leo's eyes water, and by the time he reached the Unitarian Church, his nose was runny.

The building was set back from the street, behind a small plot of lawn worn down to muddy, sterile earth where people cut the corner short. Leo hurried up to the double doors at the front of the former schoolhouse. To the left of the entrance, an unassuming sign, white with plain black lettering, proclaimed this "Unitarian Universalist Church."

The front doors were unlocked, so Leo went inside. Standing in the vestibule, he removed his gloves, found a tissue in his pocket and dried his nose with it. His sense of smell began to revive, and he noted a pleasant hint of pine cleaner, floor wax, an even fainter aroma of paint. The air was cool, but not so cold as the outside. Meager illumination came through the windows in the doors to the sanctuary. He looked through the windows, saw that the dim light inside was coming from the daylight behind translucent drapes which spanned twenty feet from ceiling to floor down both sides of the large room.

Leo pushed open the spring-loaded doors and stepped inside the sanctuary. The wooden floor creaked underneath thick red carpet on the aisle between rows of cushioned metal chairs. The room was as cool or cooler than the vestibule. A few feet down the aisle he stopped and stood. The crushing peace in the place reminded him of something long ago, but he could not remember.

"Are you a happy man?" God the Father asked.

"Ah," Leo said, his eyebrows raised in surprise. "I hallucinate a voice?" He asked this either in spite of, or because of, the voice sounding like Sid's. His eyes adjusting now to the dim light, he glanced around and saw Him in the choir loft, which was not a loft at all, but a collection of folding chairs behind a lectern which must have served as the pulpit. He was wearing a coat and a plaid hat with ear flaps folded upward. He held a paper bag molded around a flask-shaped pint bottle. From this he drank before speaking again.

"Leo, you've discovered my sanctum sanctorum," he said. "I will not share. I shall not share my orange vodka. Have you ever tried it? It's like Tang. Do you know what Tang is? The astronauts took it with them to the moon. I'll never buy this dreck again. I thought it would be easy to drink right out of the bottle. It's disgusting." He took another sip and coughed. "I'm not sharing it, though. I need the whole thing today."

Leo walked down the aisle toward Him, saying, "I thought I'd confess."

"This is a Unitarian church. We confess nothing."

Leo sat on a chair in the front row. He watched Sid drink for a minute or two, but then he felt tired. He let his head hang down, closed his eyes, wondered how to pray.

"Think of this as the world, the cosmos," God the Father instructed. Leo decided to listen without looking up. "Unless you walk out of here, or slither or whatever, out of here, through the womb there, that little vestibule at the back there, into the outside, which is life, you'll be in no position to come back, when you're done with life, back into the cosmos here."

"Is that my problem?" Leo said, loud enough that Sid might hear it.

"That is your problem," He said, and Leo heard Him suck on the bottle and then emit a quick, clearing cough. "Don't get stuck in your mother's womb, Leo, or there'll be no entity to do any walking through any doors back into any universes when you get finished with life. You don't exist until you're out of the vestibule. This I have figured out. Through which to go through it, you old sod, don't you understand? You don't drink anyway, do you?"

"No. Very rarely," Leo whispered so that He could not have heard this time.

"Good. Then my orange vodka is safe. I started to get something called Southern Comfort. But I'm not southern, so I didn't think I qualified." Leo heard Him stand up, scraping the chair. "You see, Leo, it's fine while you're alive. Alive, it's no problem."

"May not be all that pleasant, though." Leo looked up, saw Sid approaching him unsteadily. He stood in front of Leo, His eyelids so heavy they almost hid His twinkling eyes. He nodded, whether in assent or drunkenness Leo couldn't tell, but His mouth curled into a smile. He held out the paper bag.

"Therefore I give you this. Just a slug, Leo. Don't hog it," and then he sang, "Don't Bogart that joint, my friend...."

"Thanks, but no. It would be wasted on me."

Leo watched Sid take a seat across the aisle and strike a macho pose, His elbow cocked over the back of the chair, the bag of orange vodka held at the ready near His face.

"How's everything with You?" Leo asked.

"Terrible, just awful. I've blown it. I'm out of school. Blown it. I'm a dropout, without finishing, no degree. What'll I do?"

"When did all this happen?"

"Oh, last week. Or week before last. But you know, whatever your name is, Leo, sorry, there's nothing to learn anyway. What I told you, and nothing else. Into life, live the sucker, back out of life. Universe is at either end."

"Through the vestibule," Leo reminded Him.

"Yes," He said, turning to Leo with a sly smile, "and we guys spend our lives trying to get back in there. Ever think of it that way? We can only fit as far as our pubic hair, of course." He laughed and settled back in the chair, took another sip. "Only time we can't touch creation is while we're alive. Rest of the time we're fine."

"That sounds a little backwards to me," Leo said.

"No, it's a little counter-intuitive, but it's right. If you can pray, that's a way you can connect back to reality–I mean, the universe—for a short period of time. Can you do that?"

"I don't know," Leo said. "I was thinking about trying. But why would I want to?"

"There's a pull back toward the universe. It's instinctive, like dying."

"And sex," Leo added.

Sid brightened and turned to Leo again. "That's right. That's right, my man. My man."

"This seems to put women in a different position than men," Leo said, "since they don't have an appendage to try and stick back into existence."

"Maybe so, but how much good does our appendage do us guys?" God said. "Not much. So I don't see what difference it makes, man or woman. I tell you, my man. I tell you." And God shook his head side to side with a wan smile.

Leo's feet were so cold they were beginning to tingle, the last stage before numbness. His hands were getting colder, too. He looked at Sid's hat, attracted by the pattern, aware now that it was the same plaid as the curtains in the trailer house in Cannon Shoals. He knew that this was a sign from Him Who wore the hat, knew it as surely as he'd ever known anything. Without another word, he left the church, feeling, as he walked through the vestibule and back into the harsh, cold day in Springdale, that he was being born.

—

He sat in the apartment for the next twenty-four hours, preparing several small meals for himself, poking his head into the bedroom now and then to see if Leah had moved. He slept beside her during the night. She lay still, as in a coma, the way she always did when she took her drug.

A few times he tested himself, imagining doing things to her while she was unconscious to see if the imagined things would arouse him. They did not, but the test, he knew, proved nothing. *Why should I think it will be any different this time when I tell her I'm leaving, this time for good?* And he intended to do that, reserving the possibility that he might be wrong. He might try it, fail again, and be more entrenched with Leah than ever, and hopeless. But he believed that he had God the Father on his side now, and that God would see him through.

When Leah awakened late Sunday afternoon, she went directly to the bathroom, and it was her noise there that alerted Leo she was up. She then trudged into the living room and sat on the couch.

"Where am I?" she said. Leo was sitting at the kitchen table with a cup of tea.

"Anchorage," he said, "where do you think?" He found her confusion amusing. "Would you like some blubber on toast?"

She sat there for some time, frowning. Finally she looked at Leo and said, "What are you talking about? You're crazy."

Leo laughed and said, "You're right. I was kidding. We're in Chicago. You've been unconscious for three days. You must be hungry. I'll run down to the deli and get you a bagel with lox and cream cheese."

She frowned even more heavily and dismissed him with a wave of her hand. "I know where we are. We're in that town in North Carolina. Springfield or whatever it is."

"Springdale," Leo said.

An hour later, with some food and coffee in her, she was awake and aware. They were sitting at the kitchen table in the uncomfortable little dinette chairs. "Mother," Leo said, and this word caused her to look at him with alarm, her eyes wide and fearful. "While you were out, I did some thinking. I've decided I don't want to audition for the CTS production this spring."

"But they're doing *Oliver*, and you'd be perfect for...."

"I've made up my mind."

"But I thought you saw it as a chance to start carving a niche for yourself here."

"I've made up my mind, and behind this decision I have the power of God, whom I consulted about this. I have the power of God and the power of the macrocosm. Everything I thought about while you were out is resolved, with infinite power behind it."

She looked back at him. "This is not about the CTS audition, is it?"

"It is, Mother, but that's the least significant part of it."

"Well, at least I hope you're not planning to sneak off again down to that little jerkwater town and what's her name."

"Not at all," Leo said, meeting the challenge in her eyes. "This time there'll be no sneaking. And as for you, there'll be no following this time either."

She dropped her gaze to the table top. Leo reached across the table and took her hand in both of his. "Is this a thing you understand, Mother?"

Without looking up, she said, "Please Leo, stop calling me that."

"Is this a thing you understand?"

"I understand," she said to a breadcrumb on the table, "but I don't believe you."

"Then you'll have to learn how to pray to God yourself so He can tell you first hand. This is what is going to happen, and there's nothing you or any other mortal can do to change it."

"But I don't even believe in God," she said. "Neither do you, do you?"

"Oh, yes we do, Leah." She looked up at him. "We do, now that God has appeared, an avatar, and talked straight with me." He looked at her, trying to see if she was buying it. She began to nod her head.

"You can prove it to me," she said.

"How?"

Now she looked Leo in the eye. "Only one way. I'll get it for you, make it easy for you. If it's true, then you prove it."

She stood up, went into the bedroom, came back a moment later and handed Leo a small piece of paper, a prescription for chlorpromazine. "You get this filled for me, bring the bottle to me and put it in my hand before you leave me."

Even if the implication of this was unclear, the fact that it meant something should have been obvious. But Leo blocked this from his consciousness for the moment. He took the prescription, read it over and over. "Thorazine 10 mg" and the scrawl of her doctor's signature.

"I'm taking a shower now," she said, and left him sitting there, staring at the prescription as though he understood her stipulation.

Theo Demian was the doctor whose signature appeared on the prescription. Leo sat for the better part of an hour at the kitchen table playing with the little piece of paper and other paper, a pad they kept near the phone. He knew, from having been with Leah for so many years, that Thorazine came in 10, 25, 50, 100 and 200 mg. pills. Thorazine, anagram for Zane I. Roth. Zoe Thrain. No such name as Thrain. Chlorpromazine, Archie Z. Monoply with a leftover r. He copied the handwriting again and again, Theo Damian, practicing like a forger would do, not knowing why. Theo Damian. Made in Heto. The Ode in Ma. I'm One Death. It was amusing, but he gradually let himself realize that all he needed to duplicate was a single zero.

While he scribbled letters and doodled anagrams of the doctor's signature, his mind wandered through a vast landscape of memories. He lingered on events he'd never focused on before. Even though he had tried to bury them, they came back, perfectly preserved. Almost every memory was peopled by himself and Leah, no one else.

He searched the house for a black ballpoint, noting that Leah was on the bed, her washed hair wrapped in a towel. She was reading a magazine. He found a pen that matched the writing on the prescription. He sat back down with it and practiced on the note pad until he was sure how to make the change. With a deft stroke, he changed the number 10 to 100. He examined his work, and concluded that a pharmacist's unsuspecting glance would not catch it.

Leo took a deep breath, realized that night had fallen. He read until his eyes were dried out, then put down the book and stared toward the radiator.

Why is my name the same as Leah's?

The bedroom light was off. He heard nothing from Leah, assumed she was asleep. It was nine-thirty. Leah often went to bed this early, especially when the effects of Thorazine were still in her system.

He went into the kitchen and turned on the flame to heat some water for tea. When he sat at the table, he saw the prescription, as edited. Why had he done it? Changing the number was a message to Leah, a wordless one, telling her that he understood, and agreed to her condition, and would offer this little emendation to show—what?—good faith?

The water began to boil. He stood up and his thinking threatened to crystallize into words. *Overdose.* No wonder his mind had tried to protect him from seeing it.

No. I don't see anything, and I don't understand. All I know is I'm finished here.

He dropped a teabag into his favorite cup, poured the hot water over it and carried his comfort to the easy chair, and he sat all night, thinking, drinking more tea.

He dozed toward dawn, and was awakened by the sound of Leah's morning preparations and the smell of coffee, which he welcomed. When he opened his eyes, he saw Leah standing in the kitchen area in a white satin slip, white brassiere, and white house shoes, smearing margarine on a piece of bread. Finding her sexy as usual, he suppressed his arousal through an act of will.

"Coffee," he mumbled, trying to sound cheerful.

She glanced at him. "All done. Want me to pour you a cup?"

"Please," he said. He found his heavy cold weather shoes where he'd taken them off in the middle of the night. Shoes on, he stood up, padded sore and stiff to the kitchen and found his coffee. Leah brushed past him on her way to the bedroom.

He reached down for the coffee and saw that it was placed so that the cup covered the corner of the prescription, holding it in place. Pages from the note pad with his doodling were strewn about the table where he'd left them. She had made note of what he had done.

He slumped into the chair and sucked down the first cup of coffee, abandoning any notion of restricting caffeine intake today. He was sipping his second cup when Leah came out of the bedroom already wearing her warm coat and hat over a black wool skirt and white cotton blouse. Her makeup was spare and tasteful as usual. She stood in the middle of the room pulling on her gloves, her hair flowing from beneath the stocking hat, the profile of her face intent as she worked at the gloves.

She turned away from him then and toward the door, walked out without saying a word.

He tried not to listen to her receding from him. He stirred the half cup of coffee, then tossed the spoon into the sink with a loud clatter while he could still hear her on the stairs. Then he stood up, hurried to the front door and jerked it open. He could see down the short hallway to the stairway as far as the little landing, but Leah was already out of sight.

He went into the bathroom hoping to see the man in the mirror, but saw only a reflection of himself. He cried bitterly, kicking the door closed, sequestering himself in the cold hard place.

An hour later he'd eaten some breakfast, cleaned himself up, dressed for travel, and was out the door. He walked to the drugstore, where the pharmacist filled the prescription with 100 mg. tablets. Leo paid with cash, having barely enough to cover the price.

Back in the apartment, everything he altered began to take on some mysterious significance. What would his having made the bed say to Leah? What would it mean to her if he not only washed the dishes, which was usual, but also dried and put them away, which was not? Should he dust the furniture? It needed dusting, but would that tell her something he did not intend? "My God, stop it," he said out loud to himself.

When the apartment was in order, he took the bottle of Thorazine from his coat pocket and placed it on Leah's pillow. He packed his suitcase and carried it out the door.

It would be a long walk to the bus station, but he had hours. He would stop at the bank, which would be almost on the way, and take a fair share of money from his and Leah's single account. He withdrew half what was there.

44

THE SWEET AROMA OF SMOKY meat hung in the cold atmosphere when he stepped off the bus in front of the Cannon Shoals Diner. Unsteady, his back aching from the cramped ride, he squinted into the unfiltered daylight. He'd exhausted the hours on the bus trying to extirpate an insistent sense of guilt, reasoning that he could not know, nor could he control, whatever Leah intended to do. How much simpler it would be if he could hate her, and nothing would remind him of her. But to Leo, the barbecued air was like a lungful of Leah. He pictured her as she would be now, still at work, in her black skirt, her white underwear, still unaware that Leo had carried out his plan. He didn't know what she would do. For all he knew, she would take up with some guy at her office. Certainly, she would have been flirting with some of them from the day she was hired, so why wouldn't she go ahead and wreck somebody's marriage? *She could have a life without me, could she not?*

What he did know was he was hungry. Through the window of the bus stop cafe he could see the few, languid, late-lunchers, a pair here, a trio there. Leo carried his suitcase inside and sat in a booth.

No one waited on him. Three men in overalls paid up and left. Leo watched them climb into pickups in the gravel lot outside. An elderly couple made their arthritic way to the cash register where they, too, paid and left. Leo began to worry that he was being ignored.

"Honey," someone called, a woman with the rough low voice of a smoker. "Honey," she called again. Leo looked toward the voice. She was looking at him. "You order up here."

"Ah!" he said. "Thanks."

He ate the delicious smoky meat, sopped the remaining sauce with the sliced white bread, finished the potato salad even though it was bland. Satisfied and renewed, he was ready for the walk to the trailer.

The waitress met him at the cash register, flipped through her pad of checks, and quoted a price. He loved the entire ritual, the entire town.

He avoided ice-rimmed puddles and mud for much of the way out to the trailer. When he arrived, gray clouds were banking in the northern sky, the sun already low in the west.

He wondered if any or all of his things would still be inside, or if Meredith had cleaned the place out. He pulled open the door and set his suitcase onto the floor just inside. In a blur of motion, a man leapt from the direction of the stove, across the space in front of the door toward the bed, which was down in the sleeping position. Surprised and stunned, Leo froze, wide-eyed.

The man landed on the floor, and in the next instant Leo saw him holding something in his hand, then in both hands. He was pointing a gun toward the door. Before Leo could even think of moving, the man fired.

The bullet tore into the aluminum door frame near Leo's head. His ears did not so much ring as scream from the sound of the explosion. The man was still pointing the gun. Leo turned and ran, heading straight back for the road. At the road, he realized it would have been more sensible to run in a direction oblique to the doorway, out of the shooter's line of sight.

He ran down the road, into the long bend, until he was sure he was obscured behind the trees. He had no more wind and had to stop running, though he continued walking fast. He thought his heart might burst, and his ears were still screaming so that he could hear nothing else. He stumbled several times over small stones.

"Walk fast and steady," he panted, thinking that speaking words would help him regain his composure. But the eerie muffled non-sound of his voice filtering through the traumatized eardrums frightened him.

Back among small streets with rows of houses, he avoided the brighter streetlights, kept to the darker sides, heading for Janet's house.

He replayed the shooting in his mind. Had he seen the man take the gun from somewhere? Yes, he definitely saw him reach under the mattress before the gun appeared in his hands. And what else? The smell. When he had pulled the door open there had been the natural burst of air fanned from within, and it had been warm—

something that would have registered a split second later but for the shooting—and smelly. The smell was pungent, like stale grease—yes, greasy cooking from hours or days earlier, and body odor.

The man is living there. And I burst in on him.

How had he failed to consider the possibility that Meredith might have rented the trailer to someone else. It had been over two months since Leo had abandoned it. Of course she would want to rent it. All the utilities were hooked up, it was ready to occupy. Leo was astounded at his stupidity.

And what kind of person would be renting such a place? Well, of course, some loner, some misanthrope, a half-insane pariah, paranoid and likely to carry a gun, no doubt involved in drugs or some other illegal activity. Of course he would spook if his door burst open. *What an idiot I am!*

Dusk gave way to night, and Leo, nearing Janet's house and realizing he had no excuse for showing up there, changed course and walked toward Cannon Shoals Elementary School. Surely he would eventually calm down if he kept walking. He reached the school and continued again toward Janet's house. Slowing his pace, he took a deep breath and recognized an altered, yet familiar state of mind. Thinking it may have been the rush of blood to his brain that made this moment vivid now, he was not so much outside of time as existing intensely in the moment. He was once again like the neighborhood cat—the tree, the stone, the stars.

Several doors down from Janet's house, he stopped and leaned back against the smooth trunk of a birch tree, folded his arms across his chest, and continued to look from within to without. He was struck, as he had been once before, by the loose shards of time that drifted along this street as palpable as the cold air, with shapes as defined as the dark houses and the root-upheaved sidewalks.

In the dark and cold and stillness, the purity of his observation gave way to rationalizations and judgments. The pieces of time he had seen could also be construed as pockets of safety, where one might hide in the past. The trick would be to remain within the pocket forever, but of course that was impossible.

We live in linear time. The words almost formed on his lips. He walked on to Janet's house, where he sat on the porch swing for a few minutes, not knowing whether Janet was home or not, hoping she would come outside and find him.

But she did not, and he began to feel absurd sitting there, getting colder. He knocked on the front door, and there was no answer. He tried the door. It was locked.

He rounded the house, noting that almost all the lights were off. The back door was unlocked. He went inside.

No shooters, anyway.

He was the intruder, uninvited, not even welcome, but that was not important. His mind was clear—was that an illusion?—unclouded by fear, which seemed now to have been flushed from him in the aftermath of the gunshot. No one had seen him enter, he was sure. The police were not on their way. He could sit down and rest if he liked. It might be hours before Janet came home. Where would she be? Out eating dinner with friends. Meanwhile, he could take his time and decide if he wanted her to discover him in her house. He could leave her a note, tell her to meet him somewhere if she would. The barbecue restaurant. Or he could wait on the front porch, although it was cold outside.

He wandered through her house, absorbing its quiet. His ears were still ringing, but not so loudly now. He was able to sense some of the tiny sounds in the house, and its aromas, its light, its color, its ages. This house, like the neighborhood, evinced epochs recent and far in the past. The blue-mirrored coffee table was art deco, and on it was a portable radio from the disco seventies. The windows spoke of the turn of the century—their curtains, of the sixties.

He not only felt, but could almost see the waves his body created as he drifted into Janet's bedroom. He reached down and touched the fabric of the bedspread, its nappy texture like electricity in his fingertips. The room was so dense with intoxicating Janetness that it infused his body from every direction, flooded his senses, obliterated his capacity to fear. He floated around, his eyes sweeping the entire circle of the room, the wallpaper, the ancient dresser, the kitsch on the walls, the misplaced sock under the edge of the bed, a bit of dust at the baseboard—everything was outside of him, and then everything was in him, and he was merged with it, no more able than the nightstand to will himself to move.

But something moved him. He floated to the one empty corner and brushed against the walls there, ricocheting in slow motion until he was facing out into the room again. He saw his reflection in the dresser mirror, but didn't recognize the person.

Ghosts who knew about a wooden chest between the side of the dresser and the wall, pulled him down to it. It had a hasp but no lock. His hand drifted out from him on its arm and lifted the lid of this chest.

"Behold," said the disembodied voice of God the Father, and Leo's lips curled into a sweet smile at the sound, although he did not *think*.

The lid yielded to his hand, opening until it leaned back against the wall. The smile left his lips, and he still didn't *think*.

Mounted in the lid of the chest was a large photograph, a portrait of a young man. The chest itself contained several more photographs of this man, and in some of the photos, which Leo could see without picking them up or moving them, Janet was with the man. The photos were resting on some items of clothing and some smaller boxes.

Now, at last, Leo thought. *This man must be the pharmacist.*

The elation left, sucked out of him as though he'd stepped from a spacecraft into the vacuum without his pressure suit. He realized he was kneeling on both knees, and at this instant he fell to the floor, lying there on his side in fetal position, the wind knocked out of him. He could not breathe. It was like the time in second grade when Billy Pierce walked up to him on the playground, stood before him scowling and said, "You're wearing a dickie," and then punched him in the stomach with all his might.

He thought he might die before he could get his diaphragm to pull air into his lungs again. He sucked in a short breath, then the muscle froze again. He tried exhaling, but that didn't work either. Seconds passed, and he pulled in another fraction of breath, this time a bit more. In this fashion, he lay there for many minutes until he was breathing again.

He lost track of time, lying there, recovering, remembering kids from his elementary school days, sculpting their faces out of the darkness under Janet's bed. He was still there in the fetal position when he heard the back door clattering open.

His mind raced. For her to walk in and discover him there on the floor would be the worst. The best he could do now would be to soften the discovery somehow, so he called out to her. "Janet." All sounds from the kitchen ceased. "Janet," he called out again, and struggled to a sitting position on the floor. "It's me. Leo. In the bedroom." He was sure she could hear him. He managed to pull himself to a sitting position. He heard no movement. "The back door was open. I was tired," he called out.

Like a frightened child, she peeked around the edge of the doorway. Their eyes met, she hesitated a moment, then stepped full into the doorway.

"What do you want?" she asked him, her voice kind and soft.

He hung his head and shook it side to side. There was too much to tell, and nothing at all. He squeezed his eyes shut and peered into the pandemonium of emotion, searching for something, anything to say to her.

"What?" he heard her say, a gentle urging.

Something sparkled in the blackness before his eyes. It was far away, but it grew brighter, a diamond brilliance swirling, trying to take the shape of words. Finally it arrived in an explosion of light and an ecstasy of resignation and clarity.

"I love you," he whispered, searching her face then, wishing he could be lost forever in the soft dry world of her eyes. Then she turned away and was gone, leaving him to wonder if he could walk, or even stand up.

—

It had been the dash away from the shooter, the unaccustomed demand on his muscles that left his body in chaos. But he managed to walk to the living room, where Janet told him she had a pot of tea well underway in the kitchen, and asked him to sit while it brewed. She indicated the couch, and Leo was glad for its enveloping comfort. She sat in the easy chair.

"You act like you've been through something terrible," she said.

Leo nodded. "I went to the trailer. I pulled open the door and more or less tossed my suitcase inside."

"But there's...."

"An occupant. Yes, so I discovered. He took a shot at me."

Her hands went to her mouth. "Oh, no! My God!"

"I was too stupid to get out of the way. I just ran. I don't suppose he wanted to kill me, because he didn't shoot again."

"But why? Couldn't he see what had happened? I mean, that you made a mistake."

"I surprised him. I was so stupid. I don't know what I was thinking."

Janet went into the kitchen. Leo started to follow her, but his leg muscles felt like rubber bands. He sat back down and waited until Janet brought cups of tea.

"He's a stupid redneck," she said, sitting beside Leo. "He was probably rolling joints in there, or who knows what. He's some cousin of Meredith's, or a cousin's friend, or something like that."

They sipped tea. The silence stretched, Leo grateful, feeling that there was some easiness between them still.

"Meredith told me...," Janet said quietly, then she looked at Leo. "Is Leah your mother?"

"No, she's my aunt."

"And you sleep with her?"

Leo hesitated, but only for a short beat. "That's a misleading way to look at it."
He felt Janet's subtle exhalation, willingness to listen. "There has been a strange and
convoluted relationship between her and me. Well, convoluted? No, fairly simple, let me
postulate, damn it. I'm not sure. I'll tell you about it, and you decide."

"Tell me about it."

"She's eight years older than me. She lived with us—my parents and me. She's my
mother's sister. She came to me one night when I was eleven."

"Oh, Leo...."

"So, well, she came to me when I was eleven and... I've had other... I fell in love with
a girl when I was in college, but... And Leah was always there for me."

"I see."

"She shouldn't have been, but she always was."

"I'm sorry," Janet whispered.

"I'm sorry, too," Leo said, "but I've made a decision. It was difficult, but I have
left her on her own. Left her and her drugs on their own. She's got a good job in
Springdale. She may or may not make it, but her present circumstances are about as
good as they can be for her."

"You'll need to visit her often, I would think."

"I'll need to visit her never. Visits from me would exacerbate her problems, and they
wouldn't help me, either."

Janet picked up her cup, held it close to her mouth.

"When I came here before, I had run away from her. That was wrong. This time she
knows I've left. We've discussed it, and she knows there's no point in coming after me."

Janet sipped her tea. "Does she feel she's lost you to another woman, a rival?"

"I think the answer to that is yes, partly. She knows I'm gone from her, and how she
sees the reasons for that, I'm not sure."

Janet held her cup still, looked at Leo, looked away.

"What are you thinking?" Leo said.

Janet looked at him, shook her head. "I don't know."

Leo nodded. He drank off his hot tea, set the cup down on the coffee table, stared
into the blue mirror that was the tabletop. "I think I deserve a life. Whatever it is, I
think I deserve one."

Janet stared through the doorway into the different light filtering from the kitchen.
"Yes," she said. "Everyone does."

—

Janet drove Leo out to the trailer at half past nine. She volunteered to knock on the door, but Leo insisted that he should do it. Janet waited in the car, headlights on, motor running. Leo went to the door and knocked.

"Who is it?" came from inside the trailer, a thin, whiny voice.

"I've come for my suitcase," Leo said. "I apologize for the mistake. I used to live here. Didn't know it was occupied."

"You bring the cops?"

"No. I just want my suitcase."

After a moment, the voice said, "Stand over in front of the car and keep your hands where I can see em."

Leo did so.

The car was thirty feet away from the door. Standing in the headlights' glare, he could barely see the trailer door open and his suitcase appear. The redneck set the suitcase down on the step and closed the door. Leo heard him say something unintelligible. He waited a moment, then went to the step and picked up his suitcase.

"I'm taking it," he said. "I'm sorry about the mistake. I'm not reporting the shooting. You hear me?"

"Yeah, I hear you."

"But you're a stupid son of a bitch," Leo said, surprising himself.

"Meredith has your shit."

Leo hurried back to the car and jumped in. "Let's go before he opens up on us."

Janet had not been at dinner when Leo was waiting for her. She had been at a mall in Oak Hollow, the small city just over in Catalan county, returning a pair of shoes that had broken the first time she'd worn them. She was hungry now, and while Leo wasn't, he sat at the kitchen table and watched her pan broil some kielbasa, boil some potatoes, and sauté cabbage in the sausage grease until it was limp and chewy. She heated some rolls from a package, and had Leo move the table a little closer to the warm stove and set it for two. By the time everything was ready, he had an appetite.

"This deserves candlelight," he said, looking at the elegant country simplicity of the checkerboard tablecloth and napkins, the old chipped blue stoneware, the charming salt and pepper shakers—a hen and rooster this time.

"And wine," she said, setting polished goblets in place.

The wine turned out to be a half-bottle of stale Mogen David from the refrigerator. Janet, Leo was sure, didn't know the difference, and this made him love her all the more.

He ate her delicious food, swallowed wine fast before the metallic tang could assault his taste buds.

"When did you eat last?" Janet laughed. "Last week?"

"About four hours ago at the barbecue place downtown," Leo said, and they let smiles be enough.

The gentle clinking of dishes, the complaint of the chair, all the tiny sounds framed in the silence of inner places evacuated of their secrets—this quietude was so exquisite that neither Leo nor Janet spoke much during the meal, preferring instead to enjoy the peace of the kitchen.

They finished all the food except one roll, and at it they both picked while they finished off the last of the wine. Leo said, "I have more money than before. Not a lot, but I'll manage. More realistic this time. You can take me to that motel off the interstate tonight, and tomorrow I'll find a room or something."

Janet's eyes sparkled like sunlight off wet blueberries. She leaned back in her chair, cocked her head far to one side and sighted across the wine glasses at Leo. "You can stay here if you want to," she said. "Do you?"

"Well, yes," he said. "If you want me to. Or if you don't mind."

She nodded and sat up straight again. "I want you to. I don't know, sometimes these things happen. Sometimes people fit together."

"We'll try to be careful with each other."

"Yes," she said, nodding again. "That sounds right."

They stood together in the bedroom late at night, facing each other. He had not realized before how Janet's height compared to his own. The top of her head came about to his nose. She placed her arms over his shoulders, drew herself into him, her hands finding the back of his head and caressing it. They kissed, and Leo pulled her toward him.

"I'm not used to wine," Janet said. "It's given me a little headache." Then she laughed. "That's not what it sounded like."

"It doesn't matter."

As they began to disrobe, Leo felt a distance developing between them. He told himself it would go away as soon as they were lying beside each other in the warm bed. But something continued to intrude, to invade and wedge them apart. It was not, Leo knew, coming from Janet. It was originating in himself and his history. It was a fear, an evil that created no desire, no heat, but only cold isolation.

He began to get angry with himself. He commanded his body to arrive back here in bed with the beautiful woman he loved, but his body remained in a distant orbit, and the entity in bed, the thing that contained his mind, was a sweating, panting corpse.

"What is it?" Janet whispered.

Leo shook his head.

"Don't worry," she said. "We'll just lay here together."

But Leo was not with her. His eyes were wide, darting around the darkness, his gaze falling on the dim patches of light coming through the window, and from the lamp in the living room, the light some pale shade of blue-black falling in horrifying patterns on the walls, the furniture, and the enticing world he could almost make out beyond the glass of the mirror.

"I suspect most people have heard gunfire in the movies and on TV and don't realize how loud a real gun is up close," Leo said.

Janet turned toward him and placed her soft warm hand on his cheek for a moment.

Leo tried to calm himself, but he was losing control of his own body, the corpse. The corpse turned on its side, away from Janet, providing a more direct view of the dresser mirror, which seemed orders of magnitude brighter and more visible than the world it reflected, and was full of movement Leo could not define.

But even more astounding was the sight of the wooden chest beside the dresser, because it glowed with the cold blue-white luminescence of foxfire—which he had never seen. He shivered, clutched the blanket around himself so violently that it startled Janet.

"Leo," she said, "tell me. Are you all right?"

His corpse sat up on the edge of the bed.

"Leo," Janet said.

The senseless body moved around the room in the darkness, finding its clothes and beginning to put them on. Janet switched on the bedside lamp. She said something, but his corpse didn't hear it. It was slow and awkward, this corpse trying to put on clothes. Leo knew, from somewhere, that Janet was asking him questions. For a second he took control of the corpse's eyes and saw that she too was dressing—much more efficiently than was his corpse.

It staggered through the house, and Janet was holding its arm with both her hands.

She was with it, with Leo, offering soothing words, though Leo didn't understand what the words were.

Out the front door they walked like zombies. That Janet was next to him, trying to hold on to him, was Leo's only comfort. But half a block from the house, the corpse broke into a run, and soon tore away from Janet's grasp. Leo heard her running behind him, calling, "Wait. Wait, Leo."

He ran for a long time, and when he stopped running, he continued to walk fast. It was his own mind that navigated, taking back by degrees its control over the corpse. His only criterion in navigating was to turn away from the light. He walked fast toward whatever darkness the town offered from moment to moment.

He came to a high gate made of heavy wire mesh. This gate was open. Beyond it he saw the black silhouette of some structures, small buildings, along the fence, and vast empty darkness beyond. He passed through the gate, walking over hard surfaces and grassy ones, heading into the blackness until it surrounded him. He could not see his feet on the ground, and he could not see the world around him. He was neither safe nor in danger. He crouched to the ground, felt the damp soil, and sat on it. The air was cold. Beyond that, he understood nothing.

He would understand, a little later when the headlights of Janet's car lit him, that he was sitting near the center of the automobile raceway. He heard the sound of the car, heard her turn off the engine. She also turned off the headlights but left on the amber parking lights. In the glow of those lights she approached him.

"Come on, Leo," she said, standing over him. "It's not that bad."

"I'm sitting here wondering if I've just got to die, too."

She knelt beside him. "You can't die," she said, and her voice took on a strange, decidedly male aspect. The change was so alarming that Leo looked up at her face, but he couldn't make out her features because the dim light was behind her head. "You can't die because you haven't even been born," said the voice, and he recognized it, even though it was her voice, as that of God the Father. Leo laughed, but it was a crying, and Janet waited, then said, "And I'm the one who's going to birth you." It was her own voice.

"You are?" Leo said, intrigued with this prospect.

"I intend to," she said, and crouched beside him.

"The ground is cold and damp," Leo said. "Better not sit on it." But she did sit on it and put her hand on Leo's knee.

"We're going to get you straightened out," she said.

"I don't see how."

"We'll do it together. I have a good feeling about it. Why not?"

"You'd have to love me, and I'm afraid I would hurt you. And you couldn't love me."

"Sure I could, Leo. I do love you."

"Tell me. Tell me how it's possible."

"Well, it doesn't hurt that you're good looking, and tall. And when I watched you with my ten-year-olds, you crushed me. What you did for them made me have to sit down, and made me feel alive, and made me feel that there was life on the planet, Leo, right here in Cannon Shoals. I knew right then. I knew."

They walked to the car, and on the way back home, Janet said she wanted to tell Leo where she had disappeared to after the pharmacist died.

45

LEAH COULD NOT REMEMBER WHERE they kept the little pan for heating tea water. She had slept naked, having planned but then forgotten to take a bath last night. The Thorazine seemed to be wearing off more slowly than usual. Where were the tea bags? And why was her robe open?

The sash was missing, so she returned to the bedroom to search for it, noticing that her robot needed oil as never before. In the drawer, she found no sash but saw a lilac brassiere. She put it on over the robe and it held the robe closed, at least at the top. Some memory tried to make her smile, but then went away. She would not think of Leo. She didn't want to remember Leo, so she didn't.

For a while she sat at the kitchen table thinking about Lulu, how she spoke of the colors of words, the textures of emotions, temperatures of intentions and actions. Lulu's face appeared before Leah, so clear and solid that she felt she could reach out and touch it, and she sat very still to make the face stay, but after a while it vanished and Leah was staring at the top of the stove. The pan for heating water was sitting on the stove. Leah felt heavy and dizzy when she stood, but she managed to run water and turn on the flame. She used two tea bags in her mug, and drank the tea plain as soon as it cooled enough not to burn.

More Thorazine made a day or two pass. The thought of food repulsed her. She sat for a while, thoughts of Leo drifting through her mind, but then expelled, replaced with scenes from movies, then from her childhood with Cord and Lulu, and even earlier scenes with her mama, and finally, when Leo's very young face threatened to loom before her, Milton's strangely terrifying words about God's love, and his soothing caresses as some old man in the Bible raised a knife against his young son.

Sometimes it was daytime outside, and sometimes night. She wondered why she was not annoyed by what was trickling down the inside of her right thigh. She should be annoyed, she knew, but it was inconsequential, this feeling of a fly walking down, warm and then cool and then nothing. Lulu, just before she quit, or was fired, from Kimball's, had described a snake- or eel-like entity that bifurcated inside her and went down her gut and up into her throat at the same time, choking her, giving her a headache, and stunning her legs so that she crumpled onto the cannery floor. She had told Leah that the entity was angry, and that Leo—who was a baby at the time—was the only force that could fight the entity, but he was too young to do it. Leah had kissed her sister and tried to soothe her, but the loss of the job at Kimball's coincided with a sudden decline in Lulu's daily activity.

Leah had not been out of the apartment for six days. The phone had rung a few times, but she knew it was Kirk & Ghent Components, and she was all done with them. Instead of going to work, she took Thorazine, and although that made her sleep the first time she took one, the next time it merely made her stare at the stove, where there was a pot of coffee she had made. She had made pots of coffee three times, and had eaten crackers twice, or maybe more, she couldn't quite remember.

She had gone to the bathroom only once, and saw a red or brown circle the size of a dinner plate on the back of her bathrobe, but she put the robe back on anyway because otherwise it was too cool in the apartment.

In the light of dawn, she saw dark spots on the floor where she had walked. The lines of spots led from the bathroom to the kitchen and to the window where she had looked down to the street, and had seen a dog, and a telephone pole, and a broken sidewalk.

A slight itch, almost a tickling, made her reach down and touch the inside of her thigh, near where the fly had walked, and there was something there, not liquid but wet, maybe part of the eel—no, that was Lulu, but maybe it was the same thing, she thought. It was part of the eel's skin, wet from being inside her, warm, gelatinous.

She forgot about taking Thorazine. She had slept too much already, she thought. The terrible backache from yesterday, and the day before, had now given way to a pulsing numbness that stopped her from moving her legs. She needed to wake up better, and looked around for coffee. She felt lost. The apartment no longer looked the same. She saw the bloody panties she had thrown into the corner near the heat register, but now all of that seemed to be on the other side of the apartment. She was sitting on the couch, had been for most of the last week. It was daytime, and she could see filth on the couch where she had sat before. She could see a dark orange mass at her vulva, the pubic hairs all clotted with something grey, and for the life of her, she could not stand up, but she didn't call out because she was well aware that Leo was gone.

46

J ANET TRIED TO TURN OFF the alarm on her clock before it awakened Leo,
but it took her too long to reach the button. They had slept only a few hours, but
it was Tuesday, a school day.

"Should I make some coffee?" Leo yawned from where he sat on the edge of the
bed. Janet answered from the bathroom that coffee was already brewing.

"It's cold in here, isn't it?" Leo said, but Janet had turned on the bath water and
didn't hear.

Leo looked out the window into the dark. He could feel the cold emanating off
the windowpane.

By the time Janet was out of the bathroom, Leo was halfway through his first cup of
coffee. Janet bounded into the kitchen smiling. "Find everything you need?"

"So far, so good," he smiled back.

Janet poured herself a cup. "I'll try to come home at lunch."

"That sounds nice."

"I'm going to get a doughnut at school. I never eat breakfast here on school days. You
take your time and find something. We've got eggs, all kinds of things. Just look around."

"Make myself at home?"

She leaned over and kissed him on the mouth, her lips hot and tasting of coffee.
"You are at home," she said. "Can do?"

Leo nodded his assent and his happiness.

—

The next night Leo slept in fits. Janet could not comfort him much. She tried, but she was tired, and fell asleep, leaving Leo to roam the house until very late. He, too, was tired, having walked long distances during the day, but when sleep seemed near, something from outside him seemed to descend on him, frighten him. He was worried about Leah.

Fatigued, he stayed awake all day Wednesday, and that night he fell asleep exhausted.

On Thursday, a cold day under a glaring fluorescent sky, while Leo was walking to the newspaper traps located outside a pizza joint, ruminating about what the Help Wanted ads might offer, he suddenly stopped and looked up at the sky. Something had disappeared—not exactly a burden, but a viscosity in the air. Resistance to movement was suddenly absent. He stood still, feeling unaccustomed, raw and exposed, like a creature having shed an exoskeleton. He could see Cannon Shoals Elementary several blocks down to the west, downtown straight ahead to the north. To his right, the street curved away into trees, and behind him, what? The sidewalk stretched ragged, undulating up and down all the way back to and beyond the street where Janet—and he—lived.

He walked on through the rare ether to fetch *The Cadbury News-Topic,* carried it back *home.* Over another cup of coffee, he searched through the classified ads for happiness and a new kind of surrender. He made a nice meal for two, in case Janet made it home for lunch. She didn't. He ate his pasta, then nibbled at hers while he perused the want ads again, until her lunch was inside him.

By the time Janet was home that afternoon, Leo had made several phone calls, and the result was two scheduled interviews. Menial work. Simple. Good. Temp, which was probably wise. Something clerical at a travel agency—sounded like a mess of paperwork left by a former employee—and something for somewhat better pay that sounded like driving a disabled man around and doing errands for him. Janet was pleased, kissed him well. And that night, when they went to bed, they made love.

———

Saturday morning they awoke and made love again, then discovered that it had snowed during the night, enough to cover the landscape. The house felt cold, but Leo and Janet chose to stay naked except for house shoes and a blanket each. Wrapped like Navajos, they made coffee, breakfasted on toast and jam, then piled onto the couch in the living room, the blinds pulled wide open, to enjoy the snowy scene before them.

Soon, they found the edges of each others' blankets, merged them, slipped inside the nest and were together again.

In the mid-morning aftermath, they dozed, Leo's head propped up on the arm of the couch, Janet face down on top of him, nuzzling into his armpit. Peering out the window at the snow, relishing the joyous sticky trickle he hoped wasn't wetting the couch, Leo gave Janet a gentle extra squeeze.

"Mmm," she said, and kissed his shoulder.

"You told me right away that you are childless," Leo said. "Does that mean... I mean, that doesn't mean...."

She turned her head to the side toward his ear, spoke to him. "Never married, that's all."

"I don't mean to be... I'm not asking anything. I just...."

"I *could*, Leo. I mean, I'm old, but not that old. I'm not sure if.... Well...."

"Oh, I know. I'm not sure either, of anything, about things like that."

"I could."

They held each other, the question hanging in the living room air, a measure of comfort lost to their wondering.

"I could too, for the record," Leo said after a while. "I mean, I assume."

"Then we need to be careful."

They sensed each other thinking again, and it was so obvious they both laughed.

"Leo...."

"Yes?"

"You need to be the one, until I can...."

"Oh, Lord. Yes. You're right."

—

It was mid-morning on Tuesday, the last patches of snow barely clinging to existence in the shadiest spots, when Deputy Sheriff John Peck knocked on the door. Leo was out of the bath, dressed for the interview with the travel agency except for his shoes, still combing his hair. He was thinking about buying condoms, amazed that he was embarrassed, not knowing what kind of criteria to use in choosing, not knowing where to go. Leah had always taken care of contraception.

Deputy Peck was portly and polite, had his Smoky hat in his hands. "Good morning, sir. I'm looking for Mr. Leo Nobles?"

"I'm Leo Nobles."

Peck had the bearing of an official bringing sad news. Leo thought he should probably invite him in, but he hesitated and the deputy continued. "Sir, a Detective Terry Floyd up in Springdale has phoned our office. One of your kinfolks has passed away and Floyd would like to interview you."

"You mean, he wants me to come to Springdale?"

"Yes, sir. He said you might be going anyway for the funeral. This I believe is in regard to your aunt." Peck glanced at a notebook he held discretely. "Leah Bledsoe."

Leo shifted sideways so he could support himself against the doorframe. Unable to formulate words, he managed to nod and meet the deputy's eyes.

"Here's the name and phone number for Detective Floyd," the deputy said, handing Leo a sheet torn from the notebook.

Leo took the paper and said, "Thank you."

"I'm sorry for your loss." Deputy Peck was a kind man, clearly not a threat. Leo looked at him.

"Did she... was she.... Was there a note?"

"Sir?"

"Did my aunt leave a note?"

Deputy Peck looked at Leo curiously. "What kind of note? I didn't receive many details, Mr. Nobles."

"Do you know where she did it?"

"Where she died, you mean?"

Leo nodded again, and noticed that Peck was now scrutinizing him.

"She died in her apartment, unattended. Not clear why she didn't call for medical help. Maybe that's what Detective Floyd is interested in. Why she let it go on for days without calling anybody."

"Let it go on?"

"I'm sorry. Detective Floyd mentioned that she was having a miscarriage and there were complications."

Leo nodded, but his throat was constricted. He tried for a polite smile. He knew he needed to say thank you, but he could not. He just nodded again. After a long moment, Peck touched his hairline, a salute of sorts.

Leo watched Deputy Peck walk back out to his patrol car. He seemed interested in the crabgrass that encroached on the cracked concrete. He stopped on the walk near the spot where Leo had lain with Janet, placed his hands on his hefty hips, turned his head first up the street then down, as if searching for a trace of smoky guilt, listening for an echo of the anguished cry that it seemed must have wracked the air here. Leo's mind reeled. What had he said to the deputy? Had it been clear he'd assumed Leah was a suicide? Why was the deputy still standing on the sidewalk?

But the deputy was only expelling gas—so loudly that Leo heard it from the door. Then he stuffed himself into the patrol car and drove away.

For a few moments, shapes skittered in the periphery of Leo's vision, disappearing shadowy shapes. He paced through the house, had the sense to drink a glass of water.

He could not recall his phone number, Leah's phone number. Then he did recall it and wrote it down, his hand shaking. He would call the number, see if someone would be there—Uncle Russell? Cord? Would they have known where to find Cord? Would Cord be alive? Was there any way to avoid the affair altogether?

The police? Would it have to do with the altered prescription? Surely not. They would want to hear all about their relationship, why he left, and *whose child she'd been carrying.*

He began trying to pull himself together, taking his time—he knew it would take a while, but there was a long bus ride to work with. The job interview scheduled for this morning was for a position he had no intention of taking. A gesture to show Janet that he was making an effort, it was a dishonest thing to do, so to hell with that. He would need to go to Springdale without delay.

Leo went to the phone in the kitchen and called Cannon Shoals Elementary. He knew, from his residency, what a scene an incoming call made. He had to declare it an emergency, and she would be summoned over the intercom, then have to trek down to the office to take the call. He hated doing it.

"Hello?" Janet's voice was cool, a little apprehensive.

"I'm sorry to call you at work like this," he said.

"It's fine," she said, but Leo sensed displeasure, whether it was there or not.

"I need to go to Springdale, and I want to go right now. Leah has died. I need to go up there and, you know, take care of some things."

"I'm sorry," Janet said. It seemed to be for the benefit of the eager ears that no doubt surrounded her in the office.

"I know this is awkward," Leo said. "It shouldn't take long. A few days. There has to be a funeral. I don't know if my uncle is there or not. There's some question about her medical history that has come up, I think. Probably about the drugs she was taking. I'm going to try and help with whatever I know about it."

"When will you, uh...," she said. Stupidly, Leo had to think for a moment what she wanted to ask.

"I'll be back in a day or two, maybe three. Not sure when the funeral is. I'll call you. Is that what you wanted to know?"

"Yes."

"Can I go, or do we need to meet first?"

"No, it's fine. I'll talk with you when you get back."

47

L EO HAD HIS KEY—AND he wondered why—but the door was unlocked.
It did not look like the crime scene Leo had been imagining. The place
was cold, the thermostat turned down to fifty. The dishes were all done and
put away. There was food in the refrigerator, but no milk, nothing that might spoil
quickly. Leah, he remembered, liked to leave the living room window open a crack
for fresh air, even on the coldest days, but all windows were closed. There was a smell
of disinfectant.

Leo phoned the police station and asked for Detective Floyd. Sounding
sympathetic, the detective arranged to meet Leo at the apartment right away, just to
take care of some formalities.

An hour later Detective Floyd was sitting in the kitchen.

"No sir," Floyd was saying, "another party had the apartment cleaned this morning.
We'd only do that in certain cases. There's no criminal aspect here. Russell Bledsoe is
your uncle, I believe?"

"That's right. He's in town?"

"He was the only contact besides you that your aunt had listed at her job. He flew
in last night. Very nice man. Gets things done, doesn't make a fuss. You know him well?"

Leo shook his head. "I know he's a nice man, successful. Haven't seen him for years.
You know how it goes."

Floyd extracted a metal clipboard from the briefcase he carried. "Okay, let's see.
She was employed as clerical help at Kirk & Ghent Components. Had not been in or
called in for five work days. They had called her daily with no answer, and reported her

absence to police yesterday." Floyd looked up from his notes. "The door was unlocked. She'd been dead for less than two hours."

Detective Floyd looked back at his notes, then away, toward the window. "Did you know she was pregnant, Mr. Nobles?"

"I did not." Leo wanted to say more, had mentally rehearsed saying more, making it voluntary to remove suspicion from himself. But now he felt that saying more would sound like the guilty dog barking.

"I was wondering when you last talked with her. Somebody at her job said they thought it was you who picked her up daily after work."

"Yes, until recently I lived here with her, usually kept the car for errands during the day, took her to and from work. For the last year or so I've been seeing a woman down in Cannon Shoals—you know where that is?"

"Sure."

"So I recently moved in with her down there. I'm sure Leah was glad to see me go."

"Why do you say that?

"Well, I mean, assuming she knew she was pregnant, she was probably working on some plans of some sort. I don't know what she had in mind. You know, on the way here, I was trying to remember if she had sort of encouraged me to go ahead and make a move in my own life. She knew Janet and I were pretty serious. Anyway, I was under the impression I was taking charge of my own life."

"Ah, yes," Floyd smiled. "Was your aunt a sort of mother figure for you?"

"Mmm, maybe so. Yeah, I guess I looked to her for advice sometimes."

"Mr. Nobles, do you know who the father was?"

Father. Professor Gottschalk, for example?

Leo tried for a blank stare into the refrigerator door. "I don't. I'm sorry. I know she was... active." Leo looked Floyd directly in the eye now, surprised at his own temerity. "I wouldn't want to guess which...." He looked away quickly.

Floyd gave Leo a moment, then said, "Let me ask you, then, if there is any name you'd care to share. Someone who, regardless, would want to know of your aunt's passing."

"No." He knew that in saying it, he was calling Leah a slut, a woman who had sex with so many different partners that none of them would emerge as her partner in life. He knew that this characterization would fit with whatever her office mates might have said about her. *She was nice, but she was a flirt.* He would deal with his guilt, his filthy misrepresentation, at a later time. For now, this was all he could do.

"Would you mind if I used the bathroom here, Mr. Nobles?" Floyd stood up.

"Go ahead," Leo said. "Of course."

Leo quickly reviewed his lies. He remembered a story Leah had told him back in Chicago when she was working at Merchant's Mart. Like the other women in the office, Leah had taken to wearing her jeans on Friday, and had noticed approving looks from several of the men. They all thought she was "interesting," she told Leo, because of her hip way of speaking and outspoken liberalism, and also because she kept a photo of her dead sister on her desk. Or was that her lover? She could tell the imaginations of these men, especially one named Sam, sometimes spilled over into verbal slips, prodding, innuendo. *Your sister doesn't look anything like you. No family resemblance at all, hmm?*

Leah retaliated with hearty doses of frustration for these men, which she later described to Leo. Irked by Sam's insinuations, she found a reason to discuss some office issue with him at his desk, stood near him, leaned her hands on his desk, letting the neckline of her blouse fall free. Acting as though she was unaware of it, she told Leo, she revealed her breasts all the way down to the chocolate areolas and the perfect tiny cylinders of her nipples. She knew he hadn't the courage to call her on it, could tell that he was a titty-baby and would be unable to concentrate on his work for the rest of the day, and would, she was sure, grouch at his wife when he got home in the evening.

The toilet flushed, Floyd came back and picked up his clipboard. "Just another question or two so we can file this away, if you don't mind."

"Anything I can tell you...."

"Well, I ask this just because you lived with her until recently. Were you aware that she was taking medications?"

"Oh, yes. I don't know what it was, but she definitely took some kind of sleeping pill a lot. Sometimes she would knock herself out in the middle of the day if she wasn't going to work that day."

Floyd nodded. "I'm going to tell you something, Mr. Nobles, because I think you deserve to know it, even if it is unpleasant."

"Go ahead."

"It appears that your aunt was altering her prescriptions to get higher doses. The particular drug is not a narcotic, so we don't think she was physically addicted, but maybe psychologically dependent. Does that seem right to you?"

Leo stood up and walked to the window. An unwanted flash of pride in his acting experience and ability skittered across his mind. Looking down at the street, he said, "It could be. Yes, I think she might have." He turned to look at Floyd. "That does make sense. I should have seen something like that, but we kind of just led our own lives and didn't pay all that much attention to each other. The living arrangement was just an expedient, you know. We got along well and neither of us was much of a breadwinner, so we just put our financial resources together more or less."

Leo was now beginning to wonder how much more lying he was capable of. But it was over. Floyd packed away his clipboard, made some quick small talk, offering empty condolences—all that seemed appropriate. At the door, he turned one last time to survey the apartment and said, "None of my business, but which one of you had the bed, and who had the couch?"

Leo could not speak. Floyd held up a hand, dismissing the question. "Doesn't matter, Mr. Nobles." He closed the door.

—

The interview had exhausted some reserve of strength Leo hadn't known he possessed. He sat on the couch for an hour without moving, then reclined. Waking from a bad dream, Leo noted his odd position on the couch and understood the sensations of pain. His hair was indeed being pulled, but by the fabric on the arm of the couch, not by goats, the smell of which resolved into cleaning fluid. Sitting up relieved the backache, and he tried to rub the headache out of his eyes and temples. But he was not fully awake.

Dark blobs blocked out his field of vision when he stopped rubbing his eyes. One blob resolved itself into a clear image of Cord standing next to the refrigerator, leaning on it, a cigarette hanging from his lips.

Shit. Wake up and clear your head. Leo's heart was pounding as he watched the image of Cord fade. His vision returned to normal, his pulse began to slow.

He shuffled over to the kitchen area, looked around for some teabags. Once he had some water heating on the stove, he sat at the table and for the first time looked at the business card Detective Floyd had left there. It was the card of a funeral home.

48

EAH HAD LISTED TWO NAMES as emergency contacts on her job application. One was Leo. The other was her brother Russell. The personnel director at Kirk & Ghent had contacted Russell, but had been unable to find Leo, whose address of record was the same as Leah's.

While Drew was associating with criminals, becoming a criminal himself during the postwar years, Russell was looking for work anywhere he could find it during his school years, and saving his money. Leo remembered Lulu telling about Russell's metal treasure box containing cash and other valuable objects he used for trading, always to his advantage.

What else could he remember about Uncle Russell? Lulu had talked about him. After high school, he'd begun a business that the family referred to as "import export." He'd given Lulu an inflatable lifeboat and some oriental dishes. He'd moved to Abilene and lived in a warehouse. Sometime in the 1950's he invested in stocks and bonds, according to Lulu. At age thirty-four in 1965, he bought a house, and soon thereafter married a woman named Alavie. The marriage did not last long. Leo met Alavie once when Russell brought her to Brownwood, and she seemed nice to him.

At about the time Russell bought the house, he also bought a beer distributorship covering the greater Abilene area, and started making real money.

When Drew was buried in 1969, Russell invited Leo to ride with him from the funeral to the burial site, and Leo found his uncle to be a quiet but personable man.

When Lulu died in 1980, Russell was there for her funeral. Although he wasn't ostentatious about his wealth, the family knew about it. Leo noted that Russell's body weight was changing in proportion to his wealth, as he had become portly through his forties.

The last real news Leo recalled about Russell was his heart attack in 1988. Russell had been 59, so he would now be in his early sixties. After the attack, Russell retired to Cloudcroft, New Mexico, presumably to a nice, easy lifestyle. Leo wondered now, as he stared at the business card of the funeral home, how Russell would react to the death of his last remaining sibling.

In the cold apartment, Leo set the phone on the kitchen table and dialed the number on the card. A man answered coolly, "Davis-Williams...," and because Russell had anticipated such a call, Leo soon knew the name, location and phone number of the hotel where his uncle was staying. He also knew that Leah's casket would not be opened—at Russell's direction—and would, tomorrow after the funeral, be interred at Springdale's Riverside Cemetery in a plot Russell had secured yesterday.

Where is the sense of loss? Leo turned up the heat and also lit the oven, leaving its door open. Outside, the sun briefly broke through the clouds, then disappeared again. Something inside him had twisted like the breaking of a kitten's neck when he'd heard the word casket. The sensation ran up his spine and into the back of his head—and now his scalp was tingling.

He stood in front of the oven, felt the warmth issuing from the cavity. He searched inside himself again, and saw that he was a jumble of fragmented emotions. He could break down and cry at any moment. He could laugh. He could cry and laugh at the same time. Could he distract himself long enough to make the call to Uncle Russell? He thought he'd better try.

It was five o'clock, the daylight already fading. Leo picked up the phone and called Russell's hotel room.

"Hello." The voice was dry, deep, nasal, the word like two notes from a brass horn.

"Yes, Uncle Russell, it's Leo." Having said some words, Leo relaxed a little, felt the familiar wash of anticipation—an older man, a possible father—pass over him as if by habit.

"Leo, good, they found you?"

"Yeah. I live down the road about an hour. Not too hard to find."

Russell must have nodded his understanding—the phone was silent for a moment. Leo continued, "Why don't we get together. You want to have some dinner?"

"That sounds good," Russell said. Leo noted that his tone stayed poker, must be all the years of business dealing.

"You sound good, Uncle Russell. I'm looking forward to seeing you."

"Me, too."

"We could, let's see.... It's sort of cold here in Leah's apartment. Why don't we hit a restaurant?"

"I made a reservation at a place called the Messina Garden. I'll up it from solo to two. Seven o'clock work for you?"

"Sounds good. Where is it?"

—

The Messina Garden occupied the second floor of an antique two-storied building on Four O'clock Lane, a short side street downtown. Leo arrived in a taxi, not knowing where Leah had left the Chevette, which was not where they usually parked it.

A canopy discretely lettered with "Messina Garden" jutted from above the entrance. Leo opened the heavy, oaken door and stepped into a tiny vestibule leading to a carpeted, dimly lit stairway up to another doorway on the second floor.

Climbing the quiet stairs, Leo noted the aroma of baked bread and garlic, and his stomach churned.

Another small vestibule at the top of the stairs opened into the restaurant. A tall, dark-haired woman greeted Leo and led him to a table near a window looking down on Four O'clock Lane. Russell was seated there and smiled at Leo.

"Leo," Russell trumpeted, a bit too loudly for the subdued room, and offered his hand. Leo shook the hand and seated himself. The white tablecloth was already set for two places, with bread and garlicky olive oil.

"How did you find this place?" Leo asked. "It's nice."

"Guy at the hotel told me about it," Russell said, looking Leo in the eye. "How are you doing, young man?"

"I'm fine." Leo did not want to make Russell pry. He wanted to tell him things, explain himself. He didn't know how to start. "I'm living with a woman down in Cannon Shoals, about sixty miles."

"Living with her, huh?"

"Nice relationship," Leo said. "I'm lucky." He smiled and found he could look at Russell now, as the uncle was poring over a wine list. "How about you? You were in Cloudcroft, New Mexico?"

"Yeah. I retired there. I had a heart attack a couple of years ago."

"I know, I remember. How are you?"

"Have to restrict my diet to a lot of red wine and Italian food, you know. Other than that, I'm living like I always did." He looked at Leo and laughed. Leo found he could laugh as well, but checked himself as a hint of hysteria crept into his throat.

"Did you ever get married again, Uncle Russell? Living with anybody or anything?"

"I have a Mexican woman who lives with me. You know, a housekeeper. I'm in love with her but she doesn't know I exist." He laughed again and Leo smiled and nodded. "Let me ask you, Leo, how were you getting along with Leah? Y'all were living together for a long time, weren't you?"

"We were."

"Cord made some remarks about it. I never saw anything wrong with it—kind of unusual for y'all to stick together, but y'all were close to the same age, so...."

"We always got along. In a funny sort of way, she protected me against Daddy." Leo felt himself falling back into the old deceptive ways, admitting just enough of the truth to hide his real relationship with Leah.

"Do you know where he is?" Russell asked.

Leo shook his head. "Daddy? He disappeared about the time Mother went into the state hospital for good."

"I knew that, but I thought maybe you'd heard from him since then."

"No. Dead, for all I know. I have no idea where he went. Might be out in the South Pacific. He used to talk about it a lot."

"What do you say to a Chianti to start with?"

"Go for it," Leo said, and it occurred to him that Russell was not going to pry, and it was because he didn't much care to know anything about what was left of his family. He was being polite in asking his questions, feigning interest.

The southern Italian cuisine was excellent. As Leo had hoped, Russell insisted on picking up the tab—a hefty one. Then he insisted on driving them both in his rental car back to his hotel for drinks in the bar.

—

"Do you remember your granddad?"

Russell was putting away his second single malt scotch, and Leo was enjoying the comfortable bar, the comfortable old uncle, and the buzz of red wine, continuing here at the bar with a glass of Merlot.

Leo shook his head. "No, I was only five when he died. I mean, I have vague visual memories of him, but nothing about him personally. I remember Granny very well, of course. I was in high school when she died."

"She was something."

"Yeah? What was she like when you were little?"

"I don't know," Russell knocked back the last of his shot and looked around for the waitress. They were sitting at a booth on sumptuous leather upholstery. He caught the alert waitress's eye and signaled for another. "Actually, she was kind of nervous all the time. Worked hard around the house. We started off in the Depression, you know."

Leo nodded. "Glad I missed that one."

"Not Leah," Russell said. "She came right at World War Two."

"I guess you and Drew were too old to play with her much."

Russell snorted. "Drew didn't like her."

"Really? Why not?"

Russell's drink arrived and the waitress initiated a spate of good humored patter, jockeying for a good tip, Russell relishing the exchange. When she left, Leo was still wondering about Drew and Leah.

"So how come Drew didn't like Leah?"

Russell regarded Leo from behind his glass of amber liquid. "You know about Leah, right?"

"Know about her?"

Russell took down half his drink and set the glass on the hardwood surface in front of him. "I just mean, Drew didn't like her."

"I guess I didn't know that."

"No big deal. Drew was sort of Dad's boy, even though Dad was a drunk because of the depression. Did you know what Dad was going to be before the depression?"

"Not sure. He was a milkman, wasn't he?"

"Yeah, but what he was going to be, if the depression hadn't hit, was an electrician. That was how he and Ma met. He fixed their washing machine motor. Or some motor."

"So how come Drew didn't like Leah?"

Russell squinted, shook his head. "I don't know. You know how kids are. I guess he resented her being a new baby, getting all the attention."

Leo could hear the obfuscation, decided not to pursue it, wondered why he was nursing his wine, polished it off.

Russell spotted the waitress and called out. "'Nother wine for my nephew here."

They drank for a while longer. Leo was grateful when his uncle insisted on driving him home, dropping him off in front of the house without cutting off the engine.

—

It was the smallest funeral Leo had ever attended, but it was a bona fide one held in Davis-Williams' tasteful, simple chapel, with several floral arrangements, and a closed casket. After the handful of attendees from Kirk & Ghent introduced themselves to Leo and Russell, a lady performed a religious song. A real preacher delivered a brief—but not too brief—eulogy mentioning several facts about Leah, including that she had been a church-goer and was a good Christian. That her brief church-going period had ended many years ago, he glossed over. A limousine, in which Russell and Leo rode, followed the hearse to the cemetery.

As the minimal graveside service ended, Leo said to Russell, "I'm really grateful, Uncle Russell. I don't think I could've managed it. It wouldn't have been nearly as nice. Thank you."

Pulling out of the Davis-Williams parking lot, Russell told Leo, "I have to fly out of here tonight. Otherwise we'd hit a few bars."

"It's been good to see you, Uncle Russell. We should try to stay in touch."

"Do it, Leo. Stay in touch and come see me sometime. Bring your girlfriend. What's her name?"

"Janet. I'll try and do that."

—

Leo found the Chevette parked around the corner, not a hundred feet from where he and Leah had usually parked. The car was unlocked. That was unlike Leah, but supported the idea that she had been in a mental haze. Leo found the key where they always hid it behind a torn bit of upholstery.

He slipped behind the wheel and adjusted the seat to accommodate his longer reach to the foot pedals. Though uncomfortable in the jacket and tie he'd brought for the funeral, he sat for some time with his hands on the wheel. He thought about Professor Gottschalk again, and some of the discussions back in Philosophy in Literature 303. Had anything changed in all the years since those discussions? Was art the only place to find a hero, or had Gottschalk been correct to agree with Leo's assertion that a good and normal nature, however deeply buried, might, through an act of will, arise out of anyone under the right circumstances.

Leo's hands were so cold that he could barely grasp the steering wheel. He started the car and drove to a pawn shop he knew about, and with most of the sixty-six dollars in his wallet, purchased a used .32 caliber automatic and some ammunition.

49

WHAT WAS HIS CRIME? SHOOTING alley cats? The pawnbroker had answered questions about the gun. It would be louder than a .25 or .22, the man had said, but not as loud as almost any other gun. Sitting on the couch now, Leo practiced. A little lever released the magazine. Pushing the magazine back into position gave a satisfying click. He loaded the magazine and locked it in, then released it, unloaded it, looked at the bullets, felt their heft. Several times he loaded and unloaded, then left the gun, the bullets, and the magazine lying on the end table next to the couch. Leo had never held a real firearm before. He was not planning a murder, just wanted to have the power of death in his hand. More than wanted, he needed it. That was enough reason. And the metal machine did fit his hand, and it embodied the very power he required.

The wind was kicking up outside, and a bare tree was strobing the streetlight into the window. He flopped onto the couch, propped his head on the armrest, let his feet rest on the opposite arm. The heat register hissed. The strobing light hit his face, the amber glow a window into the cosmos, blinking and winking at him—*Come on in, the water's fine.*

He could have driven back to Cannon Shoals. He didn't need to spend the night here, did he?

He could phone Janet, too. No reason not to. Then why didn't he?

At midnight he made a cup of tea, drank it slowly. The wind outside had died down, and for a while he stared out the window, caught himself hoping desperately someone would come walking down the street to prove it was not just a picture, but real.

He went to the bathroom, urinated, avoided the mirror.

Leaving the lights off, he crept into the bedroom. Standing at the chest of drawers, he opened not his underwear drawer, but Leah's. In the dim light he could see that it was full, as usual. He placed his hand into it, letting his fingers burrow down among the soft materials, the tiny buttons, snaps, elastic edges brushing his palm and fingertips, the drawer's contents no longer a multicolored riot, but all black in the darkness.

He was still dressed when he awoke on the couch. His upper back cramped, he sat up, tried rotating his shoulders for relief, looked at the window. He couldn't have slept long. He'd been wide awake at four, and now it was still dark. He made his way to the kitchen, switched on the light. The clock showed 5:30.

He couldn't find any coffee, so he made another cup of tea. At the kitchen table, sipping the hot liquid, he realized that the apartment was much too warm. Instead of turning down the heat, he gulped down the tea and went to the couch, stood at the end table, pushed the loose cartridges into the magazine and popped the magazine into the stock of the gun. He found his coat, put it on, and jammed the gun deep into its pocket.

The cold was polite as he descended the stairs, but shocking when he stepped outside. The car started grudgingly, and without letting it warm up he put it in gear and drove toward the convenience store.

A man Leo had never seen before was behind the counter.

"Yes sir," the man said. He looked to be in his seventies, with leathery skin, white hair combed straight back except for an Elvis cocktail hanging down his forehead.

"Can you heat me a taco while I get some coffee?"

"One taco, heated." The man reached into the refrigerated case behind him. The microwave door snapped shut and the mysterious machinery whirred. Leo filled a foam cup to the brim with black coffee and covered it with a snap-on lid. By the time Leo reached the cash register, the taco was warm and waiting in its paper pouch.

"Coffee and a taco." The clerk punched buttons on the register. "Two ninety-seven."

"You happen to know when Sid comes on duty?" Leo said, handing the man three dollars, noting it left only one dollar in his wallet.

"Three dollars," the man said, grabbing three pennies from an ashtray beside the register and proffering them to Leo.

Leo ignored the pennies and said, "Sid."

The man dropped the pennies back into the tray. "I don't know any Sid."

"Works here," Leo said.

The man shook his head. "He might work here but I don't know him."

"Thanks," Leo said, and left the store, walking into a void where there was neither day nor night nor week nor month nor time at all. He stepped out of the void, into the car, and drove toward Riverside Cemetery.

The gate to the section of the cemetery where Leah was buried was padlocked, Leo could see from the car. It was not the main entrance, but a back way that required pulling off from the highway. He barely had room in the drive to execute a U-turn.

Taking the next exit, he found himself in a uniform and grayish housing project. He would need to navigate through several blocks of the dreary structures in order to find the other side of the cemetery.

He slowed the car as he approached a murder of crows eating a groundhog in the middle of the street. They moved out of the way as the car passed over the carcass.

Another half block on, Leo saw a man in a heavy, hooded winter coat standing on the sidewalk. As the car approached him, the man raised his hand to the height of his head, holding something small.

Leo was relieved to reach the end of the project and turn onto the street leading to the cemetery's main entrance. At the gate, a small sign stated *"Cemetery Open 6:00 a.m. to 6:00 p.m. Daily."* Though it was not quite six o'clock, the gates were wide open, and Leo drove through.

Riverside Cemetery was hilly, steep in places. Much of the vast graveyard was terraced, but some areas were too steep even for that, and were devoid of graves, though some had switchback footpaths carved into the slopes. Easing the car along the paved single lane, he entered an old part of the cemetery with looming large monuments and mausoleums. He needed the new section, all the way toward the rear, where the land sloped down toward the highway. The twisting, forking road was confusing, laid out to access the various sections of the old cemetery, not to provide a through-way to the other side. Several times Leo found himself driving along a section of pavement that he had been on minutes earlier. Frustrated, he stopped the car, turned off the lights and engine.

With the headlights off, the faint light of dawn revealed, Leo sat in the car for a while, feeling no purpose.

Soon it was light enough to make out the histories carved on the granite stones near the car. The sky was taking on a warmer, almost yellowish light now. Leaving the car, Leo looked around, guessed Leah's grave would lie beyond a low rise he could see to the west.

He was chilled after about ten minutes of walking along the paved lane, and found that he'd been wrong about the direction. The path was forcing him to make a circle that would lead him back to the front gate. Annoyed, he hurried along the road until he saw his car, parked only a hundred yards across a steeply terraced stretch of graves. He cut into the graveyard and made a beeline for the car, trouncing across graves.

He started the car and turned on the heater. In full daylight now, he put the car in gear and crept along the pavement, watching for some ingress to the new section.

Rounding a blind curve, he spotted a small house with a separate garage and a couple of small outbuildings, the compound mostly obscured in a hemlock grove. He saw some earth digging equipment parked beside the garage. A sign on a post near the front door of the house announced "Office." And about a hundred feet on along the lane he saw a man walking. Leo was sure this would be a caretaker.

Stepping from the car, he said "Good morning." He now saw the man was young, not out of his twenties.

"'Morning," the man replied, his eyes widening to invite Leo's inquiry.

"I thought I could go straight to the new section but I seem to be lost."

The young man smiled. "It's a big place."

Leo had hoped for a straight answer. "I keep driving in circles. My aunt was buried yesterday. It's right near the entrance from the highway."

"I'm going to open that gate at ten o'clock," the man said, nodding as though he were addressing Leo's concern.

"Well, how do I get there from here? I'd like to get over there now." The man continued nodding but said nothing. "I have to be somewhere else by ten," Leo said. The man continued to nod. Leo elaborated on his lie, "Have to be at work."

"I can tell you how to walk there, but you won't be able to drive to it from here. It's a whole separate section."

"That'd be great."

The young man turned away from Leo. "Leave it parked here and walk with me."

Leo fell into step with the man, who walked a few yards past the hemlocks, then stopped and pointed to a small meadow with neat rows of identical looking headstones. "Go through here to the other side. There's no path but the rows are straight. See where these military stones end?"

At first Leo could not see, as they seemed to continue to a rise where the sight line stopped.

"They only go back about halfway there," the man explained, "then they're regular headstones. See, there, that tall one?" The man pointed to an obelisk. "When you get to the end of the military rows there's a footpath be easy to see. Turn left on it and it'll take you past the Jewish section, that's where you won't see any crosses at all, and it's got hedges all around it. That'll be on your left. You go on past that and then on your right'll be some little trees look like fruit trees but they're not. Cut into those little trees and when you come out, you're in the new section."

"That sounds pretty easy. Thanks."

"You're welcome. I'd show you but I'm heading for the front gate. Opposite direction."

"No problem. Thanks again. I never would have found it by myself," Leo said, grateful as he started across the military section.

The footpath was impossible to miss, and it did lead past the Jewish section, which was obvious. Once past the hedge around the Jewish section, however, Leo saw on the right not small trees but dense vegetation, thorny and opaque. He walked on a ways, but found himself back in the old cemetery after a few hundred feet, the path now paved and lined with a curb of cobblestones. He turned back and peered into the thicket. At one place he saw what might be a narrow footpath, so he forged into it. Although the thorns tore at his coat and trousers, he was through the thicket after thirty or forty feet, and found himself in the grove of small, gnarled trees. These trees appeared to have been planted in rows, but some were missing, those spots encroached upon by thorny brush.

Leo emerged from the grove to see a comparatively barren landscape dotted with small markers among rows of otherwise unmarked grave sites—the new section. Down the gentle slope he could see the highway a quarter mile away. An eighteen-wheeler passed along, its roar reduced by distance to a low whining complaint. Sunlight reflected mauve and ochre off the industrial buildings on the far side of the highway, and off the gravestones as well.

It took him only ten minutes to find her grave. Although the terrain here was not terraced as in the old cemetery, Leah's grave was on a level stretch. The entire section of the cemetery here was shaped like a shallow bowl, something of an amphitheater tilted toward the river that carved its slow course less than a mile away.

Her grave was still shaded by the small trees when he found it, but the sun was coming into view over the thicket. Leo stood for some time staring down at the freshly dug soil. It looked surprisingly red in the blanching light, and it was wet in places, as though it had been watered down after being shoveled back into the hole.

Fatigued, Leo sat down cross-legged in the sparse, yellowed grass a little distance from the grave's raw earth. Now the sun was in his eyes, causing him to squint and warming his face. *Not chilled now, that's nice.*

If the angle of ascent were just right, the sun would rise above her grave and stay hidden behind a monument—if placed and shaped correctly—until it emerged at the top of it. At least, it would do that on a certain day of the year, *if I were sitting in the correct spot.*

His tired mind wandered to Stonehenge, and a faint glint of reflected sunlight caught his eye. It was emanating from the disturbed earth of the grave. The reflection grew brighter over the next minute as the sun continued upward. Leo decided to dig out the bit of broken glass or soda can, whatever it turned out to be, and dispose of it. But first, he would watch for a while and see how much brighter it would shine.

The light began to hypnotize him—not an altogether unpleasant feeling, and he stayed focused, letting the play of the light on his retinas do what it might.

He saw tiny figures—miniature angels, all colorful and pale like a fading rainbow—dancing in this light. The brilliance expanded in his visual field so that the scene was everywhere, yet he could watch it all, somehow, without moving his eyes. The angels danced, their flight choreographed as they circled each other, files of them passing other files, ranks rising like thermals and then diving back in all directions, not so much symmetrically as with design, esthetic perfection.

He allowed this show to continue for as long as it would. When it began to transmogrify, the angels becoming dragonfly-like insects, and then less pleasing forms, he jerked his head away, focused on something else, the remnant of a rock near the thicket. Then he closed his eyes altogether and listened to the traffic, faint and reassuring, down at the highway.

When he opened his eyes again after a moment, he glanced at the light and found that its brilliance had begun to wane.

He stood up, brushed off the seat of his pants, and walked over to the grave. Stooping down, he found the spot from where the reflection had emanated. He saw a tiny piece of smooth glass in a depression in the soil. He reached for it, gingerly working his fingers in the dirt to find an edge without cutting himself. He could find no edge through probing, so he brushed away the dirt to look for it, or to discover a shape. Not a bottle fragment, it was flat. He brushed away more dirt, exposing an area of several square inches. The glass looked black, like obsidian, and yet it wasn't opaque. He pushed more dirt off, still guarding against sharp edges as he brushed lightly with his hands until he had cleared an area the size of a saucer.

The glass was transparent. It had appeared black because of the darkness on the other side of it.

Leo checked the sun. It was above the trees now by several times its own width. He placed his face down close to the glass, cupping his hands around his eyes like blinders to shut out the daylight. He peered through the glass and, as he had suspected, there was a vast void underneath it. But not a complete void. Once his eyes adjusted to the darkness, he saw that in the almost infinite distance there were points of light—stars, or something that looked like stars.

He sat up, resting on his knees, and looked around again at the other rows of graves, noting that some were covered in raw earth, while some were grassed over. A few had headstones—modest ones. In its remote location, adjacent to the busy highway, this whole area was a sort of potters' field—modern version, of course. The cheap seats. Low rent district. One would not expect to see many visitors here. And if one were a visitor, would not expect to be seen or noticed from the highway. One would not be heard, if one made noise, by people in the more genteel parts of Riverside.

So, what I do is I flirt with giving up this so-called gift. And to do so, I'll have to deny the one thing in life that's been held out to me as my claim on dignity. That dignity, that gift, that intellect guaranteed to raise me out of the poverty of my shameful position in life, is, in the end, a sham. And it's been the legacy left to me by the one person who should have given me comfort in the face of my loss of all dignity: my mother.

Now, for her I couldn't give up, could never admit failure. And I couldn't cut myself loose from the cynicism that was welded together with my strongest concept of masculinity—my father. These remain the deepest impressions my parents delivered on rusty blades into my tender childhood heart. The bloody wounds have festered there, scabbing over year after year, never accessible, but apparent to my intellect, tantalizing and frustrating me.

All that was inside Leo and not himself came flowing up and out of him, not like vomit, but in chunks great and small, all the pieces that had settled and cemented themselves together to make a wall protecting the goodness at the center of him from all that grew around it. Chunks of Professor Gottschalk came up, dragging art along with Leo's labels and judgments. Chunks of love, some of it the fragrance of wisteria on the night air, and some of it fetid, all of it now unsticking itself from the concretion in him.

Chocolate came up in chunks and in liquid mixed with saliva, some of it digested, and as it came out, it left clear thinking, deep thinking, good ideas he might consider later. Chunks of empty space, and chunks of time also came up and flowed out of his open mouth into the graveyard, and stuff kept coming until he was empty.

Leo pushed an inch or two of dirt back over the glass. He wanted now to shove back through the thicket, back onto the main path to his car, and drive away. His heart pounded with excitement and a sense that he would be happy now, that he would be born, and that when his time came to die, he would re-enter the universe from which he had been snatched. For now, he would want to buy some grass seeds and plant Leah's grave with the thickest, softest bed of grass that could be grown. He knew what he must persuade Janet to do with him.

—

Let me clarify that. I will still write bad poems when I'm grown up. I'm not sure why I purposefully came up with some misspellings in this one—it must have something to do with the way our perceived reality is never quite the same as anyone else's:

That soft green rectangle
I imagine to be nutrishioned from underneath
by the ether of humanity,
Leo's protector,
dead and decaying,
now sustaining a green life force.
That green patch curiously the size of a bed
filled in and thickened and supple enough,
became a bed,
was the site of my conception
literatively? Figurally?
A fiction a bard pursues?
It happened.
I know because I'm here.
I'm afraid that I yam what I fear.
I think that I yam what I think.

I feel like I yam what I feel.
I act like I yam what I do.
I yam what I yam and that's all that I yam.
I'm Popeye the Sailor Man.

The early morning sidewalk was only the first venue for Leo and Janet's *al fresco* lovemaking. As different as the origins of such a proclivity may have been for each of them, they both liked it, were drawn to it, looked at each other upon stumbling across a semi-private space that called out to them, and their eyes would twinkle as they would start disrobing.

—

He stood up, pulled the automatic out of his pocket, took aim at the window into the universe, and fired. The shot was loud, but the hills swallowed up the sound. Leo sank to his knees and with his bare hands, dug the bullet out of the dirt, put it in his pocket, and buried the gun.

—

In a parallel universe, I might have been a miscarriage and never existed. But that's not the case. I do exist, I am in the fourth grade, I do love my teacher Miss Hamilton, and here we are in this universe, not another one.

"Even after I'm dead, I'll love you," Papa told me. We were in a big graveyard where a famous man was buried who was governor of the state of North Carolina. We were talking about ghosts. "I'm not sure if I can give you a sign when I'm a ghost," Papa said, "but if I can, I will. One thing I can tell you for sure is I will be watching you and I'll hear you and see you because I will never stop loving you." I was five years old, in kindergarten, I remember because it was after he picked me up at school.

Sometimes Mama picks me up but usually it's Papa.

When I was little—I know, I know, I'm little now, eleven is little, but I mean when I was a toddler—he would carry me around in one of his arms so my head was right up even with his, and we would look at things from the same perspective. He would walk us up to a leafy low hanging dogwood branch, and he'd watch my eyes. When I'd focus on a leaf, he'd say "Leaf. Leaf," and I would try to say the word. Now I'm very verbal, and will be all my life. If fourth grade had a valedictorian I would be it.

Papa says I was born into love and out of the ashes of love, conceived in his personal renascence atop the dull, indiscriminate dust of someone already dead. He added, "with apologies to Edna St.Vincent Millay," and then told me I would read her poems someday. Right now, I read poems by Emily Dickinson and Dr. Seuss, who is actually a genius, in my opinion, even though—I know, I know—he's a children's writer.

I'm telling you about my relationship with my father. I can't do that without telling about my mother also. Mama is a very pretty woman, so even at my age I can understand why Papa loves her and married her. She is older than most of the other mothers of my classmates. Papa is older than most of the fathers. That's because they didn't meet until they were old, up in their mid and late thirties. But Mama is still beautiful and not fat like so many of the other mothers, and she was a teacher until I was born, and now she's a good mother. Papa would love her even if she was not pretty, even if she wasn't smart. That's what is important, I think.

If Papa had to give his life to save mine, he would do it without hesitating. When he realized that, he was walking along the sidewalk thinking about nothing in particular. It was the biggest revelation of his life, that he could love someone more than he loved himself. He wasn't even sure he would give up his life for Mama, without at least thinking about it first—although he decided later that he would under most circumstances.

As you may know, we have a large community theater in Oak Hollow. Papa is the head of it and he has to work hard to keep it going because it doesn't pay for itself. Never go into a career where you can get grants, Papa told me, even though that is what theater is and he loves it. Most people around here don't like to go to the theater, but some of them do, and that's what matters. Papa says the real benefits of the theater are for the people who are in it. He says that all theater is a parody of nothingness, and I do know what a parody is, and I do know what farce is, and comedy, tragedy, all those things. But again, he says theater is all a parody of nothingness. He lets me go on the catwalk, run the light board, the whole works. I know stagecraft and terminology already. I'm not going to be in the theater, or maybe I am, I don't know yet. I'm interested mostly in rocketry, and I've already built two model rockets, not from kits.

I used to write books. I wrote quite a few of them, and Papa would staple them together and put covers on them which I would illustrate. Most of my books were about Papa and me, although I would change our names or just say "Once upon a time there was a man who had a little boy." I know, I know, it's pretty obvious. In these books we would always go on an adventure and get caught in rushing water, or on a runaway train, or get lost in the woods, etc. I would usually get hurt, or sometimes he would, but we would be fine in the end and Mama would usually show up right at the end, having been extremely worried about us.

But one time I wrote a different kind of book. It was all about a little Shingaru boy who got lost and fell into a wormhole and ended up in our universe. The physics of his happening to fall from his world directly into ours might be pretty iffy, I realize, but through the magic of fiction, I had him in Oak Hollow, North Carolina, by halfway through the first sentence. This book, which I called *A Shingaru Lost in the Mind of God,* was the longest one I wrote. It went twelve pages in twelve-point Times New Roman. But it was hard to finish. I started out telling another adventure story, this time without the father figure. But then I started thinking about how a Shingaru would look, and act, and experience things in our world, and of course it was basically impossible. But by that time, I had written quite a bit and I didn't want to give up on it, so after a few days of worrying myself silly about it, I started trying to change the Shingaru reality so that it would fit more into our reality. For some reason I also didn't want to tell Papa that I was doing this. I wanted him to see that I could write this book about a Shingaru in our world and I could make it work if I tweaked reality a little bit. And to some extent, I succeeded. But my success was all based on ignoring the differences between my reality and the Shingaru reality. I get a queasy feeling from that. That book is not truly done yet, but it is stapled and I'm working on some cover art for it.

We live in a house almost a hundred years old. It's like Oak Hollow, not too big but big enough. The bedrooms are small, but I like mine because it has good windows and I get to put things on the walls if I want to, and I have a big high bookshelf I keep books and videos on. We have a TV but it's old and we don't have cable. We do have a VCR and DVD player. The TV is in a little room that we think used to be a sleeping porch. We can only get one station and it's all fuzzy, so we don't watch much TV at all, just videos sometimes. Instead we read and talk and sometimes fuss at each other and things like that.

In the living room Papa and I have our "buddy chair." It's a big velvet recliner that we both sit in at the same time, like buddies. He takes up about ninety percent of it and I fit in on the side—which is how I like it. We may have to get a bigger one when I grow some more, because it's getting pretty tight in that chair. I'm happiest when we're sitting in the buddy chair, because we always talk about interesting things.

Papa shows me things he knows I'll appreciate. He showed me how to make a penny garden and gave me a book by Reynolds Price that describes one. He showed me doodle bug holes and how to say a poem to get the doodle bugs to come out. He seems to know an awful lot, and he teaches me the most interesting things he knows. He makes sure they're appropriate for my age, of course. He used to have a gun, just for a short time. A thirty-two-caliber bullet fired at the ground will penetrate one and a half feet of freshly packed dirt, such as the dirt in a new grave. You can only know this if you fire the bullet into the dirt, and then dig down with your bare hands until you find where the bullet has stopped. By that time, your hands are scraped and raw and it's a good time to stop digging, put the slug in your pocket, and enjoy your renascence. I'm looking forward to spending a lot more time with Papa.

I was in school on 9/11 when the terrorists attacked America. Papa picked me up after school that day and instead of driving home, we went out to our church. The church was closed up but it was a nice day so we sat in the graveyard on a bench. Papa said he didn't want to go home yet because I would get absorbed in my usual routine and it would be hard to talk to me. He explained what had happened, and told me we were not in any special danger, and that I would not notice much difference in anything, but that in some important ways life would be different for everybody because of what happened. He told me people in America don't understand much about the rest of the world because we are far away from it here and all wrapped up in our own lives, so we were surprised that other people could hate us. He said when someone hurts us like that, it is never right of them to do it, but our first reaction should not be to hurt them back, but to understand why they did it. Papa doesn't believe in letting politicians do our thinking for us, and I don't either. That seems obvious to me.

I'm too young to understand spirituality. This has nothing to do with the Shingaru. Papa found his spirituality after he was grown up, so he is not sure what it is I mean when I say I believe in God. It's probably that I've been told about it ever since I can remember, so I haven't questioned it seriously. That's what Papa said, anyway. I may never question it, or I might question it and stop believing it, or I might question it and still believe it, or I might do like Papa did and question it, stop believing it, and then later, when I've become wise enough, believe it again but in a bigger way. Papa said he understands spiritual things now, and I can believe him when he tells me that the spirit is as much a part of people as their bodies and their minds and their emotions, and it lives on after the body dies. He said he would prove it to me if I gave him enough time.

He said it might come to me at any time, like when I'm in my thirties or forties or even older, walking along going somewhere, not thinking about much, and suddenly wham I would understand, and it would not be a mystery any more. Then Papa laughed after he told me that and said, "I shouldn't say this, but you'll also understand that atheists are not wrong. They're just not thinking in very broad terms." That was when he told me about paradox. Understanding all this is something to look forward to, I believe.

And finally, I want to tell something else I don't know now but will later. This is not repeating anything Papa told me. Papa did not lie to me about the Shingaru when he said they live in another universe where time is not one dimension of space but has several dimensions of its own. This is about Truth, and I know to capitalize the word Truth, because then it's not one single thing but something different for each person. The Shingaru are a paradigm Papa gave me, and they are a paradigm full of paradox because they are for understanding us. And we are full of paradox, if nothing else. I won't actually know all this until much later, when I am getting old. I believe that means about fifty years from now, when I'll be around sixty. There's one simple thing that is not paradoxical, and on some level I know it even now, as a kid. It's that a man learns many things from many sources throughout his life, and some of it may be meet and may be right, some of it may be mistaken and wrong. But regardless of any of that, every man who inhabits the Earth learns the Truth from one source—his father. And with luck, his mother saves him from it.